SUMMERLAND

SUMMERLAND

MATTHEW MCCONKEY

Broken Tribe Press

Summerland
2nd Edition, 2025
ISBN: 9781965412336
Copyright © 2024 by Matthew McConkey
Originally published in 2024

Book cover art and design by Jacob Arms
Interior book design by Casey L. Jones

Published by Broken Tribe Press
Lawrence Landing Company
Raleigh, North Carolina 27609
USA, North America
www.brokentribepress.com

Broken Tribe Press is a proud member of:

Independent Book Publishers Association
 and
Community of Literary Magazines and Presses

For Carrie Turbyfill

CONTENTS

CHAPTER 1
DR. MANDY FIELDS/SUMMER OF 1991

MATT—MATTY as his dad and his friends growing up had nicknamed him—sat on his patio in a chair for what his wife, Mia, thought was forever. She had been watching him through the kitchen window above the sink for a good ten minutes. She worried about him. When he told her that he was going outside for a few he looked, to her at least, like he had just been given the most terrible news he had ever gotten in his life. She had no idea what Matt had seen on the news feed on his phone as he sat at the kitchen table that morning, eating his waffles and drinking his chocolate milk.

Scrolling the news on his phone was an evolution from when his dad used to do it. Back then, back in the 1980s, Matt's dad would sit at the kitchen table every evening after work and read the newspaper. He would read it front to back and side to side. No matter what the articles were, he read them. He even read all of the classified ads people would place in there: be it selling a car, looking for a handyman, finding a stray dog, selling eggs—you name it—his dad read it all. Matt guessed that he shared his dad's DNA because he read everything in his news feed, whether it was national news, regional, world, or local. Especially local.

Mia had cooked Matt's staple morning breakfast, the one she made for him over the last twenty-two years: waffles with light Log Cabin syrup and a tall glass of chocolate milk. It was what he ate on his off days

1

which were on the weekends from the tire factory where he worked and managed. Off days, those Saturdays and Sundays, were usually spent doing chores around the house that he was too tired during the work week to do.

In the summers, it was lawn care: mowing their acre lot and trimming around the house and down the sides of the driveway and the dreaded embankment that ran the length of their property beside the street. In the fall, mowing and trimming had switched to managing all the leaves that had fallen from not only his trees but the surrounding trees in proximity to their house. Winter, it was just too cold to get out there and do anything. It was the only time of year—those three months of December, January, and February—when he could be lazy.

Matt had finished his waffles and glass of chocolate milk and was about to get up from the table and put his dishes in the dishwasher when his thumb accidentally clicked the MORE LOCAL NEWS tab. When the news feed switched over to MORE LOCAL NEWS, there was a headline where a picture was attached. LOCAL DOCTOR KILLED IN ACCIDENT. Matt stood there, and his heart sank. He knew that face on his phone screen. He had dreamed about her so much over the course of his life—a lifetime ago that still lived in the past—that the shock of seeing her staring back at him with that ominous headline caused him to slowly ease back down in his chair.

———

Matt sat out on the patio in a chair and felt the warm summer breeze of the morning kiss his skin. He could not believe what he had read in the kitchen. It was some of the most awful news he had read in a long time. To be honest, it was a gut punch, knocking the wind out of him as he read the article further. Mandy Fields, a local doctor, had been killed in a single-car accident out on Galaxy Parkway the night before. Mandy wasn't just some random doctor on the news. For a time back in the land of long ago, back when they were kids, she was the love of his life; his reason for never missing a day of school; the girl he thought about every second of the day. For lack of a better phrase, she was his everything back when he was young.

He had not seen Mandy since their high school graduation back in 1995...thirty years ago. Looking at her picture again in that news article, she looked the same: had the same smile, the same glow in her eyes. She even styled her hair the same. When Matt saw the article and her face on his phone screen, it didn't matter how many years had passed by, how many decades, he had known that face—it was the face of a girl, the love of his life.

Matt—not a Facebook minion though he had an account—called her profile up. And there she was... and the last post she had ever made. It wished everyone a Happy Fourth from her and her staff at Fields Family Practice. Matt looked at her, and his breath was knocked out once again. Even though he had not seen or talked to her in over thirty years, he knew that he was going to miss her.

He closed his phone down and settled in his chair, looked around his backyard, and tried to grab scattered thoughts that floated around in his mind like leaves on the wave of a light breeze. Mandy was on his mind, heavy. He had not thought about her much and the older he got, the less he thought about her. He was happily married now, kids were grown and out of the house doing their own thing, and Mandy Fields was a distant memory of a time long ago. Now that he thought about it, so were his friends—his best friends from that same time as Mandy. Seeing Mandy, her face in the news article, not only brought Matt back to a time and place when he was younger, but to a particular summer that was his most character-defining time as a human being.

It was a summer that changed everything; it challenged all that he knew and held dear to his heart. It was a summer where he learned to be brave; a summer where he understood what loss was; a summer where he saw his family deteriorate even more; a summer where he laughed, and a summer where he cried. It was the summer that he confessed to Mandy his love for her. It was his last, best summer with his friends. Thinking about that summer out on his patio, he arrived at a poignant conclusion: he never had friends or times like that again...never a first love like Mandy...

2

It was the biggest day of my young life up to that point in time in my hometown of Claxton, Tennessee: Graduation Day. I was thirteen years old, and it was 1991— May 26th to be precise. It was a simpler time back then, for those of us that can still recall that particular point in time and space. Maybe it wasn't a simpler time. I guess in comparison to today's time, it *was* simpler. Our lives weren't dominated by smartphones or technology that has invaded our homes and everyday lives. This was back when TV was TV, not streaming everything online; when certain days of the week meant that your favorite shows were on, or when Saturday mornings had actual cartoons. I remember it was a great time to be a kid. Perhaps the last great time for kids if I'm being honest.

In 1991, if a kid wanted to have some fun, they had to go outside and find something to do, or stay inside and play video games, listen to CDs, vinyl records, or cassette tapes. Now it seems that kids are glued to their phones. But are they even phones? More like handheld computers that are a gateway to almost anything that you can imagine. If smartphones and tablets were back in '91, I would've been one of those kids who couldn't have put my phone down.

The morning of our eighth-grade graduation, I had gotten up early like I did most mornings and eaten a good breakfast: cold milk and Frosted Flakes, the manager's daily special around my house those days. I was kind of nervous about the day ahead of me because it would be the last day I would ever be in Claxton Elementary School. Or so I thought.

Decades later, I would return to bring my own child to attend the school. It was weird going back to that place to take my daughter to her first day of kindergarten. I remember walking inside, and it was like nothing had changed at all. It even smelled the same. Time seemed to have stood still waiting for me to come back. I remember that day after walking her to her classroom. I stood in the cafeteria just looking around at how much had stayed the same. I remember thinking to myself, *God, I actually grew up in this school a lifetime ago.*

I got my dress clothes on—black dress pants, a white shirt button down with a blue tie—and combed my hair. I grabbed my Walkman and headed out of the house. Dad was already at work where he pretty much stayed those days, and my mother was sleeping, locked away in the bedroom opposite my dad's. Neither would be attending the ceremony in the school's gym that morning. I didn't care. I had gotten used to being the forgotten kid. That's pretty much all I had become in the last few years at home: a kid who just came and went. I don't think that I mentioned my graduation to them. I think mainly because I didn't think they would show anyway.

I needed to get some nerves off of me, and the only way that I could do that was to hop on my bike and ride around my small town as the sun was about to peek out behind the treetops to the east. It was still that morning, not a lot of traffic, just people going to their early morning jobs. With my cassette tape of the Cure's *Disintegration* album playing through my headphones, I peddled down my street and past Curt's house. His house was still with no lights on just yet. It would be for about another twenty, thirty minutes until he and his family got going.

Further down the street, Tommy's house was going. Lights were on as Tommy's dad was walking out to his car, lunchbox in hand, waving at me as I passed by. I liked Tommy's dad. He was always nice and talked to me like an adult when I was over there. Mostly it was about baseball and who I thought was going to make it to the playoffs that year. When baseball wasn't going on, we'd talk about college basketball. I enjoyed those conversations with him and wished that me and my dad could have those. We never did.

At the end of the street, right before you turn either on Juniper or Saturn Street, was Pete's home. His parents were already gone for work, and Pete was up in his bedroom getting ready. His bedroom light was on and through his thin curtains, I could see him a little bit walking past the window. I thought about stopping and tossing some rocks up at his window to spook him a little but figured with my luck, I'd break his window. That was trouble that I didn't want to buy. Besides, I'd see him in a bit.

I kept riding and peddling throughout neighborhoods as Robert Smith sang his vocals in my ears. One particular street I went down was Juniper Street. That's the street where Mandy Fields lived down. She was the love of my young life although up to that point; she just didn't know it yet. The quintessential unrequited love, I guess you could say. Man, was I crazy about that girl. I always wanted to ask her out on a date to the movies or even her phone number, but I was always too nervous and shy to do it.

I was riding my bike to empty all the nervous feelings that I had pinned up inside me. I wasn't nervous about graduating and getting the hell out of the Claxton school system—it was what the ceremony itself stood for. It was a change. I didn't deal very well with change back then. I had a deep-seated fear of the unknown. As far as I was concerned, going to high school was the deep, dark unknown for me—a Pandora's Box that when it was opened, nothing good was surely to come out of it.

Changes were coming for me and had caused a great deal of trepidation of the future for me. I could feel it in the air, heavy and thick. I had ignored my feelings throughout the eighth grade school year, burying all those that I possessed of what the month of May would bring. May would be the last month of school and the last time we'd ever be students there.

It was the official kick-off to summer and we all would officially become high school students as soon as the ceremony was over that morning. That caused me a great deal of panic. I wasn't ready for that: mentally, socially, or academically. It didn't matter how I felt or how unprepared I was because after ten o'clock that morning when the eighth-grade graduation was over, we'd all be out of school for the summer and out of Claxton Elementary forever. I had two and a half months to think about what was coming next.

5

I had survived and somehow passed through the Claxton Elementary school system, and the end result was me sitting there in the hot gym on the freshly waxed basketball court amongst my peers in the eighth-grade graduating class. How did I manage to pass from grade to grade? I don't know, really. Luck mostly, I think. I had a couple of teachers who were really kind to me and allowed me to turn in work that was late without being penalized. They gave me the extra help that I needed after school and worked with me one-on-one to make sure that I understood the material. Mr. Hicks and Mrs. Trotter helped me more than they'll ever know. Without those two back then, who knows where I would've ended up?

I wasn't the sharpest kid in class. I never really tried because at home, I didn't have anyone to push me in academics. I don't even recall showing them my report card very often. Bringing home Cs and Ds didn't seem to bother my parents very much. My dad was always working, so I only saw him on occasion, mostly weekends, provided I was even home and not with my friends—which I was ninety-nine percent of the time. Mom was mentally unstable, and she was of absolutely no help. She couldn't even help herself. I guess you could say that there wasn't much expected of me on what I would grow up to become. I had no one to talk to about the future and no support system aside from my friends. They were really the only family I had...until I didn't.

My mother stayed locked in her bedroom for a good chunk of my youth and teen years. She was up and down from the bipolar issues that plagued her to even to notice what was going on around her and the house. Mom's mental problems had gotten the best of her, and she was very isolated from me and I'm pretty sure dad, too. This was during a time when words like "mental health" and "bipolar" were not in the lexicon as they are today. I'll be honest, I never heard those words and terms when I was growing up.

All I knew was that Mom was not well. She was a ghost that haunted the home, and I was the invisible kid. After a while, I just accepted the fact that my home wasn't a normal home. But whose house really is? When it came to most things, I was on my own: like cooking my own meals and doing my own laundry. I did these things early on at the age of eight. Schoolwork and trying to do good in school was a cross I had to bear. I wasn't a stupid kid by any means, but I wasn't the most academically fluent either. Was I middle-of-the-road in terms of grades? Sometimes. In my youth—and I hate to say this—I was just trying to make it day to day, at home and at school.

I wasn't like Curt, my best friend, who was the smartest kid I knew.

When it came to school and making the grades, Curt could do it. He was naturally brilliant, and there was an ease when it came to making all As. His family was about as screwed up as mine, maybe worse, but he was smart enough to get good grades. Good genes, I guess. He had to deal with his family dysfunction, as did I, but I had two different theaters of struggle: home and academics. At least he had the academics down pat. I never held it against him. Was I jealous of the ease of getting good, if not great grades, came to him? Yeah, I was. Sometimes I wondered why I wasn't as gifted as he was.

6

In the gym, I was dressed in a button-down shirt and tie just like most of the other boys in my class. I hated wearing those kinds of clothes. I was a tee shirt and shorts or jeans kind of kid back then. Looking around, I couldn't help but to feel out of place. Feeling out of place was a theme in my life up to that point in time. Even though I was dressed like most of the boys in my class, that still didn't make me feel like I belonged. I still felt like an outsider sitting there. I guess in the grand scheme of things, what kid at one time or another hasn't felt out of place? Even as an adult, I sometimes feel out of place.

I sat there in my steel folding chair slouched over, looking down at my black dress shoes and waiting for the ceremony to end. I never really understood then nor do I know now why some schools have a big graduation ceremony for getting out of the eighth grade. I guess some places see it as a rite of passage. Not me. It was just another grade down and four long ones to go. I didn't see the point in a ceremony for us to go to high school.

I had given much profound thought about the eighth-grade year there at Claxton as being our last. Throughout the school year, I remember the thought of high school creeping up on me at times, but I was quick to put it down and close the door on it. As the final Christmas break came and went and the final spring break evaporated before us, the reality of leaving our small school behind and heading for a much bigger school was at the forefront with me. I remember around April and especially the whole month of May, I was waxing on how things were going to change for me and my friends. I worried about the future and what it had in store for not only me but the dynamic I had with my best friends.

Sitting there in the hot gymnasium listening to our basketball coach/ history teacher speak about the challenges that lie ahead for the class of '91, I was occupied with thoughts of what the upcoming summer was going to be like. It was going to be different—I knew that much. Little did I know that it was practically our last one as a cohesive group. Had I known that the summer was practically the end, I would have appreciated it more and took pictures. You never know when the end comes. The end comes when no one is watching.

It was the summer before we went into high school—those small two-and-a-half months. My other summers were just plain old run-of-the-mill ones. After July and a couple of weeks in August, we knew that we were heading back to the safe confines of Claxton Elementary, not this time. After that summer recess, we were going off to another entirely new place that none of us had ever been to before but had only heard about. It was scary, some of the stuff we had heard about it. I wanted no part of it. There was no escape; we had to go.

Me and the guys never spoke about high school as a group during our eighth-grade year. We just went on our year pretending that it was never going to happen. I guess we just fooled ourselves for a short time so we could not fill our minds with dread and despair. It worked, I guess, because not a word was uttered about our new school. Do I think that my friends thought about it as much as I did? Yes, I do, but privately. Me and my friends went on that eighth-grade year and never talked about leaving Claxton Elementary School. We would have a conversation later on that concerned what was ominously towering off on the horizon. That confabulation was some time away.

My prime thought that day in the gym was a thought of what the summer break would bring. We always had adventures and times that we all recalled with hilarious vigor when we got together and told the stories. We were like old men sitting around telling big fish stories; with each story, the fish got bigger. Me and the guys had made a book full of memories that to this day are cherished and recalled with certainty, clarity, and conviction. I'll never forget those times we had.

I never knew that the upcoming summer recess would be our last *real* summer together as a group. As a kid, you think the good times will never end and that friends are forever—all it will ever be are endless days and nights. I'm glad that the summer was as good as it was. I'm thankful that I got to share it with the guys that I did, my brothers. I never had a summer like that one ever again. I don't know if the guys did either. That's what made it so special...it was the last. I remember listening to my grandparents talk when I was a kid about how they missed the good old days. I know what they mean now.

7

The graduation ceremony had finally come to a close. My three best friends and I were walking out of the gym amongst the sea of people that had flooded the halls and sidewalks outside of the building. It was hot that day, I remember—a muggy May day. The guys went over to their families and mingled a bit while I kinda stood off alone, waiting for them to join me. Eventually, they did, and we all started walking toward the front of the school. We were walking and talking, pretty much about nothing of importance, when all of a sudden, I was frozen in my tracks by the girl of my dreams: Mandy Fields.

"Why the fuck did you stop walking?" Tommy asked, not noticing the girl who was dead ahead of us who was talking to her parents and a few of our now former teachers.

"There she is," I replied almost in a whisper, not taking my eyes off her. She was beautiful. Her blue dress seemed to flow about her, making her elegant and captivating. She had brown flowing hair, her skin was slightly tanned, and man, did she smell wonderful sitting in front of me in all the eighth-grade classes. I think that the sweet smell was honeysuckle or maybe something else pleasing, like vanilla.

Some days it smelled like a mixture. Either way, her smell was utterly intoxicating to me. As an adult when I caught a whiff of honeysuckle or vanilla, sometimes in places like a grocery store or doctor's office for that matter, it would take me back to Mandy. Always back to Mandy.

Mandy had moved to our town in the fifth grade from somewhere down in Louisiana. From the first time she set foot in our school, I was hooked. The only problem was that almost all the other guys in our class were stricken by her beauty as well. I was lucky though; she had managed to be in my class for three years in a row, always sitting directly at the desk in front of me.

Every day I was privileged just to see her. It was why I was never absent from school. A day not seeing her would surely kill me, a kid that young. I know that this is going to sound crazy, I know, but she made my getting up and going to school bearable. It's crazy how much my happiness seemed to hinge on her just being at school. The days she wasn't there turned my day bad in a hurry.

In those three years, I never once dared to make my move on her or ask her to the movies. I was too shy and too socially awkward. I talked to her only in passing or when she was handing papers out in class, and then I only said "thank you" in a sheepish tone without looking at her. I know that she caught me looking at her from afar in places like the lunchroom or library. Our eyes would meet, and I would turn them away because I was too timid for her to see me admiring her.

She was the girl that I swore one night to the guys on a stack of *Batman* comic books she would be mine. Of course, my friends always mocked me because I never followed through with my pipedreams. And that's pretty much what they were back then, just pipedreams. Before that summer of 1991, I was just way too shy and backward to approach her to see if there was even a chance.

8

I told myself some whoppers, but that one about Mandy was the biggest. I remember Tommy saying on that particular campout where I took an oath on a stack of *Batman* comics, "Get the fuck out of here, man. You can't even talk to her." The rest of the guys laughed.

He was right, but there's something about being brave when the night is late and you're there with your friends—courage is readily available. That night it could have been very possible it was the Mountain Dew talking and the high caffeine intake after my sixth can. I was serious; and if Mandy would've been there, I'd asked her out to the movies. At least that's what I tell myself. Sometimes the biggest lies you'll ever tell are the ones to yourself.

"Yeah whatever, dude. Let's get going," Pete said, watching me look at Mandy on the sidewalk.

"I've got to do something this time," I said just watching her. "There's no turning back. This is…"

"…to be the summer that I ask her out," the boys all said in unison. They had heard this declaration from me before.

I turned away from looking at Mandy and at my friends, "Thanks for the support, dicks."

"Whatever, dude," Pete began, "we've heard this same shit last summer, and the summer before that I think, and maybe even the summer before that."

"You told me the same thing last week," Curt laughed, leaning up on Tommy who wasn't laughing but grinning like he wanted to.

I stood looking at them looking back at me. I *had* said that before. I had made a lot of thin promises to them and to myself over the years about asking Mandy for her phone number or to the movies many times in the past. My friends always listened to me but also made fun of me because they knew that I wouldn't ever go through with it. Maybe I even knew.

The want was there, but there was something about seeing Mandy that turned me to jelly. I always had this vision in my mind that one day I would just walk right up to her and ask her for her number. She would smile and write it down on my hand, and later that night, I would go home and call her. Of course that never happened because when it came to reality, I was way too shy to go up to her. I dreamed about it often.

"I wish you guys would be a little more helpful here," I said.

"We have been for years. But you will never do anything. You might as well forget her, dude. We're going to high school and trust me, the competition will be a lot more intense up there. Those guys can drive.

And what do you got? A Huffy? Face it, you missed an opportunity. C'mon, let's sneak into Grady's classroom," Tommy said as they made their way across the grass and into the main building.

I stood as my friends darted off towards the main building of the school and watched Mandy walk away with her mom and dad. I remember saying to myself a million times that this was going to be the year, damn it. *Tommy was right*, I thought. I had watched whatever chances I may have had in asking her out evaporate into thin air over the course of three years. When high school came, there would be more guys looking to be with her. What chance did I stand against a guy who had his own car and wasn't rocking a bicycle? I tell you what kind of chance…zero.

Mandy lived two blocks away from me, and I always made it a habit of riding my bike by her house. Sometimes I would see her out in her yard and try to make myself appear that I was just "in the neighborhood." She never saw me that I know of, and I only saw her a few times in her side yard helping her dad cut the grass. I made a vow to myself standing there on the school's sidewalk that I was going to make her mine if it killed me that summer. That was my goal. Just to talk to her and ask her to a movie or something—something, anything just to be more than the guy that sat behind her in class.

Feeling as if I had all of the confidence in the world at that moment, I quickly caught up with Curt, Tommy, and Pete who had already made it back inside the solemn main building and into the classroom of one of the most feared teachers in the Claxton Elementary School system: Grady's room.

9

Grady was one of those teachers that you loved to hate. I mean, she made you feel stupid, small, worthless, and always, always treated the most popular kids with respect because their parents contributed to the school programs. Those kids were not on free lunch like me and my boys whose parents were not rich and sure did not contribute any funds to the school's many programs. We all just barely had enough money to buy school clothes and supplies for the new school year, and even then it was still never enough. We were viewed as wretches by her—nothing more than low-down kids who would never make anything of themselves. But I guess living well is the best revenge, ain't it?

There we were: me, Tommy, Pete, and Curt inside Grady's classroom, which was as empty as a tomb except for all the desks, chairs, and of course, Grady's desk. Tommy, the adventurous one of the group, started things off by going over to the blackboard and picking up the three-foot ruler. He swung and smacked it against the blackboard so much and so hard until the wooden ruler finally snapped and fell to the floor in two pieces. For some reason, we laughed out wildly. Then, Pete went over to her desk and started ripping up her papers that sat neatly in stacks. It was beginning to be total and complete anarchy in that classroom that apparently we came in to destroy.

I don't really think that us tearing up her classroom was planned, but it sure seemed like it. I admit—it was not a very nice thing to do—but God did it feel good. It was as if we were getting some sort of revenge out of it up there in the empty room for all the things that Grady had put us through over the school year. I was at the classroom door on the lookout, making sure no one was coming down the hall while the violence was continuing.

Curt walked over to the TV and turned it on. He pressed the channel seek button until he found channel 35. Channel 35 was not just a channel; it was the destination for MTV. This was way back when they actually played music videos instead of fake reality shows all the time like they show now. I recall that while we were wreaking havoc in Grady's classroom, two music videos played: "With or Without You" by U2 and "When It's Love" by Van Halen. Every time that I heard those songs, it took me back to the time we destroyed her room. Not my proudest moment, I will attest to that.

———

We had completely totaled that room by the time we left. I mean, we had done stuff in there that by today's standards would have gotten us jail time. Could have back then, but fortunately for us, we were never caught or for that matter suspected. We were long gone, a distant memory by the time she came back to her classroom. I did, however, wish that I could've seen the look on her face when she came in and saw what had been done to her room.

Grady had lots of enemies that could've done that to her room. Rulers were broken, the blackboard was messed up with the words, "Grady, you fat pig" written by Tommy; the desks in the room were all turned over; Grady's desk was turned upside down where Pete had broken off two of the slender, metal legs. Curt had taken books, textbooks, and torn pages from them, throwing them into the air. They had beaten the hell out of that classroom while I was on the lookout. I guess now that I look back on it, it was a horrible thing to have done. I suppose that the room represented our feelings toward Grady herself.

Years later—I mean years—after I had gotten married, had Brooklyn, and softened up a bit, I wrote a letter to Grady and mailed it to the school. I wrote about what we had done to her classroom that day, which I'm sure she had never forgotten about, and explained to her why we did what we did and about how she treated us kids over that school year. I never revealed our identity, and I didn't put a return address on the envelope.

The four of us had walked out of that school for the last time in our school-aged lives. The reality of the four of us never coming back had not sunk in yet. Too early, I guess. However, I did look back at the building from behind as we walked away talking and laughing all the way down the road. I felt kind of sad, to be honest. As much as I hated being there, it was damn hard to say goodbye. I was turning a page in my life, leaving that school for good. Sometimes you never know in real time when the last time is that you're going to see someone or do something. I have always remembered the last time that I walked out of that school as a kid and how it made me feel that day. It was a time I'll never forget and even back then I was cognizant of the fact that it was the end.

CHAPTER 2
THE BOX OF PORN/DOG TOWN

1

WHEN I SAY the box of porn, it is exactly what you probably think. It was an oversized shoebox full of porn magazines we had collected starting probably back in 1989, back when we were twelve. The porn mags were gathered and placed in a shoebox that I had retrieved from home after my dad bought a pair of new work boots. The brown shoebox housed our pictures of naked women and to cover the shoebox from the environmental elements, we placed the box in a thick black sheet of plastic that was also taken from my house—my dad's tool shed to be accurate. The box was securely wrapped, preventing any kind of moisture from getting in. Curt suggested stashing the securely wrapped box inside a huge tree that had fallen who knows when. There was an enormous opening in that oak tree, and it was the perfect place to hide something.

The magazines of lust were in a neutral area where any of us at any time could look at them at our whims. The place where we hid them was deep within a forest where we played "war" all the time as kids. Those woods were also where we camped. That stretch of woods was called "Hudson's Woods" by all the old-timers. It was the most logical location when Curt proposed it, and we all agreed.

Playboy, Hustler, Penthouse, along with several more publications that I'd never heard of back then—were collected in a strange way. We didn't just go to the convenience store in our town and lay down our lawnmowing money or allowances to buy them. We were too young for that. Some, honest to God account here, we found in ditches on the sides of country roads and in garbage cans at the town park. In total, I think we had amassed around eight magazines in all at the time. That is if my memory is correct. That collection would later increase in a funny way.

On occasion, when we would get home from school, me and the guys would go into the woods and hang out in the area where most of our campouts were. Hidden inside a rotting log was our box of porn. We would be talking about the day's events at school, and Pete would take out the box and disperse the magazines that we had looked at, at least a million times. It was a ritual though. We would sit in a circle around the blackspot where campfires past had been lit, aimlessly looking at the magazines and talking about whatever. Usually, it was nothing or major concern—just idle kid chatter.

Honestly, it had gotten almost pedestrian, and the allure of the women that were posed in those magazines were not doing it for us any longer. However, we did not stop looking at them. It had become a routine for us. The thrill of looking at those women had waned each time. Our sexual education did not come from school or our parents. It came from those magazines for better or worse, and the highly sexually charged letters to the editor where the author of the letter talked in detail about their sexual fantasies or an encounter they had was where we had an idea of what sex was about. At twelve, that's where our education in sex came from.

There was never a time where my dad or mom, or any of the guys' parents sat them down and had "the talk" with them like you'd see on TV. Nope. Not us. We learned pretty much everything from those magazines: sex positions, names of things, and what the naked girls said they liked in a partner. Looking back on it now, with older lenses, it was not the best education into something like sex, but it was the best we were ever going to get at the time. I think we all knew that.

Our collection of magazines eventually did increase with new women to lust over and think about at night while we were trying to sleep. More mags had come into our possession one day by sheer accident, which ballooned our collection to over twenty-five. We had collected eight up to that point in time and were in desperate need of something new, but getting skin mags wasn't something kids our age—or any kid under the age of eighteen for that matter—could readily get.

2

We obtained those new porn mags in a strange way that makes me laugh every time I think about it. In May of 1990, the summer before we graduated from Claxton Elementary, Pete, Tommy, Curt, and I had planned on riding our bikes through a stretch in our small town called "Dog Town" during the end of our seventh-grade year.

Of course, that was the unofficial title of that particular neighborhood, but that was what we had called it. The actual name of that part of town was Pin Street, but Dog Town seemed to fit better given all the dogs that lived on the street. It appeared that the neighborhood had more dogs than people. Every time me and the guys would ride our bikes or walk down the street through Dog Town, we were greeted by dogs that did not like us one bit. We were the outsiders in their territory. They always let us know about it.

After a few near misses over the years where we were nearly bitten or worse, mauled, we had stopped going through Dog Town altogether because it was getting to the point that the dogs were getting more vicious. Even though it was a shortcut to the other side of town, we decided as a group not to go through this part of town anymore—wasn't worth the risks involved.

It is worth noting that we had only gotten all the way through to the other side of Pin Street only a handful of times. No more than two or three is the best I can remember. If you ask Curt, he'd probably say three. Tommy would say five, and Pete would declare we never made it through. The number depended on whom you asked.

It'd been a while since we had been through Dog Town, maybe a year or so at that point, and I guess that day we each had hoped that the dogs were leashed; or had forgotten about us; or even better yet, dead. I guessed that we thought since we hadn't been down that street in a while, the neighborhood dogs would have calmed down or somehow become friendly. That was a monumental miscalculation on all of our parts.

On the day we got our magazine haul, I recall being bored out of our minds. It was decided—by who, I have no clue—that we were going to ride around town on our bikes. We wanted some excitement for some reason or another and wanted to see if we could make it through Dog Town without having to stop and turn back. What was more exciting than nearly getting eaten by dogs? We were going to show those dogs that we were the bosses, not them. At least that is what I thought we were going to do anyway. We weren't taking the long way around. We were going to go right through Pin Street/Dog Town. Dogs be damned.

I remember that we each stood at the top of the hill on our bikes looking down at the long stretch of street. We knew what awaited us in the middle of the neighborhood: dogs. Not just dogs: but vicious, teeth-gnashing, mangy mutts that tried to not only bite our legs as we pedaled on our bicycles, but car tires when cars and trucks would drive by. There was nothing that those canines would not try to eat or go after full speed. And when one would bark, there came all the others in unison. That's how it always was.

3

It was hot that day, I remember. We all stood there on our bikes, looking down the street and waiting for the first one of us to start. But no one opted to be the first to begin.

"What are we waiting on?" Curt asked, looking at all of us.

"Are we all going like usual?" I asked. There was a silence amongst us. That was never good.

"I think we should see who has the biggest pair of nuts and see if one of us, by ourselves, can make it all the way through," Pete suggested. Pete always suggested things like that—stuff that was dangerous—stuff he, himself, wouldn't dare do. He liked to talk.

"Fuck that," Tommy said. "I'm not going down there by myself."

"Pussy," Pete said.

"Oh, it's pussy not to want to get chewed apart by dogs?" Tommy replied. Tommy would always call Pete out on his fake macho-ness. If anyone was willing to do dangerous things, it was Tommy. He was the risk-taker of our group back then. But he also knew when to use his common sense. "Calculated decisions," he called them.

"I think we need to just keep doing what we've always done," Curt said.

"We ain't going to make it through any damn way. How many times have we made it across? Five times?"

"It's not been that many," Curt replied.

"Oh what, like you keep a ledger, 'Mr. Math-lete,'" Tommy said, making himself, me, and Pete laugh. When Curt was selected to represent our school in the county Academic Olympics, he went in under the math event. Since that day, Tommy ragged him calling him Mr. Math-lete. Curt never showed it, but I know that it pissed him off. Tommy knew it too, that's why he did it.

"No, but I know that it's not been five times. I've done it once, Pete did once, and you did."

"Oh, so the only one that hasn't ever made it across is you," Pete said, looking my way.

"I thought I did," I said, knowing that it was a lie.

"Since we've all done it, maybe you need to show us your balls and do it," Pete said to me.

"Your mom has seen my balls plenty of times– does that count?" That made the boys laugh, even Pete. That was just me buying time. I knew that I would have to go down there, or at least try to.

I can't tell you why or what came over me; but with them all looking at me and waiting on a decision, I got up on the pedals of my bike and pedaled away down the hill. To this day, I don't know why I did it. Maybe it was to prove a point. Perhaps it was to prove something to myself. I still don't know what came over me to do it. It could've been because I was one of those kids—who even as an adult—never really took any chances. I sat on the sidelines and watched others take a risk. Sometimes they won and sometimes they didn't, but hell, they at least took a shot.

It was never my intention to attempt to go through Dog Town that day. I had tried it on several occasions, only to turn back and pedal back up the hill for safety. The dogs never followed us back up the hill, only halfway. I always found that strange. Must have been a territory thing.

The guys never knew it because I never told them, but I had a deep-seated fear of dogs. I was scared of them all: small, medium, and large. It didn't matter. For some reason, which I cannot explain now and surely not back then, I rode down that street keeping my hands tight on the handlebars and my Atlanta Braves baseball hat pulled down just above my eyes, which was the way I always wore it back then.

———

I had made it to the middle of the neighborhood and still no signs of dogs. Every time we would make it to the beginning of the neighborhood where the Wilson's house stood, the dog from the Wilson's house would come out of nowhere as he was apt to do. He was the scout and had to be better than fifteen years old, if not older. He had a gray muzzle and didn't get around very good—probably didn't see too good either.

His bark was still youthful and deep, and it was that bark that called the other dogs around the street. When he barked, they listened. It was a good feeling, wonderful actually, that I had made it past the Wilson's house and no black and tan dog.

I hoped that I could make it to the end of the street without being chased and snapped at. I thought I had a better than a better-than-average chance of doing what the guys had done in the past. At that point on my ride, I wasn't even seen by any of the dogs. I turned my head and looked back at my boys. They were still standing up at the hill waiting for me to hit the end of the street: the safe zone. Very rarely did the dogs chase any of us past the safe zone—that part of the street that spilled into Chestnut Ave.

With the wind blowing against my skin and cooling me off, I felt that I was in the clear. For the first time in a long time, I felt safe traveling through Dog Town. Maybe the owners of those mutts had leashed them up or taken them to the pound. Perhaps even the town made them do something with them. Maybe the infamous Dog Town was no longer and would be safe for kids like us.

Then it happened. The dream dissolved rather quickly. With no warning at all, off to the right of me, a dog started barking loudly and gruffly but not at the Wilson house. This dog came from the white house with the picket fence around it that stood about three-quarters of the way through Pin Street. I didn't get comfortable with that dog ever because I had seen that gray and brown dog leap over the fence once to chase Pete down the road, making him turn back. I had been spotted. My heart fell to my stomach. Suddenly, my ears were filled with the loud and terrible sounds of barking dogs—barks that told me that I wasn't wanted and if I didn't turn back, I was going to be eaten alive.

4

There I was caught in the crossfire of barking dogs because all of them came out of hiding– I think around six in total. I saw them emerge from the yards on both sides and even from the front of me. My heart raced, I was sweating profusely, and I felt myself become encircled with violent dogs that wanted nothing more than to see me chewed apart. I could not let that happen. I kept my bike going because stopping would surely get me hurt. I had no choice but to keep pedaling towards Chestnut because turning back would have been too far to go. I was at the literal point of no return.

The dogs were running alongside me on my bike, snapping at my shoes. I could feel their teeth clamping down my heels. I was scared to death. I wanted to cry. The tears were there in my eyes—that I can recall. I could have sworn that one of them had pulled at my sock. It was the first time I was ever that close to the dogs and that scared me beyond belief.

I was kibble if I did not get out of there and fast. With the dogs chasing me, I felt something pull my foot violently. I looked down at my right shoe, and my shoelaces had come untied at some point and gotten tangled up in my pedal. If this has ever happened to you, then you know that when this happens, you cannot pedal your bike anymore. Because with every revolution of the pedal, it tightens your shoelace that much more, causing your shoe to get tighter and tighter. Eventually, if you don't fix it, you can't even pedal the bike.

5

At that time I was just coasting down the street from the speed that I had garnered earlier coming off the hill. But I knew that I was going to slow down and be dog meat. I have to admit, it was the scariest time up to that point in my life. Later in the next summer, I would discover that this was *nothing* compared to what I was going to encounter by the railroad tracks.

Anyway, there I was, dogs to the left and right of me barking, growling, snapping at my feet, sometimes biting my shoes, and pulling on my socks. What was I to do? I could not pedal anymore because my laces were being twisted around the pedal, and I was slowly coming to a stop. And the mutts knew it. I could tell that all they were doing was waiting for me to stop. What was going to happen? What would they do to me when I had no way out? My mind raced, and I thought to myself, "What could I do?" Just when I thought things were not going to get any better, something happened that saved my life from the snarling dogs.

A kid by the name of Mike Napp, who was around ten—I can't remember right now—came from his house with a BB gun and started popping the dogs from the street. With each BB that hit the dogs, they howled and lurched back away from me and scattered about the street. One by one, the dogs left my side as I was slowing down. I stopped on the side of the street, at one point I never thought was an option, and stood and watched as the street was cleared of the dogs.

For the first time in my life, I had touched my shoe down onto the pavement that was Dog Town. Not many kids in that town could say that. I was the first, well besides Mike Napp of course.

"Damn dogs," Mike said as he walked over to me.

"Yeah, I thought I was dead. Thanks," I said, trying to untangle my shoelaces from the pedal and trying to calm myself. I was shaking.

"Ah, these dogs think they're so bad. Lucky I was around," Mike said, putting down his gun to help me get free from the pedal.

"Whose dogs are those anyways?" I asked, still pulling my shoelaces out from the pedal.

"Everyone's. A few of them don't belong to anybody. But most of them do," Mike said.

Just then, Tommy, Pete, and Curt rolled up from the top of the hill, "What happened?" Curt asked, looking around at the ghost town that was Dog Town. "You got too far. We couldn't see you very good."

"Mike here shot the dogs off me. If it wasn't for him, I would be dead right now," I said, finally getting my laces out.

"Way to go, Mike," Tommy said, punching him on the shoulder.

"No problem. Hey, do you guys want to buy something?" Mike asked.

You see, Mike was famous for those lines. For a kid his age, he always had a lot of stuff to sell. At school, he was always peddling something of value at a deep discount. And where he got his inventory, no one ever knew. Mike Napp was like a mobile flea market of sorts. If you wanted something, he would get it—no questions asked. Me and Curt had bought stuff from him in the past. Stuff like comic books, baseball cards, you know, kid stuff like that.

"What kind of stuff you got this time, Mikey?" Pete asked.

"Porn mags, and don't call me Mikey. I hate that name. That's for five-year-olds," he replied.

"Porn mags?" Curt asked. "How did you get your hands on stuff like that?"

"I have my ways. You want them or not?"

"Of course we do," I spoke up before anyone else did. Of course I wanted them and I was speaking for the rest of us.

"Come over to the house then. I have what you need," Mike said, walking away from us and over to his house.

6

We all followed him with our bikes, laid them down in his front yard, and stood out on his front porch, waiting for the kid to emerge. We felt safe there in Dog Town, right in the middle of it. We knew if those dogs came back out, Mike would pop them again. For a kid of ten years old, he was a pretty good shot. Mike went inside his house through the front door, and we waited for a bit. Me and the guys were talking about me nearly getting killed by the dogs and how lucky I was that Mike came when he did. The front door opened and out stepped Mike with a black trash bag full of magazines. It was surely much more than what we had stashed in the woods.

I know what you are thinking right about now, *Kids that young with magazines like that? You should be ashamed of yourself.* You have to realize we were kids—boys—and our hormones were going crazy at the time. Having something like those magazines was powerful. We already had some, but they had gotten old to look at. Something new was an exciting prospect. It was having something in our possession that we were not supposed to have that honestly made it a thrill.

"How did you get these?" Pete asked, taking the bag from him and handing out the twenty-something magazines to us.

"Picked them up a while ago. Do you want them or not?" Mikey hastily asked.

"Hell yeah, we want'em. How much?" Tommy said, not looking up from the mag he was thumbing through.

"Twenty dollars," he replied. That is when we all stopped looking at the naked women. Twenty dollars?! We did not have that kind of money; we were just kids, you know?

"Twenty dollars? We don't have twenty dollars," I said.

Mikey stood there for a minute and devised an alternative exchange, "How about games? You guys got any Nintendo games that you'll give up?"

Now he was talking. Nintendo games were just as good as money there in my hometown: Well, those and baseball cards and comic books.

Back when we were kids, you could substitute money for any of those before-mentioned items. Let us be honest here—if you gave a kid back then money, they would spend it on trading cards, comic books, and Nintendo games anyway. It all balanced out in the end.

"We've got a few. Which ones are you looking for?" I asked, ready to make the deal for the pages upon pages of naked women. I was already in love with what I saw there on the glossy pages because they were different women than what we had been looking at for a long time, and different was good.

"Legend of Zelda, the gold cartridge," Mikey replied. Anything but that, I thought to myself. "And any of the Castlevania games." No, not those. It just happened that I had the Zelda game and Curt had the Castlevania games (1-3).

"Done," Tommy said hastily.

"No, not done, dude. This is Zelda we're talking about. We haven't even beaten the game yet," I claimed to the guys.

"Damn the game, man! We have new porn right here in our hands. Give him the game," Pete said. I could tell that I was not going to win the war. I wanted the magazines badly, but not at the cost of my Zelda. I loved that game, and so did the guys. In their defense, they were not thinking very clearly.

"What about instead of Zelda we throw in Mario 3 and any Castlevania game of your choosing?" Curt shrewdly suggested. Curt was the negotiator of our group. If a deal was to be made, he was the one that would do it. He could talk anyone into anything. I mean, this guy could sell a car to an Amish person. He was that good. And when he served up my Mario 3 and any one of his Castlevania games, I knew what he was doing.

We had beaten those games two weeks ago before school let out for the summer and once we had beaten those games, they just kinda sat there collecting dust. Since we were not playing those anymore, it made sense to put them up on the trading block for something that we would use.

"Deal. I want Castlevania 3 and Mario 3," Mikey said without hesitation. What gamer could resist those two cool games? Not us and not Mikey. We went back to my house, got the games, went back to Mikey's house, and made the trade. The games for the mags. Even trade.

7

Now, flash forward to 1991...

We had each spent the night at Pete's house celebrating our graduation from the eighth grade. That night, none of us even dared to mention that we were going to have to journey to another school that was bigger, badder, and scarier than anything we had faced before in our young lives. We kept that out of the conversation. We just lived in the moment the best we could.

I guess it was in the back of our minds though. How could it not have been? But we did not say anything about the forthcoming high school years. All we did was play video games that we had rented that night at Bill's Pool Hall and Games. I think they were *Super Mario Bros. 2* and *R.B.I Baseball*. I could be wrong here, but I think those were the two games we played that night.

Pete's mom had bought us three big pizzas from the pizzeria that was in our town, Papa Enzo's. I carried the red plastic cups, and Tommy carried the three, two-liter Pepsi bottles up the stairs while Curt and Pete carried the pizza boxes. We ate like kings up there in Pete's bedroom that night.

Inside the room, we played Nintendo and listened to Pete's black radio that sat on his window sill with the window open to allow the cool summer breeze to blow in. We talked a bit as the night wore on. WIMZ, a rock station that we all listened to back then, quietly played some classic rock bangers. I sat on Pete's blue bean bag that was on the floor and flipped through a sketchbook of his. There were a lot of pencil drawings he had done over a period of time. Man, could he draw. There had to be at least a hundred or more sketches in that book I saw that night.

The night after, we woke up and ate breakfast that Pete's mother had fixed, and we decided to travel down to the woods and see our beautiful vixens that awaited us in the covered-up shoebox inside the tree. Nothing was unusual about that particular afternoon. The plan was after we hung around the woods looking at the magazines for a while, we would go to the swimming pool to socialize since the town's pool officially opened, kicking off summer vacation.

Of course, I had other motives for why I wanted to go to the pool. I hoped that I would see Mandy down there. She was always at the swimming pool getting her tan on. But the problem was that she was always there with her friends, which made it impossible for me to talk to her. Even if she was alone, I would not speak to her, and the guys knew that and mocked me for it all of the time. But when you are a kid at thirteen, how can you just go up and talk to the girl of your dreams? It was something that I wanted to figure out. I had made a declaration that she would be mine by the end of summer. I just had to try to figure out how.

———

Riding our bikes down the gravel service road that would lead us to the entrance of Husdon's Woods, Tommy, who was in front of the pack, noticed something peculiar and even out of place. He stopped, sliding his back bike tire against the loose gravel, causing him to fishtail side to side a bit. The rest of us followed suit. At first, we didn't see what he had seen through the cloud of gravel dust. But standing there with our bikes between our legs and feet on the ground, we saw what caused Tommy to stop dead in his tracks.

There in the entrance to the woods where we always went in, had bits and chunks of paper in the grass and weeds. At first, we didn't know what was going on. There was litter sprawled everywhere in the field beside us and even on the gravel road. It all looked like random bits of paper to me, strung across the tall standing grasses. We got off our bikes, laid them down, and walked over to the paper. Leaving our steel horses on the side of the gravel road, (which we never did) we followed the trail of torn pieces of paper.

We walked towards the scattered bits of paper, and it was Pete who figured out what it was, "This is our stash." When he said that, I think all of our hearts sank into our stomachs.

Each one of us had already made that claim in our heads as we bent down to inspect the chunks. The pieces that I recovered were of partial legs, a half-torn page of a woman in black lingerie. Could it be true? Could something have destroyed our secret stash of porno? Picking up the chunks of paper along the way, it became apparent that it was our beloved collection. We followed the line of bits of paper like bread-crumbs into the woods looking down at them as we slowly walked in a single file. It was our magazines, that much was clear. Or what was left of them.

We eventually made it to the place where we camped and saw the utter destruction lying in pieces around the campsite. It was worse, much worse at ground zero. Our box of porn had been torn asunder. We each stood there shocked, utterly flabbergasted by what we had seen. How could this have happened? We each stood there racking our brains trying to figure out how this could have been done. Why now? Nothing had bothered it before. It was and still remains a complete mystery. We were silent for a long time, and all that we could really do was just stand there looking at our stash—what was left of it anyhow. Some magazines were salvageable—only about four of them were intact—the rest? No chance.

Of course, we had our own theories on what could have caused the destruction. 1) Someone could have found the stash and tore it apart in an act of violence. 2) One of us on a campout could have left it out, and then a dog or something came and tore it apart. But why would a dog have gone right for the magazines even if they were left out? It made no sense. Nothing about it made no sense.

I mean, it had been a few weeks since we had last been to the woods, and everything was fine then. The box of porn was safely tucked into the tree like always from our last campout there, which was in mid-April, I believe. However, no one of the four of us was going to confess to acci-dentally leaving the stash out in the open. I know it wasn't me, that I can say for certainty. But if I had my guess as I did back then, it was Tommy. Here is how I arrived at that decision...

Every time we camped out, Tommy was the laziest person with us. If the campfire was going out, he would not get up and go get more wood. When we would clean up our trash the next morning after a campout, he would not help us even though part of it was his mess. When we would put up the tents, he would not help out. And we constantly told him to put the box of porn up after we were done looking at them. There were many times that myself, Curt, or Pete would have to secure the magazines in the shoebox and put them in plastic and inside the fallen tree. Tommy was just lazy and would never do that.

He was always the one who got the shoebox out on those campouts. I believed then that Tommy had gotten the box while down in the woods by himself, which wasn't unusual for any of us to do and did not put it back up for safety. I am not alone in this reasoning. I remember looking at the magazines during our last campout there but can't say who the last person was who put them back into the tree. That part I'm fuzzy on.

Curt and Pete shared the same sentiments as I did. We never said anything about it, but you could tell that Tommy was bothered by it more than the rest of us. It was the way he carried himself that day in the woods when he saw all of the pieces of paper scattered about the forest floor. I guess I knew then he was the one that left it out. He never confessed to doing it and we never pressed him on it. We all kinda knew anyway. We had no proof at all though. It was all circumstantial.

"Well," Pete said, "great way to kick off summer vacation."

We never restocked our collection after that.

8

A couple of years later, I'd say towards the end of sophomore year in high school, me and this guy named Abe Brooks, who I met in English class, had gotten around to talking about porn mags and the like. I told him about what had happened to our stash back in 1991 in Hudson's Woods, and he told me about this huge barn out in the country that was rumored to have dozens of *Playboy* and *Penthouse* magazines inside someplace. Keep in mind, he'd never actually seen the magazines or the barn for that matter. This was just talk he'd heard.

When Abe was telling me this, I so wanted the guys to be there hearing this, too. His story was the kind of thing Pete, Curt, and Tommy would have loved to have heard because we would have gone out there to this barn and found those mags. But the guys weren't with me anymore. We were still friends, but we were drifting apart more and more each month during that sophomore year, and our adventure days were trailing off into the sunset.

Me and Abe decided that we were going to ride our bikes to this fabled barn that he'd been told wasn't far from his house. Turns out, Abe lived about four miles from my house, out in the sticks and right before the county line. He gave me his address, and I rode my bike there. I remember it bothering me that Pete, Tommy, and Curt weren't along for this adventure. It was the last one I was ever on, *my* last adventure.

After meeting with Abe at his house, we rode our bikes to this barn that we could see from the side of this old scary-looking country road. On one side of the road was a farmhouse where no one was at home for the moment. Abe said the owners of the barn and fields around us lived there. I asked him what the best way was to get up there to the barn. The structure looked down from atop the hill it sat on for no telling how many decades. Through the cattle gate would be best, he told me. The only problem I had with that was that the cattle gate was right across the narrow road from the farmhouse. I scanned around and found a spot down the road where it looked like we could stash our bikes and jump over the wire fence. And that's exactly what we did.

9

We walked up that hill in the cow pasture, which seemed to be miles, and finally made it to the faded and dilapidated red barn. I would check behind my shoulder from time to time to look down at the farmhouse as it grew smaller and smaller the further we walked. Still no car in the driveway. Which was good; gave me and Abe some time to snoop around and look for these fabled magazines.

Were they even inside the barn? Who knew? I sure didn't at the time. But on most adventures me and the guys had back then, we didn't bother checking out the validity of the story. We just went and did it. That was the adventure.

This one time me and the guys went and stayed the night in the old abandoned McNamara Mansion outside town back in March of 1991. We had heard the stories, like most people had in that town over the years.

We didn't fact-check the stories; there was no way to, back then. We just went and spent the night there; four kids that didn't know any better. We saw some ghosts, heard a lot of footsteps in the attic and some pretty freaky voices whispering in some of the rooms. I remember seeing some odd things and feeling a presence in some of those rooms. Curt swore up and down that he saw a woman run down a hallway on the second floor and disappear into a wall—like she had gone right through it. Tommy said that someone was calling him to come down to the basement. Pete said that he saw the lawn statues out in the front yard turn and look at him while he looked out the third-story window before it got dark. It was a really freaky night staying there. One that I will never forget. After that stay, we never went back. We didn't tell anyone about it. No one would've believed us anyway. The old mansion was a secret that we kept between just the four of us as far as I know. I never told anyone what we experienced there. As for the other three, did they ever tell anyone? I don't know. This is the first time that I've even thought about the place in decades. Gives me chills just recalling it.

———

It felt strange being there with Abe prowling around the barn. I kept waiting for Pete or Tommy or Curt to come inside saying something funny. But the emptiness of the barn, other than the stacks of old wood and rusted and abused farm equipment from a time forgotten, was a cold reminder that my friends were gone; *we* were gone. All I had was Abe, and that wasn't close to being enough. Abe was a good guy and all, but he wasn't the guys, you know. It was hard for me to find a friend that was comparable to them. I never really did. You never have friends like the ones you had before high school.

Me and Abe had searched that barn from top to bottom and nothing. Just before we climbed down the rickety old ladder that led us up to the hay loft where hay had been sitting in state for years given the smell of it, Abe spied something off to the left of the floor where two huge tractor wheels stood leaning against an outer wall. Abe walked over there while I stepped off the last rung and watched. I didn't see what he had spotted.

I heard two metal clicks and then a gasp. That's when I knew he had found what we had come looking for.

I walked over to him and crouched down on my knees. The story was true. Inside a dusty black suitcase were dozens and dozens of *Playboy* and *Penthouse* magazines. We both sat there for a long time, pulling the magazines out and flipping through them all. They were practically brand new, nary a crease.

10

After a while, I told Abe that we needed to get going. We put all the magazines back in the suitcase, closed it, and I took it by the handle and carried it out of the barn. Outside, I looked down toward the farmhouse and saw a blue truck in the driveway. The owners had come back home. The old man, I'm guessing who lived there, was opening the cattle gate to walk up to the barn. Me and Abe stood there stunned because there wasn't a place we could hide except back inside the barn, and that wasn't an option. So, I told Abe to just start running.

We ran so hard down that hill that I don't think my shoes ever hit the ground. The suitcase was very heavy, but I had so much adrenaline going that I didn't mind it. I would later on that night when I could barely move my shoulder. We ran as fast as we could and in the distance, we could hear the old man scream at us to stop and come to him. And then, he started to give chase. Had he been any younger, he would have caught us for sure. He did run pretty quick for an old man.

We made it to the fence where Abe leapt over it like a deer. I tossed the suitcase over, and I crossed the fence, too. We got on our bikes—me with the suitcase in hand—and pedaled down past the farmhouse and road like a bat out of hell down the winding country roads.

When we made it back to Abe's house, we rushed inside and waited by the kitchen window to watch and see if the blue truck came down the road. It did about five minutes later. And then a few minutes after that, it went back in the direction of his farmhouse. Me and Abe both blew a sigh of relief and laughed.

11

It was, as I said, the last adventure I ever went on. I just wished it was with the guys. They were what was missing. I only took a few of the magazines from that day's plunder and gave the rest to Abe. It wasn't about the magazines for me. It was about the adventure, you see.

It was about feeling something again since the summer of 1991. And even though creeping into an old barn looking for porn mags was something that was in my wheelhouse, it wasn't the same without the guys. I knew it would be different when we all got into high school, but that was one of many stark revelations that I had back then that times had changed—people had changed.

Me and Abe remained friends through the rest of high school. But he and I never shared another adventure like that one. We always talked about that day and stuff, but we never did anything like that again. I never hung out outside of school with him again after that day. Not that I didn't like him, but because it didn't feel right, you know? The only thing I can compare it to was like wearing a pair of shoes that are a size too small. Yeah, they're shoes, but they don't fit. And Abe didn't fit. I wanted my old shoes back.

CHAPTER 3
THE SWIMMING POOL INCIDENT

CHAPTER 3

After we discovered the grisly remains of our much-cherished porno magazines, we decided to combine our money—what we had left from our few lawn-mowing ventures during the spring—and go to the local swimming pool for the day. It only cost a dollar per person back then to get in, and we had more than enough. When you think about it, it wasn't a bad deal at all: swim all day and look at girls. Even though I didn't swim, I still got my eyes full of the girls who were in our grade and even the ones in high school in their hardly-there swimsuits.

Some of the coolest memories I have took place in swimming pools and parks. I remember once, there was a special night swim a few years prior to that summer—and man was it awesome just to be there under the stars. Mandy was even there. I remember; and if I close my eyes right now, I can see her in the night under the tall pool lights, smiling and laughing with her hair pulled back. It's funny how some memories never leave you, no matter how much time has gone by. I've got a lot of memories of Mandy, but that memory is in my top five.

Going to the pool was a good way to kill time and to see other kids that you probably wouldn't have seen during the summer. Most of the kids that frequented the public pool were kids that we only saw at school. The place was like a social club of sorts—a small-town Club Med, if you will. Every kid that was somebody was there: your jocks, preps, rough ends, nerds, and just regular everyday kids like us.

You would go there and mingle with the other kids, some older and some younger, and drink your choice of Coke, Pepsi, Hawaiian Punch, or Sprite from the vending machines. Popular music from that time could be heard blaring from the speakers, usually from rock bands: Guns N Roses, Warrant, R.E.M., Poison, and even some N.W.A. Also, you would always see Stewart, the Pauly Shore-looking lifeguard from his days on MTV, sitting perched high upon his chair, watching for danger. He was a cool guy and usually chatted up the senior girls as he was just fresh from graduating high school that summer himself. I remember the girls all swooned over him.

2

I noticed Mandy started coming to the pool around the sixth grade. She had ever since her dad granted her permission to come for a few hours during the week on summer break. I made sure that I was there nearly every day, whether I knew how to swim or not, hoping she would be there.

All I wanted to do was be somewhere near her—just to see her somewhere besides the classroom. And on Wednesdays, I did during the summers of sixth, seventh, and eighth grades. I would often ride my bike past her house, and sometimes she would be outside, and sometimes not. It was a crap shoot most times. Seeing her at the swimming pool was different. God, I remember just being filled with excitement and anticipation waiting for her to show up there. And when she would, I just fell in love every time. She was the most beautiful girl there—anywhere for that matter.

Since school had let out for the summer, the swimming pool opened up the doors for the season that next day. The smell of chlorine hung heavy in the air around the pool premises; and if the wind was just right, you could smell it and even taste it around the park where the swimming pool was located. Sometimes the smell was so strong, it could burn your eyes.

Sitting on one of the plastic lawn chairs that were lined up alongside the fence facing the deep end of the pool, I watched all the kids splashing around and having fun in the water. Honestly, I envied them. I wished that I could swim. Pete had tried in the past to get me out into the pool and teach me how. But I was too afraid to do so. Even Tommy and Curt tried to get me in there; no way. I was a land lover with a high value on my life.

Sitting there without my friends to talk to, I began to think about stuff, you know, kid stuff. I thought about how much change there was going to be when we all got into high school. It's one thing to suspect change or even feel it coming, but it's a totally different thing when that change comes and fundamentally alters everything you thought you knew in life. Even if you see a change in your life coming from miles away, you don't ever fully grasp the notion until it squares up on you and knocks the breath out of you. My friends didn't talk much at all about high school coming for us; about the next four years; or the state of our friendship during that time.

I didn't blame them—it's hard being a kid going from a small school where you know everyone, even the cooks and janitors, and to a place where you are just a face in a hallway. I tell you what I was afraid of... being just a face in the hallway. I was practically one in my own home, so what chance did I stand in high school? The only thing that I had in my life back then were my friends. They were my lifeline in every sense of the word. Without them, who was I? What identity did I have for myself? When I thought about that—and I did often as you might imagine—it scared me because they were in a sense who I was. I didn't want to move to another school, a bigger school. I wanted things to remain the same.

I had creature comforts there at Claxton Elementary. I had my friends, my secret hiding places on the playground where me and the boys would hide after our class went back inside after recess. I knew the teachers, the ones who liked me and the ones who hated me. I knew the bullies to stay away from and the kids that treated me well. I knew to bring my lunch on Thursdays because I hated pinto beans and cornbread down in the cafeteria. I knew that Fridays were always pizza day and that none of our teachers assigned any homework for the weekend.

I was afraid that high school was going to be the complete opposite of all the things that I knew. And I didn't know it then, sitting out there by the pool that day, but I was right—one hundred percent correct on all of the things that I feared. I just wish I knew then what I was going to have to learn the hard way later on. There is no way to predict the future, no matter how much you wish that you could.

———

As I watched my friends play—laughing and screaming in the pool– I sat back and wondered if me and my brothers were going to be friends forever. I know that sounds all gooey and sappy, but I worried about things like that back then. I didn't have much of an emotional investment return with my mom and dad. My friends and my grandmother were about it for me. Losing them would knock me for a loop, scattering my bearings all over the place. So yeah, I did worry.

I guess at that point in time I needed them in my life for me to function well or at least as well as I could. They were my constants in this experiment that we call life. I think at the time I *needed* them more than they needed me. They were all that I had. It's sad to a degree. But that's where I was at early in my life. I had a lot of abandonment issues, I guess you could say.

Curt, Tommy, and Pete were who I was as a person—my identity. The guys were my only family as my parents were nothing but ghosts. The prospects of all of us drifting off from each other—especially them away from me—caused me a lot of distress. More so leading up to that summer. My mind was occupied with how everything was going to end in high school. I was under siege mentally on how I would handle it all when our friendship eventually blew apart. Who was I going to be afterward? What was my identity going to be going forward? A lot of questions and at that time with no good answers. Everything was just speculation, of course, but sometimes you just know.

Some days I was barely able to hold it together mentally. The depression that had gotten a hold of me a few years ago before that summer never eased its icy grip on me. It was in sixth grade when my depression hit me full-blown. I had felt low before here and there, but I was able to shrug it off—only for it to come back often much stronger. I couldn't go to my parents with any of the things going on inside my head. They wouldn't understand, nor would they have taken the time to care.

Dad was a "just walk it off" type of parent—because he didn't do feelings—and my mom was mentally out of order pretty much like an empty vending machine. Curt and I had talked about some things here and there, and it did help ease some of the pressure. But he was far from a licensed therapist. He had things going on inside his home and head, too, that caused him much discord.

I could never fully outrun my depression. At one point around Christmas time in the seventh grade, I snuck and took Dad's .45 and brought it to my bedroom. I was going to kill myself. I was finished—that young, I was just flat-out done with life. I had thought about it for a while as things had never gotten better for me. I felt like it was just time to end it all. That moment in time was one of the watershed moments in my young life. Humans have numerous watershed moments throughout their lifetimes, and that year that I held Dad's gun in my hands was one of my earliest memories where it was do or die.

I think that everything had been eating away at me all at once that night. To be honest, most of that year. By the time school had dismissed for our Christmas break for two weeks, I was mentally worn out, just over and done with it all. I couldn't handle Mom and Dad anymore. I had a mom who was a walking, talking mental case who collapsed under whatever it was inside her head, and my dad was never around, choosing work over home and family. I was failing math and science, and it didn't matter how much help I had gotten after school for it- I couldn't get it. As for my looks, I didn't even like when I saw myself in the mirror. Looking back on it, I was just a normal-looking kid at that age.

The first breakouts of acne started cropping up on my cheeks and forehead. No different than ninety percent of the kids my age. But for some reason, I felt like a freak with it. And no matter how hard I tried to wash my face, it would never go away. It seemed to multiply with no rhyme or reason. It was body chemistry, and there was nothing that I could do about it. Some kids had it worse than I did; but when I would look at myself in the mirror, I hated what I saw looking back at me. That year everything seemed to just press down hard on me, and I wanted a way out in the seventh grade.

I remember going down some pretty dark roads inside my mind around this time. I felt like all I had to do was sneak my dad's .45 out of his drawer that he didn't think I knew about, stick the barrel in my mouth, and pull the trigger—goodbye friends, Mandy, school, not perfect skin, Mom, and Dad. With one slight squeeze of the trigger, all my cares and worries would be gone.

It would be goodbye to everything with no note on why I did what I did. I remember sneaking that gun from my dad's drawer one night while he was working late and Mom was locked up in her room. I knew that it was loaded. He always kept it loaded. I took the gun to my bedroom, locked the door behind me, and sat down on the floor. My back was up against my bed, and I laid the gun in my lap.

My hand kind of just held the grip softly as I decided what I was going to do. I had given it a lot of thought and hadn't really and truly decided if I was going to do it, but getting the gun was a start. I'd thought about getting it out of the drawer many times, but that night I did it and that was a huge step. It was no longer just a thought that I ran over in my mind. That silver .45 was sitting in my lap and was ready to go if I was.

I remember that night pretty well. I had just run out of places in my mind to go. I couldn't close the door on all of the thoughts like I used to. Things had finally caught up with me, and on that night, I was at my most desperate and vulnerable. I raised the gun to my mouth, stuck it in, and closed my mouth around the metal barrel. I can still taste the metal some days. I'm sure that has been long gone, and maybe it's nothing but a phantom memory. But believe me when I say that taste is still in my mouth sometimes.

I cocked the hammer back like I had seen people do on TV and closed my eyes. Tears poured from my eyes and down my cheeks. I wasn't shaking or nervous like I thought I would be when the moment of truth—the do or die moment—arrived. I think more than anything, I was looking forward to just getting away from everything. And man, that was a good feeling there.

I placed my finger on the trigger. I don't know what really happened. But for some reason, I pulled the gun away from my mouth, uncocked the hammer, and laid it down on the floor. I couldn't do it. Even in my most dire time, I just backed out of taking myself away from the world and my problems. That act alone caused me some problems and even heartbreak because there I was, ready to end it all, and I couldn't manage to do something so simple as squeezing the trigger of Dad's .45. I remember crying myself to sleep on my bedroom floor that night. It was the last time that I ever got that close to killing myself.

———

It is often said that your actions, moments, and choices define you as a person. They forget to mention that your friends have just as much bearing on who you are and who you eventually become. There comes a time in all of our lives when you either follow your friends, or you break from them. I wondered which way I was going.

My friends had defined me just as I had defined them. If we got into high school and the band broke up so to speak, what would define me? Who would I be after the break-up? Would I just be a kid with distant friends—all of us connected with a shared past? That thought utterly frightened me. The reason was that me and my boys were like brothers, as close as actual family. I never could picture them not being in my life.

Me and my friends were destined to be together, I guess you could say. We all grew up in the same neighborhood and became friends way early on in our lives. The first of the cast that I met was Curt. He was just like me, more so than the rest. We had the same interests, same sense of humor, and even the same tastes in food. Me and Curt were like the tag team champions of our small neighborhood. He lived two houses down from me. One day in the second grade, me and him met up in his front yard and played tag. We had been friends ever since that moment. He was one of the best friends I ever had.

Later on, me and Curt met Pete and Tommy at the baseball field at the park one day playing baseball probably around the fourth grade. They asked us if we wanted to play with them, and we did. We all hit it off right then and there. They, too, had lived in the same neighborhood, just a little further down the street from me and Curt.

Pete was the type of guy who later would become a football player in high school. He was a damn good one, too. In the last game of his senior year, he was plowed by a guy who looked like a building with teeth. It was a cheap shot that got Pete that night. His college football scholarship would soon be over not too long after that injury. Too bad—he was pretty good. Pete was like the leader of our humble group. He was strong-minded and had good leadership skills, even then as a kid. He had what I called good street smarts. Pete was always there for me, Curt, and Tommy. He was as loyal as a person could get. He was a true friend and still is even if I have not seen him in decades. They do not make them like Pete anymore...at least I've not met any like him since.

Tommy was a good guy, too. He was very athletic, smart, and the funniest person that I ever knew. The guy was truly awesome. He was the mouth of our group. He always stood up for those kids who were bullied on the playground, and that would oftentimes get *him* into fights. He didn't care though; he was stopping the bullies from picking on those small kids. It was his job as he saw it.

All those fights had gotten him a notorious reputation with the teachers. They saw him as a complete troublemaker. That thought could not have been further from the truth. He fought the bullies, and everyone knew that but the teachers. The teachers just looked down on him because he was always in the principal's office after another fight. I can't recall the number of times that boy had been suspended for fighting. So much so that he nearly got sent away in the seventh grade. The teachers and the principal didn't understand that Tommy was like a protector of the meek. Maybe they did and just didn't care. Sometimes the adult view and the kid view are on two different spectrums. This is a hidden truth that no one tells you about. You find out when you grow up.

3

We had been at the swimming pool for what seemed to have been hours and still no Mandy that fateful day. But what if she did appear? What was I going to do other than just sit there, admiring her from afar as always? The guys were right; I was never going to ask her out. I did not have it in me. It was a long shot anyway because it wasn't Wednesday, and that's normally when she would stroll in. But hey, I was hopeful.

I had gotten up from the plastic lawn chair, peeled my legs from the plastic, and walked over to the Coke machines to get myself a drink. When I got there, Samantha Workman got my attention, "Is Tommy here?" she asked.

"Yeah," I replied. "He's in the pool."

"Ask him if he would call me tonight. I want to know if he wants to go to the movies or something," she asked.

Okay, here was the problem: Samantha was a good-looking girl in our class. I mean, she was beautiful. Out of every boy's league, that's for sure. But for some reason, Tommy would never go out with her, and she LOVED that kid. We never knew why, and it was not a secret how she felt. Everyone in our eighth-grade class knew about her affinity for Tommy. I remember that we used to rag Tommy pretty good about not going out with her. "What are you, gay?" Pete asked him one night at a campout. Tommy didn't reply to that question.

Samantha chased him relentlessly from fifth to eighth grades and well into our high school years. She was head over heels in love with Tommy. I think it dates back to the fifth grade, but I might be wrong. According to Tommy, he and Samantha were partners in a science project, and he pretty much did the entire volcano project himself because she didn't understand how to do it. Since that moment, she was just all about him. But he wasn't all about her. Any guy would kill to be the one she liked, but Tommy waved it off as nothing. I never knew why exactly. He never said. Later that summer, however, Tommy would tell me a secret that made me finally understand why he never liked Samantha. It made sense to me then.

"I'll go over there and ask him," I told her as I put my coins into the coin slot and pressed the Coke button. I knew Tommy wouldn't call her though. I got my Coke can and walked over to the deep end of the pool and yelled for Tommy.

He swam over to the edge where I stood cautiously several feet, "What?"

"Samantha's here."

"So?" he said, wiping the water from his eyes.

"She wants you to call her tonight. I'm just delivering the message." I told him, popping the top on the Coke can.

"I ain't calling her."

"You know, a girl like that only comes around…" I started before he cut me off.

"I'm not getting into this…" Before Tommy could finish what he was going to say, this guy named Mark Pike pushed me over into the swimming pool. My memory is a little hazy on this event. All I remember was that I felt myself get pushed violently from behind, snapping my head backward, the Coke can flying through the air and falling into the water. It happened that fast, almost in one single violent motion.

I remember feeling that extreme panic wash over me when I discovered that I was underwater. I guess I must have blacked out or something because when I opened my eyes, I was on my back, looking up at Stewart the lifeguard, Pete, and Curt hovering over me asking me if I was okay. I coughed up water, trying to catch what breath I had in my lungs. I rose from the wet concrete, looking around and resting on my elbows. My mind was trying to process what in the hell just happened.

Everything happened so fast that I had no idea what had just transpired. "What happened?" I managed to ask, trying to regain my breath. I was shaking from the shock I had just gone through.

"That prick Mark pushed you into the pool," Curt replied.

"We thought that you were a goner. Tommy pulled you out and gave you mouth-to-mouth before Stewart could get to you," Pete said.

"Are you okay, dude?" Stewart asked.

"Yeah, I think so. Just… feel a little woozy though." I said, still breathing hard and scattered, feeling like the place was spinning around.

And my chest hurt from Tommy giving me CPR. Curt, Pete, and

Stewart picked me up off the wet concrete, walked me through the crowd of kids, and sat me down in a plastic chair alongside the fence. All the people at the pool thought I had drowned. Truth be known, I probably did, but thank God for Tommy. He brought me back.

"Where's Tommy?" I asked through my labored breathing.

"He's outside beating the hell out of Mark," Curt said.

I got up from my chair and managed to walk outside while swaying side to side, trying desperately to keep from falling onto the concrete with everyone still looking at the kid that should have died. I was wobbling a lot, but I wanted to see what retribution Tommy was handing out.

Outside the swimming pool building, I saw Tommy kicking Mark, who was lying on the ground trying to cover himself from the blows. Mark– who was two years older than us, was a bully, and by the way, had a beef with me in the first place– was getting a good old-fashioned ass-beating.

Tommy knocked the bully onto the ground and then stomped on his face several times, barefooted mind you, cussing at him and promising him he would kill him if he ever fucking saw him again. Then he got on top of Mark and straddled him, with Mark on his back and Tommy started punching him stupid. Blood poured from his nose and mouth. I even heard Mark cry out for Tommy to stop.

I stood watching, still with difficulty breathing and my head still spinning, as Tommy stood up for me. That was one of the reasons that I liked Tommy; he always did what needed to be done. He always stood up for people like me. I could never thank him enough for saving my life, I mean, how could you? I was a goner, but he saved me. And to boot, he was putting the smack down on that punk ass that pushed me in the first place.

I had problems with that Mark kid in the past. He was a bully, plain and simple, with no decent friends. Most of them ended up in jail in later years. I hated him and so did Tommy and the other guys. I was so glad that he got what was coming to him. It was a long time coming. Of course, that fight had started a war between Tommy and Mark for years to come. And let me tell you something, those were some bloody battles.

Neither one would back down from the other. The first two years of high school, they went at it several times in school and out in town. I didn't see most of them, but the two I did see: one in the high school gym and the other in the high school cafeteria were epic before the teachers managed to break it up.

I stood there as Tommy finally got off Mark who lay there in the parking lot, bloodied and beaten. He didn't move at all, and the only sound that came from the thug was a low groan of pain. Tommy had thrashed him for pushing me into the pool. What a friend. This guy not only pulled my limp body out of the water and resuscitated me back to life, but he exacted severe revenge on my behalf by breaking Mark's face.

While I stood and watched Tommy fight, I didn't notice all of the swimmers that came from behind from the pool to watch. They were kids even clinging to the fence on the inside watching the brawl out in the parking lot. Hell, even the lifeguard, the person that was certified and designated to be responsible for us kids at the pool, watched Mark get his ass whipped. It was crazy. It was as if Tommy was Mike Tyson out there, and everyone wanted to see the match.

A heavy-breathing, busted-knuckled, shirtless Tommy walked away from Mark and over to me. Everyone at the pool clapped and cheered as my friend came over, "What's going on?" he asked, looking around at all of the kids clapping and cheering him on as he rubbed his right hand. He thought he had broken it on Mark's face, he later confessed.

"They watched... you beat down Mark over there." I said with labored breathing. I looked down at his bloody knuckles, and they were a mess. His hand was swollen and was already turning blue.

"Yeah, that son of a bitch! I can't believe that he pushed you in there. I should have fucking killed him!" he shouted, looking back at Mark who was trying to get up.

"Man, thanks for saving my life...you don't how much..." Before I could try to tell him how much I appreciated him saving my behind, Tommy stormed back over to Mark who was getting to his feet and tackled him. He wailed on him harder than before, busted hand be damned. What a day: our box of porn had been destroyed; I was almost drowned; and Tommy wore out Mark, a local bully. What a way to kick off summer vacation.

About ten minutes after Mark had finally gotten up off the parking lot, he staggered away for home. We watched as he slowly made his way from the parking lot and down the street. Tommy had decided to leave the pool and head over to Curt's house because nobody was there; and if he went to his house, he would be hit with twenty questions on what happened. Tommy really left because he thought that Mark would come back with an equalizer. We all left with Tommy, not wanting to hang around just in case Mark did come back. And knowing Mark like most kids in town did, he would be back with a bat, a knife, or something else that would give him an advantage. He didn't care.

4

We decided to go ahead and walk over to Curt's house and get into the medicine cabinet to help fix up Tommy's hand. I thought it was broken and so did Pete and Curt. Tommy could barely flex it there in the bathroom where I was putting peroxide on the open cuts while Pete held Tommy's hand up and over the sink. We all watched with fascination as the peroxide bubbled up white from those deep cuts.

His hand looked bad, but running it under cold water from the sink faucet helped after we cleaned his wounds. Curt gave Tommy some ibuprofen to help ease the pain. Pete walked out of the crowded bathroom and into the kitchen to get a bag of frozen peas from Curt's fridge. He brought it back to the bathroom where me and Curt were bandaging Tommy's hand. "What's this?" Tommy asked.

"Peas. We'll put it on your hand. It'll act as an ice pack for about fifteen minutes," Pete said.

"You guys want to hang here for a bit?" Curt asked. We all nodded. Curt and Pete walked out of the bathroom, through the house, and up the stairs to his bedroom.

I stayed with Tommy in the bathroom while the frozen bag of peas sat on the top of his hand. "Thanks for what you did back there," I said, finally able to thank him properly for his act of revenge on my behalf and for saving my life.

Tommy shook his head, "Nah, man, you ain't got to thank me." Classic Tommy. He was the type of kid that out of the four of us would run into a burning building to save people while me and the rest stood there watching. He was the bravest of our group.

"Well," I started, "I do. I could've died back there."

"Well, you didn't. I got you. Always will." Tommy sort of grinned at me.

"Let's get up to Curt's bedroom, so we can crack masturbation jokes on you since your hand is out of commission for a bit."

"Yeah, can't wait for that."

We got up to Curt's bedroom to hang out for a little while that afternoon. Tommy was bandaged up, and the bag of frozen peas and ibuprofen seemed to be easing the swelling. The medication had taken a considerable amount of the pain from his hand, he had told us. I still thought it was broken and so did Curt and Pete. But Tommy assured us that it wasn't. Just bruised, he said. I guess he would know; he had beaten the hell out of plenty of guys in his time.

Curt's bedroom window up there on the second story of the house, overlooking the park from his side of the street. As I watched cars pass slowly by on our street, I saw kids walking. I spotted someone in particular: Mandy. She and her friends, Courtney and Jennifer, were walking with their beach towels and dressed in their swimwear towards the pool. God, did she look beautiful.

I watched her walk past Curt's house from my vantage point and into the pool's parking lot where she and the other two disappeared into the confines of the public pool. I had missed my chance to see her there. It was okay, I thought. At least I was alive. Thanks to Tommy who was getting jokes from Pete about not being able to jack off tonight.

CHAPTER 4
CAMPING/TWO MOONS

1

SEVERAL DAYS LATER, the calendar turned to June. After my near-death experience, the fight between Tommy and Mark, and our box of porn having been ripped to shreds, we decided that we all needed to camp out to get things back to a sense of normalcy for the summer. Tommy's hand was really no longer an issue, and the blue shade of the bruise had begun to yellow a bit. The mobility also began to get better. Maybe it wasn't broken after all. Tommy could still use his hand, but he was easy about it. The jokes about him playing with himself didn't stop, however. They just got funnier.

Camping was in our blood, and it was a way for us to be out there in the wild. It was us against the elements of nature in Hudson's Woods— which wasn't far from our neighborhood at all. Plus, it was a time and place where we could feel like grown-ups, could cuss, and drink as many Cokes as we wanted without anyone telling us to stop. It was complete freedom out there in the woods under the stars and moon. I always looked forward to those campouts, whether it was in Hudson's Woods or in one of our backyards. Any of the locations was fine by me. Just being out there with my best friends—my brothers—was good enough for me.

Most of our campouts were the same, run-of-the-mill. We never deviated from our traditions or rituals, for that matter. Everything always played as follows:

I would bring the comic books that were in my collection. Sure, we had read them a thousand times, but who cared? It was something that was a staple in our campouts and was not to be left out. I think that started maybe in the fifth grade if I remember correctly. Sometimes we would go the entire night without reading them, and that was okay. Just having them was a requisite.

Tommy would bring a cooler full of ice with a case of Cokes tucked away deep inside the cubes of frozen water. In addition, he would bring sandwich meats, cheese, bread, and chips. Tommy would also bring his Martin acoustic guitar and sit and play for us when things got quiet, and the conversation was thin. I loved listening to him play and God, could he play. He was self-taught at the age of six– he told us– and could listen to a song one time and play it back without missing a chord. I remember the first campout we ever had, he played AC/DC's entire *Back in Black* album.

Pete would always bring sleeping bags for the four of us and a single tent. Why he brought a tent, I still don't know because we never slept in it. All it was, was a storage place for our stuff in case it rained or something like that. And the sleeping bags were not to be slept in. They were to be spread out on the ground for us to lie on around the campfire. The funny thing about our campouts was that we never actually slept out in the woods. I guess we were all too scared to do it, whether we wanted to admit it or not. Camping for us was more about having that distinct sense that we were alone and did not have to be bothered by grown-ups. It was as if we were calling the shots. We weren't if you really got down to it.

Curt would bring the matches to light the campfire. They weren't hard to get, those matches, because Curt was a smoker from time to time. He wasn't a big smoker but liked to do it when the notion struck him, which it always did when we would camp either in our backyards or in Hudson's Woods. Curt got this smoking idea—I call it an idea because it wasn't a habit, not yet—from his parents. They both smoked, and I guess it was eventual that Curt would be, too. I don't think he liked doing it if

I'm honest. I think what he liked the most about it was that it made him seem older. At least he looked older to me when he smoked at our campouts. The rest of us didn't smoke. Pete had tried it with Curt at a campout one night and nearly coughed himself silly. Curt seemed to take pride in the fact that he could handle those Marlboro cigarettes when Pete obviously couldn't. I never attempted and neither did Tommy. It was Curt's thing. We all had something back then.

I remember this one time, the very first time that I ever saw Curt light up, we were up in his bedroom probably in 1989, sixth grade, this was. He was smoking up in his bedroom, blowing the smoke into a brown paper bag, and then putting the bag outside his open window to let the smoke out. I laughed then as I am now thinking about him doing that. "Why not just blow the smoke out of the window instead of blowing it into a bag and then letting it out the window?" I asked. Curt seemed stunned that he didn't think of that first. By all accounts, he should have. He said that he didn't want to take any chances with his mom finding out that he smoked, but who was he trying to kid? I don't think his mom would have liked it, but she didn't put up much of a fight to curtail his nasty habit. She smoked two packs a day, and his dad smoked three, I'd say.

2

Our campouts were legendary in childhood back then. Sometimes, not always, we would have outsiders who were friends of ours join us on one of our many excursions. A campout that I recall happened on Halloween night in 1989, our sixth-grade year. We called that campout "Halloween Hell." What follows are the details of that night that immortalized our camping adventures. Side note here: For every campout that I planned, it rained. After Halloween Hell, I was forced into campout planning retirement. And wouldn't you know that for each campout afterward that was planned by Curt, Tommy, or Pete, it never rained? How about that...?

We had set up camp at our place in the woods on Halloween that year. It was the first time in our young lives that we had ever camped out on Halloween. It was like we had hit the lottery that year. Halloween just happened to fall on a Friday. It was exciting for us. Instead of going out and trick or treating—which by that year we had gotten too old to go around in costumes begging for candy—we planned to go on a campout.

Me and the guys had discussed it in math class earlier that day. Hearing that we were going camping, Buddy Martin, our mutual friend for years, asked if he could come and join us. It marked the first time that an outsider had wanted to come along. And it was the first time that we had someone outside our clique there at a campout in our spot in the woods. It was also the last time.

———

The whole day it had rained. Not a gully washer, which for those who don't know what a gully washer is, it is a heavy rain that smacks angrily against the ground causing a loud sound that numbs the ears for hours on end. Some of the hardest rain you'll ever see comes from those. The Halloween Hell rain was the worst kind of rain: an all-day drizzle that never stopped or eased up nary a bit. It just rained and rained and rained.

We met up with Buddy around 4:30 that afternoon in front of Wilson's Drugstore there in town. It was already getting dark due to the black, dreary clouds about the town. We knew that we had to hurry up and get to the woods to get everything ready and set up before it got to where we couldn't see. Hudson's Woods was dense in places and once it got just a little dim outside, the woods were nearly pitch black. That sometimes made it a scary place. Of course, the standing rumor around town was, depending on whom you spoke to, the woods were haunted, to begin with. Had to do with that huge circular clearing in the middle that people called the "UFO clearing."

We rode our bikes from the drugstore, across town, and eventually down the gravel service road to where it spilled in front of Hudson's Woods. With Buddy being new to our camping ways, we didn't ask anything of him. We told him to just meet us, and we would take care of the rest. And we did. All he had to do was show up.

We had gotten our tent set up, but we did not roll out our sleeping bags. The ground was too wet for that. All the stuff that we brought to our campouts stayed in the dry of the tent that Tommy and Pete put together. The day was waning quickly, and the woods were getting darker by the minute. We were going to have to start a fire, or at least try, through all the wetness. We had never camped in the rain like that and had no idea what we were in for, to be honest. What we were in for was never forgotten. It was brought up over the years, and we laughed about it. The night it happened, we weren't laughing about it at all.

Curt had the brilliant idea before we even went to the woods that he was going to bring some wood from his dad's wood shed.

"Supposed to be raining all damn day, and there won't be a single stick dry in the woods to start a fire with," Curt said, with all of us nodding in agreement right before school let out for the day. "Matty, why do we allow you to plan our campouts?" We all laughed because he wasn't wrong.

He loaded the wood up in this huge duffle bag that took him and Pete to carry from his house to the campsite. Before we even met Buddy at the drugstore that day, Curt and Pete had the dry wood all ready to go, and it seemed that the rain wasn't going to stop us.

3

At the campsite, we pulled the dry wood out of the bag and stacked four really good-sized logs of oak in the fire pit we always used. None of us had remembered to bring any paper to put underneath the wood for it to burn and catch. Curt opened the book of matches and struck a match head on the black, coarse striker and held the lit match onto the wood. Nothing. Again, he did it. Same result. The wood would not catch and without paper to keep a fire going under the wood, the wood would never catch.

"Well," Curt said, "ain't this a bitch?"

At that point, I thought we were doomed, and that the campout was going to be canceled because we certainly could not be cold and wet all night. We would surely catch our deaths. After standing there looking at the others and wondering what needed to be said, I walked over to the tent, crawled in, and got out some of my comic books.

The guys knew how I was with my comics. They were precious to me. I always handled those books with kid gloves, and the guys had always made fun of me for that for years. All of them, even the ones I wasn't particularly fond of, were put in a releasable bag for protection. But when they saw me tossing them into the fire pit underneath the wood to use to start the fire, they knew that the situation was serious.

With several of my less desirable books in the fire pit—the ones that I could do without if I had to—Curt struck another match and knelt and held the flaming matchstick next to the colored paper. Instantly, the books went up, and a little later, the wood that was above the burning comics caught. We had warmth and light at the expense of some of my collection. I was okay with it. Now, if all I had brought with me was my *Batman* comics– forget it– we would have suffered the entire night or just left. Nothing could make me burn those. I had limits, for God's sake.

4

Not much went on like it usually did that night, I remember. It was too wet and too cold. The temp, which had been hovering around 60 nearly all day, had dropped to around 45 by sunset, and I'm guessing around 38-40 degrees as night fell. It felt colder than that. The rain was cold, and the mood was miserable. We basically stood around in a circle around the fireplace shivering and talking about how bad this sucked. The fire was warm, but we were too wet for it to really help. But at least the fire was something.

I hated it out there that night. I wanted to call it and go home but didn't dare say it. This was my idea, and the captain had to go down with his ship, right? Besides, we couldn't get any wetter or colder. Why not just stay, right? We were already there—already in the soup. Leaving then would have been us giving up and me looking more like a fool than I already did. I did have the best intentions. As I looked around at the guys' faces that were dark and glowing red and orange from the campfire, I could see how miserable they were that night. They weren't having any fun—none of us were—especially not Buddy. I could tell that he wished he would have stayed home.

5

As the night progressed, it got notably worse. It rained—sometimes hard, sometimes light—and everything that we normally did on campouts had been ruined. All we could do was sit on the wet logs, bundled up in our coats and other such warm apparel, and talk about mostly the weather that had dampened the spirit of the campout. Here we had the new guy, Buddy, whom we had invited to our campout, and all it did was rain.

I'm sure that he was hoping to go on and spin tales of what we all did that night. Our campouts were the stuff of legends. I'm also sure he thought that he was going to have fond memories of his first campout with us. And I guess for all intents and purposes, he did. He was a part of something that had gone down in our history called Halloween Hell.

———

Later that night, probably around 3 or 4 o'clock in the morning, we all mulled over the decision of whether or not to call it a night. It would be the first time that we even considered leaving a campout. I was hesitant and did not want to leave. The others clearly did, especially after Tommy had taken off his very own jacket and used it to start another fire after the first one finally died. By that time, I had burned the comic books that I wasn't afraid to part with, but what was left there was no way I was tossing into the fire. Me and Pete got into a war of words—mostly because we were tired and aggravated by the circumstances of the night —about my tossing the rest of my comic books into the dying fire. That was not going to happen. I actually thought that we might get into a fist-fight there for a moment over it. Then Tommy took his jacket and settled the argument by putting his jacket into the fire. It caught and the flames fanned up, making things bright and warm once again. But only for a little while.

We had resorted to burning clothes that night. I think that was the last straw for them. I told the guys let's just tough it out until sunrise; then we would pack up camp and head home with a good story to tell on the next campout. By saying that, I did something that I had never done before or since. I crawled inside the dry two-person tent and fell asleep inside covered by nothing more than my soaking wet coat and clothes. It was the first and last time that I had ever done that.

6

I awoke from my slumber finding the right side of my face lying in a pool of cold water. Quickly, I rose from my position only to find myself lying in about what seemed to be two inches of water! The tent that was advertised to be waterproof was not. I found that out the hard way.

As my teeth chattered from the cold and wetness, I unzipped the tent door and crawled back outside. I looked around at the shadowy images that were the logs, and I discovered that my friends, my boys, had left the woods and gone back to the dry confines of their homes. I looked at my watch and could make out that it was 5:30 in the morning. It was time to go home; at least it was close enough. I just could not believe that they left me in the woods in a tent alone in a forest by myself.

Anything could have happened to me out there by myself alone in the woods. I stood there weary-eyed and scanned the darkness of the woods thinking about how eerie things seemed when you're by yourself in a place like that. Hudson's Woods crackled from the rain falling off the tree limbs and onto the leaves on the floor, making things much scarier than they probably were. That's when the stories of the woods being haunted flooded my mind. It's crazy how scared you can make yourself when you're alone.

I was angry that they had left me in the woods, sleeping in a pool of cold rainwater. I vowed to thrash them when I saw them the next day. But first things first; I had to get home and warm up before I caught the flu. That was the absolute coldest I have ever been. The second coldest came in March of 1993 during the blizzard that hit the area. I, along with some newer friends I had met at high school my sophomore year, went sledding down Big Hill there in Claxton. We were all doing stunts and tricks, and all of us were rating each other's efforts. I, for whatever reason, decided that I was going to sled down Big Hill with no clothes on to try to get a perfect score from my friends. Why? I don't know. Let me tell you, that was cold, but nothing as cold as that walk home from Hudson's Woods that early morning, soaking wet in mid-twenty-degree temps.

———

I was getting ready to leave the campsite when I thought of something: was I going to walk through the woods alone? I mean, we *had been* playing in those woods for years. I knew every turn; every tree that had fallen; and even knew the winding pattern of the path that cut through one end of the forest to the other. But traversing through the woods alone in the dark was not something that I was willing to do, especially not without a flashlight.

So, I did the only thing that I knew: I sat there in the drizzle wrapped up in a wet and cold jacket shivering wildly, praying silently that the day would break, so I could walk out of there. I was going to kill my friends when I saw them, I kept telling myself.

The day had broken, but it was still dreary and rainy. It was good enough light for me to feel safe enough to walk through the woods where I could at least see. I had decided that I wasn't going to break the tent down because there was stuff still inside it. I couldn't carry the tent, the cooler of drinks, and the sleeping bags. I figured that it would be safe until later on that day.

As I was about to follow the trail out of the woods, I noticed something that I had never seen in the woods before: a raccoon, a young one. I stood there, and me and the animal locked eyes. It could not have been any more than ten feet from me. I didn't see it at first when I crawled out of the tent. I guess my eyes weren't focused enough there in the darkness that was diminishing little by little in the break of day.

The raccoon was sitting like a statue and I stood there still. I had never been that close to a wild animal before. And I'm sure the raccoon had never been that close to a human before. A first for both of us. I raised my hand and gave a slow wave to the animal. It just looked at me, having no idea what I was even doing.

We stood there, locked in this stare-down of sorts in the woods. Light from the cloudy day was growing—still rainy, overcast, and cold. I could see my breath in the air. The raccoon sat looking, breathing, not knowing what else to do. I honestly didn't want to make a move toward the animal because I didn't want to scare it off. For some magical reason, I was entranced by this young thing. Then all of a sudden, with no warning at all, the animal darted away, running through the woods. I never saw it again. I never told the guys about it either. It was the first and only time I had ever gotten that close to a wild animal.

I eventually made it out of Hudson's Woods and made my way back home on my bike, which was hidden in the bushes next to the old service road. I stripped out of my clothes and jumped into a hot shower. Man, did it feel great. It was not long after the shower that I hit the bed and slept most of the day. Later that week, I came down with a nasty cold, all thanks to my friends who left me in the flooded tent.

When I did see my best friends the day after, I asked them why in the red hell they decided to leave me alone in the woods. The response that I was given was that I was sleeping, and they did not want to wake me. That was a lie, and I knew it. I think they left me there to suffer because I was the one who planned the campout anyway, and this was payback—a punishment. Like I can control the rain?

7

Our first campout in the summer of 1991 had started just like all the others. We were all sitting on our sleeping bags, propped up against the logs reading comics, eating, talking, and looking at the nice blazing fire that flickered about. It was dark, and the only sounds that came from the woods were from the night creatures that called the forest their home.

On that particular campout, me and the guys had a lot to discuss. I mean, the whole summer had to be mapped out. "I can't believe that you whipped Mark that bad," Pete said, chewing on his ham and cheese sandwich.

"I hate that fucking dude. He thinks that he's so tough," Tommy said, breaking small twigs into pieces and tossing them into the campfire absently.

"Well," I began, "thanks again for saving my life out there. I was a goner."

"You don't have to thank me, man. We're all like brothers here. I would have done the same thing for any of you." And Tommy would have. That was the kind of guy he was. He was perhaps the most noble of the four of us, and that was and currently is a virtue that's practically obsolete these days.

"I'm going to go after Mandy this week," I simply said after a few silent moments between us all. I waited for the guys to laugh and wave me off as usual. Eventually, they didn't disappoint.

"Yeah right!" Curt said quickly and laughed.

"I'm serious this time."

"You were serious the last time and the time before that," Pete pointed out.

"Dude, I almost died. I've been given a chance to do something with my life. I'm going to stop being scared and just go up to her and ask her out. Her phone number first and then a movie or something," I said, feeling my confidence meter going up.

It was easy to say stuff like that out there; simple to be bold when you were around friends out in the woods under a blanket of stars making statements about people when they weren't around you. It was, however, a whole other ball of wax when you had to do it when the daylight came. A lot of nighttime promises are broken in the daylight.

"No, you won't. You'll get close to her, and you'll back out like you always do. A chick like that won't be around forever," Pete warned. "High school is just around the corner, dude."

"I mean it this time. I just got to figure out how to do it. Timing has got to be primo. This is going to be *my* summer. So, yeah, there it is," I said wishing that she was there in the woods with us at that very moment so I could ask her out while I had a handle on my emerging courage. The guys looked at me seriously for about a second or two and then laughed wildly. I gave them the bird and looked off into the dark recesses of the woods.

———

Later on that night, me and the guys played several rounds of spades and talked a bit. We spoke about things that thirteen-year-old boys talked about back then in 1991: who would win in a fight between Batman and Spider-man; what girl would we like to do; what we wanted to be when we grew up; where we thought we would be in the next fifteen years—just stuff like that.

What I treasured the most on those campouts was the sense of belonging, the bonding that went on between the four of us. I never had those moments when I reached adulthood. I mean, how can you? You never have friends like you did when you were thirteen—there's no way. Those years when I was a kid, our friendship was authentic. Our brains and hearts had not yet been poisoned by the trials of adulthood. When you're a kid, things just are—you take things and roll with them at face value—not because you want to, but because you don't have a choice. The one choice we each made back then, the four of us, was to choose to be friends with the other. Even though I haven't seen those guys in decades, I'm thankful that I made the choice to be with them, to call them my best friends.

We all had that comfort zone with each other. It was good having people that you could talk to about things that were going on in your life—the ones that would understand and not judge. Looking back at my life, I don't know how I have made it without them for as long as I have. To say that those guys were my emotional crutches is a complete and utter understatement. Maybe if I had them as an adult in my life, perhaps things would have been different to some degree.

Not that my life has been bad, but having at least Curt around would've maybe given me a different perspective on things that came up. As it stood, all I had was just me when faced with life decisions. My wife has been great—don't get me wrong here—but sometimes you need someone who you've known your entire life who knows you and how you think.

When you grow up, you have friends, but mostly they're just work friends and get-bys. The friends I had back then were honest-to-God friends: brothers. They were what friends are supposed to be by definition. And I know that we didn't really hold that bond, but I will say this:

if I really and truly needed them, or just one of them, I know in my heart of hearts that they would've been there for me. I know that. We all had a connection deeper than any ocean.

8

It was around one in the morning on that first campout of the summer of 1991 when I saw something in the night sky over to the right of where we were camping. It was a light—a silver light just hanging off in the distance—breaking through the tree limbs from high above. It seemed far away.

I had noticed the floating orb of light ever since it had gotten dark and had assumed at the time it was the moon. I never really paid it much attention at all. I happened to look over when I opened my fifth Coke can of the night and saw that the light I had seen earlier in the night had still been hovering in the same place off in the distance.

Over to my left was the moon, the actual honest-to-God silvery moon! What's going on here, I asked myself. "Look over there," I said standing up and looking over at the light off in the distance. I then looked back over to the real moon to the left in the sky.

"What the hell is that?" Curt asked, finally putting his comic book down and joining me on his feet.

"I thought it was the moon earlier. But over there is the moon," I pointed out, showing the guys what I was talking about.

Tommy and Pete had gotten up by this time and looked in the direction that we were looking in, "Two moons?" asked Tommy.

"No way. We're not on an alien planet." Pete replied, not taking his eyes off the strange, white light off in the distance and the moon over to the left of us.

"Is it possible to have two moons?" I asked aloud to anyone that wanted to field the astronomy question.

"I don't think so. Mars has two moons, but not Earth," Curt said intelligently. Good old Curt, he was the academically intelligent one of the bunch. If anyone would know an answer to a question, he usually knew. Not that he was a know-it-all, mind you, but the kid was smart.

"Then what the hell is that?" Tommy asked, looking back at the moon and then back at the silver orb.

"How long has that light been there?" Curt asked.

"I noticed it when it got dark," I replied.

"I've never seen it before," Tommy stated.

"Me neither. And we've been camping here for years. What if it's aliens or something? Maybe that's their spaceship hovering there waiting to abduct us so they can...I mean, the UFO clearing ain't far from us," Pete said.

"Shut up," Curt said. "It's not aliens."

"You don't know," Pete shot back.

"Then what the hell is it?" I asked. I stood with my brothers looking off into the distance. "It hasn't moved since I started watching it a little while ago. It just stays in place."

"I don't know, but we need to find out," Pete said walking off toward the direction of the light.

———

We had walked toward the light with our flashlights in tow. The four of us started to make a trail in a part of the woods that we had never been in before. The place in the woods was grown up with thick patches of thorns and walls of small trees that made it almost impossible to pass through, but we were able to get through it all. Some cuts and deep scrapes on our arms, legs, and shirts that had been torn a bit, but we got through. It was kind of neat walking through a place in the woods we had never been to before.

By the time we had made it out of the woods, through the other side, and into a field that ran parallel, all four of us were cut and bleeding in various places. I had even torn my Braves shirt trying to make it through the walls of thorns and brambles. I was not happy about that. Pete had a nasty cut down his forearm, and Curt had to have me and Tommy help pluck some thorns out of his left hand.

There we were, standing out in the sage field that was waist-high in the dead of night. We looked off into the distance to where the light was clearer and more visible against the dark backdrop of the starry night sky. From our position, none of us could make out what it was. All we could tell was that it was circular and just seemed to sit there off in the distance, hovering. One thing, it was not a spaceship; at least I didn't think it was at the time.

"How far do you think it is from here"? I asked.

"Hard to tell," Curt said. "It looks like it's someplace out across this field."

"You think we should cross this field and get closer?" Tommy asked, shining his light around the field.

"I don't know. We've never been out this far before. Who knows what's out there in this field? Snakes could be slithering in there waiting for something to bite," I said.

He was right. The possibility of snakes lurking in that field was high. However, so were the woods, and we really never gave that a moment of thought in the past. Thinking about it now, it's a wonder that we never got bitten. I never saw a snake in there, and I don't think the guys did either. I'm sure they were in there though—had to be.

"But we can get bitten in the woods just as easily as we can out in the field," Curt said.

"True," Tommy said. "But what if there's like this big fucking old well in the field, and we fall in. We would die in there."

"Candy...ass," Pete said, taking steps toward the light.

"Where are you going?" I asked with our lights poised on him as he began to make his way through the waist-high field.

"I'm going to see what in the hell that light is," Pete replied.

Before we could talk him out of it, Pete screamed and fell, disappearing from our lights. I remember that we all screamed in panic. Here we were, four boys out in an unknown field, trying to figure out what a strange light was, and our best friend had been pulled down by someone or something.

We each stood there, holding our lights on the spot where Pete had plunged. I was so scared. I had no idea what had happened to our friend. I was ready to start crying when all of a sudden Pete sprang up, laughing and making fun of us, "I can't believe you guys! God, you are soooo easy!

Candies," Pete said, walking through the field toward the light. He was laughing at what he had done. I think our collective hearts began to come up from our stomachs as we followed Pete slowly in a single file line.

"I hate that kid sometimes," Curt said absently, shaking his head.

———

The only compass we had was the light in the sky that had gotten closer and closer with every step we had taken. Still, from our position there in the field, none of us could make out what it was. It still looked to me like a light hovering there in the night sky.

With us being in unknown territory and heading in the direction of something unidentifiable, I was scared a little—I have to admit. I didn't know about the others, but I feared what awaited us when we made it to the light that hung up there without any sound or movement.

I kept my eyes fixed on the light as we walked up an incline in the field. I wanted to see what it could be—wanted to see if it darted away if we got too close to it. *Could* it be aliens? I had no idea at that point. All I knew for sure was that we were four crazy kids who were walking across a field that was waist-deep, toward something that looked like a moon. The real moon, however, was behind us at that point.

As we approached the top of the hill, we were finally able to see what the light was. The light, the whole reason that we hiked across a field and up a steep hill, was determined to be nothing more than a night light that hung on the side of a tall standing pole. The light belonged to a house that sat on top of the hill that overlooked the sage field and Hudson's Woods. We had always known about the house because Dr. Maddix had lived in this huge three-story home that he had built about twenty years ago. I guess he finally put a light outside. We should have known, but in our defense, we were just stupid kids.

"Not a moon," Curt said, turning and looking down at the hill we just climbed.

"Not a spaceship either," Tommy also said.

"A night light? I can't believe we came all this way for a damn night-light," I said disappointed. I guess standing there, I wanted it to be some-thing more, something worthwhile. But all it was, was a simple night light positioned on a twenty-foot pole that gave light to the dark surroundings of the huge house that sat there.

"Well, at least we know what the light is now. They must have just put this thing up the other day. That would explain why we hadn't seen it before," Curt said.

"Well, let's go back. I'm kinda hungry," Pete said.

But before we could turn and march down the hill and into the field, a man from the house yelled something that to this day, I still cannot make out, and then a shot was fired from a shotgun that I'm guessing that the man was holding. He must've been looking out one of his windows, saw our flashlights, and thought we were prowlers or some-thing. It's the only thing that I can figure out.

We were trespassing on his property in the middle of the night in a remote location. I would be scared, too. Screaming, we ran down the hill as fast as we could, trying to hurry and dodge the pellets from the shotgun that we thought was coming after us.

Tommy had fallen and rolled down the steep hill quite a distance before he regained his footing and ran rabbit-like across the field. That was one of the several times in my life that I was truly frightened. I thought that we were going to be shot dead while running back to the woods.

In retrospect, we should have known better than to creep around a man's property, especially in the darkness. But then I stopped to think: we were just kids back then, that was all. We meant absolutely no harm. All we wanted to do was to see what the bright, white light was that seemed not to move but just sat there hovering. One thing it was not was a moon—certainly not an alien spaceship.

CHAPTER 5

THE TODD EXPERIENCE/MANDY'S NUMBER

1

IT WAS SATURDAY MORNING. I had just finished watching cartoons for the morning—reruns of the season past. That was okay with me because I liked watching *Garfield and Friends, The Real Ghostbusters, Beetlejuice,* and *Teenage Mutant Ninja Turtles* while I ate my Fruit Loops or Honey Combs or whatever cereal we had in the cabinets at the time. Very rarely did I ever have a hot breakfast. Sometimes my dad would cook eggs, bacon, and toast, but those days seemed to be lost to time. Honestly, I can't remember the last time Dad cooked breakfast. I might've been ten, eleven years old maybe? I don't know. Mom cooking breakfast? That was back in the Stone Age. I think she stopped doing that on a consistent basis when her mental health had gone sour.

I had gotten my clothes on and put on my Atlanta Braves hat, making sure to pull it down low, just like Steve Avery did his hat when pitching for the Braves. I liked watching him pitch; and when I would play baseball at the park, my delivery was just like his. It was difficult to emulate, but I was getting the hang of it each time I pitched.

I had almost made it out of the house—right there in the kitchen to go out the backdoor—when my mother came walking from the hallway from where her bedroom was. She looked tired, which was how she always looked back in those days. Most of all, she looked like she wanted to quarrel. I could always see it in her eyes and the way she used to grin. I hated that grin of hers. It was sinister, and it always scared me, especially when her bipolar episodes began. Dad would later that day confess to me that he thought she had schizophrenia as well. I never knew, nor did my dad, which woman we were getting that day. Turns out, I was getting the not-so-nice version; the full-blown psycho; the woman that scared me.

"And now, where might you be going?" my mother asked in that matter-of-fact way. I swear her voice changed when she got like that. It made my skin crawl. Does even now as I recall it.

"Just to the park to play some ball."

"I think it's way too hot to be out there. You'll catch a sunstroke. Just stay in your bedroom for the day."

I knew that this was going to be a fight—a battle of words which I was probably going to lose. I always lost when she was like this. I did have an ace up my sleeve though. My dad was home and was outside working on his car.

"It's not going to be that bad," I replied, hand on the silver doorknob.

"It's going to be well past a hundred today, and I don't want to hear it!" she said with her voice rising. Before I could say something in rebuttal, my dad twisted the doorknob from outside and pushed it open, scaring me. I backed away from the door and watched as he entered.

"Hey, Matty," Dad said as he came inside and walked to the kitchen sink.

"So you're going to have to just miss playing baseball today. No place for kids outside today. Tell him, Terry. Tell him he ain't going out in this heat. That's all we'd need, ain't it? Have to load him up and take him to the hospital for sunstroke. Good luck with that. Good luck on paying that doctor's bill with money we ain't got. I see what you're trying to do. Oh yeah, you may not think I see, but I know."

I was scared at that moment because I had absolutely no idea what she was talking about. It was clear to me and my dad that she was going down that rabbit hole again. When mom got like that, it was best to ride the wave as long as possible. But this time, Dad was here with me, and I didn't have to ride it alone. Most times I did because he was gone to work or wherever it was he went to on the weekends. Thank God he was there.

"I think he'll be fine today," Dad said, wiping his hands off on a towel at the sink.

"Oh you do, do you?!" There was another sharp rise in her voice. She was getting angrier by the second. Her face was getting redder too.

"Yeah, he will. He's a kid. Let him go do kid things. He gets too hot, he's got enough sense to get something to drink or get into the shade. But you know what,? I'm not doing this with you today, okay? I'm just not."

"Who do you think you are?! Like you're his hero or something?! Like his personal Jesus?! There's only one Jesus, and you certainly ain't him! Fuck both of you! Don't talk to me ever again!"

Mom shouted at the top of her lungs, turned on her heels, and ran down the hall. She slammed her bedroom door shut, leaving me and Dad standing in the kitchen in bewilderment. She had gotten crazy before—gotten loud—but she was steadily getting worse. I think me and Dad both knew that and most of all felt it. I'll be honest with you, I didn't feel safe in my own home anymore. Me and Dad looked at each other, locked eyes, and in that moment, I could see how desperate he was. For a long time, I felt alone in that house. So did he.

It wasn't until at that very moment there in our kitchen that I came to understand that Dad had felt alone too. It was true that the woman I called Mom was slowly slipping away into something that I didn't recognize anymore. I hated her for that—hated what her mental illness had done to her. Hated that she refused any kind of help whatsoever. But Dad had lost too.

He had lost the woman he had fallen in love with; the woman he married; and the woman he wanted to grow old with. I remember a few months ago before that kitchen moment. There was a conversation I overheard with Dad and my Aunt Shey. Shey was Dad's sister. He didn't know I was in the living room, and Mom was at a yard sale. I remember my dad saying, "I can't force her to get help. I've done all I can do, and there are no more cards to play here. I'm just...I'm at a loss. There are no good options for this to end the right way."

When I heard Dad's voice, it was the voice of a tired man, a man who had given up after years of trying to punch through. I hated it for him—hated it for all of us. We were once a good family, but those days were long behind us now. We never got back to good. I wish that I could say in the end we did. Sometimes stories end badly.

I looked at my dad in the kitchen and him back at me. I nodded to let him know that I understood his pain to a degree that only a thirteen-year-old can. My dad didn't talk about his feelings; he was never that way. But he didn't have to say anything he was feeling at that moment. I could see it on his face—feeling it radiating off him in waves. He was tired. We both were.

2

Sandlot baseball. For us, it was a ritual nearly every summer day out there on the baseball field that sat parallel to the swimming pool in the town's park. The four of us would hit the ball field early, usually around 11:00 am or noon, and play up until we were tired or thought of something else to do. Those games would last usually til about three in the afternoon, at the least. Sometimes we played up until it had gotten dark if there were enough people to play, and the game was good.

The sandlot where we played always drew in those sunbathing and swimming in the adjacent pool. After the water had pruned their bronze skin, the youth would migrate over to the baseball field where we played and join us in a game. Throughout the afternoon, we would have around fifteen to eighteen kids that came from the pool to play. It was enough to split up the kids and have an actual game. It was always mixed ages and sexes. Sometimes the girls were better than most of the guys.

We had no worries about equipment. Pete's dad was a high school baseball coach and had about a hundred old and messed up baseball gloves and aluminum and wood bats out in his shed. There was also beat-up catcher's equipment. That was a huge thing to have: an entire treasure trove of equipment for us to use at our games. We just had to make sure and bring every bit of it back so it could be accounted for. Believe me, Pete's dad knew how much of everything he had; and if something was missing, which a catcher's mitt last summer did, Pete would get grounded for two weeks. Pete never lost another piece of equipment again, that's for sure.

We pillaged his dad's shed one day and discovered the treasure trove of used and abused leather. Pete asked his dad if we could use them and he said yes, if we could repair them. And that is what we did one day. We re-laced, re-tied, and rubbed the old brown and black leather down with a leather treatment that made them look as if they were new. We each had brand new gloves (new to us anyways) and took them with us on our baseball games out in the park.

———

That particular day in mid-June of the summer of 1991, it was hot. It must have been around 100 degrees before 2:00 pm and the humidity caused the sweat to just stick to your skin. I was up on the pitcher's mound, laboring to throw Pete a pitch that he could hit. Of course, the object in baseball was to get the batter out, or if you're the batter, to get a hit.

Every time that Pete had gotten up to bat, he would not swing at balls that came straight down the pipe or that would nip the corner of the plate. If we had umpires they would have called them strikes. I'd bet you a million dollars they would. We didn't allow walks in our rulebook there on the sandlot; so you either struck out swinging, or you put the ball in play and got out that way. Even getting hit by a pitch, we didn't allow a trip to first base.

With Pete, he would stand up there until he hit the ball. That refusal to swing at perfectly thrown baseballs made us out in the field angry, especially on hot, humid days like that one. I hated pitching to him. And as much as I hated pitching to him, Curt and Tommy hated being out in the field standing like scarecrows waiting for him to finally put the baseball in play. Pete would drive a crazy man even crazier. I'll admit, there were several times he had me so mad that I wanted to peg him right in the ribs. I never did though. The thought did cross my mind.

I had already thrown nine pitches to him on that particular hot afternoon. I admit, some of those balls were low and outside, maybe a couple inside. I wouldn't have offered them either. But the five that I did manage to get in the strike zone, he just looked at. I'm like, "What the hell?!"

"C'mon!" I screamed out, tipping my cap up, wiping my forehead from sweat and hearing the groans and jeers from Tommy and Curt in the field. "Swing at the fucking ball!"

"I will when it's in the strike zone!" he barked from the batter's box.

"This sucks, dude! One more pitch, and you don't swing at it you're fucking out automatically!" Tommy claimed from second base.

"No, I'm not! He's got to get it in the strike zone! I'm not swinging at pitches that are way outside!" Pete yelled back.

"You have no strike zone! Ken Griffey, Jr. ain't that selective! He just threw three right down the middle!" Curt yelled from the outfield. "You remember last summer when Mike was at bat, and we started that ten-pitch rule?" Curt recalled.

"The Mike Rule," I said. We came up with it the summer before because I had gotten tired of pitching to our other friend, Mike Dye.

"That's right!" Tommy said. "I totally forgot! We're evoking the Mike Rule! Starts now!"

The three of us stood out there and waited for Pete's response. I didn't think that he would give in, but he did...reluctantly. Probably because we were getting mad, and I would just stop pitching to him anyway. I was almost to that point. I was getting mad at Pete, but it could've been the heat too. Hot temperatures made the blood pressure go up.

"This is pitch number ten," I said to Pete. Climbing back up to the mound, I tugged on the bill of my Braves hat, and I wound and pitched the ball. He lined out to Tommy, who laughed as he caught the ball and ran slowly to the batter's box for his turn at bat.

"I was pressured! This is bullshit!" Pete said, slamming the bat down in complete disgust.

"You had good pitches to hit all day. Can't help it if you suck," Tommy said, grabbing the wooden bat and digging in at the batter's box.

Now, I liked pitching to Tommy. He would not swing at bad pitches. He would, however, swing at pitches that were in the remote area. Most times, he would drive my pitches over the fence and into Hudson's

Woods. Tommy was just a good all-around athlete. I remember that we used to make fun of him hard when he would be up to bat. His batting stance imitated that of Ken Griffey, Jr.'s stance.

Sometimes he would swing, missing badly, and then Pete would scold him for trying to be like Junior. Of course, Tommy would yell back for him to shut his damn mouth; all part of the game out there on the baseball field between us guys. It was all in fun—frustrating at times—but still fun.

3

As we played with just the four of us, kids from the swimming pool came over to the baseball field in small numbers as they always did. By 4 o'clock that afternoon, we had enough to divide into 2 complete teams. It was always an exciting time for me, I got to admit.

As I was getting ready to take the mound once again in an actual game, I turned my head and saw Mandy sitting on a wooden bench that ran alongside the first base side on the outside of the chain link fence. Man, I couldn't believe that she was there! My heart was in my stomach, and I had so much of an adrenaline rush seeing her.

She had never, ever come there during our games to watch. My God, I was so nervous. It was like I was pitching in the major leagues or something. Curt walked up to me from first base before the game got underway, "Do you see who's over there?" He was blowing pink bubblegum bubbles and then popping them loudly with his tongue.

"How could I not? Man, she looks awesome, doesn't she?" I said, rubbing the baseball between my hands nervously while standing on the mound and looking at her chatting with her friends. I had no idea if she knew who I even was. As far as I knew, she didn't. Not really. To her, I was probably that kid in her class at school.

"Yeah. Ask her out when we get out of this inning."

"Are you serious? Man, I can't do that. This ain't the right place," I said.

"When and where is going to be the right place? You made a vow, an oath. Remember? You can do this. Now let's get out of this inning, and then you go talk to her." Curt said and retreated to his position at first base where he played every time we had those big games where everyone joined from the pool.

———

It was the longest first inning I had ever pitched there at that ball field. Every time that I pitched the ball to the batter, I would sneak a peek over at Mandy who didn't seem to even notice me up there on the dirt mound. She sat there and laughed and talked to her friends. As far as I knew, I don't think she even watched me out there.

Mandy—I remember back in school—never did anything out of the ordinary there in class, just talked to her friends who sat beside her and answered the teacher's questions when called upon. She had no idea how much she meant to me back then. The simplest things that she did caused me to stir with so much happiness and love that no kid my age should even be privy to. I was her secret admirer and hopefully, one day if I could only be brave enough, I would be more than that.

The first inning did not go as I had planned out there on the field. Bobby Ringer, the first batter, had gotten a hit up the middle. A kid named John Beavers scorched a ball down the third baseline. Jeff King knocked one over the fence, bringing in everyone that I had put on base. Honestly, I was too nervous to even play. I wasn't even thinking about getting those guys at the plate out. All I was thinking about was talking to Mandy and how I was going to do that. And then it happened. Todd.

4

Todd Lowe was one of the meanest kids that I had ever known. He was around eight or ten, went about five-foot-three or four, cussed like a sailor, and would fight anyone, no matter how old or how big. He was so tough and mean that older kids didn't fool around with him much. His reputation as a bruiser was well-documented and extensively discussed. He knew it too. He had that swagger about him when coming to a place. He reminded me of the bad guys in those old Western films. They would walk into town, guns hanging loosely off the side of each hip, people moving out of his path in a hurry. That's how I saw Todd.

I had seen him beat up kids, teenagers in high school, who were a foot taller and a hundred pounds heavier than he was; didn't matter. Todd still beat them down. If he was losing in a fight, he would pull out all the stops: he would bite, poke out eyes, use sticks, and whatever else he could grab that was around him. I had heard one time that he was getting his ass whipped out in the school parking lot. When he was knocked to the pavement, he got a handful of fine gravel and threw it into the guy's eyes. Then he beat the hell out of the dude.

Todd fought dirty. He was a formidable opponent for anyone stupid enough to tangle with him. He was like an insane garden gnome and even had elfish features to boot: like sharp pointed ears and a sharp pointed nose. Maybe that was why he was so mean. I honestly can't say. You couldn't let his short stature fool you. He was dynamite in that small frame. A little Mike Tyson.

I was struggling up there on the mound. I had only recorded one out. I didn't care though. All I was doing was looking over at Mandy, who seemed to be having a wonderful time sitting on that bench. I had sat on that bench a million times at night by myself looking over across the darkness that consumed the park and thought about life. The bench was my special spot in the world. And Mandy was sitting there. How awesome was that? I appreciated the gravity of that moment seeing her there.

———

Lester Kincaid had gotten a hit in left field, and that is when Todd started running his mouth like he often did in any situation. I honestly didn't even know Todd was there on the baseball field. I never saw him coming from the pool to play. He never played with us thankfully. We weren't his usual crowd. His crowd always hung around the pool hall back in town.

My ears caught him from behind me out in the field. "Get off the mound, you suck! Son of a bitch!" Todd shouted in disgust, pacing about second base with a baseball glove on top of his head.

I turned around to make sure that the voice I heard that gave me butterflies matched the body I saw in my mind's eye. Yup. It was Todd standing behind second base because no one wanted him in any position. So he just inserted himself there. Nobody wanted him there, but they were all too scared to say or do something about it. Seeing who it was, I let it go; didn't want any drama because things with Todd could get really crazy, really fast. I let him continue to run his mouth. I wasn't fighting him. I'd lose anyway.

I went back to thinking about Mandy and how I would carry out my plan. Pitching was on the back burner in my mind at the moment. I looked to the catcher, Jimmy Butcher, wound up, and threw the ball across the plate. By the sound of the bat, I knew it was gone, long over the fence and into Hudson's Woods. I didn't bother even turning around. I knew it was going, going, gone.

"You suck! Get somebody up there that can fuckin' pitch! This is bullshit!" Todd's ranting had gotten the attention of everyone on the field, even Mandy and her friends over at the bench. He was getting louder and to me, looking for a fight.

Before I knew it, Pete had thrown his baseball glove at him from shallow center field, hitting him in the face.

"That hurt you bastard!" Todd yelled. It was about to be on.

"Shut up, dude! All you do is cause fucking trouble. Why don't you go home and run to Mommy, you sawed off prick! Nobody wants you here!" Pete shouted to him.

Todd stood there, slowly rubbing his stinging jaw and looking at Pete who was approaching him from center. I just knew that they were going to mix it up. I think everyone out there knew it as well. I was stunned that Pete even did that. Tommy I could see doing it, but Pete? No way. It was like I was watching this in a dream.

We all stopped and held our collective breaths because everyone just knew that Pete and Todd were going to fight. Nobody—and I mean nobody—messed with Todd the way Pete just did. And I think Pete knew that, too; because from the pitcher's mound, I could see on his face he knew that it was a mistake to throw his glove at Todd. It was too late to turn back now. The situation was well past the point of no return. The heat makes people do crazy things, and tempers get inflamed when it's hot. It certainly did that day for sure.

"You want beef?! You want fuckin' beef?!" Todd asked, violently holding his arms spread apart inviting Pete to charge him. Of course, Pete was much taller and outweighed him by eighty pounds or so, and you would think that it wouldn't be a fight at all. But no one ever underestimated Todd.

"I'm not fighting you, Todd," Pete said, knowing that he had already wished he could go back in time and not throw the glove at him.

"I'll fight you right here, bitch! Any of you!" Todd said, pointing at all of us on the baseball field.

"Just go on home, you midget," Pete said, making everyone laugh at the remark. I could tell that Pete was getting nervous about the situation.

Feeling bested, Todd started again, "Let's go right now!" Todd took his shirt off and charged Pete with great speed. Before I could get any words out of my mouth, standing there on the mound watching the impending fight, Pete threw a right cross and caught Todd across the jaw, knocking him down. He couldn't have timed the punch more perfectly.

It was just dumb luck, Pete would later tell us. Todd went down like a sack of potatoes. Everyone there at the ball field was stunned as a hush swept over all of us kids. Pete just stood there, not realizing what he had done. I don't think any of us did—it happened so fast. I imagine for Pete it was like being in a car accident; you try to remember what happened, but it all happens so fast that you can't remember everything.

All the kids stood there and watched what was unfolding. I had forgotten all about Mandy being over by my spot on the bench and watched my friend take out a kid who was infamous throughout the school as the toughest little kid ever.

Todd rose from the dirt and rubbed his face. From the corner of my eye, I saw Tommy slowly lurch over to jump in to save Pete, if need be. Todd was hurt. I'd never seen anything like it before. I don't think anyone there at the baseball field did either. This was historical, to say the least.

Todd stood, looked at Pete for a bit, then dropped his head some, and turned around to walk across the baseball field. No one there knew what he was going to do next. Something, right? He had to, right? I mean this was Todd we're talking about. Todd was not the kind of kid just to let things go unanswered. I knew that he would say something back or do something to exact his revenge. I cannot for the life of me recall who it was out there that started laughing out wildly. Then, just like wildfire, everyone started laughing. It broke the tension, that's for sure.

With all the kids laughing and pointing and calling him names, Todd proceeded to run to the on-deck spot next to the fence and picked up a baseball bat. I thought for sure he was going to run amuck on all of us. He had that crazed look in his eyes. Maybe he always had that look— who really knew? I never got that close to him to tell beforehand.

Yelling and screaming at the top of his lungs and cussing every, single step of the way down the chain-linked fence row, Todd pounded an aluminum bat down the top of the fence all the way to the end of the field, a good sixty yards of chain link fence. All any of us could hear were the cuss words: fuck, shit, damn, son of a bitch, bastards, motherfuckers, over and over again until he reached the end of the fence.

Then, he turned and screamed, cussed all of us kids again who were laughing at him from far away, and he climbed the twelve-foot chain-linked fence, got over to the other side, and walked away. Wow! I had never seen anything like that before, especially from Todd.

He was such a bruiser that I was taken aback as well as others that he just walked away as he did. I was expecting him to absolutely destroy Pete with that bat when he ran over there to pick it up. Never knew why he didn't. It certainly fit his M.O., that's for sure. Pete must have been living right that day or something.

In fact, it was the last and only time that I had ever seen Todd get knocked down in a fight. Todd eventually dropped out of high school and spent a lot of time in and out of county jail. Eventually, he hit the big time and robbed a bank two towns over in his twenties. He went to federal prison for that one. I don't know if he ever got out. If he did, I'd only assume that he got back into trouble at some point. It seemed to be in his DNA.

5

After the Todd experience, no one wanted to play baseball anymore. I was tired anyway. The sun had drained nearly all my energy. I had been knocked around the field and couldn't get anyone out. My right arm felt heavy, and my mind was not on the game anyways; it was set on the girl who sat on the bench.

The kids that had played at the baseball field were beginning to file away across the park and go elsewhere. Gathering all the baseball equipment in the oversized green bag, Curt started in, "You going to talk to her?" I stood there beside Curt and looked over at Mandy, considering his question. She was leaving with her friends, Courtney and Jennifer. It seemed not to be the right time.

Maybe tomorrow, I thought. "Nah, she's with her friends."

"Whatever, dude. I'm going over there and talking to her myself," Curt said. "I'm not going to hear about Mandy all summer. Fuck that." I guess he had gotten enough of my procrastination.

He left me and rushed over to Mandy across the way. He had managed to break her away from her friends for a few moments and stood there speaking to her on my behalf. I tried not to look at them in case she looked over at me. *How pathetic am I,* I thought about myself.

I had finally gotten all of the equipment placed into the bag and stood waiting for Curt to return. He stayed over there and talked to her longer than I ever thought possible. What in the world could they be talking about? The thing with Curt acting on my behalf was that I had no idea what he could be discussing with her.

I was scared because there was no telling how he was painting my love and affection for her. Standing there watching them talk and sometimes looking over at me from across the baseball diamond as she did with a smile, I wished I would have just talked to her myself.

I stood waiting for Curt to come back over. "What in the hell could they be talking about over there?" Tommy asked, coming up to me pulling the heavy equipment bag over his shoulder.

"With Curt," Pete started, "who knows? He's probably trying to ask her out himself." We all three chuckled at that.

The three of us started to walk down the hill from the baseball field, figuring that Curt would follow behind after he was done with Mandy. Before we reached the end of the hill, Curt came running from behind and declared that he was successful.

"What?" I asked, feeling butterflies swirl around in my stomach. Had he broken through for me?

"Yeah, she gave me her phone number to give to you. Said you need to call her tonight. She likes you, dude."

My heart was in my throat, "Where's her number?"

Curt tapped the side of his head with his index finger, "Up here." I looked over at Tommy and he gave a half shrug.

"Oh that's right," Tommy laughed. "The math-lete doesn't need a piece of paper to remember numbers." We all laughed. Curt just leered at us.

6

After the baseball game, the plan was for all of us to go over to Curt's house to hang out. Mostly, they wanted to be there to bear witness to me finally calling Mandy. That filled me full of anxiety. I don't know what scared me more: calling my dream girl or the guys watching me do it.

I told Curt that I'd be over at his house after I showered. Taking that shower meant that I was going to have to go home where my mentally ill mother was swinging on those mood vines. I hated when she was like that. I never knew what mother I was going to draw. And Dad, man, he never knew which wife he was going to get from hour to hour; which is why I'm guessing he stayed at work all the time, at least as much as possible.

I walked from the park up the street past Curt's house and over to mine. Dad was sitting on a milk crate under the walnut tree in the shade. I'm pretty sure that he had been out there working on his car—a car that never had anything wrong with it—the entire time I was playing baseball in the heat.

"Hot enough for you?" Dad asked.

"Yeah, a little bit, I guess," I replied, walking over to him to catch the shade.

"Going to be a hot summer, I reckon."

"Yeah, I'm sure it will be. Already is," I said. I hated small talk with my dad. In the last year or so, that's all the two of us ever did. Sometimes it was like talking to a neighbor rather than my dad. I always wondered if he felt the same way about me.

"Car is running good. In a couple of years, she'll be yours."

This was news to me. I stood and looked at him and then the car, his precious 1981 Malibu Classic, pearl blue in color. Man, I loved that car. "Are you serious?"

"Well, yeah, I'm serious. I knew as soon as I bought it ten years ago, I was one day going to give it to you. That was always the plan. I didn't tell you?" Dad had a sly grin on his face, which made me grin.

"That's awesome! Wait til I tell the boys about this!" I was excited. I can tell you that for certainty.

"Still got a few years, but we'll be out practicing your driving out on 550 before you know it."

He and I were silent, looking at the car for a few moments before I asked, "So, is Mom still..."

Dad took my question and mulled it over for what seemed forever. At first, I didn't think he heard me, and I was about to repeat it. I wanted to know what I was going to walk into beforehand.

"She's calmed down. Mood changes like the wind direction. She brought me some sweet tea about an hour ago. She seemed fine then, I guess. One extreme to the other. Can be sweet as she can be and then flip a switch and be like she was earlier in the kitchen. Sometimes you just never know."

"What are we going to do with her?" I asked. It was a big question—a much bigger question for a kid my age to have to ask—but I asked it anyway. It was the elephant in the room so to speak.

Dad sat on his milk crate and considered my inquiry at length. I think he honestly didn't know what the end result was going to be. Neither did I. "I don't know. I really don't anymore. She's um...she's bipolar and I...I think she's getting schizophrenic, too."

"How do you know about the schizophrenic part?" I asked.

"Don't worry about how I know. I just do." Dad didn't say this hatefully. He was compassionate about it. But he was also worried. I could see it on his face and hear it in his voice. The once rock-steady man I had known forever was now a forty-year-old man who was uncertain about the future, uncertain about his wife. Maybe Dad was uncertain about everything about life at that point under the shade of the walnut tree.

"I hate living here," I blurted out unintentionally. I never meant for that thought to get past my lips, but there it was, out in the open, not being able to be taken back much like Pete's haymaker to Todd's jaw.

"Well, I do too. But," Dad said, "she's still your mom and my wife. And it's my job to try to get her the help she needs. There are doctors out there who can help your mom. But I got to convince her to go see them. She did once, a long time ago. They gave her some medicine, pills, and they worked really good. This was back when you were probably six or seven. And then one day, out of the blue, she said she was cured, and she stopped taking them. That's when she got worse. I've never been able to get her back to see her doctor since."

"Are we just going to have to keep dealing with this?"

There was a pause in my dad's response. He was thinking about, it but I know the man had thought about it for years. Even still, the answers didn't come easily. "Eventually something's got to give. It won't be like this forever. I promise. So...what do you have planned for this evening?"

"I'm actually going over to Curt's to call this girl."

Dad's eyes grew wide and he smiled, "Ohhhh, man. That's awesome! My son is growing up on me. Lady killer," Dad said playfully, punching at me. We both laughed. "I love you, Son. Come here, and give your old man a hug." I reached over and hugged my dad. "Now get out of here, Steve Avery. I don't know how in the hell you see anything with that hat pulled down so low."

Dad made me smile. He always knew how to when he was around—which back in those days wasn't much. I remember my dad fondly. One of those memories I cherish was back when I would get sick with the flu and be in bed. I had the flu several times growing up before I was twelve.

Dad would come into my bedroom and check in on me. I'd be lying there sick, not having any energy to do anything, and Dad would put his hand on my forehead to gauge my temperature. Then he would position me in the middle of the bed saying, "Why the hell have a bed this big (a full size) if you're not going to use the whole thing?"

He would then take all my covers off of me and then fling them high above me so they would land softly, covering me and the entire bed. Then, from his back chino's pocket, he would pull out a twenty-ounce 7UP. It was cold to the touch and smooth going down.

"Here, raise up just a bit. This will cool that fever down some." Dad unscrewed the cap, and I would take a sip of the cold 7UP. God, I can still remember how good it tasted back then. Did it ever cool my fevers? I don't honestly know, and neither did my dad. But that's one of my favorite memories of him.

As an adult, I've only had the flu a few times—three at best—and each time when I was lying in bed with a fever, sick as a dog, I would remember my dad's visits to my bedroom from when I was a kid, and I would smile. Dad's been gone five years now, and I'd give just about anything I have to see him in my bedroom, sitting on the edge of my bed, holding a cold bottle of 7UP to cool me down.

7

Later that evening, we all retreated to the one place where we all felt at home: Curt's house, more specifically, up in his bedroom. We all sat there doing our usual thing. Pete and Tommy were watching MTV; Curt was listening to his Walkman and playing air guitar like Eddie Van Halen; and I was sitting there on his bed flipping through a *Punisher* comic book.

The whole time that I was sitting there, I was holding the phone number of the girl that I longed for. Curt had finally written it down for me. It was the closest that I had ever gotten to her, and thanks to Curt, I was on the verge of getting her to be mine. Thanks to Curt, the ball was in my court. All I had to do was take my shot.

Was I nervous? Of course. I turned to jelly every time that she was around. At thirteen years old, I felt that this girl was the answer to every question that I ever had about life and the way it worked. I don't know exactly how to explain it. When I thought about her, I saw my future. Sounds crazy, but at that time it was the gospel.

Of course, I just could not come out and tell her that I was deeply, madly in love with her and felt that she should be with me forever. That would come off as insane to her, like I was a stalker or something. No, I had to approach her like a normal thirteen-year-old kid. It was going to be difficult, let me tell you. Brave I was not.

———

I had killed time there in Curt's bedroom, and everyone in there knew it. They were just silently waiting for me to grab the phone and call Mandy. I stalled of course. I was hoping that no one was watching the clock to see what time it was. I was hoping that time would expire on the night and my excuse could be that it was too late for me to call her, but I would swear to them to the heavens above that I would do it tomorrow. No such luck. Tommy looked over at me when whatever it was they were watching on TV went to commercial, "You gonna call her, man?"

"What?" I asked, acting as if I was deep in reading the comic book that I had been holding for almost an hour.

"You gonna call her? It's getting late," Tommy asked.

"Yeah," I said. "Here in a minute,"

"He won't call," Pete said, watching the commercials, not even turning his head in my direction.

"I'm going to call, dude," I said while Tommy got up from the floor and walked over to Curt's nightstand.

He picked up the cordless phone and handed it to me, "Do it now." I sat there stunned. Here was Tommy holding out a phone for me to call her. I wish that I had his resolve about things. I always did.

Feeling all eyes on me there in that bedroom, I slowly put the comic book down and reached for the phone in his hand. I breathed in deep, "I can't do it with you guys all up in here." They looked at me for a second. They knew I was right.

"Come on, guys, let's give him some privacy," Tommy said. He smacked Pete in the back of the head. Pete got up and grabbed Curt while he was jamming, playing air guitar. I was alone in the bedroom, trying to calm my nerves. I was sweating like a pig up there, trying to tell myself this was like a movie, and all I had to do was say my lines—that's it.

The moment of truth had finally arrived. I paced around up there in Curt's bedroom, going over and over in my head how and what I was going to say to Mandy. I had waited years to get the chance to talk to her and the chance to realize my destiny was at hand. Sure, I had prepared myself for years for that very moment in time in front of my bedroom mirror at home, but the funny thing was that when me and the moment had finally met, I was at a loss for words.

I walked over to the bedroom window and saw the guys all standing out in the front yard passing a Nerf football around. I could barely make them out but the streetlight gave me enough light to see the dark shadows of them. At least they were trying to give me as much time as I needed. I had already pissed away around ten minutes trying to get my nerve up to call her. I was nervous.

Drawing in a deep breath and blowing out a mighty wind, I started to push the number pad of the phone. I had already committed her seven-digit number to memory. I started jumping up and down, trying to get rid of those pesky butterflies that swarmed like locusts in my stomach. I was so scared, trembling uncontrollably.

The phone on the other end rang and rang. It didn't seem like anyone was home. Just as I was about to hang up the phone, the other end finally picked up and a man's voice came over answering, "Hello?"

I was stunned and was not expecting a man's voice on the other end, "May I talk to Mandy please?" I managed to ask, feeling my heart in my throat.

"She ain't here. She went to aunt's house for a while," the gruff voice on the other end told me.

"Okay, um...thank you." I hung the phone up and stood there in Curt's bedroom feeling relieved. My shaking hands had calmed down, and the adrenaline had started to subside. I noticed that my forehead was damp, and my tee shirt was sticking to my back.

I could not believe it. I had almost thrown up over calling her; and when I mustered up the courage, she was not even there. Damn it. I tossed the phone down onto Curt's bed and stood there beside myself. Did she send word for me to call her, knowing the whole time that she was not going to be home? Or was it by sheer coincidence that she had to visit her aunt?

At any rate, I had at least conquered dialing her number. That was a big win for me up to that point. *Baby steps*, I thought to myself as I walked out of Curt's bedroom. Baby steps.

CHAPTER 6

THE GOLDEN TAN/ANOTHER
BULLY/ANOTHER TODD EXPERIENCE

1

ME AND CURT were sitting on his back porch, talking a couple of days later about what had happened with my phone call with Mandy. I was doing more of the talking; Curt just sat there, listening. After hearing me complain and vent relentlessly about what had happened over the last couple of days, Curt finally broke in with some insight. I had gotten on Curt's last nerve, that much was clear. I couldn't blame him. I would've gotten tired of hearing about the same subject over and over too.

"Dude," Curt began, "she went over to see her aunt. You're reading way too much into this."

"Maybe it's a sign, you know? Maybe I'm not supposed to be with her. Maybe all of this is just life playing…"

"There you go again, taking something small and making it into something huge," he interrupted.

He was right though. Always was when it came to my trains of thought. That was the thing about Curt—he got me.

When it came to Mandy, no one had listened to me go on and on about her more than he had. He was like my therapist– a thirteen-year-old therapist but without the salary.

"Just call her back tonight. You got her number. I don't know why you didn't call her last night. Hell, or even ride past her house and see if she was out in the yard," he said, leaning back in his chair while drinking his favorite brand of chocolate milk.

"It's not that easy. I have to plan for this. Have to get my courage back up again. You know, I thought that I was going to throw up in your bedroom before I pushed the number pad. This girl has me all sorts of messed up."

"God, all you have to do is call her and talk about stuff. You're never going to get with her if you don't stop being a pussy about this." He was right.

I had to be something of a semi-adult about the situation. I mean, she was just a girl, right? She was just one of the most popular girls in the eighth grade, so why was I sweating calling her? Maybe it was because— at that moment in time—she was my everything. She was the biggest crush that I ever had in my life.

"Maybe you're right," I said, finally thinking about what Curt was telling me for a moment. "I'll call her tonight. But I'm doing it here. I need your support though."

"You got it," Curt replied.

I was about to say something else to him on the subject when I noticed something about my friend—something I should have noticed earlier that day but had not.

———

Curt had been on something of a strange quest ever since the seventh grade. And that quest was getting the perfect tan. I know it sounds crazy, but honest to God, that was what his mission was. My quest was getting the girl of my dreams and his was getting... his skin the perfect golden brown that he wanted. Strange but true. I don't know where the odd desire came from, and neither did any of the guys. But a lot during that summer of '91 Curt would lounge around outside with no shirt and some really short shorts. I remember specifically when this quest began...

One day last summer, me, Tommy, and Pete walked over to Curt's house to shoot basketball. We knocked on the door and no answer. I twisted the door knob and was going to walk right on in like always, but the door was locked. His mom's car was in the driveway, and I told the guys that she must be asleep.

We jumped off the front porch and walked to the backyard, expecting him at his basketball court already warming up for our friendly game of horse that we'd set up the day before. Me and the guys turned the corner of the house, and we found Curt lying flat on his back on a lounging chair with sunglasses on, no shirt, and really short shorts listening to music from his stereo.

"What the hell is this shit?" Pete asked as we walked over and stood before our golden hopeful.

Curt looked up from his aviators. "What's up, guys?"

"Oh my God, you're gay," I said as we looked our oiled friend over.

"Whatever," Curt said, getting up. As he stood there, we saw how short those red shorts actually were—not a good sight. "I'm going to get the perfect tan this summer," he said, stretching out, arms high in the air.

"The perfect tan? For what?" Pete asked, feeling sickened by Curt's oiled body.

"I was watching a rerun of *MTV Spring Break,* and it seems that chicks go for the guys that have the perfect tan," said Curt, feeling a pang of confidence.

"Go put some longer shorts on, dude. I think I see your sack," Tommy said, turning his head while me and Pete stood there, trying to see if indeed his scrotum was out. It wasn't, thank God.

"Whatever. And...and I'm going to start lifting weights out here in the yard in the sun and get ripped and golden at the same time. Next year at school, chicks will be all over me."

"Then all you have to do is shave your head, and you'll look like a trophy," I pointed out to our golden friend.

"Whatever, dude," One of Curt's many famous lines. "Anyways, what are you guys doing?" he asked, reaching down to turn off the U2 music that was pouring from the speakers.

"Well, let's see," Tommy began his sarcastic tone. "We have a basketball here...maybe we could play football."

"With a basketball?" Curt asked, looking at us with those damn aviator sunglasses on.

"All that oil soak into your brain?" I asked, making the other guys laugh.

"Whatever, dude. You guys can go play. I'm going to lay here and tan my backside," he said, laying back down on the lounger on his stomach. "Anybody want to oil me up? No? Okay then."

We all stood there and looked at Curt. We laughed and played horse without him.

2

Anyways, back to the matter at hand. We both sat there on the back deck of Curt's house, looking out into his enormous backyard. He was sitting there, sipping on chocolate milk in his short shorts with no shirt and those damn aviators on. I must have been so focused on Mandy that I had not even noticed my partially nude, but yet, golden friend. Before I could say something else about my problem, we saw Ricky and his friend, Todd Lowe! *The* Todd Lowe!

"Oh, hell," I said, watching Ricky and Todd walk from the right side of the yard.

"What?" Curt asked, looking in the direction that I was staring.

"Since when did Ricky and Todd become friends?" I asked.

"I don't know. Surprising though," Curt said, sipping the last of his chocolate milk.

Ricky was Curt's little brother. He was ten years old, and man, could he fight. He was one of the strongest ten-year-old kids that I had ever seen, besides the great Todd of course. Ricky could put me, Curt, and anyone else on our asses before we could blink our eyes. I never saw Todd and Ricky fight, but I would imagine that it would have been a good one. Ricky and Todd were built about the same and both had a temper and both saw red when angry.

One time, several years ago, I saw Ricky and Curt mix it up out in the backyard where the little brother pulled out a knife from his shorts pocket and tried to stab Curt with it. And the knife was not one of those regular pocket knives that a lot of kids had back then. No, the knife he tried to stab Curt with was a large kitchen knife like Michael Myers carried around. Ricky did not play around, even at that age. But I always liked Ricky and considered him one of my friends. He liked me too. Thank Christ for that.

Ricky did not take anything off anyone and neither did his new side-kick, Todd. Those two together could be terrible. Curt already had a violent history with his brother, and the two never really talked much like you would think brothers would talk. And with Ricky pairing himself with Todd, things could get very crazy, very fast.

We both sat there watching as the two of them ambulated across the yard. Todd was not looking my way, but suddenly I caught his eye. He stopped, and then, Ricky stopped. Me and Todd locked eyes. He remembered me from the ballfield the other day when he and Pete had gotten into it.

He recalled me laughing at him when he was shown up for the first time in his young life by mine and Curt's friend. Then, just as if I thought the worst was going to happen there in the backyard, he and Ricky began to walk toward the front of the house. I thought me and Curt were in the clear, but then Curt yelled out to his little brother, "Mom's gone, so no friends over!".

Seconds passed by and then Ricky, with Todd in tow, appeared from the corner of the house and stood opposing at the end of the deck stairs, "We're going in. It's hot out here." he told his older brother.

"No, you're not. When mom's gone, I'm in charge." I knew where the conversation was going. I had seen it a thousand times over, and it always ended with the two brothers at arms. Sometimes Curt would win, and sometimes Ricky would. Each time they would fight, it was rough.

Usually, I would not mind that the two brothers fought. When it got too wild, I would step in and break it up. Somehow, with Todd standing there with Ricky, arms folded across his chest, I knew that things could get out of control. Sitting in my chair, I could feel the tension between Curt and Ricky. It was like an Old West draw—who was going to draw their gun first?

All I was doing was waiting for someone to throw the first punch. I was getting nervous. Curt against Ricky was always an epic battle. Neither one of them would give in. Back in the early days, Curt would be able to beat Ricky because of the size differential. But Ricky had gone through a growth spurt and was able to now hold his own against his older brother. I mean, the kid put everything he had into scrapping with him.

And then there was Todd. I had seen his fury around town and heard about his legendary brawls with guys three, or four years older than him. I'm talking about high school kids, for God's sake. Even though he didn't fight out there on the baseball field that day, didn't mean he wouldn't throw down, there in the backyard.

Anyways, there we all were: me and Curt, Ricky and Todd. Curt got up from his chair in an opposing manner, and I just sat there. I wanted no part of the twosome that stood waiting at the deck steps. Sure, they were smaller and younger than me, but they would put everything into a fight and absolutely would not quit until someone fell unconscious.

"I don't care what she said! You've got guests," Ricky pointed toward me as I sat there and watched what was going on.

"He's been my friend for years. How long have you and this troll known each other? A couple of days?" I could not believe that he called Todd, *the* Todd, a troll. I was truly scared for my life at that point. I sat there and thought that Todd was going to leap up on that deck and tear Curt and eventually me apart if he was not tired. I couldn't believe the balls on my friend for calling Todd that. First Pete decked Todd and had just now Curt called him a troll. Wow.

"What did you fucking call me?" Todd spoke gruffly.

He stood there alongside Ricky with the look of kill in his squinted eyes. The tension on that hot summer day was thick. I slowly got up from my chair, looking at Ricky and Todd. I had no idea why I even got up, to tell you the truth. It felt like the right thing to do.

"What are you, deaf?" Curt returned, standing there looking down at his brother and the brawler. "He ain't going in. We barely know him. We don't need people like him in our house." he said, pointing his finger at the two of them sternly.

It was the first time that I had seen Curt act like a father. He was stern and meant what he said as he stood up there on that deck and looked down at the kids in the yard. His voice had changed, too. It wasn't his brotherly voice that I had always heard when he addressed Ricky, but a booming authoritative voice, like a parent— like his dad.

At that point, I felt that Curt could have taken both his brother and the infamous Todd. Ricky, Todd, and Curt all three stood there in silence, staring at each other and waiting for something—a move, a spoken word, anything. And then, out of the blue, Ricky and Todd walked away without any back-talk or hateful warnings about Curt's health or future. Craziest thing I had ever seen. I was impressed. We both sat down as the two of them disappeared around the corner of the house. Things seemed to calm down substantially. I kept waiting for them to surprise attack us, but they never did. Why? I don't know. I'm just happy they didn't.

3

Later on that day, me and Curt found ourselves in the side yard at his house that ran parallel to the small street that cut to the right of the fork in the road. We were passing baseball, a time-honored tradition that we shared just between us. Sure, we played baseball with Pete and Tommy all the time; but when we passed the hardball around, it was something special. I guess looking back on it now—it was kind of our thing—like most things were growing up.

We did not just pass baseball like you would think two boys would: we pitched to each other out there in the yard. This type of practice tied into our Little League baseball days when we were both pitchers a summer ago: me with the Yankees and him with the Tigers.

In the summer of 1991, we had aged out, unfortunately, from Little League, but it didn't stop us from still doing what we loved. Once you get baseball in your blood, it stays there. We would play a game that we had invented some years ago to keep us in pitching shape for our teams. It was the only way, really, for us to practice our craft. I think we made each other better pitchers.

The game went like this: I would squat down like a catcher, and Curt would pitch to me like we were in a game. While he pitched, it was my job to call his pitches either balls or strikes like an umpire would. If you walked a batter, then it was the other's turn. Basically, whoever recorded the most strikeouts won the game that was set to nine innings. Of course, all of that was based on the fact that we called the pitches fairly. I can tell you that he screwed me out of several strikeouts and wins. I guess...I cost him some too.

That day in his sideyard, Curt had pitched first and got eight strikeouts in a row before he walked the imaginary batter. I suppose that I could have called his 3-2 pitch a strike, but honestly, my legs were growing wobbly and tired from the muggy heat. I called a borderline pitch on the outside a ball. It infuriated Curt because I had been calling that very same pitch a strike the entire time. The bottom of the first came, and it was my turn to pitch on legs that were like jelly.

I stood up on legs of jelly; he assumed the catcher's role; and I began my start. I stood there, facing my friend about forty or so feet away. I looked into his glove and wound up, kicked my leg Steve Avery-like, and fired my first pitch. Ball. Bastard called it a ball just because I called his borderline pitch a ball. It was payback. As he threw the baseball back to me, we heard the high-pitched hum of a scooter coming up his driveway. Curt got up and stood there, looking at who it was that was coming into the yard. It was Tony "Big Red" Bartlett. This was not a welcomed sight.

————

Tony Bartlett was a sophomore in high school after that summer and was like 6'4" with bushy, red, fire-like hair. He was huge and just as mean to boot. He was one of many bullies in our town, and he had thrown his weight and height around to the smaller kids like me. For some reason, Tony did not like me, nor did I like him. I was one of the very few brave ones that somewhat stood up to him. I never was truly afraid of him. I should have been by all accounts. But with Tony, there was not really fear that I had of him. It was more of an annoyance. I wasn't a fighter, by no means. But for whatever reason, I thought I could take Tony on—square him up. I recall our first encounter when made me and him enemies.

It was my sixth-grade year and Tony's eighth at Claxton Elementary

School. During recess, sixth grade through eighth always went outside on the enormous playground to play or to do whatever it was that kids did out there. Our recess time was always after lunch. Sometimes we had fifteen minutes, and sometimes we'd have thirty or forty-five. It all depended on the teachers who watched after us. If they got to talking while sitting outside on their chairs, we could be out there for a long time.

Some played football; some played basketball on the court; and some just walked around and talked about the complexities of being a kid at that time. Me, Curt, Tommy, and Pete were at the basketball court shooting around keeping to ourselves– pretty much like we always did during recess. I remember it had been raining that day, and the precipitation had stopped long enough for us to venture outside to play.

We had been shooting around on the wet court, talking about what was on tap for that day and other such things of kid importance when my brush with Tony began. Pete had shot the basketball, and it ricocheted off the red plastic rim and bounced off to the left.

The court sat on top of a hill that overlooked the entire playground. Many a time, when kids would play basketball on the blacktop where the court sat, an ill-shot basketball would roll down the very steep hill and all the way to the jungle gyms across the playground. It sucked chasing balls that rolled down that hill, and every kid—no matter how old—always tried to save the ball and their time from that hill. I was no different on that overcast, chilly day.

The basketball bounced off the rim with a quick furry and was heading off to the left of the court. The next stop was at the bottom of the hill unless I did something about it. With no one standing on that side of the court, I saw what was about to happen, and I rushed over, trying to catch the ball from going over with one amazing leap of faith.

I leaped across the court and grabbed the basketball with my right hand, tossing it back to the guys who stood in awe of my physical prowess. Larry Bird would have been proud of that save. The ball bounced back onto the court and right into Tommy's grasp.

Now, me saving the ball from the clutches of the hill was nothing really. But what was different about all of that was that after I jumped, saved the ball, and slung it back onto the court, I landed into a rather large puddle of water that had accumulated due to all the rain that we had earlier in the day. Landing in a puddle of water that sat right between the grass at the top of the hill and the concrete of the basketball court, I was soaked from head to toe with water for my actions.

Standing there in the water puddle and trying to figure out what had just happened, I turned to my left and saw Tony and some of his boys standing there beside me with water on them. "You splashed me, prick," Tony said in his intimidating voice. Honestly, I did not see him or any of his friends standing there on that side of the court. I don't know how I could have missed them, to tell you the truth.

There I was, stepping out of the standing water, looking at Tony and his boys, wiping their faces with their shirt tails. "I'm sorry, man," I said, apologizing to the bully. I really was sorry that I splashed him with water —didn't mean to.

"Sorry don't get it," Tony said inching closer to me with hate in his eyes.

"What else do you want me to say?" I stood there and asked, getting annoyed with Tony's bullying tactics.

I didn't like the kid. Tommy and Tony had swapped words with each other before, but nothing ever came of it. Tony usually didn't do much when Tommy was around because Tony knew who Tommy was. I wasn't afraid of Tony. I can't say as to why I wasn't, but I just didn't think he was all that. To me, he looked like a rat in the face, and it always made me laugh. Maybe it was hard for me to take him seriously since he looked like a fucking cartoon rat with red hair.

Of course, I was not much of a fighter, but something about Tony just made my blood boil. For some reason, I was not afraid of him like other kids were. I was just not. Now Mark, one of the other infamous bullies in town—the one who pushed me into the water at the pool earlier—I was afraid of him. He was plain mean and had a way about him that let you know he could crush you. I stayed my distance from him whenever possible. Or at least be around Tommy when Mark was around.

Tony lacked that certain bully requisite to me. He might have had it displayed with everyone else, but not me. I didn't want to fight him because I knew that deep down, he would perhaps mop the floor with me. But that didn't mean I was going to back down from the building with yellow teeth either.

"You could buy me a new shirt," Tony said approaching me. By that time, my boys had stopped playing basketball and walked over to me for backup.

"Well," I began, "that ain't going to happen."

"Let me tell you something. If you don't bring me a new shirt by tomorrow, your ass is mine," Tony warned.

"I'm sorry, I don't date guys," I said questioning his last four words. It was a funny comeback, probably one of my best at the time.

"You want to fight, bitch..." Tony said, getting up in my face.

I don't know what came over me that day out there on the basketball court, but something washed over me, turning me red with rage. I didn't like people crowding me, especially kids who were an entire six inches taller than I was.

Standing my ground, I summoned up all of my might and pushed him as hard as I could. Of course, it only knocked him back several steps. Not the dramatic showing that I thought it would have been. If all else failed, I knew that Tommy, the bully beater, was in my corner with the rest of my clique.

Tony stood there looking at me as did my and his friends. They were all stunned by the recent events. I didn't move, not one muscle. I was ready to start swinging on him if he flinched toward me. Me and To just stood there eyeing each other—neither one of us blinking. I was ready for him to swing; I honestly was.

Some time had passed by, and Tony looked around, chuckled to himself, and started walking backward, looking at me the entire time. He was mad, madder than hell, but he didn't want to tangle with me on that day. I have no idea why he didn't make his move. He could have killed me if he wanted to, I'm sure.

Over the next few years, Tony and I would run into each other and switch hateful words with one another, but no blows ever came to pass. He would always see me out in town after he graduated from our school that eighth-grade year and promised me that my day was coming when I got to high school. But all he did was blow words past me—that was it. No tactic changes at all. I, of course, stood my ground and didn't allow myself to get intimidated by the "Big Red" machine.

4

On that day out in Curt's side yard in the summer of '91, Tony pulled up on his little scooter and walked toward us with a purpose. That scooter that Tony drove made me laugh every time because he was so big, and the scooter was so little. He looked like a gorilla riding a kids' tricycle. Seeing him drive it in town was hilarious. But there was nothing funny about "Big Red" coming into Curt's yard, eyeing me the entire time.

"We got problems," I said to Curt who stood there alongside me.

"I want to ask you something," Tony said, walking over to us.

"What?" I questioned as I took my glove off my hand, dropping it to my side on the ground. I was ready to swing on him.

"I hear you've been running your fucking mouth about me around town," Tony said.

"No, I haven't said anything," I replied. I hadn't said anything about him—never wanted to stir up trouble with him. The only thing that I ever said about him was the stuff that I said to his rat face.

"I heard you called me a son of a bitch the other day at the pool," Tony claimed.

I looked at Curt in wonderment, "I never said that. You know if I have anything to say to you, I say it to your rat face. Like 'you're mom is like a shotgun—one cock and she's ready to blow.'"

"That's it! Me and you, right now!" Tony said.

"No, not here," Curt interjected. It was a big day for the kid: He had told Ricky and Todd what to do, and now he was giving Tony Bartlett orders. "You ain't starting any shit here, Tony. You can take it someplace else."

"What are you going to do if I don't leave?" Tony questioned.

"Then I'll call the police," Curt replied. "I ain't got to do shit. You pick how this is going to go."

Tony stood there for a moment, considering what Curt had told him and looking at the both of us while walking away back toward his scooter, "I'm going home and getting my fighting clothes on. And when I come back, both of you bitches are going down. Call the cops, mother-fucker! You're going to need them." Tony hopped back on his small scooter and peeled out of the driveway and down the road where the hum of his engine grew distant. Curt and I stood there, looking at each other with that "what now" look.

5

We looked at our watches and waited for Tony to come back. We both ran over possibilities on what we were going to do. Curt calling the police was a bluff and only bluff to scare away Tony. It worked, but only temporarily, because Tony promised he was coming back with his fighting clothes on.

"You think he's really coming back?" Curt asked me.

"I don't know," I said looking around. "Maybe. Who knows with that red-headed freak."

"He comes back here he'll kill us, you know that," Curt pointed out. I could tell that he was getting a little scared and that the courage he had earlier that day was waning.

I wasn't afraid of Tony. But I didn't like fighting. Mostly because I wasn't coordinated enough to throw down like Tommy did. Tommy, now he could fight. But me, not so much. I ran my mouth to Tony just because that seemed to work on him. Plus, it saved me from having to brawl with him over the years.

"Probably, but he'll have to take on both of us. Surely he can't take both of us on. God, I wish Tommy was here." I said.

Before we could go any further into probabilities and scenarios, Ricky and Todd emerged from the street and into the yard once again. More trouble, I thought.

The two kids walked over to us, "What's going on?" Ricky asked, sensing that something was wrong. Brother intuition, I guess.

"Tony Bartlett says he's coming over here to whip our asses," I told him.

"Tony Bartlett? Big, tall, red-haired bastard?" Todd questioned in his southern drawl.

"Yeah, that's him," Curt said.

"When's he coming back?" Todd asked, looking at all the garden gnomes in the summer sun.

"He said that he was going to get his fighting clothes on and come back. That was about ten minutes ago. Maybe fifteen," I replied.

"You leave that pecker to me. I've got a score to settle with him anyways." Todd said.

Were my ears deceiving me? Did Todd Just say that he was going to take care of Tony for us? Awesome!

———

Here's what happened on that day: Todd devised a plan that would take out Tony, at least for that day anyway. After he ran the plan by us, it was bound to work. The only thing that had to be on the money was timing. The entire plan hinged on timing.

Timing had to be primo for Todd's insane plan to be executed. There was a road that ran alongside Curt's side yard. The road ran down a hill, making Curt's sideyard into a very steep bank. We all stood at the edge of the yard, looking down from atop the bank while Todd jumped from the bank and down onto the small, one-way street.

He searched the ditches on both sides, looking for his weapon. Then he found it: a forty-ounce Colt .45 glass bottle. Laughing, Todd climbed back up the fifteen-foot bank and joined us at the edge looking down. Todd told us to crouch down and hide behind one of the bushes as he looked down the road from his position in the yard.

The plan was for Tony to come driving down that very road on his scooter like he had earlier. From the top of Curt's sideyard, Todd was going to throw the glass bottle, hitting Tony in the head where he would jump from the bank, onto the street, and beat him up. That was the plan.

The only worry that any of us had was what if he came the other way where the road forked in front of Curt's house. We brought that up to Todd, and he told us to shut up. Who was going to argue with him?

We sat there for what seemed an eternity waiting for Tony to surface. And then it happened. We all heard the low hum of a struggling scooter engine making its way up the small road that ran parallel to Curt's side yard. The plan so far was on schedule. Todd hid himself behind a tree at the edge of the bank and gripped the mouth of the glass bottle tightly in his small hand.

He reared the bottle back behind his head and when we saw Tony drive past us, Todd threw the bottle striking Tony on the head and shattering the glass all over the road. I didn't know what was more impressive: Todd hitting him square in the back head with accuracy or the plan going exactly the way Todd drew it up. Tony wasn't wearing a helmet. I don't think it would've mattered, honestly.

Tony Bartlett swerved about the street due to the hit and ran into the neighboring ditch. He propelled off his scooter and crashed head-first into the side of the bank. By the looks of it, I thought he had broken his neck. It was as bad as a wipeout any of us had ever seen.

Todd jumped down from the edge of the bank and landed on the road. He rushed over to the dazed Tony and began beating him with everything that he had with his fists. Blows about the body, kicking him with those red shoes that he always wore, spitting on him, cussing him with every breath that he had. And all Tony could do was lie there and scream for help. He was bleeding from his mouth and nose, which I thought might have been broken from the wreck or by Todd's fists. I mean, here was this kid, smaller than we were and younger to boot, beating this mountain of a teenager with his bare hands. Damnedest thing I ever saw that summer.

We all stood up at the edge of the bank in Curt's side yard and laughed until we cried. Then, if things were not going funnily enough, Todd pulled his belt from his pants and started whipping Tony, who by that time had gotten to his feet and was staggering down the road, trying to get away from Todd. Blood poured down from the back of Tony's head from the glass bottle. I honestly don't know what hurt Tony more: the glass bottle busting his head, causing him to crash into the ditch, or Todd beating the hell out of him. Maybe it was a little bit of all three.

With Tony fleeing the scene, Todd cussed Tony loudly as he made his escape. Todd looked up and noticed that we had been watching and laughing the whole time. He raised his arms high in the air as his belt dangled loosely in his right hand.

To rub dirt in Tony's face, Todd walked over to the ditch, picked up the scooter, and started it back up, "Come on, Ricky, let's go!"

Ricky jumped from the bank and hopped on the back of the seat. He and Todd rode off down the road toward Tony.

Later on, Ricky told us that they had chased Tony down the road and harassed him some more, all the way to his house. But they didn't give up the scooter. Days later, Tony found his scooter. The wheels had been taken off of it and only the frame and small motor remained in his front yard. I suspect Todd and Ricky did that.

CHAPTER 7
ROCKY TOP/BASEBALL CARDS/THE STEEL GIANT

1

A WEEK HAD ELAPSED since the Todd incidents. June was approaching its last days, and soon June of 1991 was going to be a memory. Things around town—especially our quiet neighborhood—ran about the same as every summer had. The days and nights had a routine about them, and so did the four of us. Sometimes we didn't even know what day of the week it was. There was no need really because when you're a kid, time doesn't matter; time seems to be endless on those summer days and nights.

During the summers when I was growing up, there was some sense of security with knowing what to expect next. We knew that we would wake up, eat some cereal, watch some cartoons, go outside and go to our friends' houses, and then embark on some sort of adventure that would last practically the entire day. I was just fine with that. I think that was the best part of my childhood: always having something to do—something to get into.

I had not dialed Mandy's number since her dad had told me that she had gone to see her aunt. And of course, I had taken that as a sign to just completely stop trying to get with her. But did I really feel that way? Did I really feel like her not being home that night was a sign? Apparently not, because lucky for me, she didn't live that far from my house. I rode past hers on my bike ever since the ill-fated phone call, hoping to maybe catch her outside. Even if I did see her outside, would I have stopped to talk to her? I don't know. I'd like to fool myself into thinking that I would have. Sometimes you don't know what you'll do in a situation until it presents itself.

I couldn't help myself because I was a teenager in love. It's hard being a thirteen-year-old kid, and the girl of your dreams is just out of your reach. I mean she was right there; I could almost smell the honeysuckle scent of her brown hair, but there was just something keeping me and her from getting together. I suppose every kid in the world has felt like I did at one point or another with his crush. There's nothing like unrequited love.

It was absolutely killing me when school was over that May. And the way I figured it, high school would make it nearly impossible for me to see her—much less be in a class with her. The odds were not in my favor for that unless the fates made us have a class or two. That was a slim chance because I had overheard her and her friends talking one day in class that she was taking honors classes her freshman year. I was in no way smart enough to do that.

The thought of not seeing her daily for hours on end crushed me. I mean, it made my heart dip down into the depths of despair. My reason for not ever missing a day of school for three years in a row was just to see her. And when she was out or when she was sick, I was lost like a boat out to sea.

During those elementary school years, unbeknownst to her, she was the most important thing in my life. How was I going to handle the fact that when August came, we all would be thrown into a bigger school where I probably would never see her or my friends? If I was lucky, I would maybe pass her in the hallways. That question stuck in the back of my mind every day like a splinter in my hand the first part of the summer of '91. I knew it was there, and it only hurt when I recognized it.

I had to make an effort, a calculated leap, to make Mandy mine forever. I stayed up virtually all night long after the days of my call to her. I tried to figure out and examine the situation from the outside of my heart. I needed a plan—a plan that would work—something, anything that would help out my cause.

I paced a lot during those nights, constantly turning the wheels in my mind on how I was going to get the girl who weighed so much on my heart and soul. The calendar on my wall was in June: the twenty-fifth to be exact. I had time, at least I told myself that. I mean, come on, if I could not come up with a way to get her by the end of summer, did I even deserve her?

I had vowed a thousand times there in that very bedroom of mine (and to my friends a million times over) that I was not going to stop. There had to be a way, and I was going to unlock the possibilities; I just had to figure out the *how* first. With Mandy always on my mind, I had other business to attend to that late June day. And that business was baseball cards.

2

Me and my friends had assembled at the one place where we could always hang out in peace: Curt's upstairs bedroom. It was big enough to accommodate all of us for our activities. On that particular day in June, we were there on business. You see, me, Curt, Tommy, and Pete were hardcore sports card collectors. We took the hobby seriously, and our books upon books of plastic-protected cards told the story. The four of us were like a syndicate of sports trading cards.

We would meet every month, like a real club, to view each other's cards for show and most times, for trading. This, mind you, was back during a time when sports trading cards were worth something, and collectors from old to young alike went after them with a frenzy. I could remember going to baseball card shows, and there would be more adult collectors than kids. That time of sports cards was the Golden Era, at least it was to us.

I never thought the industry would ever slow down. But it did, eventually. I still have all those baseball cards in my attic. They ain't worth anything really. But from time to time I'll go up there, pull out the binders and boxes, blow the dust off, and thumb through them all from that era. God, how they always took me back to my childhood. The only thing those cards were worth were the memories they evoked for me.

Between the four of us, we perhaps had amassed over two hundred thousand cards from basketball to baseball and even football: all the common players to the superstars of the game. We had, at the time, almost every card from every company. That was before the card companies that are around today decided to make two hundred sub-sets from every major card company, making it nearly impossible to collect every single card or your favorite player.

Back then it was easy to collect every single card of your favorite team or player. Now, these days, there's no way. They will always be that card (or a thousand) that you cannot find of Greg Maddux, Ken Griffey, Jr., or Roger Clemens. But God, do I miss those old days of buying cards, opening up the boxes and single packs, and looking to see what I got. I miss trading with my friends the most. I miss just sitting around making trades with them, trying to get what they had.

3

There was a store in our town that catered to our needs. It was a store called Rocky Top. Rocky Top was like a convenience store but almost could be mistaken for a restaurant. Not only did they sell beer, candy, smokes, chips, and all that other convenience store staple, but they also had a hot bar where they served chicken strips, potato wedges, pizza, onion rings, soda fountain drinks, and a cast of others. And over in the corner of that store was an arcade machine of *Street Fighter II*. We fed that machine quarter after quarter to play until the bigger kids came to play. Then we were forced to leave.

Rocky Top had all the newest card sets, single packs, and factory boxes. It was a Mecca for us there in the small town and especially for those who didn't get a chance to go into the bigger towns near us. We would spend a ton of money there every week from money we had either earned hauling hay for the local farmers, allowances, or our lawn mowing ventures.

Usually, we would go buy the cards and something to eat, and then head over to Bill's Movie Rental/Pool Hall to rent our favorite Nintendo games for the whole weekend. It was a ritual we repeated every weekend back then. Of course, those places don't exist anymore. Time and progress have done away with those places we used to go as kids. The only way they exist now is in my thoughts. Bill's Movie Rental/Pool Hall is now a bank, and Rocky Rop is a Subway. It's almost as if they never existed at all.

———

We had a good collection going, all four of us. And that late June afternoon, sitting up in Curt's bedroom doing nothing but being lazy and talking about cards, Tommy said something that made us look at him strangely.

"You know," he started, as we were watching *MTV Spring Break* with Pauly Shore, "I know a guy that can get us all the cards we want from Rocky Top for free if we wanted them."

"Who?" I asked, watching Pauly Shore interact with some bikini-clad girl on the beach.

"Jerry Gillis," Tommy said. The three of us turned and looked at Tommy. Jerry Gillis? *The* Jerry Gillis? No way! Not that guy.

"You hanging around Gillis?" Pete asked what we were all wanting to know.

Jerry was a wild kid. And I mean *wild*. There was nothing that the kid would not do to someone or to himself, but it was all in the act of just for laughs. Once, I remember out on the playground at school in the sixth grade, he had brought a lighter from home and was showing it off to us at the basketball court. He lit the lighter and placed the flame to his hair after Tommy had dared him to.

He did and instantly the flame caught a hold of his blond, dirty locks and burned a huge chunk of his hair off. A few days later, he had to shave his head and try to re-grow the burned hair. Oddly, there was a patch, right where he burned it that never grew back. It always made me laugh when I saw it. I mean, there's all this blond hair, but on the right side between his temple and ear, there was a barren patch about the size of a dollar bill. Another episode was that during lunchtime in the school cafeteria, on a dare, Jerry took off all of his clothes and sat there at the table, eating his school lunch naked. The boy had no sense at all.

"Jerry's going to steal cards from the Rocky Top, I'm guessing?" I asked.

"He said he would."

"He could go to jail for that if he gets caught. And why would he risk that getting us cards?" Curt asked.

"I don't think he cares," Tommy said. "He says he goes in there and steals condoms and candy all the time. Told me cards were not different."

"Condoms? Jerry Gillis?" Pete said in disbelief that a kid like Jerry was even sexually active.

"That's what he told me the other day at the park, dude. Listen, why should we go and buy cards when he can go and steal them for us?"

"We ain't thieves?" I returned, saying aloud what the other two were thinking.

"I'm not one either, but I say let Jerry do what Jerry does. Just a one-time thing. Boost our collection a little." Tommy said, trying to pitch his idea to us. Now, I had never stolen anything in my life. But was it wrong to knowingly take stolen merchandise? I don't know; maybe, maybe not. Part of me didn't like being an extension of stolen stuff; but the other part of me, the kid part who loved sports cards, didn't much see the wrong in it, especially if we weren't doing the stealing.

After a long back and forth between us all, Tommy had finally talked us into Jerry stealing the cards. I was not one hundred percent sold on the idea, and I don't think Pete and Curt were either. We went along with Tommy anyway hoping that things did not go sideways on us. I felt that it was risky dealing with Jerry on anything. He was a complete wildcard if I ever saw one. You just never knew what that kid was going to do next.

4

We left Curt's house and rode our bikes to the basketball court in the middle of town where Jerry was seen ninety-nine percent of the time, playing hoops. Playing the odds, Tommy led the way as we rode down Church Street and into town where there we saw the insane Jerry Gillis, flying through the air screaming while making a rebound over some kids that he was playing with.

We pulled up onto the side of the court that served as the First National Bank parking lot and sat there, waiting for Jerry to stop cussing the kids that he was trying to clearly hustle. To no avail, we learned.

"Jerry!" Tommy shouted to get his attention. Jerry looked up from his argument with a smaller kid and saw us. He slammed the ball harshly against the concrete, and the ball bounced high in the air, hanging there for like a minute or so.

"What's up?" Jerry spoke as he neared.

Jerry, who was never known for his fashion sense, was wearing a Guns 'n Roses tee shirt with purple and black striped shorts. Plus, the notable characteristic about Jerry was his head. It seemed disproportionate to the rest of his body. He had stubby legs, long arms, and this watermelon for a head. He was an odd-looking kid. Oh yeah, he had a mullet, too. Plus, don't forget about the burnt spot on the side of his head. Jerry, for all that I remember, looked like a cartoon.

"You going to Rocky Top anytime soon?" Tommy asked.

"Hell yeah, dude. I need some rubbers," Jerry said, chewing on his gum.

"Good, is that offer to steal us some cards still standing from a while back?"

"Sure, I guess. How much do you want?" Jerry asked.

"Whatever you can get," Tommy replied.

"What do you want in return?" Curt asked.

Jerry shook his head, "Nothing. I just like stealing." He laughed, making us laugh for whatever reason.

Jerry looked around the street and the basketball court, "Yeah, those cards are going to be hard to get because they are right up next to the register."

"Can you do it?" Tommy asked.

Jerry, without hesitation, says, "Yeah, let's go."

"We ain't going in," I told Jerry.

"We'll stay over at Reedy's Market across the street, okay?" Tommy said.

Jerry nodded, walked to his bike on the other end of the court, and hopped on. He peddled toward Rocky Top with us behind him. I remember his bike was pretty beat up. It had no seat and two different rims– an orange one in front and a black one in the back. The handlebars were missing their hand grips, and the paint job on the bike was scratched and chipped everywhere. That bike seemed to match Jerry's personality.

5

"This guy is crazy," Curt said, looking around at all the grown-ups who were minding their own businesses coming in and out of the market. We all sat on our bikes, looking across the busy street from Reedy's Market. Jerry pulled up to the store, dropped his bike on the sidewalk, and went in like everything was normal. I had butterflies in my stomach watching this happen.

"He's probably going to end up in jail before he turns eighteen," Tommy remarked, sitting there on his bike and looking at the store.

Tommy was correct on that assumption. Jerry, an eighteen-year-old high school dropout, had gone inside a store two towns away from Claxton and robbed the place at gunpoint. Before he could get out with what little cash he had gotten from the cashier, he was brought down by a few of the store's employees. Then the cops came and things got worse. From what I was told about that episode and a few others, Jerry was in and out of jail so much that they had a cell reserved for him in the county lock-up.

Before any of us could say another word, here came Jerry Gillis, hair flying behind him with an armload of packs of cards. Behind him was the store manager, chasing him at top speed. As Jerry ran full sprint across the street and toward us—forgetting all about his bike—he screamed, "Run! He's gonna get me! He's gonna get me!"

The four of us panicked, turned our bikes in the opposite direction, and peddled the hell out of there from Reedy's Market. I was lagging behind, and I looked back and saw packs of cards falling from Jerry's arms as the manager closed in on him, maybe within arm's reach.

We must have done about sixty miles per hour to reach back to Curt's house where we stopped and sat on his front porch to gather our composures and breaths. After we caught our breaths, we laughed so hard that we all had tears in our eyes.

It was not supposed to go like that, not at all. We could have gotten caught; and since Jerry came running out yelling at us to run, it made us look like we were a part of it. The store manager probably thought that we were stealing from him too.

Man, that was so scary. I was shaking like a leaf the whole dash back to Curt's house. While we sat there on the porch talking about how lucky we all were, I noticed that the other guys were shaking as well. Important to say that we never got the cards because Jerry had dropped them all, fleeing from the man in charge. I never knew if Jerry got his rubbers or not.

We ran into Jerry a little later that summer in town, and he told us that not only did he lose all the packs of cards for us; but when he tried to sneak back to the store later on that night, the police were called on him by the store manager. Jerry did not seem to mind though.

6

Sitting up there in Curt's bedroom later that afternoon with our cards displayed and listening to ZZ Top on the radio, me and Curt were in talks about a possible card trade while Tommy and Pete sat back and watched. We decided to look at our cards, the ones that we already had looked at a million times over. It would have been nice to have a new batch come in-some newer ones maybe. The bad part about buying cards was that when you bought a lot of the same company, you'd get doubles of the same player's card. I hated doubles. So did the rest of the guys. Sitting there, I remember thinking it would have been nice to see what Jerry could have gotten us.

Now, I hated dealing with Curt. He never wanted to trade anything. I could not understand it. I don't care if he had three of the same card and I wanted it, he would ask for blood in return. He was a tough negotiator. Tommy and Pete hardly dealt with him at all. And if they did, they would end up giving more up than they would get in return. However, Curt had come into a card that he had gotten out of a pack several weeks ago that I wanted. I bought pack after pack of that same card company and never got the damn card he had that I wanted.

The card was a Chipper Jones Topps Number One Draft Pick card. At the time, it was not worth much, and I really did not think it would be worth any more than fifty cents at its peak. Chipper Jones didn't even play for the Braves yet. I only wanted it because I was a huge Braves fan and loved collecting Braves baseball cards. Out of that whole Topps Braves team set, that Chipper Jones card was the one that I was missing. And the one that had the card was Curt. Damn it.

Here was my proposal: I offered up a Cal Ripken, Jr. Score 1990, a Ken Griffey, Jr. 1990 Topps, and a Roger Clemens 1990 Bowman—good cards, fine cards. As soon as I offered them up for the Chipper, he looked at them, then looked up the cards in the price guide, and then back at me. "No." he rejected. I always hated it when he consulted *Beckett Baseball Card Monthly*. Me and the other two guys never did; we just made the trades if we wanted. Not Curt. Hell no, God forbid- back to the drawing board I went.

I knew that he loved the Minnesota Twins and especially their center fielder, Kirby Puckett. He had almost every card that was made of Puckett. But Tommy had one card that he did not have, and he tried like hell to leverage it away from Tommy for some time. Tommy never gave up the card, knowing that Curt wanted it so badly. He gave Curt some of his own medicine. That was the break that I needed.

In that same room, I offered Tommy a Michael Jordan 1990 Skybox card, Frank Thomas 1990 Topps (Rookie card,) and this Ted Williams flashback card that I got out of an Upper Deck pack for the Puckett. I knew if I threw the Williams in there, Tommy would bite because the dude was a huge Williams fan.

He had learned about Ted Williams from his dad who was a Red Sox fan himself. If I'm not mistaken, his dad was from the New England region. I sat back and waited for Tommy to make the deal. Curt was waiting to see if the Puckett card would change hands. I knew that if the deal went down, I would turn the Puckett over to Curt and get the Chipper card.

And just as I had hoped, it did, and all three of us were happy. It took some doing, but that was how all of our deals were done. You'd think we were general managers of real teams, trading players up there in his bedroom.

7

By far the riskiest thing I ever did was something me and Pete did a week after the Jerry incident. The idea was crazy, and I honestly didn't think I had the fortitude to even do it. Nor did I expect Pete to really come through with it. Pete liked to talk a good game, but sometimes when the rubber met the road, he very seldom could back up his words. On that night, we climbed the water tower, sat, and looked around at our small town. He actually surprised me in more ways than just one.

The idea came when the four of us were up in Curt's bedroom playing Nintendo. I think we were playing *Castlevania,* maybe *Castlevania II*. I'm a little fuzzy on which game it was. Curt's parents were gone, and Ricky was God knows where. The house was all to ourselves. It didn't matter anyway because we all stayed up in Curt's bedroom.

We were taking turns playing the video game and having to wait and watch which was usually boring as hell. I would go through Curt's cassette tapes, looking for music I wanted to put in his stereo and listen to. After going through his extensive tape and growing CD collection twice, I decided to just turn on the radio and listen to our favorite rock station, WIMZ.

Curt was on the floor beside Tommy, watching him play the game and giving him pointers as he often did, much to Tommy's consternation.

Pete was lying on his stomach on Curt's bed, playing with his brand new Gameboy his dad had gotten him a couple of weeks prior. I opened Curt's window and sat in the unseasonably cool night summer air. I could see our entire neighborhood from my vantage point. Streetlights cast a grayish-white artificial glow about the place, making it look tranquil.

I sat there thinking absently of Mandy—wondering what she was doing at that moment—when Pete said, "You know, I wonder if anyone has climbed up on the water tower?" Pete was referencing our 144-foot water tower that stood like a steel giant dead center of Claxton. Tommy and Curt were too enthralled in fighting the undead to respond. But I did.

"Probably a long time ago. But I've never heard anyone doing it since I've been alive."

"Wouldn't it be cool to climb it?" Pete asked, keeping his eyes down on his Gameboy.

I scoffed, "Yeah, right. You know how high that thing is?"

"144 feet tall and was built in 1937. It was put there in the middle of town so water pipes could spiderweb through the town, making the tower a central hub for water. Still in use today," Curt said, not taking his eyes off the TV. Me and Pete looked at Curt who I guess could feel us.

"What? Was I the only one in Mrs. Huckabey's local history class in sixth grade paying attention?" he replied.

"I say we do it," Pete said.

"I'm totally out. I don't want to die falling off that thing," Curt said, taking the controller from Tommy who had just been killed by a flying bat.

"Yeah, I'm afraid I have to agree with Curtis here. I know, it pains me to say that. But I'm out," Tommy said as he stretched his back.

"Matty? You going to chicken out?" Pete asked me.

Right then, "Bark at the Moon" from Ozzy started playing on the radio. I had never once considered climbing up that metal giant. That would be the most badass thing I'd ever done. It would put calling Mandy to shame. I wasn't afraid of heights. I figured that I could handle it for sure. But I wasn't going to do it alone. I wondered if Pete was just being Pete and talking about something that he knew good and damn well he'd never do? Or was he legit wanting to do this?

"Sure, I'll do it. You serious?"

"Bullshit," Tommy began, "he's not serious. When has he ever been serious?"

"I've been serious plenty of times," Pete replied.

"Name one time? I'll wait," Curt said, making me chuckle.

Pete was silent, still playing his Gameboy. Finally, he spoke after some reflection. "Well, it's not like I write everything down in a journal like Matty over there. But there's been times where I walked the walk and talked the talk." We all laughed hard at him. This wasn't the case at all, nowhere near.

"Okay," Pete said, putting his Gameboy down on the bed, "let's me and you do it. Tonight. Let's go climb that thing."

Curt and Tommy laughed, but I didn't this time. I could see that Pete was actually serious about something for a change. That made me really consider what he was wanting to do. Sure, it was impulsive, and not one time did I try to talk myself out of climbing that 144-foot steel giant... especially in the dark. Curt wasn't trying to be the voice of reason because he would say later he didn't think there was a chance in hell we'd go through with it. Pete was looking at me awaiting my answer.

I was sitting there on the window sill, looking at our neighborhood and the dark and stillness of the night. There's something about the nighttime that makes you brave—makes you feel invulnerable, like the rules don't apply to you. I was thinking how cool it would be to actually climb that water tower and look over at our small town. I wondered what it would look like from a 144-foot high. God, I bet it would be breathtaking, to say the least.

That summer I was bold—bolder than I had ever been up to that point in time. I wanted this summer, the last—I feared—with my best friends before high school took them away, to be something that I could remember for years to come. I wanted to feel alive and feel life running through my veins. That is how I felt after the nerves settled when I dialed Mandy's number that night in Curt's bedroom. I had never felt that much life in me before. I also felt *life* that night after I nearly drowned in the swimming pool. Climbing that water tower would surely give me a rush that I was subconsciously lusting after. I was going to do it.

"Yeah...let's go," I said.

I didn't think about any of the things that could go horribly wrong. We had Curt for the entire walk to the water tower that night, reminding us how badly things could go. He had gone over everything—and I mean everything—that could happen. It didn't matter. I think by the time me and Pete arrived at the water tower and looked up at it—its silver barrel disappearing in the dark sky—nothing could have stopped us. He had his own reasons to ascend it, and so did I. And that's what we did.

8

Pete went up the ladder first, and then I followed. Tommy and Curt stayed on the ground on the grassy area that the tower's legs had stood on since 1937. The odds of someone driving by or seeing us outside their windows in the many homes along Church Street were high. But it was one in the morning. Claxton usually went to sleep around ten.

The police—we always noticed—didn't patrol much around our town. They mostly stayed at the station and did whatever it was officers of the law did late at night in a small town. I thought we would be safe. Curt, on the other hand, ran over all the legalities of us trespassing on private property—if it really was—and said that we could be taken to jail. Then he started talking about him and Tommy leaving because he didn't want to get caught either. That was all he talked about was getting into trouble by just being there.

"Then go home," Pete said, tired of hearing it before we started to climb up. "Just you and Tommy walk back home while me and Matty do this. We get caught, it's us. We get hurt, it's us." He sounded harsh towards Curt, and Curt felt it. So did Tommy and I.

"I was only trying to tell you..."

"I don't care, dude. Don't care. Shut the fuck up or leave. We're not asking you to climb up here with us." We all stood in the shadowy night looking around. Curt, I could tell, was trying to figure out what to say next. I think me and Tommy were too.

"I'm staying," Tommy said, breaking the awkward silence between us. "I mean somebody has got to call for help when you two dumbasses fall and kill yourselves."

After a few moments, Curt said, "Yeah, Tommy is right."

For whatever reason that made us laugh, which I don't think was Curt's intention at all, but it did break the tension. We all gathered in close and did our special handshake with each other. All it was was a high five, us smacking the tops and backs of our hands and then shaking hands like gentlemen. Pete and Curt were fine with each other, it seemed.

9

Pete went up first, and I was a few rungs behind him. The old steel of the water tower was cold, hard. I could feel the rust in my hands and feel it falling from Pete's shoes as he climbed the rungs, hitting the bill of my Braves hat. Had I looked up, surely I would have gotten rust in my eyes. That would have been terrible. I couldn't imagine having something like that in my eyes. That thought alone made me lag behind Pete some, putting some distance between us. What we were doing was unsafe, but the rust getting in my eyes, or the potential of it, was enough to scare me more than climbing the steel ladder or falling to my demise. Crazy what scares you.

I don't remember thinking much during our climb up the water tower that night. I do recall that the higher we got up, the windier it had gotten. The June night was a little chilly, unseasonable for that time of year. I felt that in Curt's window earlier before this water tower business started.

We were nearly two-thirds up, and everything was aces. No issues. There was that one instance where I did what they told you in the movies not to do. Yup, I looked down. I got dizzy almost immediately and had to close my eyes and hang there on the steel ladder to gather myself. Looking down was a mistake and one I did not make again going up or coming down later. I will say that was a tense moment. If I was going to fall, it would have been right then. Thank God, I didn't lose my grip on that partially rusted steel rung and plunge to my death.

———

After we climbed up the ladder, there was this catwalk that was about six feet wide and wrapped around the barrel of the water tower. The hard part was over, and we both stood there, marveling over not only what he had just accomplished, but at the sight before us. "Damn, I thought I was going to lose it on that ladder at one point," I said.

"You looked down, didn't you?"

I nodded, "Yeah, bad mistake."

"Well, I did too. Then my foot slipped on a rung. I thought I fell." I could see the fear that was still attached to Pete—could see it in his eyes. "I can't believe we fucking did this." Pete was surprised as was I that we climbed the local landmark.

We stood on that catwalk and took in the scenery, dark as it was, but it was still cool. It's difficult to describe how beautiful everything was— how peaceful and calm—from the water tower. We looked down and didn't see Tommy or Curt. Maybe we were too high, and it was too dark. Perhaps a mixture of both. Standing on the catwalk, our backs against the steel barrel full of the town's water, Pete and I looked all over our town. We could see downtown, the shops, all the buildings, and all the houses.

"God," I said, "how many street lights do we have in this town?" *Has to be thousands,* I guessed in my mind.

"I don't know, but it looks like a million. Is this cool as hell or what?" Pete asked, mesmerized by what we were looking at. I could only nod in reply because I, too, was under the spell of our town at 144 feet.

10

Eventually, we sat down beside each other on the catwalk—our legs dangling off the edge—while we hung our arms over the thick handrailing. For a long time, we didn't say anything. We just looked and took in all that was Claxton. It was funny to me that down there were thousands of people in hundreds of homes, doing whatever it was they did in the dead of night. Mostly sleeping, I supposed. Some were probably at work. Across the dark landscape, there were several homes where the lights were on, indicating someone was up or the lights were left on because they were at work or whatever. Maybe the houses that had the one light on—which were several—were serving as a night light for scared kids. Whatever the case, it was awesome to be sitting high up on the water tower, looking around like nighthawks.

I was lost in thought of nothing in particular when Pete spoke. "I don't want to play football." Those words by my friend brought me back to reality. Not because it had broken the silence that held us for probably the better part of thirty minutes, but because Pete and football had gone hand in hand over the years. At least as long as I had known him up to that point in life.

"Really?" I asked, looking over at him with curiosity.

He didn't reply for a few minutes. It was as if he was considering telling me the rest of his secret—a secret he had not uttered one word about, especially to us, and especially not to his dad.

"Yeah, really."

We sat on that catwalk, looking around the town under the stars that night as Pete confessed his biggest secret—a secret that had been chewing him up on the inside. He had no one to tell, and there was no way he could go to his dad with this—at least not beforehand. It was an honor to be the one that he confided in. He and Tommy were closer than me and him, but maybe he needed a different opinion—a different perspective.

"Why not?" I asked.

Pete didn't reply for a few moments. Then he said, "I hate it. I hate the work you have to put in to be good. I hate the summer practices. I hate the two-a-day practices. I hate getting the hell knocked out of me every time. I hate being in the locker room with those idiots. I hate the headaches I have from getting hit in the helmet so much. And after the Fourth, we report to Central for summer practice. Man, I just don't want to play anymore."

"How long have you wanted to quit?"

"Since sixth grade," he replied.

"Wow," I could only manage to say.

Pete was really good at football. He was the running back for our school and was the best in the district during our eighth-grade year. Man, that football season he was a beast. He scored twenty touchdowns—not only a school record but a county record. "Paydirt Pete" is what they called him. I could never tell that he hated it. I always thought he enjoyed it. Usually, you're supposed to like the things you're good at. Not Pete. He had the talent—lots of it—but didn't want it.

"Football is my dad. He wasn't very good at it growing up, but he loves it so much. When I was four, he had me out in the yard doing drills. I don't remember this, but there are pictures. He talks about football constantly. He doesn't even know *me*. He doesn't know what my favorite movies are. My favorite bands. My favorite foods. Doesn't know that I get scared sometimes when I'm home alone while him and Mary are gone on their weekend trips sometimes. He doesn't care to know that I struggle in math. All I am to him is what he couldn't be as a kid. And that fucking sucks."

That was a heavy assessment of the status of the house he was living in. I wish I had known earlier how he was feeling. Maybe I could have helped in some way. But I was there now, high up on the steel giant in the cover of darkness, looking out across our town talking about what was bugging him. By the sound of his voice, he was down about it. I could relate. I think we all had something back then at home that weighed us down. We all had situations where nobody was listening, and the ones that were in charge—the ones that were supposed to listen— couldn't be bothered by our trivial teenage bullshit.

"What do you think the end result is going to be? Like, what do you want to do about it?"

"I want to quit– just go in the house and tell Dad that I'm not playing any more football. I can still watch it with him. We can still talk about it and be fans, but I just ain't wanting to get back on a field."

"How's Mary feel about it?" I asked.

Mary was Pete's stepmother. She had married Pete's Dad, Bill, a few years after Debbie, Pete's mom, was killed in a car wreck on her way from getting her hair done. This happened before we all met. Pete was barely in kindergarten when it happened, so he basically had no memories of her. Just pictures. One time, Pete told us on a campout when his mom got brought up—which was verboten most of the time—that when he looked at those pictures, it was like looking at a stranger.

"She pretty much lines up with Dad. She's not going to go against him. Never has. That's not going to change. Trust me, if I thought she could help, I'd have gone to her to see what I could do a long time ago."

"Your dad is crazy about football, that's for sure."

Pete chuckled, "Yeah, he sure is. That's why if I tell him it's going to kill him. And then things will get weird between us."

"Maybe not."

"They will. I think he only loves me because of what I can do on the football field. That's where my value is." Pete said this, and his voice cracked.

I'm pretty sure that he started to cry. I didn't reach over to console my friend. I just allowed him his time. The best thing that I could do was sit there and be his friend—to listen. At the end of the day, that's all people truly want—to be heard.

"Sometimes I wish I was dead. There was that night where I didn't score any touchdowns—this was last year against Polk County—and that man wouldn't stop talking about how much of a pussy I was for not getting through the line when we were on Polk's goal line. I wanted to score that night, believe me. Not because we would've won the game, but because I didn't want to hear what critiques my dad would have about me after the game. He records the games from the sidelines and makes me watch the tapes every Sunday morning. I fucking hate that. Nothing I do is ever good enough. You have no idea how much I have grown to hate the sport because of him. Sometimes I even hate him."

When Pete said that, it made me question why he wanted to climb the water tower. Did he do it hoping that he would slip and fall to his death on what would be looked at as stupid kid shenanigans gone tragically wrong? I wondered then as I do now. And honestly, I don't know. I really don't. I do know that Pete was tormented and had been by his dad's push for him to be the best—to do what he could not as a kid. To have a relationship with his dad, Pete had to do what his dad wanted. I don't think Bill came out and said it had to be that way, but Pete sure had picked up on it over the years.

"You obviously don't want to play football anymore. But you don't want to have to deal with your dad. You're going to have to pick a road to go down. Live for your dad, or live for you? Do you think taking some time off would help any?"

Pete shook his head, "No. It's everything or nothing at all with him when it comes to football. There's no middle. I brought it up earlier this year that I'd like to maybe take my freshman year off because I wasn't going to be starting, you know? He just laughed, thinking that I was making a joke or something. I didn't bring it up again."

"I think you need to sit him down and just tell him the truth; that you don't want to play anymore. He'll get over it eventually."

"We'll see, I guess. I haven't decided what I want to do yet. I know eventually something has got to happen though. I can't keep doing what I'm doing."

11

We sat up there for another hour in silence before we climbed down. Both of us thinking about the current state of our beings. Neither of us had much control over our lives. We both had to just ride the waves. That's the bad thing about being a kid; you have no control over what happens to you. Grown-ups make the decisions and rules, and you have to deal with it. I realized pretty early on that kids have no voice.

Thankfully, the four of us had each other to rely on in some aspects. Looking back on those days, I wonder how much differently things would have been in my life had I not had my friends when I did. Things would have been different, that's for sure. I wish that I had them during my high school years because God, did I ever need them then. I knew deep down in my soul this was going to be our last good summer together—all of us as a group. I held out a fraction of hope, just a glimmer, that I was wrong. But even then I knew better...I knew better.

Pete told me later in the summer that he told his dad that he didn't want to play football anymore. As expected his dad threw a fit about it. His dad made him feel less than zero and called him a quitter, a little bitch, and that oh-so-magical word that was supposed to make Pete angry: a pussy. None of that worked on Pete. At least, not at that point.

The more visibly upset his dad was, the more Pete dug in his heels. Eventually, his dad started treating him differently around the house. There were more times than not that he wouldn't speak to his son. Pete was okay with that, he told me, for a while. He said he could handle it, although it was hard—his dad basically kicked him out of his life over something like playing a sport that summer—but he didn't have to put on football gear anymore...or so he thought.

"There's a freedom in knowing that," Pete told me.

Then he added something I'll never forget. "You know, I think my dad would've accepted it better if I was on drugs or an alcoholic than quitting football. And that's sad." I think it was then that my friend realized for the first time a harsh universal truth: sometimes people only love you for what you can give them.

Eventually though, during that summer, as it got later on and closer to the start of school, Pete caved and started playing football again. His dad was elated Pete told me and their dynamic returned. He was back on his dad's good graces once again. Pete traded what he *wanted* for the love of his dad.

CHAPTER 8

YARD SALE/DREW FROM VIRGINIA BEACH/THE CAMPER/TAPE CITY

1

AS THEY GROW UP, a kid has things that they consider theirs. What I considered *mine* were my old G.I. Joe and Transformers action figures, my Stephen King hardback book collection, my comic books, sports cards, and my movie posters that were hung on my bedroom walls in frames. All that stuff I had collected over the years during my short life. Those items were things that gave me great joy. So you can imagine how I felt when I came into my bedroom after riding bikes with Curt on that Wednesday afternoon to find my bedroom empty save my twin bed and my desk.

After I had gotten up and foraged for breakfast at 11:30 that morning, I had gotten dressed and gone over to Curt's house for a bit. We ended up riding bikes around town for a few hours. Nothing major: just rode around and went to Wilson's Drugstore to read magazines and buy something to drink. We cruised by Mandy's house a few times. I was hoping that she would be outside doing something, so I could pull in and say hi. She wasn't.

"I was thinking. What if we do something for the last time and have no idea of it being the last time we do it."

"You mean like, will we remember the last time we did a particular thing when we're old men thinking back on it?" Curt asked.

I nodded, "Yeah. Like that. But will we know it in real-time, you think? Like, in that moment, will we know, *this is it*? We're out riding bikes and we know we'll never do this again. That kind of thing."

Curt considered my question for a moment. "I don't know. I'd like to think we would. Be kinda sad doing something for the last time and not being aware of it, you know." We both rode beside each other in silence, both thinking about that. "That would be sad," he added.

"Hopefully we'll know. Maybe I need to start writing stuff down."

We turned down Dodson Ave. and coasted down the slight hill through the neighborhood. It was a nice neighborhood: nice houses on either side of the street. People down this way were always friendly, always tipping us a wave from their porches or yards they were working in. I liked that neighborhood a lot. There was nothing at all wrong with ours, but that one seemed more idyllic to me, like one you'd see on a TV sitcom.

"My cousin Drew is coming down for a quick visit," Curt said.

"Oh yeah? I like Drew. He's always got cool stories from the places he's been."

"Man, I'd like to be him when I grow up. Just living life," Curt said.

"Me too. Here's a question. Would you do Christina Applegate from *Married...with Children*?"

"Hell yes, I would!" Curt replied with a smile. "What about you?" Curt asked.

"Not even a question. What about Tracy Gold from *Growing Pains*?"

"Oh yeah. No doubt. What about Tiffany Amber Thiessen from *Saved by the Bell*?" Curt asked.

"Every night when I close my eyes," I said. We both laughed as we turned from Dodson Ave. onto Green Street as both of us rode a smooth, newly paved street.

"If you could only watch five movies for the rest of your life, what would they be?" Curt asked.

I thought for a minute. *"Ghostbusters*, of

course...*Beetlejuice...Batman...Back to the Future...The Goonies.* What about you?"

Curt took about as long as I did to answer. *"Major League...Batman...Big Trouble in Little China...Halloween...Nightmare on Elm Street."*

"Good movies between us both," I said. We didn't talk anymore until we got onto Whitman Road. "You ready for your honors classes in high school?"

Curt was the only one in the group that signed up for honors classes. The rest of us, well, we took the basic stuff and some easy classes for electives such as: Shop and Introduction to Art History. I found out pretty quickly in my freshman year that Art History wasn't an easy class at all. I passed that class by the skin of my teeth.

"Yeah, I think so. Hope so anyway. I want to get into a good college one day." Curt had his life planned out. Or thought he did. I think we all had our futures planned out back then. But out of all of us, I felt that Curt would make good on his blueprint. The rest of us, well, I didn't think we'd hit the mark we would set. Who really does what they say they're going to do when they're thirteen?

"I just hope I can get by," I said. It was the truth. I had barely scraped by in elementary school and figured high school was going to be much worse—higher stakes, academically speaking—than what I was accustomed to. I was not a smart kid, by any means. I got by in school. Curt? Straight As just came easily to him. I always thought he'd be a lawyer or scientist or something like that. He probably could've been.

"What?" Curt asked. "You're plenty smart. You just don't try. Good enough is good enough for you."

"It is. Look, I can sit and study and study for days for a math test and fail or just barely make a 70. You? You don't even have to look at the book. How does that happen?"

Curt shook his head, "I don't know. I can read something usually once and commit it to memory. Kinda like how Tommy can listen to a song one time and then play it without missing a cord switch."

"Yeah. See? I ain't like you guys. I'm just there in school."

"You just have to apply yourself harder than I do. I got lucky when

God was handing out brains, is all. There's no trick to it. I just got lucky." And Curt was authentic about that statement. He never boasted his intelligence to me or the guys. Mostly because we'd knock him down a peg or two if he did. But we all knew he was smart.

We turned down Sunnyside Ave, our street, on the long side of it. I saw a kid walking on the sidewalk who was carrying what looked like a huge framed something. A poster maybe? As me and Curt rode our bikes closer, I kept looking at the kid and what he was carrying. It was a poster in a frame and it was as big as he was. It was a *Beetlejuice* movie poster. I stopped in the middle of the street. Curt stopped too, wondering what I was doing.

"Hey, let me see that, would you?" I asked the kid. He was younger, probably in fourth grade, maybe fifth. I'd never seen him before. He walked over to me and showed me the framed *Beetlejuice* poster.

"Where did you get this?" I asked.

"At a yard sale up the street. Got it for five bucks. Ain't it cool?"

I kept looking at it curiously. "I think this is mine."

"How do you know that?" Curt asked.

"There's a small tear in the upper right corner where the lady at the video ripped it, taking it down for me when I bought it. This is mine!"

"No way, dude! I bought this fair and square."

"What house was this yard sale?"

"The white one on the corner with the big trees." The kid turned and walked back on the sidewalk and away from us.

"You think she's selling your stuff?" Curt asked.

I simply nodded. There was nothing that I could say. My stomach had that feeling when you go down a hill really fast. I knew that when I rode my bike to the end of Sunnyside, I'd see a yard sale in my yard, and I just knew all my stuff would be sitting out there for people to buy. If they hadn't already.

"I'm going to let you deal with this one. I'm going to go home. Maybe my parents are somewhat sober today," Curt said. He drove off, leaving me in the middle of the street on my bike wondering how off the deep my mother had gone that day. She was getting worse—progressively worse—that summer. Looking back, that summer of 1991 was the beginning of the end of her mental condition.

2

I could see the front of my house from down the street. And yes, just like the kid said, there was a yard sale in front of my house. My mother was sitting on the front porch steps, smoking a cigarette while a few grownups milled about a couple of tables looking at stuff. There was a guy in the driveway putting boxes into the back hatch of his green Honda Civic. That feeling in my stomach had only gotten worse when I reached the front yard and tossed my bike to the ground.

I didn't even say anything to my mom, nor did I look at what was left on the tables. I ran to the backyard and up the back porch and through the back door inside. I noticed pretty quickly that our microwave was missing and so were the four bar stools that were in the kitchen. The pictures that hung on the kitchen wall had gone missing too. I ran through the dining room and down the hall to my bedroom. I opened the door and was shocked with disbelief that it was nearly empty except for my bed and my desk. Everything was gone.

My TV, Nintendo, and all its games were gone.

My stereo that sat on a small end table next to my bed was gone, as well as all the music cassettes I had that sat next to it. She even took the table for her yard sale. I looked over at my desk and figured the only reason that it wasn't gone was that she couldn't take it out of the house. I could tell that she had tried because it had been moved back but not in the same exact spot. It was about a foot more to the left than normal.

My movie posters, the ones I had framed from the video store there in town, had been taken off my wall and sold in my mom's yard sale. I had four of them in total: *Beetlejuice, Ghostbusters, The Goonies,* and *Back to the Future.* They were all gone.

The top of my desk was empty, too. I had some Marvel Comics and Batman collectible plastic statues on it. One was of the Green Goblin on his glider holding a pumpkin bomb, and the other was of Dr. Doom standing there with his arms folded across his chest. There was also a

Batman statue with him crouched down with his cape around him. Over to the left of the desk, where my Atlanta Braves coffee mug used to sit, was nothing. She had taken it too.

I opened the drawers to my desk hoping to find my sports card albums. They, too, were taken. All seven books and thousands of cards—gone. I rushed over to my closet, hoping to at least find my comic books that I had kept in a huge box that my dad had gotten me to store them all in. All I found in there were just a few clothes—some of those she had taken as well—and no box. My mom had taken my comic books as well. I kneeled down in my closet, looking for another box that had my action figures stored away. Nope. It was gone, too.

The bookshelf on the other side of the bedroom was empty too. On there sat all kinds of books that I had collected over the years. My favorites were Stephen King's hardbacks. I had every one of them up to that point in his career. But they were gone...all of my books. Everything that I had as a kid, everything that had given me joy, my mom had taken and sold at a yard sale without my permission.

I was stunned. I didn't know what to say. I surely didn't expect to come home and see that my childhood had been practically stolen from my bedroom. I was left with nothing. Everything was gone. How could she take everything that I loved so much, stuff that had given me joy? With tears in my eyes, I sat down on my bed and cried in my bedroom.

———

After I got a hold of myself mentally, I walked out of my bedroom and through the house. Not only had she taken my stuff, but some of the stuff inside the house too. Pictures were no longer on the walls, the throw pillows on the couch and loveseat were gone, bar stools, the coffee table that was once in the living room, Dad's magazine rack that sat on the floor next to his recliner. She had taken everything that she could carry outside for her yard sale. If she could have gotten the stove and fridge outside, she would've sold those too.

I walked outside as the last of the grownups were leaving, carrying stuff in their hands. I saw one guy carrying Dad's work boots while a fat woman was carrying a box of pots and pans. I stood in the yard, looking at what was left. Wasn't much—just some trinkets and such that sat on the tables in the house and up on top of the kitchen cabinets. I was standing there, not able to say a word until my mom broke me out of my silence and awe.

"You need to help me carry the rest of this stuff back inside. I think I've sold all the stuff I can today."

"Why did you sell my stuff?" I asked, feeling rage building inside me slowly.

My mom got up from the front porch steps and flicked her cigarette into the grass and marched over to me. She had that grin on her face that scared me. Before I could turn and run away, she grabbed me by the collar of my shirt and knocked my Braves hat off my head. She crouched down a little and got into my face. I can still smell the cigarettes on her breath even now.

"First off, your stuff was *junk*? You hear me! *Junk*! Second off, that *junk* was bought with *my* money, which makes it *mine,* and *I* can do whatever *I* want to with it! You got me, punk! Don't you ever question me again!" She pushed me to the ground violently. I lay there looking up at my mom—with that crazy grin on her face—wondering what to do next. She stared at me for a few minutes as cars lurched slowly down our street, looking at what was going on. She didn't pay any mind. She was too hyper-focused on me lying there. I was honestly hoping someone would stop and get out to help me. Because at that point, I wasn't sure what she was going to do.

"Now, get off your ass and get this back inside the house. RIGHT NOW!" I scrambled to my feet as quickly as I could and started getting what was left of the yard sale into my hands. I was shaking as tears once again came.

"And you're grounded for the rest of the week for back talking! You understand me?! Oh....you better!"

———

After I had gathered all the stuff from the yard sale and put it back into the house, I ran out through the back door, got on my bike, and headed for Curt's. There was no way in hell I was going to stay there with that lunatic roaming the place. I feared for my safety that day. I have no idea if my mother called for me or tried to stop me. I just ran out of the house and away. I wasn't planning on going back until my dad got home…whenever that would be.

Eventually, Dad got home around dark that night. Me and Curt had been passing football in the street under the streetlight, waiting on Dad. He got home, and I let him get settled in for a bit because I was sure that he was going to have to deal with whatever version of Mom was there at the time. After about an hour, I told Curt I was going to go home and see Dad. "Well, come back here and spend the night if it gets too bad," he told me. I nodded my head.

I got home but didn't go inside. Some of the lights were on inside, but there was no way I was going in. I walked around to the front of the house, and there was my dad. sitting on a rocking chair while smoking a cigarette and drinking from a bottle of Jim Beam. He saw me appear out of the darkness, got scared, and then realized it was me. He put the bottle down on the porch floor beside his rocking chair in hopes I wouldn't see it. Too late, I already knew. I had known for a while that my dad had been drinking—stealing sips—around the house whenever he could. I didn't blame him. He was doing it to numb himself from life.

"Hey, Matty. Come up here and have a seat."

I walked on the front porch and sat on a rocking chair beside him. Our street was quiet that night. It usually was when it was that late. We didn't say much for a while. I think we both knew there really wasn't anything that could be said. We both knew what the score was. But that didn't stop the kid in me from saying what I wanted to say.

"Dad, Mom took…"

Dad stopped me right there before I could get any further, "I know. I already saw your bedroom. I'm sorry. I'll try to replace it as quick as I can."

"How?"

"I don't know. We'll figure something out."

"Where is she now?" I asked after some more silence.

"Asleep. Or at least I think she is. I don't know. I don't know much of anything anymore."

I was going to say something else about the subject of Mom's mental condition worsening but decided against it. Even as a kid, I knew what was what. Me and Dad talked about Mom not too long ago, and here we were again, same issue but a different incident. Honestly, what was talking going to do at that point? Nothing.

"Am I grounded?"

Dad turned his head to look at me, "Why would you be grounded?"

"Mom said..." Dad cut me off again.

"Forget what she said. You're not grounded. Wasn't your mom that said that...wasn't your mom that sold our stuff. That's someone...different."

After another one of those silences that were famous between Dad and I, I asked a question before I could catch it before it left my lips. "Do you think she could hurt us? Like maybe kill us?"

Dad took a long time to reply. He was in thought, deep. Finally, he said, "I honestly don't know."

After Dad smoked another two cigarettes with us not talking, I got up from my rocking chair, "I think I'm going to spend the night over at Curt's. Is that okay?"

Dad just absently waved me off, "Sure. Have a good night, Son. I love you." I went over to hug my dad, and he hugged me back. It felt good doing that. We were on the same team, facing the same kind of challenge. It was nice just to have that human contact with a parent. In my ear, Dad whispered, "I'm sorry." I nodded my head. It was all I could do. I was crying by then. He was too.

3

The introduction of the heavy metal band Danzig came about to us by way of Curt's cousin, Drew, who was a huge Danzig fan. I had no idea who Danzig was at that time and had not ever heard of them before

Drew. As for my three friends, neither had they. But we were about to get schooled on what Danzig was all about.

The four of us were up in Curt's bedroom watching MTV—like we always did back then—when a knock on Curt's door disturbed us from the latest re-run episode of *Totally Pauly* on MTV. Curt got up and opened the door, and there stood his cousin Drew, smiling and spreading out his arms wide while holding a white plastic bag in one hand. The two of them squealed like girls when they saw each other and hugged as Drew was invited into the room.

We knew Drew—an awesome guy. He was like 6'4", 250 pounds, twenty-three years old, and looked like a tree of a man. He had long, dark hair that just grazed the tops of his shoulders. He came in that day wearing what was to be later identified as a Danzig tee shirt that had the skull on it, like the cover of the first Danzig album.

"Long time, no see, man!" Drew said, walking into Curt's bedroom and sitting on the bed.

We stopped watching *Totally Pauly* and gazed upon the dude who walked in. Drew was a guy that I wanted to be like when I reached his age. He seemed carefree as if nothing ever bothered him. You know and seen the type, I'm sure: a surfer dude, hailing from the West Coast who had a walk and aura about him that nothing ever bothered him and that everything broke his way.

"How's Virginia Beach these days?" Curt asked his cousin as he came in high fiving us all before taking a seat on Curt's bed.

"Oh, man," he said, moving the hair from his eyes, getting ready to tell one of his famous beach stories, "the girls up there are awesome, but not as awesome as at Laguna Beach in Cali. Like the other day, I was walking around on the beach, you know, looking for money or stuff like that with my metal detector. All of a sudden, I stumble on this girl who's wearing nothing but suntan oil." We all gasped at his description. "So, I'm like 'Excuse me, I didn't mean to almost step on you'. She looks up at me with this awesome smile and says, 'It's okay, would you mind rubbing some oil on my back'? And I was like, hell yeah! So I did! Man, it was awesome! We later went out on a date," Drew said, high-fiving all of us again in the bedroom. We laughed in triumph with him. Why? I don't know exactly. Drew had that magnetism that just lured you in.

I loved hearing stories from Drew. He always painted a vivid picture to us horny teenagers. *God, his life must be exciting,* I sat there and thought. Those stories he told were legendary. Pete said one day last year that he thought that Drew made them up, but I didn't think so. Drew had this honesty about him. Authentic would be an adjective I'd use to describe him. I never got the vibe that Drew was lying about his experiences. I guess when you're built like Drew, have good looks and a million-dollar smile, the world just comes easy for you.

By looks alone, he came across as the ultimate beach bum. I don't think that he ever worked a day in his life– not consistently anyway, maybe odd jobs here and there. But either way, a guy like that could get by on his looks and his charm until they evaporated over time like they always do.

"Hey, I brought you something," Drew said, holding up a plastic bag.

He put his hand inside the bag and pulled out a CD. He showed us the first Danzig album. I noticed that the cover of the CD looked like the front of his tee shirt. "This band is called Danzig. The lead singer's name is Glen Danzig, and he rules! He used to front The Misfits and Samhain." Drew said, handing Curt the tape.

We all got up and gathered over to Curt to see the CD he had just gotten. You'd have thought that Curt was just handed the Holy Grail or something.

We were used to Drew bringing Curt music. Every time he would come to visit Curt's mother and father, he would come up to Curt's bedroom and tell us an awesome story and give his cousin a CD or a concert tee shirt from one of the many concerts he attended since the last time he was in town. Looking at the back of the CD at the song names, Curt called them out loud: "Am I Demon, Twist of Cane, The Hunter, Mother...?"

"Yeah, those songs kick ass, dude," Drew told, cutting Curt off. "Got to turn that shit way up on the volume."

That night after Drew left– but not before telling us a few more stories about him, the beach and of course college girls– we put the CD into Curt's stereo and started to listen. I could tell right away that this band was great. Good music, great guitar, good drum beats, and the lead singer sounded like a souped-up version of Elvis. I was as hooked as we all were.

I'll bet you a million dollars that we listened to that CD twenty times that night. We had almost every song memorized and could name all the members of the band from the liner notes. We loved the band so much that the four of us right then and there started calling ourselves the "Danzig Boys." Of course, no one outside our clique knew about it. It was very hush-hush and exclusive. Mostly because people would think we were crazy.

Curt came up with the "Danzig Boys," so we called him, Glenn Danzig, after the lead singer. I was called Eerie Von, the name of the bass player; Pete was called John Christ, the name of the guitarist; and Tommy was called Chuck Biscuits, the name of the drummer. And for a long time, that was how we referred to each other until the novelty wore off—which it did after that summer.

The day that Drew brought the first Danzig album changed us forever to a degree. I was not into that kind of music at the time. I stuck with bands like R.E.M., 80's New Wave, U2, The Cars, and bands like that. But hearing Danzig for the first time, I decided that they were on my playlists for good. I guess you could say that they were an instant classic with us. Danzig was part of the soundtrack to our summer back in '91. I still own that album after I bought it on CD many, many years later.

4

The next night, me and Curt sat inside the pop-up camper in his parents' backyard. Inside the camper was a small fold-out table that hinged on the wall. On the table was a Coleman battery-powered lantern that was really bright. It was the same one that we had used on some of our campouts in the woods. I brought my small portable cassette player and had been playing the hell out of The Cure's, *Disinte-*

gration, album most of that summer. "Plainsong" started to play very softly as Curt dealt the cards, seven apiece, for our game of Rummy. We didn't keep score; we just played to have something to do while we talked– to pass the time.

This was the first night that summer that we didn't hang out with Pete and Tommy. The two of them were off with Pete's cousin, Heath, doing whatever it was they went to do sometimes at his house. It was late June and hot as hell that night. Even with the windows unzipped in the camper, it was still muggy and hot. My tee shirt was sticking to me, and I hated that.

As we absently played the card game, I asked Curt how things with Amanda were going. Amanda was his on-again, off-again girlfriend since the latter part of sixth grade. They were a good couple– looked like they fit together. Their relationship didn't make it past the mid-way point of freshman year. Curt foresaw this coming.

"Oh, man, who knows?" he replied, laying down a suit of three kings. "Sometimes she calls, and sometimes she doesn't. Gets frustrating."

Curt only saw his girlfriend at school because her parents didn't allow her to date at thirteen. She would sneak off to see Curt at the movies sometimes on Friday nights, telling her parents that she was going with her friends to the old American Cinema in the next town over. Her mom would drop her off, seeing her friends standing outside the building, but inside, Curt was waiting.

This summer so far had been bothering him for a lot of reasons: troubles at home– which I could relate to– and trouble with his eighth-grade girlfriend.

"You guys seem to work pretty good; seemed happy at the prom." I referenced the eighth-grade prom that was held in the school's gym not too long ago in May. I drew from the deck of cards and looked around in my hand. Nothing I could work with. I discarded a lousy two of hearts.

Curt, chewing on a toothpick, drew from the deck and shifted the pulled card into his hand of cards and tossed one into the pile. "We do. It's just that not seeing her sucks. High school is coming, and we enrolled in all the same classes– all the honors ones– but I doubt we'll get any of them together. We can't see each other until she hits sixteen because of her dad's strict rules. We just have to sneak around. Dude, that gets old."

"I bet. But when high school rolls around, you guys *might* have classes and stuff together. See each other some more." I replied.

"I don't know. Maybe. Depends on what times the classes fall. We have the same classes, but maybe not at the same times. But man, things have changed with us. I mean, like really changed."

"How so?" I asked, looking at him from across the small table in the glow of the Coleman lantern.

What Curt told me that night he had sworn that he was going to take to his grave. I mean, he told no one what he was about to tell me. I had been his friend for a long time up to that point, and I had no clue what was eating away at him. But there in that pop-up camper, Curt confided in me. We had talked about some serious stuff in the past, but this summer, Curt was going to lay some revelations down on me. Some things I knew; some I didn't. The camper story was one that I didn't.

"You got to swear to me...this stays between us. No Tommy or Pete." Curt said.

I nodded. I shifted around in my semi-cushioned seat, getting ready for what it was he was going to tell me.

"I had sex with Amanda a few months ago at her house." I sat there in shock. He was the only one out of us that I knew of who had gotten anywhere with a girl. Pete always lied and said that he had sex with his sister's best friend while she spent the night at his house back last summer, but none of us believed him.

Tommy called him out on it several times, and we all made fun of him relentlessly. Pete just wanted to be the first one of us to have sex; and if that meant lying about it, so be it. But I could see that Curt was for real. Curt didn't lie, not that I ever knew of. He had what I called honest eyes; those eyes, when you looked into them, told a story—an honest story for those who wanted to know.

"That's awesome," I replied, stunned. I had so many questions. I could tell that he wasn't really happy about it like I thought he should have been. Not like I would have been, that's for sure. He wasn't about to

136

brag about it like Pete's fake sexual escapade. There was something painful in his tone.

"Yeah, maybe. I guess so." He put his cards down on the table and looked around the small camper.

After a few moments of silence, I finally broke it, "What happened?"

I knew something had happened by the way he was acting. He had gotten quiet, somewhat morose. I had no idea what was weighing on him. Sometimes he talked, and when he did, we covered a lot of ground on things that were bothering him. But I knew there was a whole bunch more going on with him. We'd been friends for a long time; sometimes you just know. A bad side to Curt was that he didn't talk a whole lot about his feelings. At least not to me. He was the type that would hold it in sometimes. Sometimes he would talk about things, sometimes not.

Curt chewed on the toothpick that was poking out from his mouth, took it out, and flipped it across the camper. "Dude I thought that I got her pregnant. Like for real."

I sat there in silence. At first, I thought he was fooling around with me; he wasn't. He was clearly bothered by it. He had kept this pent-up inside of him for a long time, and I wondered why he didn't tell me sooner. Maybe he just wanted to not speak about it. I don't really know. After a few minutes of listening to Robert Smith singing the lyrics to "Plainsong" in a low gloomy fashion, I finally spoke.

"What happened? I'm guessing that she ain't because you talk about it in past tense."

Curt sat there trying to figure out if he wanted to even go down the road with me on this subject. I was betting that he did, or he wouldn't have even brought it up. Sometimes I had to fish it out of Curt. When I did, he would spew like a fountain, telling me what was going on inside that head of his.

"Amanda's parents were gone for the evening, like to Nashville. Her dad's mom had a stroke or something and had to be sent there to Vander-bilt. So, Amanda stays home, right? She calls me while I'm doing home-work, and we're talking on the phone in my bedroom about much of nothing really. Then she asks if I want to come hang out. Keep in mind, this was around 8. It was dark. I was like, absolutely, you know?

"So I get off the phone and sneak out of the house. Which ain't hard when your parents are passed out drunk in the living room. I managed to make it past Rick's bedroom and out of the house. So I made it to Amanda's, and it's so weird because I wasn't supposed to be there. There was like a certain magic to it or something. It was the first time I'd ever been there.

"We're sitting there on her couch watching TV and all of a sudden we started making out. Neither of us had ever kissed anyone before. I mean, we had been going together for a while now, and we just didn't have the right time to do it. We held hands and stuff at the movies, but that was as far as we went. Well, we just went at it, trying to do it like they do in the movies, you know? I mean it's getting intense. Our tongues in each other's mouths, her rubbing my junk, me rubbing her tits. Man, it was awesome. I was shaking, and she was, too.

"So we went to her bedroom. She took off her clothes, and I got mine off and dude, I know we should've stopped, but we didn't. We did it right there. No rubber. I thought I pulled out of her before, you know. But we both wondered if I did fast enough."

Curt tailed off and sat there lost in his story for a bit. He looked sad, like the memory of that night hurt.

"A month later," Curt started again, "she told me at school that she hadn't had her period, and it always came at that time of the month like clockwork. I told her not to worry about it, that maybe things were just off."

Curt stops his story again, just looking down at the small table.

"For three days, I thought I had gotten her pregnant. She started. Finally. But dude, I don't want that shit on me ever again. I was a fucking nervous wreck."

We both sat there quietly. I soaked in what he had just revealed to me. I mean, this guy could have been a father at thirteen, for God's sake. How would that have changed things? How would it have changed Amanda, her family, and Curt? Hell, how would it have changed our friendship?

"I think she's slowly breaking up with me," Curt concluded. There was a sadness in his voice.

"Why?" I asked. It was the only thing that I could think of to say.

Curt shook his head and didn't answer me at first. He knew why, he just didn't want to say it out loud.

"I was her practice guy, I think. Now she's had sex. Now when we get into high school, she's going to go out with older guys and won't be a virgin anymore."

"You think that's what it is? Because how is she going to be able to do that with older guys and her work around her dad?"

Curt continued to consider my question. I could tell he had thought about this over for a long time.

"She snuck around with me, didn't she?" Curt pointed out. He was right.

"Good point."

"Yeah, just a practice guy," he said. "Things have been messed up ever since that night. Maybe I'm messed up, too."

I sat there with my cards lying face down on the table. Robert Smith had switched to another song while Curt and I had forgotten about the game that we weren't really paying any attention to anyway. I couldn't believe how close he had gotten to being a dad. Neither could he.

I could tell just sitting there that Curt was glad that he had told someone—to offload that weight that he had been carrying for months. I wished that he would've told me sooner. Maybe he would've felt better.

"Dude, this might sound stupid, but I'm going to say it anyway. I don't care if I have sex anymore or not. Especially not after all this. All the nerves just ain't worth it. Maybe it would have been different if I had a condom, but I didn't think we'd be having sex when I went over there. At best, I thought we'd just make out, you know. Maybe some under-the-clothes stuff."

I sat and thought about something that made me laugh on the inside. I wasn't going to say it at first, but I figured that I needed to break the gloomy scene in the camper, especially with The Cure playing in the background.

"You could've gone and found Jerry. I'm sure he had some rubbers lying around that he'd give you."

He looked at me and we both laughed, remembering on cue the day Jerry stole from Rocky Top.

5

Later in the week, me and Pete had finished mowing Mark Neefler's yard which, by and large, was always a chore. It wasn't that it was too big for me and Pete, but every single time we would mow it, Mark would come out there and inspect it. Jesus, you would think he was a governmental inspector for nuke plants in Iran the way he would go over everything. I had been mowing Mark's yard for a few years now—every two weeks from March to October just before Halloween. I could've quit at any time, but he paid pretty good, and I always could use the money. Besides, I needed to start replacing my stuff that my mom had sold at the yard sale.

Dad had taken steps to fix things around the house. At least for me. He installed a new doorknob with a lock and key. "Now," he said to me on the day he gave me the key, "keep this locked when you leave. If she wants to get in here, she'll have to bust the door down. Which I don't think she'll do. But always lock it when you go out, okay?"

Right then and there, I nearly told my dad about an incident earlier in May before school let out. Mom had come into my bedroom while I was sleeping and that was the night I thought she was going to kill me. I never said anything to Dad about it. Why? I don't know exactly. But it scared me to death. I had asked Dad earlier if he thought she might hurt us. I think, even then, he thought the possibility was there. After that night when Mom crept into my bedroom with a knife, I slept with my desk moved to the door so she couldn't open it. As a secondary precaution, I opened my bedroom window just in case I needed an escape hatch if she did get in. That's how I slept until Dad installed the new lock on my door.

Dad had taken me shopping at the comic book store where I bought some comics to replace what was sold, and I bought some new plastic statues for my desk. I got a new Green Goblin on his glider, but Spiderman was with him. It was okay; I like my old one better. I also got this cool Batman one and a Joker one as well. Dad even bought me a new stereo with a few CDs to get me going.

We went to a pawn shop and bought me a new-to-me TV and a Nintendo with some games. Then we hopped on over to Wal-Mart and bought a small TV stand. I felt good again about getting my bedroom back to normal. I never did replace my movie posters. Nobody had those old movie posters around. The Internet wasn't a thing at the time, and you couldn't just go order them. Dad was trying to make it right, and he was.

———

Every time I cut Mark's grass, I had one of the guys help me. Mark paid well, thirty dollars each time. I used to do the yard and the trimming by myself, but I got tired of doing it—tired of being out there in the sun. I got the bright idea of getting one of the guys each time to come and help. I told them I'd give them fifteen bucks, and all they had to do was mow. I would take care of the trimming.

Curt tried to argue that I had it easier than him once, and I switched it up on him: he trimmed the bank down on the street, around the house, the flowerbeds, under the trees, along both sides of the concrete drive-way, around the edges where Mark's grass and the city's street met, and around the front and back porches. I had finished up mowing, sat on the front porch, and watched Curt labor out there with sweat pouring off him. It had taken me about an hour with a self-propelled walk-behind mower, and Curt was about an hour from being finished. It was the last time that he ever challenged me on having it easier on the trimming.

This time it was Pete's turn to help out, and things went pretty smoothly. He had mowed Mark's yard with me several times before and knew the flow of the yard, where to make the turns, and how to actually cut time off by mowing in a different pattern. When Pete and I did Mark's yard, he and I always finished up fifteen minutes quicker than the rest.

When we were finished, Mark came out and inspected every single spot in that yard. That day he didn't have us touch anything up; it was good as is—another first for me. He paid me with a check, and Pete and I took it to the bank and cashed it: fifteen dollars both ways.

———

Standing outside of the bank discussing what to do with our new fortune, I suggested that we head over to Tape City and look around. Pete wanted to blow his cash on pizza at Pappa Enzo's—which was fine, I didn't care—but I wanted to buy the new Van Halen CD. I had heard the first single off that album, "Poundcake," and really wanted that song.

We went inside Tape City, and everything about it screamed music. They sold tee shirts from various bands that hung on racks that were scattered throughout the building. They had wall posters of said bands decorated throughout, and ones you could buy were rolled up in a tube in cubbies, where a movable swatch of framed posters hung. All you had to do was find the poster you wanted and look for the cubby that matched the letter on the upper right of the frame.

A few months ago, I bought a Guns N' Roses, *Appetite for Destruction*, wall poster from Tape City. I had not gotten around to taping it up on my bedroom wall before my mom went and sold everything I owned. Good thing. But it was up now on my closet door. It was the only wall decor that I had.

In the middle of the store, pretty much as you walked in, there were seven aisles of music: tapes, CDs, and even vinyl records, all sectioned by genres, and in alphabetical order by artist. Above, on the store's speaker, was Van Halen's new album playing, *For Unlawful Carnal Knowledge*. Such a great album.

Pete broke away from me and went down the metal section. He loved Iron Maiden, and every time that we went inside Tape City, he walked over there to browse the tapes and CDs of the ones he had not gotten yet. I thought he was going to buy one of the ones he didn't have that day, but for whatever reason, he passed. I guess he wanted a pizza and to rent some Nintendo games.

I walked over to the rock section and to where the Vs were. I quickly spied the new Van Halen CD right away. I snatched it from the stack as if it were the only one left and held it in my hands. I carefully read off the tracks, all eleven of them. I was so excited about having their newest album in my hands. I turned to walk away from the V section,and my eyes came up from the back of the CD to Mandy. She had come in through the door with her friend Jennifer, and they were laughing and talking, not paying much attention to anything. The two of them walked in the direction of the band posters.

My heart fell into my stomach as "Man On A Mission" from Van Halen, off the album I was holding, played on the stereo speaker above me. "Oh my God," I whispered, watching Mandy and her friend walk across the store.

I frantically turned around and looked for Pete. I needed him and fast. I rushed down the aisle I was on and over two more to where he was still standing looking at Iron Maiden CDs.

"Dude...dude. She's here."

"Who?" he simply asked, not paying me any attention at all, thumbing through the CDs.

"Mandy, man. She's here with Jennifer."

Pete took his eyes off the CD shelves and scanned the store. He found them from the shoulders up across the CD racks, looking over at the posters. "This is awesome. Go over there and talk to her. This is your chance."

"Man, I don't know. This is crazy," I said, already feeling that high anxiety of the moment.

"All right, listen, I'll walk over there with you. We'll just act like we don't even notice them, okay? You follow my lead." Pete smacked my shoulder and smiled. "We're all over this." I nodded and exhaled with the force of a hurricane.

Pete and I walked up the aisle and turned left to where we could see Mandy and Jennifer. They had their backs to us, turning the framed posters to look at. Me and Pete looked at each other and nodded. I felt as if I could do it, talk to her. Here's my chance, don't blow it. Not watching where I was going, my eyes locked in on the backs of Mandy and Jennifer, I ran face-first into a spinner rack of sunglasses and key chains, knocking it down as it made a loud crashing sound.

I know everyone in the store turned to see what was going on, and I even heard some people laughing. I looked up and saw Mandy and Jennifer looking at me, giggling. With a face that was burning red with embarrassment, I bent down to pick the merchandise up. Pete crouched down and helped raise the spinner rack upright while I picked up the sunglasses and key chains that had spilled onto the floor.

I was so focused on getting that situation cleaned up that I didn't see Mandy and Jennifer walking toward me. "Thanks for that. Made my day," Mandy said to me as she walked by, laughing. I looked up and caught her smile. God, she had such a beautiful smile.

"At least you made her laugh, dude," Pete said. "If you can make a girl laugh, you're in."

"Yeah, well I just made myself look like the biggest spaz out there. God...I can't believe that I knocked this thing over."

Pete and I finished the last of the key chains and fit them all helter-skelter into slots and hooks where they probably didn't belong. I didn't care. I was happy to have that mess cleaned up. I watched as Mandy paid for the poster that Jennifer had in her hand, and they walked out of the store through the exit glass door. Before she disappeared into the summer sun, Mandy turned her head and gave me a wave and another smile.

"Got to watch that guy over there," Mady said to the dude at the cash register. He laughed and so did Mandy and Jennifer.

"Dude? Did you just see that? That was awesome."

"I did," I replied. "Wow."

CHAPTER 9
THE BIG CAT COMETH

1

THE BIG CAT. His name was Mike Dye, and he was one of our best friends. Our relationship started way back in 1984 when his mother and my mother were friends. This was back in my mom's good mental days— back when her mental stability was sure and true. His mom used to babysit me, and my mom used to babysit him. Our friendship predated mine and Curt's. We never really knew the origin of our mothers' friendship and never thought to ask. We just assumed that it always was.

Mike's parents had gotten divorced somewhere around 1987 or 1988, I can't really remember the precise year. When it happened, Mike went to live with his dad in another town. But he would come back to town for a couple of weeks during the summers to visit his grandmother who lived three blocks over on Alkaline Drive. When he did come back to Claxton, it was like a reunion. I always missed him when he was gone.

Was I surprised by his folks getting divorced? Absolutely. To me and the guys, his mom and dad seemed like one of those families you'd see on TV sitcoms. We were all jealous of what Mike had. None of my friends had been immune to the trials and tribulations of marital issues that spilled over to us kids. It was established as the norm with all of us. Each of us just dealt with it the best we could back then. I think Curt's was the most volatile although he never spoke much about it. I was there, and I saw firsthand some of the stuff that had gone on. My home life was a close second because of my mother's mental issues and my dad's purposeful absence. Pete and Tommy's home wasn't great either, but it was substantially better than mine and Curt's.

When Mike said he was moving away—back when we were in the third grade—due to the divorce, it caught me by total surprise, I can tell you that. I thought the kid would stay in town but no. His dad moved them away to the neighboring city. It was weird not seeing him at Claxton Elementary School afterward.

And as the days went on, I became acclimated as most young kids do to new situations, especially with Mike not being there. I'm not exactly sure if Mike had any advanced warning or not. If he did, he never told me. Maybe he couldn't handle saying something like "divorce" out loud. I know that it was such a profound event in his life. But he adapted the best he could to the situation that he was handed. Sometimes you have no choice but to work with what you have.

———

I wondered often—as all of us did back then—if our parents would divorce, would that be better than the status quo? Eventually, Pete's did in October of our sophomore year in 1992. Tommy's parents had been killed in a car accident at the start of the summer of 1994. After that happened, Tommy was gone, living with his aunt in another town. Curt's parents split in our senior year, or so I heard. By then, none of us was really around when it happened.

My parents stayed together. I was the only one of us who would go on to have a complete set—a broken set, but a complete set nevertheless. My dad stayed with my mom through all the bad times, and believe me, there were many. She wasn't well mentally. I never asked him why mom was so messed up, so depressed, so unstable most of the time. Mom was like this terrible secret in the house that neither one of us talked about before that summer of 1991. I kept my friends clear of her and after a while, they asked why we never hung out at my place.

Reluctantly, I told them on a campout in Curt's backyard earlier in March during Spring Break at our school. It was a true confession. They listened as I told them all the things that had happened within the four walls of my home. By the time I was finished, I felt that I needed to cry, but I had stopped myself. I had cried so much over my mom's mental state over the years that I was just so exhausted from crying. Eventually, the tears stopped coming and numbness replaced them.

Mom was on the road to getting worse and when the summer of 1991 came, she was already there. Dad was driving himself deeper and deeper into his work by that time, causing me to be abandoned in that house. I used to think that maybe if Dad had tried harder and was more stubborn about getting her the help that she needed—maybe forced her back to her doctor—the meds could've straightened her out. Maybe things at home would've been much better. I don't know. I like to think so.

That summer she was getting worse. The house became a place that I hated having to go to or even stay in. I stayed with my friends or at their houses as long as I could. When I got into high school, I did the same until finally, it was all over after my freshman year in the summer of 1992. That's when things got better but at what cost?

———

My parents didn't divorce like my friends' parents had, but I still lived in a house of horrors. With mom getting worse- more manic by the month it seemed- dad, it was discovered, had been seeing another woman he worked with. That's where he had been this whole time, not working late, like I thought he'd been doing. Mom found out like most wives often do, crazy or not, and nearly killed him out in the backyard one night with a very large butcher's knife in June of 1992.

The police came that night from a call from Mr. Wilson, our neighbor from across the street, and it was big news around the neighborhood. Mom was eventually taken to a psychiatric hospital—Leyland Hills—for evaluation, and Dad kept seeing his girlfriend. She didn't go to jail for attempted murder—although Dad had nearly bled to death out on the front lawn that night of the attack—but she was remanded to stay at Leyland Hills. It would eventually be a place where she died years later. I wish that I could say that my mom had gotten better while there. That wasn't the case.

My high school years at home were better because I didn't have to keep my bedroom door locked anymore after Mom was put into the mental home. She was gone, and I'll be honest, I breathed a little easier knowing that she could go off and maybe hurt me not meaning to. During those high school years at home, Dad was never really there. I was at that point of raising myself the rest of the way. My newer friends that I made—was forced to make—in high school thought me pretty much living by myself was totally awesome. I guess it was on the face of it. On the inside, I hated it. No kid should have that kind of freedom.

Dad would go see my mom at Leyland Hills once a week for a long time. Then those once-a-week visits became bi-weekly and then once a month. By the time I graduated high school, I hadn't been there to see her in several months. I'd ask how she was doing and Dad would always say fine– the meds she was on were helping while she was at Leyland Hills. But the doctors had told him that her mental decline was still going, and eventually, the meds that she was taking would stop working. In other words, the meds would hit the ceiling on working to where nothing would work. That was a dire warning. It wasn't a case of IF but WHEN the ceiling would be reached.

Dad had asked me if I wanted to go see her. I declined. I know it sounds bad of me for not going, but I didn't want to see my mom like that. I had seen enough of her at home being the way she was. Plus, I knew that it would hurt me to see her. I'd wanted the mom I used to know, not the one that nearly killed my dad that night out in the yard, or the one that scared me to the point where I feared for my safety at home. I never saw her again after the judge remanded her to Leyland Hills' care.

I was a freshman in college at Auburn University when I got a phone call about my mom's death years later. I had gotten a job at a grocery store and stayed in my dorm at college. I was set up pretty well there. I got along okay. Sometimes late at night, I would think about home—about Mom and Dad, my friends—and wish that things would have been better. But you work with what you've got—Dad's old tried and true axiom. I used it a lot in my own life as the decades rolled by: work with what you've got.

I stayed in contact with Dad, just routine checking in and such. I'd go months without talking to him, but then out of the blue, he'd call to see how things were going on my end. Not much had changed back home as I was on my way to becoming a man. Maybe that was a good thing, I didn't know. I'd ask about Mom, and Dad would tell me that she was about the same. But I honestly don't think he ever went to see her. I had suspicions that he had only maybe twice since she was there. What could I say? I never even brought myself to go. How do I feel about that? So much time has gone by that I don't even feel ashamed anymore, to be honest.

Dad had moved his girlfriend into the house, the one that he had seen way back when. I didn't care though. He was fifty when the news came about my mom, and what did I care what he did with the remaining years of his life? Dad stood and talked to me outside in the backyard that evening after the funeral and told me that Ava, his soon-to-be wife, and my soon-to-be stepmother, was moving in. I didn't care one bit. I wasn't happy or sad about it. Hell, I was indifferent to my mom dying in a mental institution. Talking with my dad was like talking to a stranger with a shared past. After that night in our yard, it was the last time I ever saw my dad alive. We had spoken on the phone here and there: Merry Christmas, Happy Birthday, when are you coming for a visit? How are my grandchildren? That was it—our relationship in a nutshell. Sometimes we'd talk about our sports teams. Mom was never brought up. It was almost as if she was forgotten, erased from our shared past. Maybe she was.

———

I never knew what triggered my mother's mental issues. All I knew was that she grew more and more imbalanced as I got older. I figured out as I got older myself that mom's issues weren't environmental but something in her DNA. She didn't have a choice in her schizoaffective disorder. It was all in her makeup as a person, probably passed down from the family gene pool. I remember my mom's mom, Grandma Bobbie Jean, was mentally ill, too.

I had been told a story once at a family reunion—well, overheard it I guess is a better way to characterize it—that Grandma Bobbie Jean tried to kill my mom and her sisters down by the creek when they were just little kids. I didn't get a lot of the backstory there that day, but I poked around like a good investigator does and found out that it did indeed happen. Dad told me that. But he refused to get into the particulars. I wasn't ballsy enough to ask my aunts about it. I left it to the imagination afterward.

I recall back when I was a kid- like maybe ten or eleven years old- Mom and Dad were talking in the living room. I had gotten up from my bed late that night and had gone into the kitchen to get a drink of water. They were in there talking, and I remember Mom saying she hoped that she didn't end up like her mom. I had no idea what they were talking about. What kid does at that age when adults are talking? Dad promised her that he'd make sure that she got to a doctor before that ever happened. Looking back on it as I did as I became an adult with rational thought and reasoning, I put two and two together and looked at the signs. My grandma had mental issues as well. I never saw much of her, and neither did my mom and dad. Mom stayed away from her as much as she could. In the end, she became her mother. Sometimes we become the people we hate and fear while trying not to. Sometimes things are just eventual.

2

Mike moved away when we were in the third grade, and the only contact that we had during the school year was by phone. When school was dismissed for the summer, Mike would return to town for a few weeks to visit his grandmother, me, and the guys. It was always a welcomed return when the kid would come back. It was as if we picked up where we left off the last time he was around.

Having Mike around injected something new into our very routine group. Just when things were getting stale with us, here came Big Cat to ratchet up the fun. The summer of '91 was not any different than the others.

Mike was given the nickname, Big Cat, by Pete one day last summer, in 1990. We were at the park, on the baseball field to be accurate, playing just as we always did on an idle hot Thursday afternoon in mid-June. The swimming pool over to the side of the baseball field was humming. I was pitching, of course; Mike was batting; Tommy played the outfield; Pete patrolled third and short; and Curt guarded between second and first.

Mike—who was a terrible baseball player—could not hit the ball, no matter how slow I pitched it. I would throw it straight down the middle, and he would miss it. One time, I tossed it to him underhanded, and he was so mad that I did that, he swung the bat so hard he almost came out of his shoes. We all laughed. He still missed the ball, even underhanded! We laughed about that for a long time. Mike, not so much.

I had already fired two good, live fastballs down the middle, and he swung and missed at both of them. I could hear the whiff of the bat as he swung. He wasn't even close! The guys out in the field knew what would happen with Big Cat up at bat. He was not going to hit, and they were going to have to stand out there bored out of their minds.

"This sucks!" Tommy screamed from the outfield. "Hit the damn ball!"

"I'm going to put one right out there!" Mike barked loudly, practicing swinging the bat in the batter's box.

Wiping the sweat from my forehead, and adjusting my Braves hat, I wound up and fired another pitch down the middle. Just like the last two, Mike took a mighty swing... and missed.

"Come on, damn it!" Curt yelled, kicking dirt around.

"I'm trying!" Mike defended.

"Okay, hey!" I said walking off the mound to give the guys my suggestion to resolve Mike's hitting woes. "For the rest of the game, each batter gets ten pitches. After ten, you're out in the field, and someone else comes at bat. This includes foul balls. Fair enough? Ten pitches." The guys seemed to be okay with what became known as the "Mike Rule."

I climbed back onto the pitcher's mound and adjusted my Braves hat once again and looked in at an invisible catcher giving me signs. I kicked my leg high, wound up, and released the ball right into Mike's wheelhouse. Before I realized it, Mike swung the bat with one of those hard swings of his, and the barrel of the bat and the baseball collided in mid-air. All I heard was the crack of the bat as I saw the ball soaring, towering, over us kids there on the baseball diamond.

Taking everyone off guard, Tommy realized that the ball was going over his head quickly out there in the outfield. He turned and started to run backward, trying in earnest to flag down the scorched baseball. He was playing too far in, thinking that Mike would never hit the baseball over his head. None of us out there ever thought that Mike had that much power.

With everyone stunned—including Mike who had forgotten to sprint to first base—Big Cat shook the cobwebs from his head and started lumbering down the first base line. As he was running as fast as his legs would carry him, all that was heard was him screaming, "Speed of the puma! Speed of the puma! Speed of the puma!" I swear to God, this was what was coming from his mouth as he touched first base and cut to run to second.

The baseball finally dropped and rolled to the fence and died in the grass. This allowed Tommy to retrieve it and fire it back into the infield where Mike had already touched second base and was heading for third. He was nearly out of breath, and his face was beet red.

Pete caught Tommy's throw as he cut it off, and from there, he rifled it to me as I ran from the pitcher's mound to cover third. Pete threw the ball to me, I caught it with my glove and tagged the head-first-sliding Mike on the arm. He was out on that play and most notably, out of breath. He lay on his stomach, sprawled out in the dirt, a heavy dust cloud covered us both.

After that play ended, the guys and I screamed in joy that Mike had finally connected. After several summers of pitching to him out there on the baseball field, he finally ripped the ball and almost put it over the tall chain-linked fence. By my crude calculations, I think Big Cat was 1-120 in the batter's box against me. He did have some foul tips along the way.

I was proud of him as were Curt, Tommy, and Pete. Mike got up from the dirt at third and dusted himself off while the guys gathered around me and Mike for a quick time out.

"Man, you almost put that one out of here," Curt said, fanning himself with his sweaty Minnesota Twins hat.

"I just closed my eyes and swung the bat, you know?" Mike said, trying to get his breath at its normal rhythm. I looked down at his legs and noticed a rather large strawberry burn appearing on his knee. Blood was already mixing with the dirt and streaming down his shin.

Tommy took the baseball from me and looked at it, "You hit this thing so fucking hard that Bo Jackson's autograph now says Yo Johnson." Tommy showed us the baseball that had the baseball player's replica signature. We laughed.

"What was that you were saying running down the line?" I asked.

"I don't remember," Mike dismissed.

"It sounded like 'speed of the puma'. I heard it," Pete replied answering for Mike.

"Speed of the puma? What the hell does that mean?" Curt asked.

"It's nothing," Mike said, dusting his shirt off.

"Speed of the puma?" I said, looking at our friend.

"It's something that I say when I want to run fast, like a puma, you know? A big cat?" Mike cleared up for us, clearly embarrassed.

"Big Cat? That's what we'll call you from now on, "Big Cat." I like it." Pete said smacking his hands together with excitement.

Thus, Mike's new name was born, and we have called him by that name ever since. I wonder if he ever heard after we all grew up and went our separate ways? Nah, probably not.

3

Seeing Mike for the first time since he left last summer felt good. It was always great seeing him. His appearance seemed to unify us all. It was like he put us whole. He showed up unexpectedly at Curt's front yard on the day of his return while the four of us sat on the front porch trying to conjure something worthwhile to do on that miserably hot day.

We weren't expecting his arrival until later on in July, but Mike said that his dad had to go away for business in Alabama and gave Mike into the care of his grandmother. That was awesome because it meant that Mike was going to be around for a little while longer than normal.

After we all caught up a little bit, we sat there on the front porch and discussed what the adventure of the day was going to consist of.

"We can go to the swimming pool and hang out," Mike suggested, sitting there with me on the porch swing.

"Nah," Curt said, dismissing the idea. I don't think any of us wanted to go, especially after what happened to me earlier there.

"Well…" I began. "Let's go buy some cards at The Top. That's always fun to do."

Pete, Tommy, and Curt all turned and looked at me.

"We can't," Pete said. "That store manager could remember us and call the police for Jerry stealing those cards, thinking we were in on it."

"I don't think he even saw us, dude. He was too focused on Jerry running like hell out of there," I said.

"Doesn't matter. I'm not back in there at least until December," Pete replied. "And just maybe, I go in there with a disguise."

"Hold up! Stealing cards?" Mike asked, wanting to know what happened.

"Tommy had this crazy guy named Jerry go into Rocky Top and steal us a bunch of cards," I reported.

"What happened?" Mike inquired as he laughed.

"Well, we went over to Reedy's Market and sat there on our bikes and waited for Jerry to come out to give us the cards he stole from Rocky Top. The only thing was that Jerry came running out of the store with an armload of cards with the store manager chasing him. Jerry goes, 'Run!

Run!' We didn't have a choice because Jerry was running right toward us! So we took off and got out of there!" I told.

"So you guys didn't get the cards?" Mike asked.

"Nope. The cards that Jerry had in his arms fell out as he ran across the street," Curt replied answering Big Cat's question.

"Sounds like you guys have kicked the summer off in good fashion," Mike said, snapping his fingers and smiling with those big white teeth.

"Yeah, we sure did. Plus, I nearly drowned, and Tommy beat the hell out of Mark Pike for pushing me into the pool," I said.

"And don't forget our porno mag stash getting torn all the hell," Tommy reminded us.

"Oh and Tony Bartlett getting the hell beat out of him by Todd," I said. We all laughed at that one.

Mike sat there and looked amazed. "And I've missed all of this. Nobody went to jail though, right?"

"So, what are we going to do today that requires no money?" I asked.

We all sat there and thought about our options, which weren't many. We had gotten tired of all the things we did up to that point in the summer and needed something different—something new. This was pretty usual for us at that point during the summers past.

We were going to have to settle on the routine as badly as we hated it lately. Our routine did cause us some distress each summer, but it always was bound to happen.

"Let's go shoot some pool," Tommy said.

"Money, idiot. We have none," Curt said.

"Let's go in the house and play Nintendo," Tommy said.

"We've already beaten all the games that we have. We need something new to play– something that we hadn't beaten yet," Curt said.

In order to play something new, we were going to have to have money to rent a game. And money did not grow on trees for us.

Looking around listening to the guys just make idle talk there on the porch, I spotted an opportunity for us– a financial opportunity.

"What are you going to do with that old ten-speed over there?" I asked Curt, looking at the neglected ten-speed that was leaned up against his house. I remember that bike from years ago. I also never recall Curt ever riding it. The thing had literally been sitting there in the weather for at least four years, maybe more.

"Nothing, it's a pile of junk. I don't even think it has a chain anymore," Curt replied.

"I'm going over there for a second."

I got off the porch and walked over to the side of the house to inspect the bike. Yeah, Curt was correct: it was junk. But with a little oil here and there, a wash, and some rigging, I felt that we could get this bike back to its glory days, whenever that was.

"What are you doing over there?" Tommy asked from the porch.

"We can fix this bike," I said, still looking at the bike and checking it out like I knew what the hell I was doing.

"And?" Curt asked.

The four of them sat silent on the porch, awaiting for the rest of my plan, "And... sell it so we can go rent some games or something."

"Sell that thing? To who?" Pete quizzed.

"You know who?" I said, knowing that they all knew whom I was speaking of.

"Jason Barker!" They all said in unison. Even Mike knew Jason Barker.

———

Jason Barker was the kid in town who was like a pawnshop to us kids. He was the opposite of Mike Napp. Instead of selling things to kids in town, Jason bought things. His family was flush with money, and the kid had like an insane amount for a weekly allowance. You could bring him junk, and he would buy it. No questions asked. It was rumored a long time ago that he and Mike Napp went into business together buying stuff and flipping it to sell for profit. I never saw them together; it was probably just local chatter. They did hang around each other a lot though.

The five of us repaired and washed that old, red ten-speed as best as our small hands could that day. After we were done, we stood back and looked at our work. It looked a little better, but not much. The tires were thin and worn and the chain was too tight, and it snapped the master link every time we stood up on the bike to peddle. The seat was dry-rotted and showing its insides of nasty yellowed foam that was probably once white. The chrome was speckled with rust and had seen its better days gone by. Would Jason buy the ancient bike? We were going to find out.

Jason lived on the other side of town where the well-to-do lived. It was not far from where we lived, but our families didn't make enough money to live in that part of Claxton. The five of us walked to Jason's well-maintained home at the end of a cul-de-sac in a subdivision called Fox River with the ten-speed in tow. The front tire, I remember, was warped, causing Mike to have to keep it straight as he walked beside it.

None of us rode the ten-speed to Jason's house. Tommy and Pete had gotten on the bike and tried to peddle, both cracking their nuts on the frame when they stood up on the pedals and broke the link of the chain. We decided for the sake of our future children we'd just walk it to Jason's place.

"What if he wants to take it for a test drive?" Mike asked while we walked to Jason's.

"We'll figure that out when it gets here," Curt said.

"We'd better figure it out now because you know he's going to want to ride it first," Tommy replied as we all walked slowly up the road.

None of us had a good idea worth mentioning as we approached Jason's house. We had no idea what we were going to do. I guess we hadn't thought that far ahead.

We had made it to Jason's lavish home and rang his doorbell. The front door finally opened after several ding-dongs. I asked his beautiful mother if we could speak with Jason. We stood outside on the walkway and lowly discussed how good his mother looked while she fetched Jason.

"Do you think she was wearing a bra? I don't," Pete remarked.

"Dude, did you see how she looked at me?" Tommy said. "That's not the first time she's looked at me like that."

"Oh, yeah, right," Curt said. "She looks at you the way we all do: 'What's this stupid kid with the little dick want?'" We all laughed hard.

"Ain't what your momma said last night," Tommy replied. We all laughed again, still laughing from Curt's cut on Tommy.

"Probably not if she was drunk enough," Curt said, making us laugh even more.

As I stood there listening to the guys switch to talking about how hot Jason's mom was, I looked at the bike we were trying to sell as something worth buying. It was junk—a piece of garbage that I wouldn't even buy if I did have the disposable income. I would rather buy a notebook that already had all the pages written in it than buy this bike.

But who really knew what Jason would think? I had seen this kid buy things at school that I never thought he would. Like the one time he bought a baseball card that was autographed by Darryl Strawberry for like forty bucks. Doesn't sound so bad, does it? The only thing about it was that a kid we knew had signed Darryl Strawberry's name to the base-ball card and sold it to Jason who was more than happy to take it off his hands. I have to admit, the signature that the kid forged *did actually* look like Strawberry's. But before the age of the internet, who really knew back then what Strawberry's name looked like, you know? It looked authentic to me and more importantly, to Jason.

The front door opened again and out stepped the rotund Jason Barker. "What's happening, guys? Mike, you back in town?" Jason asked, shaking hands with every, single one of us. He was like a miniature version of every car salesman you've ever encountered in your life; black hair slicked back, polo shirt tucked in.

"What can I do for you gentlemen this fine afternoon?" the nerdy kid asked us.

"We have a bike we'd like to sell?" I proposed.

Mike was holding the bike up on the lawn because the kickstand had managed to fall off while in transit to Jason's.

Jason walked over to it and gave it the once over, "Is it stolen or something?"

"No," Curt said. "I had it in my garage, and my dad wanted me to get rid of it. So...here it is. We figured that you could buy, and it flip it later for more money. You're really good at that kind of stuff."

Jason, the professional young businessman, knelt on his knee and inspected underneath the seat and gears that were on the back wheel, "How long has it sat in storage? Looks like it's been out in the weather for a long time." he asked, running his chubby fingers across the red-orange speckle chrome.

"A few years, I think," Curt replied. "Been in and out from the garage to the side of it. Depending on how Dad was that weekend, you know?"

"Ride okay? Not bumpy or anything like that?"

Christ, was this kid buying a car or something, I thought to myself.

Jason knelt again and looked at the spokes of the front wheel and the tread on the paper-thin tire.

"Yeah, it's okay. Rides like you'd expect," Curt lied.

"The rims aren't warped or anything?" Jason asked, rising up to his feet and looking at the bike as a whole, hands in pockets.

He pushed down on the tires to see how much air was in them. "Tires seem to be nearly dry-rotted."

"Rims seemed okay to me," Curt said. "You want this thing or what?" he cut to the chase, putting the pressure on Jason.

"Yeah, maybe. If the asking price is right. I mean, guys, come on, this bike is not in great condition. Going to be hard to turn a profit. I mean there's a lot of money I'm going to have to put into this vintage piece," Jason said, walking around the other side of the bike to look.

"What would you give?" I asked.

Jason rubbed his face with his right hand as if he was strongly debating in his mind how much the bike was worth, "Twenty? Sound good? Best I could do. And I might make after what I put into it maybe fifteen and that's been generous."

Of course it sounded good! Great! Twenty dollars for a bike that when you pedal it, the chain breaks?! Twenty dollars for a bike that you can't even sit on the seat without it falling off? Awesome!

"Yeah, I can do that," Curt happily accepted.

"Wait. Mike, do you mind riding the bike around for me to see how it handles?" We all looked at each other.

"The chain will break," I mouthed to Curt who was looking right at me with fright in his eyes.

"You should ride it, Jason. That way you can get a good feel for what the bike has to offer," Mike offered.

Jason stood there and looked at us. Then he dug into his pants pocket and pulled out his black money clip. A money clip? This kid has a money clip, honest to God above. *Crazy*, I thought to myself. He handed Curt the twenty-dollar bill, and he quickly took it from his hand.

We told him goodbye in haste and started hurriedly walking away, leaving Jason there alone with the bike. Our quick pace walk became a jog and then a mad run down the street. I looked back while we made a break for it and saw Jason get on the bike and stand up to start peddling.

When he put all his weight on the left pedal to start riding it, the pressure that Jason applied to the metal foothold broke the chain, causing him to fall and crunch his nuts on the straight bar that ran from the dry-rotted seat to the base of the curved rusted chrome inward handlebars. All I saw after that was Jason falling to the ground with the bike lying on top of him.

Oh well, we had the money that we needed to have a good time with, and we probably wouldn't see Jason until high school if we even saw him then. Turns out, we never saw him again after that summer. Not because he died or moved. He ended up in a private school for four years. Eventually, he made it to Harvard. And then to Congress. I wonder if he ever thinks about that piece-of-shit ten-speed we sold him in 1991 that he cracked his nuts on?

4

With the money that we received from Jason—let's be honest it was ill-gotten gains at best– the five of us went to Bill's and rented three Nintendo games at a buck twenty-five each and had enough money left over for us to buy drinks, chips, and candy for the impromptu sleepover at Pete's house.

We were going to hang out at Curt's place, but he brought me over to the side at Bill's while the guys went to the counter to pay for the games, and told me that his mom and dad were drunk and at it again. So I went to Pete and suggested that we have the night over at his house. He was fine with it but had to clear it with his mom. It was no problem.

His mom was cool with all of us staying the night, but she wanted us to make sure that we cleared it with our parents. No problems there—never really were. I never even tried to ask my mother if I could spend the night at Curt's or any of my friends' houses because what was the use? She had no idea if I was coming or going. She stayed cooped up in her bedroom ninety percent of the time and knocking on her bedroom door was something that I didn't even want to do. With our food, drinks, and entertainment set for the night, the guys and I were ready to let the good times roll.

———

It was ten-thirty that night up in Pete's bedroom. We had been playing *Friday the Thirteenth* on Nintendo for two hours, and we were on the verge of beating that game and its villain, Jason, the hockey-masked supernatural movie monster and 80's pop culture icon. It was getting hot in his room, as it did every summer. I was feeling dizzy from the stale heat inside the room, and I went over to open the window to let some fresh night air in. It had to be at least ninety degrees up there, no joke. The breeze—I still remember—felt good against my face.

Curt and Pete sat on the floor in front of the TV, taking turns playing the game; Tommy was fooling around with the small radio that sat on a table; and Mike looked through our eighth-grade yearbook while lying on Pete's bed. I stood in front of the window and hogged the cool breeze that flowed in from the night. It felt good against my damp skin. Man, could it get hot up there.

Turning away from the window after I was comfortable, Tommy finally decided on a radio station: WIMZ was the station of choice that played classic rock and new rock from the classic guys. The first song that we heard on the station that night was "Road to Nowhere" from The Talking Heads.

I sat down on the blue bean bag and watched Curt fight Jason in a cabin on the game. Pete and Curt—taking turns after the other died—

were getting close to beating it; they both could tell and were dialed in. Nothing could break their concentration.

I was sitting there just mindlessly watching the game being played when Mike broke in, "Do you guys realize that we'll all be at the same school next year? I can't wait for that. Going to be rad as hell." I could. I didn't want to go.

I didn't want to go to high school. Was not happy about the thought, I can tell you that. I don't think any of us were except Mike. Mike was used to change. He always adapted well to any environment and was never intimidated. His strong mental ability would not allow it. I wished I had his resolve back then.

"So, have you and Mandy ever gotten together yet?" Mike asked. From the other side of the bedroom, Tommy giggled.

"Not yet," I said, hoping that he would drop it.

"Not yet? What do you mean not yet?" Mike looked up from the yearbook. "You've been talking on and on about this chick for years. Not yet? Get out of town."

"Just haven't...I'm working on it, okay?" I said, knowing that I was a liar.

"What's the problem?" Mike prodded.

"I don't know," I sat there, looking down at the floor. *Yeah, what was the problem*, I thought to myself.

"Man, you've been talking about this chick forever, and you haven't done anything to get her?" Mike asked, dumbfounded.

"Hey," I said starting my defense, "I called her, and she was gone to see her aunt."

Mike sat there and looked at Tommy and then at me, "And what else?"

"That was it," Tommy injected.

"So, you called a girl that was gone, and you never called her back? That's pretty lame," Mike told me. He was right, it was lame.

"Yeah, but Mandy ain't like other girls. She's...she's..."

"She's just like every other awesome girl in the world. They're so pretty that guys like us don't ever ask them out because we think they'll turn us down. That's why you will never be with her, dude," Mike laid out.

God, he had only been there for just a few hours, and he already had me backed into a corner. His words stung me a bit, but they did have a ring of truth to them.

"I don't know what's wrong with me," I said after a few quiet moments of contemplation.

"Nothing. You're a good-looking guy, and you can get this Mandy girl. Don't think that you can't," Mike said.

"Gay," Curt said while beating his thumbs against the A-B buttons on the Nintendo controller.

"Shut up," Mike said. "Listen, why don't you call her up right now and start talking to her?"

"She might be asleep," I said, giving another excuse for why I would not call her.

"I bet you don't even have her number, do you?" he asked, knowing that I did.

"I've got it memorized," I replied.

"Bullshit," Mike said. "Your memory sucks."

I repeated her phone number, showing him just how good my memory was. By doing that, I sealed my fate. Mike tricked me. He was good. He went over to Pete's nightstand and picked up the phone, making sure no one was on it. "I'm going to call her if you don't."

I knew that he was not bluffing. Mike had no filter and never got embarrassed. He did things by the seat of his pants and never regretted anything he did. I knew what he was about to do. I knew that I was facing one of the most stressful situations that I had ever been in up to that point in my young life. Mike was about to call Mandy on my behalf right there in front of all the guys.

He meant well, honestly, he did. But that still didn't mean I had to like it. Sitting there on that bean bag, I clung to that sliver of hope that Mike might change his mind about calling Mandy. How wrong I was.

Mike started pushing the number pad of the cordless phone. Of course, I just sat there on the bean bag and watched with a mixed bag of emotions that contained anticipation and fear. *Had I sunk this low*, I thought to myself watching Mike listen to the ringing on the other end of the phone. He had actually called her!

There was silence between us boys in the bedroom. Only the music from the radio played. We all watched while Mike stood there looking up at the ceiling, waiting for someone to answer the phone. The tension was so thick, you could've cut it with a knife.

My fate hung there like a piece of meat over a hungry dog. I was scared. Did I really want to know how she felt about me when Mike asked her? What if she didn't have the faintest amount of affection toward me? What would I do? I mean, I have liked this girl for so long that if she shot me down, how would I ever recover from the rejection? And then there was Curt telling me the other day when he got her number at the baseball field that she felt the same as I did. Could he have lied about that just to make me feel better?

Sitting there, I had almost convinced myself that maybe I was okay to live in my fantasy world where I had a chance with her. Maybe it was okay to love her from afar like I had for so long. There was a sense of safety in staying a great distance from her, although I didn't want to. Mike, my dear friend Mike, was going to get me a gauge of how she felt toward me.

If everything was positive, then I could plot my next action later to win her heart. If not, I had the terrible task of moving forward, knowing that she and I were never meant to be. That was a hard pill to swallow as I sat there on the bean bag running over things in my head and watching Mike at the same time.

After numerous unanswered rings, Mike gave up, turned the cordless phone off, and placed it back down on the table.

"No answer. Lucky you." Mike said to me, sitting back down on the bed. Excitement over and crisis adverted.

Everyone else resumed their activities, and I sat there and felt relieved. *That was close*, I thought to myself, *too close*. It was right then and there that I decided that I was not going to be that kid where his friends had to ask a girl out on his behalf. No, it was time for me to grow up and start acting like a thirteen-year-old. Little did I know that I was going to have to deal with a grown-up situation or two in the coming days.

5

A few days later, me and Mike went out to a pond that I knew was off County Road 183. We had to cross a waist-high field to reach it, but it was well worth the excursion. Mike was afraid that we were going to get bitten by snakes walking in that field and to be honest, that thought had never occurred to be when me, Curt, Tommy, and Pete walked through it to go fishing. Once Mike told me that as we were walking, I started to panic a little bit because I was very afraid of snakes. I began to high step and walk faster through the field. Now that I'm thinking back on it, I never went back.

We had finally reached the pond, getting out of the field with no snake bites. Mike stood there alongside me and looked out across the enormous body of water. "Man," he said, "this place is awesome."

"Yeah, it is. Lots of different kinds of fish in here, too. We've pulled cats, bluegills, large and smallmouth bass out of here."

"How did you find this place?" Mike asked as he walked closer to the edge of the bank where me and the guys went every time we came.

I sat down on a log and placed my tackle beside me. "My Uncle Jim brought me here back when I was a kid," I said "kid" like I was an adult at the moment.

Mike sat down beside me on the log, and I handed him my extra fishing rod that was already baited with a nice green diver lure.

"It's so peaceful out here, ain't it? I mean, there's no noise," he remarked.

"Yeah, it really is. I've come down here a time or two without the guys during the fall, like in October, just to sit here and think about stuff."

I stood up and cast my line dead center into the pond. The line spooled out, and I turned the crank, taking the slack out of it, and sat back down. Mike stood up and did the same motion I did, but cast his line off to the right side of the center and sat down. He put the rod between his legs and reached into his front jeans pocket and pulled out a pack of Malboros and a lighter.

"Since when do you smoke?" I asked incredulously.

"A few months ago. You're not going to get all after-school special on me, are you?"

"No, I guess not. Curt does it, too."

"I don't smoke like my dad does...just every once in a while," he told me, holding the stick between his lips as he reeled his line.

"So, ready for high school?" I asked, changing the subject.

"Hell yes. I get out of that place and with you guys. It's going to be awesome." I didn't share in Mike's enthusiasm. He hated his school with a passion and couldn't wait to get to Central High. I, on the other hand, wished it was never coming.

After reeling my line in, I stood up and cast it out again, dead center, and sat back down and slowly cranked it back toward me. "Heard from your mom lately?"

Mike's mother had left him and his dad a few years back to pursue a life with another man. Mike was still reeling from that, but in the times I talked to him on the phone, he tried to act all hardcore about it. Deep down, I knew that he was hurting from the abandonment.

"Nope. I hope I never do," he said, standing up, reeling his line in so he could sling it back out again.

"Do you want to talk about it? I mean, we really never really have talked face to face about it."

Mike sat back down and considered for a minute my offer. "There's really nothing to talk about, is there? She walked in one day and told my dad she was done and had met someone else, and that's it. I didn't even get a goodbye hug. She just packed her shit and left with no explanation. What kind of fucking mom does that? Oh well, that was years ago. No big deal."

"How's your dad been dealing with things over the years?"

Mike laughed a bit, "In typical dad ways. He drinks when he comes home from work... stays in front of the TV, watching sports. I did get to meet his new girlfriend though. She's nice."

"You think they'll get married?" I said, reeling my line back in and slinging it back out to dead center.

Mike shrugged, "Who knows. I don't care either way. I'm just counting down the days I can turn eighteen, go to college, and move out. I fucking hate my house." I could relate. I hated mine too.

I wanted to run away most of the time and forget them both. I was too young still, too young to make it work. If my Uncle Jim had still been alive, I know that I could've moved in with him. I don't think my mom or dad would've put up much of a fight if I wanted to.

"What about your mom and dad? Things any better from the last time we talked?" Mike asked.

Now, it was my turn to laugh. "Yeah right. Mom has gotten worse. Dad is a ghost in the house. He never comes home hardly anymore. He says he's pulling double shifts. I don't know. I think he just doesn't want to be home anymore or he has a woman on the side."

"You think he's cheating on your mom?" Mike asked, reeling his line in and this time not standing up when he cast it back out to center-right.

"Probably. I mean, who could blame him? I can't. But it sucks that I don't get to see him. I think if he ever leaves, I'll never see him again. I get scared that if he did finally call it quits he'd go and leave me there with her." I felt a little sad about that because I had been thinking about that possibility for a couple of months now, the more and more I didn't see my dad.

"I'm sorry, man. I am. I know how you feel," Mike said. I know that he was being genuine because he understood exactly how I felt. Curt did, too. It seemed like we all came from some sort of home that was broken to varying degrees. "Has your mom gotten any better?" Mike was referring to my mother's psychosis

"No. I think she's getting worse. The other night while Dad was at work, she had taken all the light fixtures apart."

"Why?" Mike asked, blowing more gray smoke into the air, slowly reeling his line in.

"She thought that someone had put listening devices in them while she was at the grocery store."

"Son of a bitch, dude. That's bad."

"I know. Last month she..." I couldn't even finish what I was going to say because the memory of what happened to me that night was still fresh, still haunting.

"What?"

I sat there, my fishing line slack, and considered telling Mike something I had not told Curt yet. "I thought she was going to try to kill me last month before school let out for the summer."

"What?! How?" Mike asked, turning his attention from the water to me. I didn't look over to him. I could feel his eyes piercing me, wanting answers.

"I was sleeping in my bed, nothing out of the ordinary, you know. I got woken up by someone getting on top of me. I open my eyes and it's Mom. She's on top of me in the bed, and she's got this kitchen knife to my throat. I was about to scream for Dad, but she put her hand over my mouth and told me that if I screamed, she would kill me right then and there.

"I'm laying there scared to death, right? I've got tears in my eyes because I'm thinking this is it, you know? She slowly takes her hand away from my mouth and leans into my ear and whispers, 'I know what you are. You're one of them. I know now. But I'm here to tell you, I'm watching you. I got to you once, and I can get to you again.' She gets off me and leaves the room."

Mike sat there while the ash on his cigarette grew in length, eventually falling off without having to be flicked. He was at a loss for words and for a length of time, we didn't say anything. I don't think he knew what to say. I mean, what could anyone say? We sat there in silence as thunder rolled dully off in the distance. Storm clouds were gathering in the west.

"Damn, dude, I don't know what to say about that...wow...I mean...damn."

I sat on the log, not even looking at my fishing line, just looking out across the pond and replaying the fear of that night in my bedroom. It was hitting me hard like it had just happened. "I know. I still don't know what to say about it."

"Did you tell your dad?"

I shook my head, "There's no point. He knows how crazy my mom is. It's the reason he's looking for a way out. But it sucks that he won't take me and him away from there and force the issue of mom getting help. It's like he's just unplugged from the whole thing. I feel a little safer now because he put a lock on my bedroom door now. This was after she sold all my shit at a yard sale."

"Son of a bitch! You think one of these days she'll try to kill you?"

I had actually thought about Mike's question a million times before but not considered it much. Honestly, I thought I'd come home from school and find her dead from suicide but after that night in my bedroom, all bets were off.

"Sometimes, yeah. She's getting spooky." Just then, my fishing line got tight, and the rod that I was holding loosely in my hand began to tug. I had a fish. I stood up and started to reel the slack line in. It was a fish all right and a fighter. Mike stood up with me while I reeled him in. It was a three-pound smallmouth bass.

———

"You think you'll ever see your mom again?" I asked, as the excitement of the fish I caught dulled over the next twenty minutes. It was silent between us before I asked him my question. The only sounds came from the wind that was blowing the approaching storm from the west and the thunder that sounded closer than it was before.

Mike took a long drag from another cigarette and blew gray smoke into the air, "I don't want to. If she can turn her back on her only child...I don't want to deal with someone like that. I know that if I ever have kids, I'll never do them like she did me. And it's not that I even hate her, I mean I should, you know, it's just that..."

"You're hurt," I finished for him.

"Yeah, that. I mean, she really hurt me. We were good, and the family was happy; her and Dad were getting along pretty good. I guess she wanted something more, but Dad didn't understand what the more was. I didn't either at the time...still don't, I guess. She had it all. Crazy what she had."

"I'll be honest with you," I said, reeling my line in and slinging it back out, this time left of center, "me and the guys were always jealous of you."

"Why?"

"Because you seemed to have a happy family...like the ones you'd see on sitcoms."

Mike sat there and thought about that for a few moments. "I guess in a way we did, yeah. You know, I used to blame that guy she ran off with. Like I focused my anger on him for so long that one day I realized that it wasn't just him. My mom pulled the trigger and made it happen. It takes two."

"You think she regrets what she did? Leaving like she did?"

Mike shook his head, "Nope. You know, she's never called me to wish me a happy birthday or wish me a merry Christmas? Nothing. It's like I never existed. That hurts, too. Now, Dad is with his girlfriend most of the time, and I'm like invisible there at home." I could relate to that as well. "I thought about moving in with my grandma, but I don't know if Dad will let me. I thought about asking him when I get back."

"Man, that would be kick-ass you living down here with us."

"It would, wouldn't it? Imagine having me all the time," Mike laughed, finishing his cigarette, and snuffing it out under his shoe against the ground. I laughed, too. It would be great. It never happened though. I don't know if his dad vetoed Mike's wishes or what happened, but Mike never came to live at his grandma's house. I wonder if it would have made a difference in my life had he come to Claxton to live. Like with me before, Mike's fishing line began to pull. He had himself a fish on the other end. Reeling it in from the water, he pulled it out and it was another smallmouth bass, nearly identical to mine.

He released it back into the water like I had mine and a crack of thunder rumbled. "I think we'd better get going. Looks like it's about to come a howler," I said, reeling my line in for the day.

We walked through the field back to the fence on the side of the road where we ditched our bikes. I turned and looked at the field we had walked through. Off in the distance, in the backdrop of dark, stormy clouds, I could barely make out the body of water we fished in. I smiled as if somehow I knew that it was going to be my last time there. It was. After Mike and I fished that day, I never returned and me and Mike never had another summer like the one we were in. That was our special moment, much like mine and Pete's up on the water tower and mine and Curt's in the camper.

CHAPTER 10
EUREKA MILL/ GRANDMA DIXIE

1

IT WAS hot the day my grandmother died on July 1st, 1991. The Fourth of July festivities were being set to begin there in my town. Claxton was decorated in patriotic red, white, and blue to commemorate the town's events and the nation's birthday. It was and still is a big to-do in my old hometown. There was something Rockwellian about Claxton back then. Yes, it was the 90s, but in some aspects, Claxton never lost that small-town charm. I always appreciated that about my hometown and appreciated the people in charge who did their best to keep it that way.

Everything from telephone poles, shop windows, homes, and churches were soaked in the colors of the U.S. flag. Of course, the town had always celebrated the Fourth grandly from way before I was born. My hometown had like a whole day of activities planned for the citizens: first, there was a huge pancake breakfast that was held outside one of the biggest Methodist churches in town. After that, there was a softball game at the park where we played our baseball games during the summers. It was always between the city workers and a team of guys in town that were really good, called the Taxpayers. Usually, the city workers lost the annual game. But it was all in good fun and cool to watch. It was always neat to be there and to hear the cheering and jeering from the fans in the stands while walking around eating a hotdog from a food truck.

Later on that day, there was a riding lawnmower race through the streets of the town. Now for that, the city had to close off two blocks of the downtown area for the lawnmowers to race. It was the slowest ten laps you'd ever watch in your life, but there was something fun about it. There was also a horseshoe tournament at Faith Baptist, a baking competition for pies at the community center, an arts and crafts show downtown after the lawnmower race, and some Native Americans came down representing different tribes to tell stories about their people.

When the night came and the streetlights lit up, there was a square dance in the middle of the town square. A local country western band usually played and could be heard for miles, it seemed. For the closing number that night, there was a huge, colorful fireworks show at the park that lit up the night with beauty and wonder. Me and the guys used to sit up in the northeast corner of the park far away from all the townspeople and watch. I can't tell you when we first started sitting there to watch the fireworks show. Might've been around 1989, maybe. I'm not sure. But it was magical sitting there with the guys and watching the night sky boom and pop with all the colors of the rainbow. There was something peaceful about it, something intangible.

2

My day started like most of the others had so far that summer. I got up late, around ten or so, to go into the kitchen for some cereal. I had no idea if there was any left. It was always a gamble if anyone ever went to the grocery store during that summer when Mom was slipping and sliding down that hill of mental wreckage. I came down the hallway from my bedroom, still blurry-eyed, when I noticed the house was dark inside on that bright morning. I saw my mom sitting at the kitchen table with her hands peacefully folded on the table, sitting perfectly bolt upright as if she had been waiting for me. Where was Dad? Gone to work, I guess. So that left me and my mentally ill mother. I was about to turn and go back to my bedroom and lock the door behind me when she spoke. Her talking had frozen me in my tracks.

"Son, don't open the shades today...they're out there watching the house," she said.

I stood there holding my breath, my heart beating forcefully against my chest. I could even hear it in my ears, the beating. Staring at her from across the kitchen, I finally spoke after a few moments. "Who, Mom?"

She smiled, not that sinister grin that scared me, but a smile of compassion this time. A smile that said I should know who she was talking about. "The FBI, silly. They're out there surveilling the house. It's because I didn't pay taxes on my yard sale. I don't know how they knew that I didn't, but they know. You didn't call them, did you?" That's when her smile turned to that sinister grin that I was frightened of. I began to tremble at the sight of it. I began to slowly back up, back down the hallway.

"Mom, there's no FBI outside"

"You sound just like your dad! You're just like him! Even look like him! You certainly don't look like me, do you?! I wonder if you're even mine!" Mom's voice boomed through the kitchen and within my head. I turned and ran down the hallway, slamming my bedroom door and locking it. I pressed my back up against the door, shaking like a leaf. Then, I heard her laughing from the kitchen. I can still hear that laugh today.

About an hour had passed by, and nothing came from my mother. I had no idea if she was still even in the kitchen. I wasn't going to chance it. I got dressed, opened my window, and hopped out into the bright and cheerful morning. It was already hot, and the heat attacked me at once. This hot this early was going to mean it was only going to get hotter.

I got on my bike and headed down the street to Curt's house. He had gone grocery shopping with his mom, his dad told me when he answered the door. His dad was slurring his words when he talked, and I assumed he was already drunk this early. Curt had told me they—both his mom and dad—stayed in a constant state of intoxication to deal with each other and to avoid their own issues.

With no luck there, I pedaled over to Tommy's house. His parents' car was gone out of the driveway, and there was no answer at the front door when I knocked. Strike two.

I rode my bike over to Pete's. He never went anywhere except with us. He, too, was gone with his family. There was no car in the driveway, and no one answered when I knocked on the door for a good three minutes.

Mike, I knew, was gone for a couple of days because he and his grandmother had to travel to Nashville to see her sister. Big Cat hated that trip but was forced to go.

3

The guys being gone—all of them at the same time—had never happened before. That should have been my first notion that things that day were going to take a turn for the worse—as if my mother's behavior at home earlier wasn't enough of an indication. Looking back on that day- and believe me, I have a lot- I should've maybe just gone to the swimming pool and hung out. There was safety in numbers.

The pool was a possibility, a faint one, but I quickly put it down because I was afraid of being pushed in again, and this time around, no Tommy was there to bring me out. I should've just found a crowded place to hunker down. Be that as it may, I tried to figure out what I was going to do—how much time I needed to kill—to when my friends would be back.

I had no idea what to do from that point. I had never been by myself before on a summer day. There was always one of my friends around. Always. The only things left for me to do were to either go home—which was a dangerous idea within itself, given how Mom was doing—or ride my bike around town. I chose to ride my bike around to kill time until the guys came back home. That decision nearly cost me my life.

4

My town was small compared to others close by, nothing big at all. You could hop on your bike and ride to the end of town in just about ten minutes or so in any direction. I had done that in my short life up to that point several times over. There was not anything in that town I had not seen before. The landmarks were all the same, the same as they ever were. I had gone down every street, every side road, and every country road.

I knew who owned all the buildings and shops in town; what neighborhoods were safe and which ones were not; I knew practically everyone who lived in every house in town. I guess you could say that at thirteen, I was an expert about my community. I knew the history of the town pretty well, too, having studied it in the town's library a year before in my spare time. The town's history was something that Curt and I had an interest in. For a small town, it sure had some crazy things happen in it over the years. Even after that summer of 1991, weird and horrible things continued.

I had been riding around town that fateful day on my trusty bicycle for hours. It was another scorching hot day, and I sought refuge from the angry sun in the local drugstore: Wilson's. I always loved going there during the summer. The place inside was always clean and most of all, cool, giving us boys a place to beat the heat. One of the other pharmacists, Mr. Jones, was always kind to the local kids, especially me and the guys. He and I shared an affinity for the Atlanta Braves. In the fall, that shared affinity was college basketball.

Often, me and the boys would go in there and buy candy and something to drink—usually a Pepsi or Sprite—and walk to the other end of the store to sit down where several old, and very used restaurant booths were. In the mornings, the elders of the town would gather there and talk about their creaking knees, their failing backs, and big fish tales that only old men could tell. Me and the guys did a younger version of complaining—not of creaking knees and bad backs—but of mean teachers and girls that we liked.

On that particular summer day with everyone being absent from the roster, I didn't feel much like sitting by myself in the drugstore, especially when I noticed that Mr. Jones wasn't behind the pharmacy counter. Mr. Wilson was. I didn't like him very much. Maybe it was the way his glasses sat on the tip of his nose and that shark-like grin he had. Something about him just gave me bad vibes. He wasn't a friendly man at all.

After Dottie, the old lady behind the checkout counter rang up my Pepsi and Milky Way, I paid her the buck fifty and walked back into the heat of the day and looked around at the town before me. Not much at all going on, not until the Fourth anyway. I stood there leaned up against the brick building and ate my candy bar quickly and washed it down with my twenty-ounce drink. I was hungry—starving, I guess is a better way to describe it—since I wasn't able to eat breakfast because of Mom earlier. I figured that would hold me over until one of the guys got home, and maybe I could get a sandwich or something from them.

———

I had been on my bike for at least an hour and a half maybe, passing the same old places and riding down the same neighborhoods. I was ready to head back to our neighborhood to see if any of the guys had returned. Before I went back, I turned off a side road from the main street. I rode past all the houses along the way and toward the old Eureka Textile Mill that lay in ruins at the end of the dead-end road.

It was a place where me and the guys used to gather after school on occasion but had stopped going there for some reason or another. Never knew why, actually. Maybe because we had discovered Hudson's Woods, can't say for sure. At any rate, I had not been to the huge abandoned brick building in a spell. It wasn't a place that I particularly felt safe at, but I really never gave it much thought as to why. Just a vibe I got. Why I was even compelled to go there in the first place was and still is a complete mystery to me. That trip to the Eureka Textile Mill was my final trip there. I never went back after what happened.

I pedaled past the homes and saw the enormous, dilapidated brick structure waiting for me. I stopped at the side of the old building—in an alley, to be exact—where on the other side of me was a long-running brick wall that no doubt belonged to the mill some decades ago. Above me, trees reached over in a canopy and provided some much-needed shade. I sat on my bike there and rested for a bit, back turned against the main road, looking out towards the railroad tracks. I was a good fifty yards from the main street in that alley.

I still remember sitting on my bike and looking at the trees that were trying to push back the building and the vines that had grown wildly alongside the outer walls. Parts of the roof were falling in on that old mill, and the numerous windows had been busted out by careless kids over time, leaving nothing but glassless frames.

Tired bricks had fallen or had been busted out over time, making it to where you could see inside some. Colorful graffiti decorated the outer walls with cuss words and expressions of love. The old textile mill was a complete and utter wreck. It wasn't always like that, though. Back in the day, it was a hub of the town and county. It was once a titan of Southern industry. But looking at it as I was at that moment, it was difficult to believe it.

I had read in the town books that long ago—before my dad was even born—that the building that I was looking at had once been a pillar of employment for not only the town but the region as well. It employed over five hundred people, maybe more, and distributed its textile to points all over the country and even the world. Sometime in the seventies, the owner, Mr. Kirby, passed away and left the business and his people to his son, George. The Kirby family in our county were big in farming and textile. Everyone knew them.

George did not want any part of his dad's legacy and let it go, selling it to outside interests. Those interests—I read—sold them out someplace overseas, thus giving the employees that had worked there, some their entire lives, a pink slip with no place to work. After years of neglect, the building was let go, and the place became a safety hazard, garnering frequent visits by kids like me and sometimes transients that come through town. I used to hear all kinds of wild stories—mostly on Halloween—that the sprawling building was used for devil worship and witchcraft.

It needed to be torn down, but perhaps it was more trouble than it was worth. 'Dozing the building and cleaning it up would cost a pretty penny, and the town didn't have that kind of cash on hand. It was easier to just let the mill slowly wither away. Eventually, the old mill was torn down after the town, which had ceased ownership of it, decided that something else needed to go there in its place. The town's new fire department took the spot sometime in the early 2000s.

Some of the kids that I knew would go in there and explore that old mill. Some would even say they saw ghosts, and the high schoolers would tell stories about the place being haunted by the original owner, Mr. Kirby. Me and the guys went inside one night to check on these so-called "ghost sightings" on Halloween night back in the fifth grade.

Being inspired by *Ghostbusters*, we all four went in there and took a look around. It was spooky, and there were a lot of creepy sounds and such, but we never saw anything. And those sounds? Most likely animals moving around or the usual moans and groans from the rotted wooden floorboards and the roof joists. I'm sure the sounds that we heard in the walls of the enormous mill were packed with rats and raccoons to boot. I don't think it was haunted. I believe it was just more wild tales from kids with overactive imaginations who liked to spin yarns.

———

I had been sitting in the alley by the building and brick wall for some time and was getting ready to turn my bike around and head for the main street. All of a sudden, this creepy-looking white car barrels onto the small, narrow service road that I was parked on. The car screeched to a halt about twenty feet from me, and a cloud of dust from the dry gravel poured toward me, covering me. I couldn't see anything, and I was coughing, gasping for air.

Through the dust, this guy—tall and lanky in a white tee shirt and jeans—got out from the passenger side and started running in my direction. It all happened so fast; it was like I was watching it on TV. I mean, I'd never experienced anything like that before. It was like my brain went into some hard pause or something. For some reason, I couldn't move. I was frozen. My fight or flight response was warning me to run and run fast, but nothing was working. The danger was coming—the stranger danger we were taught in school—was barreling right toward me.

I finally panicked. I told my legs to pedal, and I started riding up the narrow road ahead of me. At the end of the narrow service road was a dead end. But at that dead end lay a decommissioned railroad track that ran parallel to the main street behind me. You could follow that track all the way back into town—in the middle of town to be exact—back to safety where people were, people that could save me.

I remember feeling scared. That's about all I could recall while pedaling for my life. Why was I being chased? Had I done something? I looked behind me as I pedaled at top speed to get to the tracks, and the man who was chasing after me was within arm's length behind me. I could hear him gasping for air and felt his fingertips reaching for me as they touched the back of my Braves shirt. He was that close to grabbing me.

Frightened beyond reason, I made it to the abandoned railroad tracks and took off on them—to the left, towards town. I don't even think I was breathing at that moment. I was frightened, pedaling on pure adrenaline, hoping that my feet didn't slip off the pedals. Looking back, had my foot come off one of those pedals, I would've been done for. I would've crashed down onto the tracks and maybe broken my arm, leg, or neck. Maybe all three.

Then what would've happened to me? Would the man chasing me still see me as something he wanted? Would he have done something to me? I used to have nightmares after the near-kidnapping where I fell off my bike, and the man got me and dragged me back to the white car, with me yelling for someone to come and help me. Living with Mom and her mental illness was scary, don't get me wrong. But being on the verge of being taken, for whatever reason, made Mom seem like a picnic at the park.

Riding in the middle of railroad tracks is not easy. It takes a required skill, and thank God above that I could handle myself on a bike. I rode in the middle of the tracks as fast as I could, bumping violently with each revolution that my wheels took on those rocks and wooden ties. I knew I was slowing down- could feel it because the wind was not whipping my face as it had on the smooth, forgiving roads that I had been on earlier. I kept pedaling that damn bike of mine on nothing but adrenaline and fear. I had to get away from my abductor, whatever it took. I was fully aware in the moment that my life depended on it. There was no maybe about it. My life was at stake.

———

I just knew that the man in the white car was going to catch me. And for what? What was he going to do to me when he did? It was thoughts like that that spun around in my mind as I raced down the tracks for what appeared to be the race of my life. I think I was screaming for help. I don't know. I think, maybe, I had tears in my eyes. I can't say for sure. At that moment, my brain was in nothing but flight mode. You hear the "fight or flight" a lot in school, especially in psychology classes. Let me tell you, that's real.

I had not looked behind me for a few moments. I was too scared. I kept my eyes concentrated on the nearing downtown ahead. I could see it just around the bend of the tracks. I could see Wilson's Drugstore off in the distance, the small city hall building, and Bill's where we rented our Nintendo games. I was almost there.

My mind was in some kind of automatic drive, and before I knew it, I had reached the bend of the tracks and into the middle of the town square itself. Cars passed by on Main Street like nothing else in the world was going on. Feeling safe, I slowed down and looked behind me. Nothing. The guy that was chasing me must have gotten exhausted and quit somewhere back. At what point? I don't know, exactly. I didn't care.

I had gotten off the tracks and waited for the cars to pass. I pedaled across the somewhat busy street and rode over to the park benches that sat in a small rose park that was right next to a taxidermist building. I laid my bike down on the grass, sat there on the bench, and watched as the town fluttered with life. I was safe. That's when I broke down and cried.

I was shaking. I took my Braves hat off and wiped the sweat from my forehead and sat there wondering what in the hell just happened. I had never had that happen to me before—not in my town. You heard about that kind of stuff happening in big cities like New York or someplace like that, but not there in my neck of the woods. I watched from that bench for a white car to pass by. My heart dropped a few times when a white car did come by, but it was not the one that flew into that service road in the alley.

Some time passed by—I'd say maybe forty minutes—as I sat there trying to calm down. I was still waiting for the white car to pass me by on the street, maybe even making another attempt to snatch me. I never saw it again. It was as if it never really happened at all. But it had; I had the jumping heart to prove it. I never told anyone about the incident—not Curt, Tommy, Pete, Mike, or my dad. I went the rest of my life not ever going down that service road where the old Eureka building sat again. I avoided it completely. I guess I never said anything about my near abduction because I wanted to forget it. It was by far the scariest moment in my life.

It is safe to say that I never went riding without my friends ever again for fear of seeing that creepy, white car. I saw creepy busted, white cars during that summer but never *that* creepy busted, white car. I always kept a sharp eye out, nevertheless. They wanted me once, seems to reason that they might want me again. I was very cognizant of my environment after that day. Even as an adult. I realized that my small town— the one where I lived and felt safe and secure—hid monsters, monsters that weren't afraid of daylight.

During the rest of the summer, I kept a watchful eye on everything around me. I waited to see the car again in town but never did. The funny thing was, I don't recall what the guy who was trying to do me harm looked like. It happened so fast—like in a flash—that I wouldn't have been able to pick the guy out of a lineup if I had to. All I knew was that it was a guy, with shaggy dark hair, a white tee shirt and jeans, and slim in build. That is the best description that I could offer. He was like a monster out of a horror movie but in the daylight.

I wish that I could forget that day, but it has haunted me for years. Even though the old Eureka Textile Mill has been long torn down, and the dead-end service road was made into an actual passable road; I can still see myself being chased by a faceless man with no name.

You can change the environment, tear buildings down and erect them, and cut down all the trees and bushes, but you cannot change what happened there. That place in town will forever be the spot where I almost was kidnapped or possibly worse, murdered.

Feeling that I was relatively safe at that point, I pedaled my way back to familiar territory: my neighborhood. I could tell from the top of my street that some of my friends' parents' cars were still gone from the driveways. With my legs feeling like jelly, I decided to duck out at my house as much as I didn't want to. I figured that I had already dealt with a devil I didn't know, so why not deal with one that I called Mom?

5

I pulled into the backyard and saw my dad's car in the driveway. I laid my bike down and up the back deck stairs I went. I opened the door. It was right then and there I knew something was wrong. I never saw the man cry; not even at my mother's funeral. I could hear the wailing long before I opened the back door, and that scared me.

At that moment in time, I knew something was wrong. My dad was not a crier. He just plainly was not. The first thought that sprang into my mind was that Mom had killed herself, and he came home to find her. That was always on the table in my mind back then. She had talked about it some to my dad previously, and she meant it. I always waited for it to happen. I thought I'd be the one that found her, like when I came home from school or something.

I remember back in 1990—around March of that year—my dad had found my mother lying unresponsive on the kitchen floor while I was at school one day. An empty bottle of pills and booze lay beside her. The only reason I didn't find my mom dead coming home from school was because, by chance, my dad came home for lunch from work to check on her that day.

She hadn't been doing good and had a bad run mentally, and something told him to go check in on her. She hadn't answered the phone when he called, He left on his lunch break and came home to find her nearly dead. He saved her life that day, but barely. Her mental state had only grown worse over the months leading up to her getting really bad in the summer of '91.

———

I stood there in the doorway and saw my dad sitting down on one of the kitchen chairs with his face in his hands, crying. My mom—being a person of support it seemed—stood over him motherly stroking his back and trying to comfort him. That scene threw me for a loop because I hadn't ever seen either of the two of them doing what they were doing. Looking at my dad, I felt helpless. I mean what do you do when the strongest person you know is crying? I had no words to offer. I was powerless.

Sometimes words cannot describe the feeling that you have in situations like those. You just kind of feel the moment—feel the authenticity of emotion. Words would've probably gotten in the way. My mom looked up at me, and for that moment, I saw in her eyes a calm, mentally stable woman. I saw my mom for the first time in years, not since I was a little kid. She was beautiful, and she was in her right mind that hot day in July. I could see she was back—just for a while—and I can't tell you how happy that made me. If it was for only a little bit, but I wanted it— wanted it to feel like my mom again, like home again in the days of old.

6

I stood there in the funeral home a few days later with relatives I had not seen in a long, long time. It was aunts and uncles and cousins who were there to see my Grandma Dixie off. There were even some relatives that I had never seen before in my life. The whole death thing was new to me. I had never known anyone who died before. And my first taste of death was my Grandma Dixie, dad's mother.

It didn't seem real, standing in the grieving halls of the funeral home. The entire scene seemed fake—like it was all staged—as if all of it was like in a sitcom that had taken a serious turn. I felt nothing but numbness the entire time there. I could not believe that she was dead, lying lifeless up there in that black casket with flowers towering in the backdrop. I could not bring myself to go up there and face her, just could not do it. I had just talked to her on the phone several nights before and had planned on seeing her sometime later in the summer. I was going to spend the night with her or maybe even two if my cousin, Whitney, was going to be there.

I think the reason I couldn't go up there to see her was because none of that seemed real, and seeing her would make it real. I was thirteen years old, and seeing someone dead was not something that was on my to-do list—especially my grandma. Although I considered myself a grown man at thirteen, I couldn't do what the grown men at the funeral home were doing: going up to the casket where she lay and giving her one last good look before they closed the lid forever. For days after the funeral, I wished that I would have gone up there to see her. I should've, I guess. It's gnawed at me since.

————

I remember the day of the graveside service distinctly well, too. It was raining, an all-day drizzle to be exact, that seemed to make the day even muggier and hotter. The graveyard that we had to walk through to get to my Grandma Dixie's grave had muddied our nice shoes and made us slip and slide all over the place. It was just nasty to even walk to the graveside service. The overcast, rainy conditions fit the somber mood that we were all feeling very well. The rain hid all of our tears. I would glance over at my dad from time to time, and he was just devastated. Of all the things the man had going on at the moment, his mom dying was going to be too much—the proverbial straw that would break the camel's back.

When we made it to her gravesite with all of the other relatives, we all stood underneath a green canopy and listened while the minister gave us words of comfort. Those words were meant to soothe us in that time of death, but they did not comfort me. I was still trying to understand why things like that had to happen to good people. Why could not it have been some drug user or murderer? Why not the man who tried to kidnap me? Why did God take my grandma?

I spoke to God the night I learned of her death. It marked the first time in my life that I prayed. I was alone in my room that night, stunned by the news of her sudden death. No one had any answers, especially my mom and dad. They were too emotional to give me any explanation on why she had to go. So, I turned to the only person who knows why things are the way they are: God.

I locked my bedroom door, got down on my knees, closed my eyes, and started talking there in my room. I asked him what happened to her. I asked Him why it was her time to go. I wanted answers and quickly. But as I was there alone in my bedroom, the only thing that answered my questions were the ear-numbing sounds of silence. I was angry at God for taking her, taking her away from me, taking her away from my dad.

I had seen my Grandma Dixie during Spring Break from school earlier that year. Christ, it was just several months back. She seemed fine, you know. She was working in her garden like she always did during the spring and summer. I would sometimes help her break beans while sitting on the front porch, pick tomatoes, or whatever else she needed me to do there. I didn't mind. I rather enjoyed it, working beside her—me in the splendor of my youth and her in the winter of her life.

She called me her little helper although I was not so little anymore. I was always happy to help, though. On that front porch way out in the knobs, a slang term for being way out in the country, she always told the best stories, and it made the time pass very well as we broke beans and tossed them into white five-gallon buckets. I would later help her can them in Mason jars and store them away for later. Usually, she canned way more than she needed. In those frequent cases, she would give the food away to neighbors and to people who came for a visit.

My grandma was always nice to me and never scolded me even when she probably should've. She used to take me to town and buy me things when I would spend a few days and nights with her on Spring Break. The Braves hat I wore all the time was one that she had bought for me. I had gotten it good and broken in and sweat-stained, and my grandma would see it and say, "Got it broke in pretty good, don't you?" I would smile and nod.

Grandma Dixie was a hell of a cook. When I would stay with her, it was a steady diet of fried chicken; cheesy, mashed potatoes; green beans; and all the German Chocolate cake that I could eat. She knew all of that was my favorite meal, and she cooked it every time that I spent the night or weekend with her. She also made these really thick chocolate shakes, too. God, I can taste them now. Nobody made them like she did. They were so thick that I couldn't use a straw. I'd have to scoop it with a spoon.

I would spend the night during the summers too, and we would turn her TV on to the TBS Superstation and watch the Atlanta Braves games. She never missed a broadcast. Then, around 10:30 on those evenings, the two of us would lounge on the front porch, listen to the crickets play their nocturnal music, and make idle talk. I was going to miss those nights with her: the Braves games on her floor model TV in the living room, the smell of fried chicken in her house, and the chirp of crickets outside at night while we sat on the front porch and talked about nothing at all. Even now, although it was decades ago, I can still get a sense of being back there sometimes when I sit outside at night to unwind from the day.

———

I stood there amongst all of my family, staring at the closed casket that lay atop the grave that was to be her final resting place. The drizzling rain that sprayed about camouflaged the tears that streamed down my face. It was the first time I had cried about her being dead. I tried not to. I have no good reason why I tried not to. But the tears came like I knew they eventually would. And when they did, it was like a dam breaking. It was okay; no one was watching. If they did, what did it matter? You're supposed to cry at funerals.

I guess standing there I realized, at the young age of thirteen, the gravity of the situation. Her death hit me hard. She was not coming back —ever—and my last cognitive recollection of Grandma Dixie was of her standing on her front porch, waving me goodbye as I waved back to her from the passenger seat of Dad's car. That was Spring Break. That was the last time that I saw my Grandma Dixie alive.

CHAPTER 11
SEXUAL ADVANCES/DEW BASH/NIGHT SWIMMING/A TRIP TO MANDY'S HOUSE

1

MY GRANDMA DIXIE'S funeral came and went, and so did the Fourth of July. It was now mid-July. High school was getting closer—coming more into focus. Things around the house were still at that point...strained, odd, emotional, place your adjective here. Dad was still mourning Grandma Dixie, and Mom snapped back to her mental illness roller-coaster ride. Her run of stability didn't last too long. But it was nice while it lasted.

I wasn't the only kid on the block having problems at home. Curt's house was not much better than mine and was heading for worse. The nice-looking, normal Rockwellian family was falling apart behind the front door. It wasn't a known fact to a lot of people. Perhaps close family might've known. Pete, Tommy, and Mike didn't know a whole lot about Curt's home life. It was something that me and Curt kept only to ourselves. That was our secret, but I'm sure the others knew what was going on. Sometimes things are hard to miss, even if you think no one is looking.

We might have been kids, but we were smart enough to sense when things weren't right. Maybe it was because we each had something going on in *our* homes. I never asked Curt why he didn't talk to the others about what was going on at home. I figured it was his business. Sometimes Curt was private like that. I was really close to the kid for a very long time, and there were things I'd bet you a million dollars on that I didn't know about him. Curt only told you things he wanted you to know.

Curt's family had been falling apart for a while, and I knew some of the particulars but not all the intimates that are between a married couple. His dad had a drinking problem, and so did his mother which made for a combustible combo; "gasoline and fire," as Curt once described it. I was an unofficial member of the family and by proxy, I was involved with and witnessed some of the issues over the years. Those issues usually began on Friday afternoon around five o'clock and didn't end—if they ever did—around Sunday evening when everyone had to go back to work for the week. Then, when Friday came about, so did the cycle. It seemed neverending. We all would hang out at Curt's house quite a bit, but I honestly think we all had gotten so used to the way things were at our houses that hearing his parents fight and cuss each other wasn't that big of a deal. It never spilled over onto us up in Curt's bedroom room. I think most times they had forgotten we were even there unless we had to come downstairs for something.

When the fighting, the yelling, the glass breaking, and the pushes evolving to shoves began, Curt and I—when it was just the two of us—would sit up in his bedroom trying to play Nintendo, turning the volume up on his TV so the music of the game would drown out the yelling downstairs. It never worked. The marital discord would go on for hours with one of them leaving and slamming the door shut behind them. Then, the family car roared to life and peeled out of the driveway. That was usually how things ended on the weekends when I would spend the night, which was often.

His mom and dad used to fight once a week it seemed. As the summer of '91 marched along, the fighting became more than just weekend arguments; it became near-daily events. Could have been the heat of that summer because God, it was HOT. Heat brings people's blood up, including his parents' blood was up—way up—that summer.

———

I remember a few weeks before Grandma Dixie's death, I had gone over to see Curt. Usually, I opened the front door and allowed myself in like I had a million times in the past because I was there most of the time. It was never weird for me to do that, nor was it strange for me to raid their cabinets and fridge for food. There were times when Curt's dad would be sitting in his recliner watching a ball game, and I'd walk right in and sit on the couch and talk for a bit. This only happened maybe a couple of times that I remember. He was always nice to me but distant to Curt. I could never figure that out. Maybe it was because I wasn't his son. I don't know.

I opened the front door that day and walked right in as usual. I saw his mother slumped in her recliner, snoring in the middle of the after- noon on a Tuesday with a dozen or so dark brown beer bottles standing empty on the coffee table beside her. A few were lying still around her feet. I tried not to stare as I crept by her, trying not to wake her as I made it to the stairs and up to Curt's bedroom. It was the first time that I had seen his mom in that state, and it was the first time that I saw how exactly bad Curt was having it. I had heard the fights but seeing her in that condition hit me differently.

I had seen her drunk before and even felt the weirdness of how relaxed she had gotten when intoxicated. She would always get close up to me and talk, her breath smelling like Pabst Blue Ribbon, touch me on the arm, smiling, playing with her hair– flirting with me. One time– I remember that summer of 1991—she even grabbed my crotch while I was in the dark kitchen rummaging through the cabinets.

On that particular night, the kitchen light was out, and the only light was coming from the bathroom where the door was half open. She came out of there wearing these really short shorts and a tank top. I remember her breasts were too big for that small tank top. I heard her walking behind, bare feet on hardwood. I didn't turn around to look at her. I knew that she was coming for me. She got behind me and slipped her hands around my waist, slowly ran them down to the front of my basketball shorts, and asked if I'd fucked a girl yet as her hands went under my shorts.

I got so red and flustered that I could feel my heartbeat pounding in my ears. I couldn't catch my breath. I got hard, but I didn't want to be. At thirteen, you can't just decide when you get an erection. It just happens. Her face lowered down to behind my right ear, and I could hear her slow breathing as she rubbed my crotch. I shut the cabinet quickly—forgetting all about being hungry—and slipped out of her grasp and walked quickly across the kitchen and up the stairs back into Curt's bedroom. I didn't go back downstairs for the rest of the night.

It scared me that she was thinking about me like that in a sexual way. His mom was a beautiful woman, and I'll be honest here and say that there were plenty of times when I thought about her in sexual ways when I tried to go to sleep at night. But fantasy and the real world are much different, especially when you're thirteen. In my teenage fantasies, I was more than ready and willing to take her anywhere—her bed, across the table, or even on the couch—but in reality, where it counts, I was afraid.

When she wasn't drunk, she never acted like that around me. Ever. When I saw her sober, I would try to act like nothing had ever happened. For the most part, I was able to. I never told Curt about those times and yes, there were several more than the reach around in the kitchen that night.

The last time she tried anything with me was when I had come down to use the downstairs bathroom because Curt was in the upstairs one down the hall from his bedroom. I couldn't hold it anymore. I had drunk like a whole two-liter of Mountain Dew and just had to go. I came down the stairs. It was quiet and dimly lit. I raced across the living room and through the kitchen to the bathroom. God, it was the best piss I ever had in my life.

When I opened the door, feeling the best I'd ever felt, I walked through the kitchen and there was his mom standing there wearing a black silk robe with nothing underneath. I froze in my tracks. She walked over to me slowly, as if it were a dream, and stood right in front of me. She took my hands—which were shaking like crazy at this point—and put them on her chest. "Before you go to sleep, I want you to come play with me in my bedroom." She leans in close and licks my lips. I could taste the alcohol on her tongue and smell it on her breath. She turned and walked away back towards her bedroom. After that, I never came back down without Curt, no matter what.

As I said, I never told Curt any of this. He had too much on him as it was, and adding to his misery wasn't something that I was going to do to him. It would be humiliating for him to know that his inebriated mom had tried to get at his best friend. I kept my mouth shut. Besides, she never remembered any of it the next time I would see her. She was too drunk. That was good. It made it less awkward.

———

His mom had started drinking, according to Curt on a midnight tearful confessional there up in his bedroom back in January of that year, to keep up with her husband, Curt's dad. But Curt saw that as a cop-out and rightly so. Curt hated his mother for her alcoholic ways. She was the last parent that he had because his dad had pretty much stayed in a bottle, leaving Curt only one parent: his mother. Then, she began to binge, too. Eventually, Curt was on his own for parents.

His dad drank a lot more than his mom from what I was told by my friend. But I didn't see much of his dad. I had very few experiences with him. When I did, they weren't much in the way of profound. He didn't talk much, and I can remember a couple of short, topical conversations we ever had in all the years that I knew him; one was about the Braves' chances during that summer of '91 and how school was going. That was it. Those short, topical conversations took place in the living room while he sat deep in his recliner, red-eyed and buzzed from the brown liquor he drank.

You wouldn't think of it to look at him, but he was a highly intelligent man who worked at a nuclear plant three counties over in the accounting department. His two degrees hung with pride on the living room wall: a degree in psychology and another in business. I always wondered even as I got to be an adult how someone so smart could make dumb decisions. I still don't know the answer. I never asked Curt what had led his dad down the path he was on. Maybe Curt didn't know. Back then, as kids, we didn't just go up and ask our parents questions like that.

They came from a generation where they didn't feel the need to explain much of anything to us. At least, that's how my experiences went with my own. My friends' parents were the same way, so I guess maybe my estimation is right when I say they came from a generation where they didn't need to explain much of anything to us. It would've been nice to know why the ones in charge of us did the things they did. Some sort of explanation might have gone a long way, who knows?

The more memorable experiences with his dad that I had were of the loud, verbal kind that started on Friday nights downstairs in the living room when he and his wife would start in on each other. They had some really bad shouting matches, I can tell you. It had gotten so bad that Curt would come over to my house and spend the night some nights because the behavior was starting to spread throughout the week instead of being saved up for the weekend as usual. I thought it was ironic that he took shelter from the family storms at my house where it was nothing but a rollercoaster of emotion on the daily.

Curt said to me once, "I'd rather deal with an unstable person who has no choice than with people who choose to drink and fight." We all had crosses to bear. Curt was right and usually was. Mom's problems weren't her direct fault. It was genetic. She couldn't help it, but she could have gone to the doctor and gotten help like before. So in a way, it was *her* fault. Curt blamed his parents for the way his family was. They chose to act the way they did, and he hated them for that. "When I graduate high school, I'm going to college far, far away from here. I will never come back. I swear to God." he once told me.

He did just that. After high school, Curt was accepted into the University of Pennsylvania, one of the eight Ivy League schools. I wasn't around when he packed up and left for good. The only reason that I knew that he had gotten into that elite school was that I had run into him at Papa Enzo's right before he left. I was going in there to get a pizza, and he was coming out carrying one. He and I talked for about forty-five minutes that July evening on the sidewalk—catching up a bit like old friends with a shared past do—and that's when he told me where he was going and what school he had gotten into. Before that chance meeting after high school at Papa Enzo's and throughout our high school career, Curt and I had become just barely friends, nothing like we were in 1991 and before. He and I had become just another kid in the hallway going from class to class. I didn't like it, but I guess things happen that way. It was the very thing that I worried about that summer in 1991, and it happened—not with just Curt, but with all of us.

I didn't see Curt after that night. It was the last time. It was and still is a sad ending to what was a fantastic friendship and brotherhood. We were brothers back then, back in the midst of our unencumbered youths. High school had its evil way with us, breaking all of us, and scattering us into the four winds. I never had friends like the ones I had back then. What was the point?

As the summer of '91 ended right before we went to high school, Curt's parents split. It was probably for the best. Some things– I had learned at that young age—cannot be repaired. His dad eventually got remarried and so did his mom. I remember going over there just like I had before high school, but not so much as time went on during my sophomore through senior year.

When I did go over there, I'd walk right in through the front door, as always, and there were no empty beer bottles, no slumped in the recliner forty-year-old mother that liked to booze it up and make sexual advances towards me. She was normal.

His dad had even cleaned up after getting away from Curt's mom. He moved away, and when I would ask Curt how his dad was when it was his turn to spend a weekend with him, he told me his dad was great; no more drinking, and that he'd cleaned up. That's when I figured out an important life lesson: Sometimes the people that you love are the worst for you. Combustible. Toxic. Insert your own adjective here.

2

I desperately needed to get back to some sense of normalcy after Grandma Dixie. With my boys at my side, things were starting to feel somewhat stable after a few weeks since she passed. I wasn't over her death by no means, but I had cried so much and ran over so many memories with her that I was empty—shot, played out. I was still hung over immensely from her death, but being around Tommy, Pete, Mike, and Curt was a welcomed break from the dark cloud that was hanging over me.

It was funny because when I was with them, it seemed that my grandmother had never died at all. They took my pain away by being just as they always were before the death in my family. Their craziness was just what I needed to escape my grandmother and my house of horrors.

They were sympathetic towards me, as they felt they should have been. I appreciated it. Really. It was the first time in our history together that any of our family members had died. I was the first to garner that distinction.

I told them that her passing had been rough, but I was ready to start feeling normal again- something that I had not felt in a bit. And of course, the guys accommodated that request. I needed them so badly to pull me out of the creeping depression that I felt was trying to make a power grab for me. Not only was I dealing internally with the impending doom and utter fear of going to high school, but I also had my home life falling away, and then Grandma Dixie's death on me. There for a while things never seemed to let up. It was always something, always another mental obstacle.

Being around the guys back in 1991 was something magical, something more than mere words could describe. They were more than friends to me; they were something that I could count on, and lean up against when things got rough for me. They were like brothers to me—irreplaceable. Shaking the webs from my grandmother's death from my mind, or at the very least as best I could, the guys and I decided that we would hold a Dew Bash out at Tommy's backyard later on that night.

———

You are probably wondering what a Dew Bash is. It was really simple and silly, now that I think about it. We would all gather at night at somebody's house and sit out in the backyard under the stars in lawn chairs or whatever we could find to sit on and drink a cooler full of Mountain Dew once a month. That was it. It really was no different than us camping out, but it made us feel important out there for whatever reason. I never understood why we did it other than us having something to do.

The name Dew Bash had been introduced by Tommy one day while we were all standing at my house drinking the said soda. And from there, it became a tradition of sorts to gather once a month someplace and drink Mountain Dew while talking about life and all the issues that we had going on collectively or solitarily.

That night, me, Mike, Curt, Tommy, and Pete all sat in Tommy's backyard on lawn chairs around a small campfire, talking about things and sipping on Dew. It was good to get back to basics after my grandmother's death. Anything that resembled normalcy was a welcomed emotion.

The summer was slipping away, almost too quickly. It was July sixteenth as we sat under the cloudless night sky having our first Dew Bash of the month. July was marching onward, and the reality of high school was getting closer with every passing day. Still more than a month away, but now the approaching storm that was high school could be seen on the horizon—closer than it was on May 26th.

June was the past, and July was heading down the track full speed ahead. After the Fourth of July, it always seemed, at least to me, that summer would zoom by, and you wouldn't catch how fast it came and went until you were in August. July Fourth was and still is the unofficial beginning of the end of summer. Don't ever let anyone tell you any different.

Knowing that things were going to change was pressing down on my chest, causing me to lose my breath sometimes. I wasn't any good when it came to change and never adapted to it well. But growing up is all about change. Change is in the very DNA of getting older. But we have to change with the change, right? If we don't, we'll get left behind.

I wasn't ready to go to high school. Neither were my friends. Of course, they didn't talk about it much because I guess they were too scared. But I wasn't too frightened to utter the words that everyone thought to themselves. I was so emotionally spent that I had to start unloading my mind somehow after Grandma Dixie, or I was going to explode. I had so much on my mind that summer, and I think everything finally came to a head that night of the Dew Bash.

"Guys, things are going to change soon," I said, looking at everyone who sat there looking back at me in silence.

I did not have to say the words high school. They already knew what I was talking about. I hated to be a wet blanket on the Dew Bash because it was going so good, but I needed them to tell me that I was scared over nothing—that everything would be okay; we would be friends forever; and that we would leave that place intact, maybe better than before. I needed to hear that so badly.

I wanted someone, anybody, to tell me that things were going to be okay even if they weren't going to be. I'd believe the lie if I had to. I just needed someone to tell me that things were going to be okay. Sometimes when you're a kid, hearing that things will turn out okay even if deep down you knew they probably weren't going to, helped some. I guess that's what I was looking for when I spoke through a momentary pause in conversation. I was fishing for that.

Could they do that? Could we as thirteen-year-old kids sit there under the supervision of the brilliant moon above and say with certainty that things would stay as they are?

"Maybe not," Pete said dryly diving into the cooler for another Dew, breaking the silence finally.

"Guys," I started, "we're going to be in high school in several weeks. Things are going to change whether we want them to or not." Now the ball was rolling. We had avoided the subject as a group up until that moment, but how could we any longer? High school was coming. It was closer now.

"Only if we let it," Tommy said.

Tommy was always right, it seemed. Every time that he spoke, I listened. Except when we got us mixed up with Jerry at the Rocky Top that day. But other than that, I listened to him. Tommy once said that don't commit to anything until you see that it's permanent. Of course, that good piece of advice was not given until our freshman year toward the end. The kid always had a calming sense about him. He seemed unflappable the whole time that I knew him. I don't know if he was frightened by the prospect of going to high school or not. I really couldn't ever tell. He was hard to read at times when it came to that.

"Are we still going to be friends during high school?" Curt popped in.

We all looked at each other, waiting for the other to come up with an answer. None of us had one, at least not a truthful one.

"Hell yeah," Mike said. "We've been friends this long– why would anything change it now? Stupid damn question."

"I just hear that high school changes people," I said lowly, trying to get them to at least talk about what was coming in the future. I was hoping that talking about it would help.

"We're going to be fine, dude. Stop asking stupid questions," Pete said.

"What if we ain't?" Curt asked. "What if things change so much that we don't do things like this anymore?"

"You act like we're just friends because we have to be or something," Tommy said, getting aggravated.

"No, I just don't want things to tear us apart," Curt said. I was glad that someone else other than me was spilling his guts about the fear of high school.

"We all have been friends for so long that nothing would break us all up. Not high school, not anything," Tommy said, trying to convince us that things were never going to change. Maybe he was trying to convince himself more than he was us.

"I hope you're right," I said finally after a few moments of silent reflection, looking at Tommy from across the campfire. I wanted to believe him that night. I wanted to completely give in and just not worry about high school and all that stuff. But I couldn't do it. I just could not bring myself to believe that nothing was going to change.

I think deep down, Tommy was afraid of high school just as we were. He never really said much about it. But I think that was because he didn't want us to know that he had the same fears we had. Sitting there in silence while we quietly thought about what had just been debated, I told myself to leave the future for another night. There would always be another night to toil in the world of the unknown.

I perhaps should not have even brought up the whole high school thing out there, but I needed some word that things were going to be alright. I kind of sort of received that, but not enough to calm my fears. If anything, I wondered about the four of them. What was really going on inside their heads as it concerned high school? What was going on inside their heads as it concerned anything?

3

Another tradition that the five of us had was sneaking off to the park at night. The park was in our neighborhood, just between Curt and Tommy's house. After we got tired of sitting around Tommy's backyard, we decided to extinguish the fire and go off to the park to walk around in the dead of the night. That night, the dying campfire was extinguished by Mike pissing it out... literally. There was so much smoke swirling around him as he did it that Curt remarked that Mike looked as if he was in a Whitesnake music video. I still laugh every time I think about it.

I don't know why we went to the park at night, but we would go down there and just hang out. It was really cool to be cloaked in the darkness, milling around the town's park, just us stupid kids. It always brings a smile to my face when I think about it. It was just a park at night, but there was something majestic and magnetic about being there in the darkness—being the only ones there. Maybe it was the stillness of the night.

I guess if I had to pinpoint an exact reason why we went to the park after hours was because we weren't supposed to be there after the gates were closed. It was as if we were breaking the law or something. It really wasn't a law to break, I surmise, but when you're thirteen small things like that seem incredible and fantastic.

We had cleaned up our empty cans from our Dew Bash and made sure the campfire was done. It was only smoldering now. The five of us cautiously snuck out of the dark recesses of the yard and down the street, dodging the streetlights above. It was twelve-thirty as we lurched down the quiet street, looking around and making sure that no one was watching us from their windows. I mean, most people were asleep in this town by ten, but you always had those people that stayed up all hours of the night for whatever reasons.

We had snuck to the park many times in the past, and each time we acted as if it was our first. We didn't want to get caught and have the law called on us. We were careful—extremely careful—when walking to the park through the darkness. We acted like it was our first time because it kept us on our toes—made us look around and not dismiss things. We were always on high alert.

The gate was always closed up tight at nine o'clock sharp by the local police department. I never knew why they closed the gate and locked it. It never prevented us from getting in. Anyone who knew about the hole in the fence on the northeast side could get into the park after hours. Of course, we were the only ones who had known about the hole in the fence because it was made by us one night as we tried to figure out how exactly to get into the park.

We ran alongside the street that was parallel to the park's fence and up the hill to where the hole was in the chain-linked fence. Looking around making sure that no cars or people were about, we one by one got on our stomachs and crawled under the fence while one of us held it up. Not really a big opening, now that I think about it. I can tell you that we each went through several shirts getting ripped before we perfected our crawl under the sharp, pointed metal fence.

The park itself was mysterious at night. It was quiet with nothing but the nocturnal creatures that ambulated about. I always liked going in there at night. It seemed peaceful, not buzzing as it did during the day. We were the masters of our universe walking around in the darkness. The coolest times were when we would walk around when it was really foggy. That was rad and scary at the same time. We each would play a game where we would look around the darkness and fog and think of the best places Michale Myers would be standing. Then, later on, we would play hide and go seek. Those foggy nights at the park have a special place in my heart.

The swimming pool that was across the park sat there invitingly as we walked down the hill from the fence and past the swings and monkey bars. We had never been into the swimming pool after hours before, especially during the dark. It was going to be a first for us even though we had many night trips to the park. Mike had actually brought it up about us going into the swimming pool. Not a bad idea, we all thought. So we did it.

The swimming pool was on the other end of the park, next to our baseball field where we played. The pool itself was sectioned off by another tall chain-linked fence that seemed too tall for us to scale—nine, ten feet maybe—too tall for any of us to even think about climbing. Standing there looking up at the swimming pool from the swings, an idea came from an unlikely source.

We ran up the hill towards the swimming pool as fast as possible. Before we knew it, we were standing by the fence looking in at the water that sat still in the pool like a mirror. I looked up at the fence, and yes, it was too tall for us to climb. Besides, I didn't like climbing fences anyway, not since that time I got hung by my pants leg by those twisted parts that are always at the very top of most chain-linked fences I've ever seen. I hated those things. I still have a scar on my right leg where I got a nasty cut that went deep back in 1990.

"How are we going to get in there?" Curt asked as we stood there looking at the swimming pool twinkle in the moonlight.

"I have a plan," Mike said walking away from us and into the darkness of the community park.

———

"This ain't going to work," Pete said after Mike unveiled his plan.

"Why not? It's the only way we're going to get in there," Mike said, leaning up against the ladder he'd just "borrowed" from one of the houses that we passed on our way to the park. His plan was to leave the park; go quietly into someone's tool shed; and "borrow" a ladder. And he knew just the place to get a ladder: Red Raper's tool shed.

Everyone in the neighborhood knew about Red Raper. He was like a guru when it came to do-it-yourself stuff like landscaping and home repairs. The old man refused to have any outsiders come into his house to fix something. As a middle-aged man who liked to fix things himself, I admired people like Red Raper: a man's man.

His tool shed that sat behind his home harbored numerous tools from every kind of manufacturer known to man, and everyone in town knew it. There were tools in there that he hadn't even gotten out of the box yet. On the outside of his tool shed hung a steel extension ladder. And it was that very ladder that Mike "borrowed" from the man's building– took it right off the metal hooks, where it hung parallel to the ground.

"I can't believe you stole a ladder," I said, looking at my thief for a friend. We had carried that ladder through the night, slid it under the fence of the northeast corner, and carried it across the park. Mike leaned it up against the fence of the swimming pool, smiling with pride.

"I didn't steal anything. We're just borrowing it," Mike replied.

"We ain't borrowing nothing," Curt said, not wanting anything to do with the borrowed tool.

"I'm going to take it back. It's not like the old man is going to get up in the middle of the night and use the damn thing. It's cool—Mike told us—trying to get us to understand it wasn't stealing but just borrowing.

"We're supposed to climb the ladder and jump over to the other side?" Pete asked.

"Yeah, something like that," Mike replied.

We all stood there and looked at Big Cat. "Oh, like you guys have a better idea," he asked, knowing damn well none of us did.

"Maybe we shouldn't do this," Curt said, getting nervous about breaking into the town's public pool.

"What's the worst that could happen?" Mike asked. Famous last words?

————

We climbed the ladder reluctantly, one by one, and hopped over the fence while trying in vain not to make any sounds. Everything is louder at night time, for some reason. Maybe it was the stillness of everything. But we had made it over without being cut up or calling attention to ourselves. The landing from up on high to the concrete hurt a little bit. It was strange being in the confines of the swimming pool at night. Just like the park, there was something mysterious about the swimming pool being swaddled in darkness.

I wasn't a swimmer like the other guys in my group, but that didn't stop me from appreciating the time that we were having. The guys stripped down to their boxers and slipped into the cold water of the pool. I, of course, stayed around the sunbathing area, looking around at the night that we were playing in. It was muggy as hell—the kind of thick air where your clothes just stick to you, and I'm for sure that the water was a welcome relief for the guys.

Sitting down in one of the chairs that leaned up against the fence, I sat back and watched the guys swim in the moon-kissed water. I watched them splash water at each other and laugh, oftentimes getting too loud to the point where I waited to see the cops come into the park or the swimming pool parking lot. Tommy's words from earlier that night rang in my ears, 'Nothing would break us up'. Sitting there smiling, I hoped to God that he was right because there was no way I could ever have friends like those or times, for that matter, ever again.

————

Later on that night, tired of night swimming, Curt climbed out of the water and came over to me dripping wet. He sat down on the concrete and used Tommy's shirt to dry his face and arms off.

"What's up?" he asked.

"Just sitting around," I replied, lying on my back on the concrete and looking up at the millions of stars.

"Yeah. It's always interesting when Big Cat comes to town, isn't it?

Something wrong?" Curt asked, getting down onto his back to stargaze beside me.

"Just the norm, I guess."

"Norm as in what?"

"I don't know where to start," I said. "Mom...Mandy...high school... grandma dying. Just seems like things are changing, man. Can't seem to shake this feeling, you know?"

"They are. But what are you going to do about it?" Curt asked.

Good question, I told myself, looking at a very bright star that I thought was a planet off in the distance. It might have been Venus.

"I don't want them to change," I told my best friend, wanting to break down and cry. "I don't want times like these to end, you know?"

"Dude, we're getting older. In several weeks, we're going to be freshmen in high school. Like it or not, things are going to change. But don't think for a second that things between all of us will change. We'll always be friends, all of us," Curt advised.

His words were sincere, thoughtful, and hit the mark. He meant them that night at the swimming pool. I think he was trying to convince himself because he had some of the same questions I had earlier that night at Tommy's. He was worried too, but his goal right there at the pool was to calm my thoughts.

"You really think so?" I asked, wanting so badly to believe him in his prediction of the future.

"Yeah, I do. Man, times are changing. We're changing. Have you seen, Tommy? He's getting facial hair now." We both chuckled at his peach fuzz that Tommy thought was just the best thing ever. "But seriously, we just got to roll with the changes wherever they lead. And how we do that is together."

I knew that Curt was right. He usually was. It still didn't settle things inside me. "I miss her, man," I said, feeling the tears in my eyes and looking at the stars while thinking about Grandma Dixie.

Curt lay there beside me looking at the same stars, staying silent, allowing the moment that I needed, or even how long it would take to go down this emotional road. "I wish she didn't have to die." By then I was crying, tears streamed from the corners of my eyes and down the temples of my head. The hurt that I felt the day I heard the news was fresh again. I can't say as to why, but it was there. Curt just laid there beside me, hands folded on his chest, listening to me weep. It was the only thing that he could do, really.

After crying it out for a few minutes, I switched gears. "Mom is getting bad again, too. She was decent there for a bit after grandma died, but now she's right back where she was," I said, hearing the splash of Tommy, Pete, and Mike goofing around in the water.

Curt replied, "Yeah I thought she was, too. I could tell she was getting worse. I didn't want to say anything, though."

"I don't know what to do, man. Grandma Dixie died. Dad is falling apart and is never home. Mom is getting worse. High school is coming. It's like it's too much right now." I wanted to cry again, but the tears weren't there. They had dried up, I guessed.

Me and Curt lay there on the cool concrete on our backs for a few minutes before Curt said something, breaking the silence between us. "I think my mom is cheating on my dad."

That hit me kind of hard. "You really think so?" I asked, keeping my eye on a star that I thought maybe was the planet Venus.

"Yeah," Curt replied after some careful thought.

"What makes you think so?"

"She's been on the phone with a guy every time Dad is at work. I'll come downstairs for breakfast or something, and she'll be laughing and acting different. She stays on the phone all day, nearly. Except when Dad is home. She goes out for hours at a time getting groceries, but she never comes back with anything. I think she's going to see him or something. I don't know. She just acts differently. Not like she does when she's drunk. Just different, I guess."

This was a heavy revelation, to say the least. All the stuff that Curt was dealing with within his house as it concerned his mom and dad, now this. I was shocked. Maybe I shouldn't have been. I don't know. But I was. I could tell he was hurt and confused by what he thought was happening in his house. It turned out later on that he was right, though. That was one of the reasons for the split. Maybe the cheating was the catalyst for the boozing by his dad. "Does your dad know, you think?" I asked.

Curt considered my question for a few seconds. "I doubt it. Maybe. I don't know." Curt said with frustration. "He might know something is wrong. I mean, he drinks a lot. Maybe that's why he does it. Drinks to cope." Curt's voice was sad and thick.

I could tell that he had been thinking about this for a long time. How long? I haven't a clue, maybe since before the summer. Curt sometimes had a way of keeping things bottled up even though he and I shared a lot over the years. There were still things that went on with Curt I probably never knew about. We all have three lives: a public life where everyone sees everything. Then, we have a private life where we only invite a few people in to see us. And then there's a secret life where no one is allowed in. Curt exposed that secret life of his, or at least some aspect of it, there at the swimming pool that night.

"What do you think will happen eventually?" I asked.

Curt lay there, and I could hear him considering the question before he answered. But I'm sure that he had asked himself that question a million times before he told me. "I'd say Dad will find out. Then they will get a divorce. And that'll be that, I guess."

Letting that sink in for a bit, I asked another important question, "How are you going to be with that?"

"It'll be fine," Curt replied. "I've been watching them tear each other apart for so long that I'm ready for it to be over. You've seen how it is at my house. It's just...it needs to be over. I don't ever want to be home anymore. Sometimes I don't want to be anywhere anymore."

"What do you mean?" I asked, thinking I already knew the answer.

There was a pause in Curt's response– so long in fact that I was about to ask him again– until he spoke. "I thought about killing myself. Like just end it all because man, I can't take much more." Now it was Curt's turn to cry. I didn't turn to look at him. I didn't need to. I could feel his pain radiating off him. I kept my eyes on the stars above. I didn't go into a whole yarn about how he was so young and that things would eventually get better. He knew that. He didn't need me to dole out clichés about there being much more life to live and that this too shall pass. I just did what he needed at the time: I lay there on my back beside him and looked at the star that was probably the planet Venus and listened to him cry and talk. That's what he needed: just to be heard.

Was he serious about suicide? I don't know. Maybe. It's really hard to say what goes on inside the mind of someone. Curt looked stressed that summer of '91. He was carrying a load on his back that no thirteen-year-old kid should have to carry. I think we all did back then.

After several minutes of Curt crying and sniffling, he finally stopped. He had gotten it out like I had and that emotional release helped. "What about Mandy?"

"What about her?"

"The summer is winding down, man. Your window is closing every day," Curt asked as we both watched a shooting star rocket across the night sky.

"I know. I've got to get something going. I thought about riding by her house again, hoping to catch her outside. Maybe trying to talk to her or something. Try her again on the phone, but it seems she's never home or something. Even when I ride by there, there's no car in the driveway."

"I think you should do something. A girl like that only comes around once in a lifetime. She likes you, dude. She told me. The opportunity is there for you if you want it. You just gotta get up and go," Curt said.

I thought about what Curt had said. I had to do something, just anything, to get things going with her. I had been putting things off for so long that I guess I thought that things would just come to me. Doesn't work that way, and life is no romance novel where the love of your life just comes walking in and sweeps you off your feet. You have to go out there and actually work for it. I learned that nugget of infallible truth that summer.

If I was going to win the heart of Mandy, then I was going to have to be proactive. After some lengthy consideration, I finally was struck with a bolt of inspiration. "You know," I said, rising up feeling the bravest that I've ever been at that point in my young life. "You're right. Let's get out of here and ride to her house."

I don't know where that sudden blast of courage came from, but man, I was ready. Maybe it was sneaking into the pool at night, gazing up at the stars and feeling as if everything that I did was insignificant in the grand scheme of things. I don't know, but I had to hang onto whatever it was pushing me at the moment.

"Tonight? It's late," Curt said.

"Don't tell me about 'late.' We went to the water tower."

"I don't know, man."

"If I don't do something now, I'm going to regret it."

Curt looked at me, and he could tell that I was serious. "Then you should do it. Seize the night."

———

We left the swimming pool about thirty minutes after my and Curt's conversation through the front door, which wasn't such a bold move on our part. Back then alarms weren't in vogue, and just unlocking the door and walking right out didn't seem like a bad idea at all, seemed elementary. But Mike, yet again, made a decision and did like Nike and "just did it."

Mike unlocked the heavy metal door and walked out. We followed closely behind, keeping our eyes on sharp lookout for any passing cars or people. I made sure that no one from the homes on the other side of the street had any lights on with people standing and looking out the windows. So far we were good as gold.

We all quickly rushed around to the other side of the swimming pool, along the fence from where we climbed earlier, and took the ladder. We took the ladder with us across the park with Mike and Tommy carrying it. Me, Curt, and Pete crawled under the fence, and Mike and Tommy took the ladder and slid it under the opening. So far everything was perfect.

Cautiously, we walked down the dark street. Tommy and Mike carried the ladder and returned said ladder back to the side of the tool shed on Raper's tool building. No muss, no fuss. Things went off without a hitch—couldn't have planned it any better.

We all hurried back to Tommy's backyard and retrieved our bikes. I had told Tommy, Pete, and Mike about my plan, and off we went down the road, the five of us, heading to Mandy's home in the middle of the night. It was the craziest thing that I had ever done up to that point in my life, certainly the bravest. To be honest, it was one of those spur-of-the-moment things that was born out of fear of time slipping away. *Curt was right,* I thought as we rode slowly and quietly down the streets of our town. My window of opportunity was getting smaller, and I had to at least try something to win the girl.

We stopped at the crest of the street where she lived and looked down at its dark patches, where street lamps didn't shine from the overhanging tree limbs. Her house was not that far from where we stood, maybe a few houses down. I had memorized where her house sat and was pretty sure that I could find it with my eyes closed. "Well?" Pete asked, breaking the silence between the five of us.

"Well, what?" I asked, looking at him.

"What's next?"

"I don't know," I said, sitting on my bike. I had never done anything like that before. I had to think about what my next move was.

"You don't know?" Pete said. "We came all the way out here, sneaking around trying not to get caught by the law, and you don't know?!"

"Did you even have a plan before we came out here?" Mike quizzed.

I could tell that the guys were upset by my indecisiveness. Who could blame them? They supported me by riding the streets in the dead of night to help me go to the girl of my dreams' house. I had to do something, kind of forced to, at that point.

"Do I look like a kid that has a plan?" I asked them.

"If you don't come up with one, we're going to kick your ass," Tommy said.

I looked at the others, and they looked serious about it there in the darkness. I looked down the dark road and let out a deep, relieving breath. I started to pedal my bike and pulled away from my troop.

"Good luck," Curt said almost in a whisper but loud enough that I could hear him.

———

I coasted my bike down the street without having to pedal at all. The summer night wind kissed my face as the slight hill gained me speed. I was nervous—actually scared to death. There I was, going to the house of the one I loved in the dead of the night. But the closer I got to the two-story home that sat on the right, the faster my mind raced.

What was I going to do when I got there? What could I do in the dead of night? I had no idea, probably wouldn't know until I got there. One thing that I did know was that I was not going back up the street to face my friends without having done something. They would beat me down and perhaps shun me for the rest of the summer. I didn't want to lose face with them because I had already lost their respect when it came to Mandy. I had to earn it back—for them and more importantly, for me.

Coasting my bike to a stop in front of her house, I was going to earn their respect back; and at the same time, get Mandy's heart. I called it my "double-pronged attack," as I sat there in front of her house.

I looked at her house. It was all dark. All the lights were turned off except for the downstairs bathroom light. I knew that Mandy slept upstairs in the last bedroom on the left. I knew that because I had ridden my bike by her house a thousand times in the past and saw Mandy through the upstairs window from the street. I looked up at her window and of course, her light was off, just as the others were.

I looked around, making sure that the neighbors were not looking out their windows. Feeling somewhat safe, I got off my bike and laid it down carefully at their mailbox, and trod across the dewy, newly mown lawn. What was I going to do– go up there and ring the doorbell? No way. I had to do something different to get her attention.

Standing there by an oak tree and shielding myself from anyone who might see me, I looked over at the driveway and came up with a terrific idea. I looked around—checking to make sure things were clear—and darted over to the driveway to grab a handful of rocks, small ones. I had seen what I was about to do in a movie once, where the guy threw rocks at the love of his life's window to get her attention. It worked then. Should work now.

I stood out in her front yard and positioned myself there in front of her window. I tossed a rock, and it hit her window, making a clanging sound. I thought it was too loud myself, but nothing happened. Standing there waiting for her to emerge from the window, I tossed another smaller rock against the window about thirty seconds later, another loud clanging sound. Nothing. I was about to throw another rock, harder, when all of a sudden, her light came on, and her silhouette danced by the light through her curtains. It was her, finally, just like in the movies.

She opened her window and looked down at me, not knowing who I was, "Who's there?" she asked, frightened. This all felt like a movie I was in. It was like I was watching this unfold from a movie theater and not there in real life.

I couldn't believe that my rock-throwing worked like it did in those sappy love story films. I was dumbfounded, almost so much so that I didn't answer Mandy. Snapping back into reality, I cleared my throat and dashed away the butterflies that swarmed around in my stomach, "It's Matt. From school." *Why did I say from school*, I scolded myself there on the lawn.

"What are you doing here?" she asked with a loud whisper from her window confused. I could tell she was stunned by my actions. She sounded still asleep.

"You know, I really don't know. Um...so, how's it going?" I asked, not knowing exactly what to say to her now that I was face to face with her. I was trying to whisper but talk loud enough where she could hear me.

"Well," she began. "I've been sleeping lately." It was a sarcastic reply, and I could see that with the grin on her face through the darkness.

"Yeah, me too. Hey listen, I've got something to ask you, and I don't know how to ask you this but..." Before I could get out what I wanted to say, the downstairs lights came on, and her dad opened the door, wanting to know what was going on out in his yard.

"Who's there?!" he roared, walking outside in the night in his red robe. I started running back to my bike, nearly slipping in the wet yard. I had to get out of there as fast as I could.

I got on my bike but before I did, I looked back up at Mandy who was still leaning out her window, and shouted, "I love you!" as loudly as I possibly could. I had no idea if she heard me or not.

I pedaled my bike as fast as I could up the dark street while Mandy's dad stood in his robe, watching me flee the scene like a thief in the night. Man, I had done it, I really talked to her. I can't describe the euphoria that I had rushing through my veins as I pedaled my bike at top speed back up the street. I couldn't wait to tell the guys. I felt good about what I had done even if I nearly got caught by her dad. It was totally worth it.

CHAPTER 12

A TRIP TO GRANDMA DIXIE'S/A SECRET/POOL BRAWL '91

1

SEVERAL DAYS HAD ELAPSED after me and the guys snuck off to the park, and I went to Mandy's house that night. I felt like I had accomplished something; felt proud of finally talking to the girl that I dreamed about for so long. Even though it was outside on her lawn in the dead of night, and she was coming out of a deep sleep—it didn't matter. I had done it and was able to prove myself to my friends, and mostly, prove something to myself. They looked at me a little differently that night and during the next several days. It was like I had gone up a notch on their scorecards or something.

The night after I threw rocks at her window, I called her. Can you believe that? I most certainly did. But the phone just rang and rang. I called her house several times a day for days, and no one would answer the phone. The guys told me that she was probably away or something; I was calling when she was outside; or she and her dad was gone. Yeah, I guess that could've been the case. But deep down inside me, I was getting the feeling that she was looking at the caller ID each time the phone rang and decided to not take my call. This prompted me to ride by her house after the first day of unanswered calls.

I cruised by her house and, oh no, she wasn't home. The full-sized black F150 that I assumed was her dad's wasn't in the driveway. So I guess she was gone like the guys said. The next day I called and called and just like the days before– nothing but ringing. Again, I rode my bike down her street, and the black truck was still gone. Something didn't seem right. I would later find out what that was.

2

Later on that week, me and Tommy were together riding bikes at night around town. It was late, getting close to ten if my memory serves me right. The two of us had been hanging out most of the day together. It wasn't unusual for us to do that. Pete, Curt, and Mike had gone to Carl's Billiards Hall to shoot some stick. I wasn't about going in there, and neither was Tommy.

The last time Tommy was there, there were several people who wanted to fight him because they had heard how tough he was. It was a reputation Tommy had gotten, which was fair. Tommy could handle himself pretty good. He didn't like to fight and hated trouble. After that night at Carl's—where there was nearly a fight with some kid from a high school in another county—Tommy told us he was finished going in there.

It was not a place really for a kid, especially at night, but Carl didn't seem to mind much. As long as people were decent and didn't start any trouble he didn't mind for kids to come in there. For the most part, Carl ran a good place. But it wasn't a place that I liked going into. I had been a few times with Curt because he loved to shoot pool. I never much liked pool because I was never good at it. Curt was. He would play adults there and take their money sometimes through the thick cigarette smoke and country music on the juke.

Me and Tommy found ourselves on our bikes, riding around our small town with nothing much to do that night. I remember the summer night was sticky. It had been raining off and on that day, and the air was so moist that you could reach up and grab water. We had been down Barker Street, Slack Drive, and up around Winder Road. What we were doing was just passing time until the boys decided to leave the pool hall. But who knew how long that would be?

We didn't talk much riding through the night. I was still stinging from the death of my grandma and was thinking about her. I had been thinking about her a lot lately– thinking about everything at home, too, if I'm being honest. I had not been to my Grandma Dixie's house since she died. and that bothered me. I had talked to Dad about going there a couple of days ago, and he said what he usually said when I asked him to do something that he didn't want to do: "We will later on," he would always say. Taking me to my grandmother's house was one of those things that he said we'd do "later on".

I stopped my bike at the stop sign on Amhurst Street as Tommy rolled up beside me. "We've been everywhere. You ready to call it a night?"

I sat there and looked around at the night. Everything all around us was quiet. It usually was around ten except downtown where Carl's was. I looked up and could see all the night bugs swarming around the street-light. I wondered for a few aimless seconds how many bugs were flying up there. "No, I don't want to go back home."

"I would say we'd go to my house, but I don't want to go there either. You want to go hang out at the park?" Tommy asked.

I kept looking up at the night bugs flying quickly around the street-light, thinking really of nothing at all. When I answered Tommy, I was surprised at what came out of my mouth.

"No. I think I'd like to go to my grandma's house."

"For real?"

I took my eyes off the bugs and the streetlight and looked at my friend. "Yeah, I think I do."

"Where does she live...I mean, lived. Sorry."

"It's okay. I forget sometimes, too. About seven miles from here out in the country. It takes me and Dad ten minutes to drive. Probably take us a good twenty, twenty-five minutes to get there."

"Well," Tommy said after some silence between us, "let's go."

3

That night, the countryside was a tranquil bike ride that I have always remembered. You have moments in your life—profound events—that you never forget; either because they were so bad and traumatic, or they were so peaceful and serene. That night, when me and Tommy rode to my grandma's house, there was something in the air—a sense of being— not just in my mind, but as if I belonged to the wind, the moon, and the stars. There was this sense of self like I knew my place in the world at that precise moment in time. I wasn't thinking of anything pedaling on those country roads and being guided by nothing more than moonlight and memory. It was the most whole I had ever been in my life, and it happened at thirteen on a night ride to my dead Grandma Dixie's house.

We didn't meet any cars on those backroads that curved and switch-backed to straightaways. We didn't need flashlights as we went from our town and into the darkness of the country. The full moon above us, the Hay Moon, as the old timers called it that July, gave us enough. God, it was so big that night. I remember just coasting down the roads, not paying any mind at all to the roads we were on. My eyes were fixed on the full moon in front of us. The whole landscape around, as we rode to Grandma Dixie's that night, was washed in an eerie grayish-silver moonlight.

I remember looking at Tommy for a second, who was coasting beside me to my right, and he was awestruck at where we were. He had never been out this far on his bike before. Hell, neither had I until that night. I could see on his face that he was enthralled by the utter beauty of the country. He would look at the moon and then over at the woods and empty fields around us, bathed in that grayish-silver glow. For a moment in time, if just for a moment during that bike ride to my grandmother's house, I was at complete peace. There was no home life bothering me; Grandma Dixie's death wasn't in my head at all; and high school wasn't rattling around in there either. I think Tommy was too.

We didn't talk that entire bike ride to my grandmother's house. We didn't have to. Words would have tarnished that experience, I think. Sometimes, things are better left unsaid because we both knew—both were self-aware—at the ghostly world we were in at that moment. We never spoke about that bike ride to her house. I thought about it often growing up and even as an adult.

Sometimes, when I couldn't sleep or when the kids had me up all night sick, I would close my eyes, and my mind would be whisked away to that night me and Tommy took off to my dead grandma's house. My God, how lucky was I—both of us—to have experienced something so mundane yet magical at the same time? I'm sure that Tommy felt the same way I did and always looked back on that bike ride with nostalgia and a sense of peace, of belonging. I like to hope so.

4

We pulled into my grandmother's driveway, and there her house was. Her house was positioned some thirty yards or so off the country road. And what about neighbors? Her closest neighbors were acres away from her in any direction. I was sure that no one saw us coming down the road. I snuck a peek at my watch. I had to tilt the face of it toward the moon and could make out that the hands were on the ten and six. It was right at ten-thirty when we got to Grandma Dixie's home.

We rode our bikes up to her front porch and got off. I stood there in the front yard and looked around. The house was big, and the moonbeams seemed to bounce off the metal roof casting the home in a grayish-silver glow. Shadows painted the corners and recesses of the home's structure here and there as well as the yard. Tommy, I could tell, was a little bit scared.

"This is a big house," he managed to say.

"Yeah, it's bigger inside. If that makes any sense."

We stood for a few moments looking around. I wish that I could say what I was thinking at that moment, being back at my grandma's house. But I can't. I honestly don't know if I was even thinking anything at the moment. I was just there—along with Tommy—standing before the house and looking around as if I had never been there before in my life.

"So what are we going to do?" Tommy asked after a few minutes of silence between us.

"We could go in, I guess," I said.

"But it's got to be locked up, right?"

"She kept a key hidden," I said.

I broke myself free from where I was standing and walked slowly over to the front porch. Grandma Dixie was constantly locking herself out of her house, and Dad had told her that she needed to place a key somewhere to the front door just in case she did it again. The key to unlocking the front door was underneath a flower planter of petunias to the right of the door. I bent down, lifted the planter, and found the key she had put there.

I got the key and eased the flower planter back down. I looked at the purple flowers in the dirt, and they looked nearly dead in the moonlight.

"She'd freak out if she saw this," I said. "I'll water these as soon as we get inside." Tommy, who had walked up on the porch behind me, nodded. I stuck the key into the doorknob and turned it. The latch clicked. I gave the door a small push, and it opened.

———

It was dark as a tomb inside as we stepped in. That was scary, I remember. The smell of lavender hit the two of us like a tidal wave. She always made sure her house smelled good, and lavender-scented candles were her scent of choice. The smell nearly brought tears to my eyes because I was half expecting her to come into the living room from the kitchen and greet us.

"You think the power is still on?"

"I don't know," I said.

I ran my hand over the wall next to the front door, trying to find the light switch that I knew was there somewhere. Finally, I found it and flipped the switch. The lights came on stunning me and Tommy. I wasn't expecting that, by no means, but looking back on it, I guess her bill was still paid up for the month.

"Awesome," Tommy said.

"Yeah, but we can't keep them on just in case someone was to drive by and call the cops or my dad."

"How we going to see around here then?" Tommy asked.

"She had a few of those Coleman battery-powered lanterns in case it stormed and knocked the power out. I remember seeing them in the back bedroom the last time I was here."

The lanterns were exactly where I remembered them being in the back bedroom. There were three, but we picked up two and turned them on. They were really bright and gave us the sense that we were treasure hunters or something in a lost mummy tomb. Tommy had made such a reference, and it made me chuckle.

We walked around the house, me giving my friend the ten-cent tour of my Grandma Dixie's place. I showed him all the bedrooms, downstairs, and up on the second floor. We opened the attic hatch and pulled the ladder down to climb up. The attic had all kinds of neat things tucked away up there that had been forgotten for decades. We spent probably an hour up there rifling through old, dusty boxes, opening up drawers, and pulling the sheets off of other items. I even saw Dad's old baseball glove up there in a drawer with some old baseball cards from the sixties. The attic was a time capsule of sorts.

We went into the kitchen and opened up her cabinets. She still had some food left in them– nothing had expired as of yet. She hadn't been dead very long, and everything was still good. Even in the fridge, she had sandwich meat and cheese that was still good. Also, there was an unopened two-liter bottle of A&W root beer. I took all of that out and got a loaf of bread that was still soft from one of the cabinets and made us something to eat.

Tommy was wandering through Grandma Dixie's house with his lantern looking around. He walked into the den and found an old record player. He also spied the crate of old records beside it. Tommy placed the lantern down and thumbed through her collection of music. I was in the kitchen making us some sandwiches when I heard Sam Cooke's voice come softly through the still house. Sam was Grandma Dixie's favorite.

I remember being there, and she would be playing that record all the time. She told me hearing him made her think of when she was young, back in her forties. She and I would dance in the living room to various songs of his like, "Having a Party," and "Wonderful World." "Wonderful

World" was what was playing when Tommy dropped the needle. He came into the kitchen and sat down at the table. I slid his plate with the sandwich I made over to him as I handed him his glass of A&W. I took my sandwich and A&W and sat down across from him. With the two lanterns on the kitchen table, we sat there and ate in silence while Sam sang to us.

"You miss her, don't you?" Tommy asked, sipping on his second glass of A&W root beer later on through our late-night snack.

I sat back in my chair and looked around the kitchen. "Yeah, I do. It sucks, man. I really loved her. I mean...she um...she really made me feel good when I was around her. Much better than my own mother these days, that's for sure."

"I'm sorry, man. I really am," Tommy said.

"Why couldn't it have been my mom who died instead of her," I said rhetorically.

Tommy sat and looked at me and then down at his nearly gone ham and cheese sandwich. He didn't know what to say. I don't think there was anything to say, honestly. I had given that statement a lot of thought after she was buried and wondered why God took the good ones. Maybe he needed them for whatever reason. I don't know. Still don't.

"I still think about Grandma Dixie a lot, man. I wished that I could tell her how much I loved her."

"I think she knew," Tommy told me. "You guys were really close. I mean, you used to tell me that you and her would sit over in that living room there and watch the Braves play when you'd stay up here."

On the verge of crying, when Tommy said that, I smiled and the tears receded back into my eyes. Those were great memories. She taught me about baseball before my dad really did. "Yeah, she was a huge fan. We'd sit there and watch the game, eat some popcorn, and drink A&W. I was just up here not long ago and now...she's gone. I still can't believe it."

"What do you miss the most about her?" Tommy asked.

I sat and thought about his question for a bit as the Sam Cooke record spun on. "Everything. There wasn't just one single thing but a bunch. The way she laughed, her perfume, the jokes she told me, the stories she told me about when she was younger. She'd tell me stories about my grandfather. You see, he had died when I was born, so I never got a chance to know him. But she always made sure that I did through stories and pictures. She told me once that I looked just like him when he was a kid."

"How's your dad been taking it?"

I shrugged my shoulders, "With Dad, I never know. I don't think he's doing good with it all because now he doesn't have any parents left. He and Grandma Dixie were pretty close. And the stuff with Mom...Dad is just existing."

"So you two haven't talked about it?"

I shook my head, "Nah, not yet. I keep waiting, but...he's like a ghost. Stays at work most of the time. He does that to stay away from Mom. Do you know that he never has once asked me how I was handling this? Not once. It's like I don't count. My feelings don't matter. I might as well be a piece of furniture in that house. It's hard being someplace where you don't fit in or where you're not wanted."

Tommy shifted in his chair and stared at his glass of nearly gone A&W. "I know exactly how you feel about not fitting in."

"How would you know?" I asked, kind of irritated that he was trying to compare himself to me and my situation.

For a few minutes, Tommy said nothing as Sam Cooke continued to sing. I thought maybe I had made him upset by my tone, and maybe that was my intent. Finally, Tommy said something that changed everything. Not only for me but more importantly, for him.

"I know how you feel about not fitting in because I don't fit in... because I'm not like you, Curt, Pete, and Mike."

"What do you mean you're not like us?" I asked.

More pause in our conversation. I could tell that Tommy was struggling with something while sitting across from me in that lantern-lit kitchen at the table. I sat and leaned back on my chair, waiting for him to say something because to me he was making no sense.

Tommy cleared his throat, "I'm not like you guys...because I'm gay."

At first, I thought he was joking, and I was going to say something to the effect of, "Oh, we've known that for years." But I didn't. I could tell—better yet, sense—that Tommy was being sincere. It took a little bit for me to realize that Tommy was telling me a deep secret, one that he kept in a dark room away from all of us. When Tommy told me he was gay, his eyes never left his glass of A&W. I guess he was afraid of catching my eyes and seeing the absolute confusion in them. Or maybe he was afraid when he caught my eyes, there would be judgment in them.

"Are you fucking with me?" I asked, wanting to make sure that this wasn't a joke of his or something. Deep down, I knew it was not a joke, but for some reason, I needed some sort of shallow confirmation, I guess.

Tommy just kept his eyes on the glass of root beer and slowly shook his head, "No, man. I'm not fucking with you. I'm gay. I like dudes," he told me in a slow, quivering voice.

When Tommy told me again, that stunned feeling of when he first told me abated. This was real, and Tommy was telling me something that I doubted he had told anyone else. I didn't know what to say. Here was one of my best friends sitting with me in my dead grandma's kitchen telling me over ham and cheese sandwiches that he was gay. I was speechless.

A few more moments passed, and the Sam Cooke record finally went off. All was silent in the house and the two of us sat at the kitchen table in a state of wonderment; Tommy because he finally confessed something he probably never thought he would, and me having to take in what his secret. I didn't know, to be honest, what to say. The longer I sat there, sometimes looking over at him, the more questions that I had for him. But I didn't want to push the issue and keep asking him things. Thankfully, he broke the silence.

"Don't tell the rest of them. I don't want them to know. I'll never hear the end of it from Pete."

I nodded, "You're safe with me."

"I know," Tommy said. "That's why I told you and only you."

"How long have you known that you were gay?" I asked, clearing my throat beforehand. I wanted to talk about it and make Tommy feel comfortable at the table.

Tommy—seeming to consider my question for some time—looked up from the glass and caught my eyes.

"For a while now. I just don't have feelings for girls like I do guys. You know how you feel about Mandy? I feel that way about Connor McCord. I know he's not gay. But I really like him. And he's someone I'm never going to have. At least you have a chance at Mandy. It's frustrating for me sometimes because there's not any people that I know of around here that are like me."

"You're the only one that I know," I said dryly.

"Are you freaked out?" Tommy asked.

I considered his question for a few seconds and then shook my head, "No. I was shocked when you told me, but I'm not freaked out. Should I be?"

"I figured you, out of all of them, would be the most level-headed about this. Pete would harass me about it and wouldn't be my friend anymore. Curt would make a big deal about having a gay friend, and I'd hate that shit. Mike...I end up whipping his ass because you know how he'd be. So no, I don't think you should be freaked out. I'm still the same ol' Tommy. I just like dudes, that's the only difference...so are we okay?"

"Yeah, nothing has changed with me," I said.

I was thunderstruck that he felt safe enough with me to tell me something so big. In 1991, being gay around our town and in our school would not go over well, and Tommy knew that. I never had any inclination that he was gay. I still look back at that night at the kitchen table with honor because my friend—my brother—told me his secret. That in itself takes a lot of trust for someone to do, especially back then.

"Are we still friends?" he asked. I think there was a fraction of him—and who could blame him—that thought that I would turn on him. I was kind of hurt by him asking if we were okay and if we were still friends. But I knew sitting there that he had to ask.

"Yeah, man," I said. "Yeah, nothing has changed between us."

"Thanks," Tommy said lowly after some thoughtful silence between the two of us.

"Don't thank me. We're friends here. All the way to the end of the line," I told him. "So you're never going to tell the others?"

"No," Tommy quickly said. "Never, ever, in a million years."

"I won't either."

———

The rest of the night—up until about three that morning when we locked up and left—me and Tommy talked some more about his sexual preferences and about life and what lay ahead for the two of us. We didn't know it as we sat on my grandmother's living room floor playing Monopoly by lantern light, but some bad times were coming for the both of us in the future. When it's the future, you never know what is coming, what can change your life to its basic, fundamental core.

5

A couple of days later, it was Big Cat's last full day and night with us there in town. July was now in its twenties. We would all spend Big Cat's last day together. Actually, it was no different than any other day during the summer, but we said it out loud that we were going to do all this stuff for him to make it seem official or something. Mike was going to head back home and visit some more family that was scattered about the South before the summer died, and school was born. I hated seeing him go. I really did.

It seemed that when he left, it broke our rhythm. But Big Cat had reminded me that in a few short weeks, we would see each other every day since he was going to be going to the same high school as the rest of us. That was good news to hear, but I dreaded going to high school and began to fear the calendar even more than I had. Soon, July would flip over to August, and two weeks into it, school began again. I decided that I wasn't going to look at the calendar for the rest of summer break. I kept that vow.

6

I woke up and unlocked my bedroom door and walked down the hallway for breakfast. It was around ten-thirty that morning, and all the blinds were open, letting sunlight in. Mom was in the kitchen; it kind of scared me when I saw her at the counter making toast and coffee. She turned to me, smiled, and said good morning.

I replied in kind, hoping that this was going to be a good start to the day. She went over to the table with her toast and coffee and sat down while I rummaged through the cabinets for a box of cereal. Finding the Fruit Loops, I pulled a bowl from another cabinet, got a spoon from the drawer, got some milk from the fridge, and made myself breakfast. I was going to go back to my bedroom and eat, but I decided that I was going to chance it by sitting with Mom at the table.

"What do you have planned for today?" she asked.

With my mouth full of Fruit Loops, I said, "Maybe go to the pool. Mike's last day here in town, so we're going to all hang out and do stuff."

"So a normal summer day then?" She asked while giving a good-natured laugh.

It was nice to hear that coming from her honestly. I felt a little more at ease sitting there at the table. "Yeah, it is."

"Friends are an important part of life. I used to have friends growing up. We were like sisters."

"Where are they now?" I asked, spooning more cereal into my mouth.

Mom sat there and considered my question for a few moments. "I don't know exactly. When we graduated high school, everyone kinda went their separate ways. Stacy got pregnant in high school, so she couldn't hang out with us like she used to. I think she ended up moving to California with her husband. Carly went off to college in Ohio. Never saw her again. Then there was Emily, who I was closer to out of the group. She ended up getting a job right out of high school at a dentist's office as a receptionist somewhere in Knoxville, last I heard. Sometimes you think your friends will be there forever, and then you grow up and realize that's not the way the world works."

That was perhaps the most poignant thing I had ever heard my mom say. Sitting there, she knew exactly what I was going through in thinking about how high school was going to potentially demolish my friendships with my friends. Sitting there, she and I talked a little more that morning. It was a good conversation that covered friends, school, and even Mandy of all things. For a brief moment in time there at the kitchen table, it was like my mom was back—fully back—from the edge of the darkness that engulfed her mind. She wasn't the woman that I was scared of. She was the mom that I used to have.

I got up to wash my bowl out and put it in the dishwasher when mom —the mentally unstable mom—came back. It was like her brain had just switched channels. I turned, and she had this look on her face. It was a look I'd seen before. It looked scared and confused. I was just glad that she didn't have that sinister grin on her face. "I don't want to scare you," she started saying, "but I think your dad might be in the mafia. Might be why the FBI is watching this house."

7

We kicked off Mike's last day by meeting up like we always did at Curt's house. With a scant few dollars still between us from the ten-speed sale to Jason and some lawn mowing money I had made, we decided to go to the swimming pool since Mike had not been there during normal times of operation. We were going to give Big Cat a good send-off like we did every summer, but going to the swimming pool, I had other intentions. It was a dollar to get into the pool and between us the five of us had five bucks. Most of it was in change.

I was hoping that I would run into Mandy there. Maybe she had gotten back from wherever and decided to hit the pool. On that last day of Mike's visit, I didn't call or even ride by her house. It wasn't that I had forgotten her, rather just tabled it until Mike left. If she was back in town, there was a huge possibility that she would be at the pool with her friends, and I would just happen to run into her by accident. That was if I didn't lose my confidence which I was prone to do.

We walked to the swimming pool, the five of us, and paid our dollar to get in legally. We walked out from underneath the roof of the entrance and into the bright sunlight that bounced off the water and wet concrete. They were kids all over swimming and splashing and having just a good old time. A lot of kids, mostly girls, sat sunbathing on the perimeter of the pool along the fence in Adirondack chairs.

I stood and scanned the area for Mandy while the guys got down to their swimming trunks. She wasn't there, but I was hopeful. I walked over and sat down on a bench by myself while the guys scattered about; Curt and Pete climbed to the high dive board and started acting a fool while Tommy and Mike ran across the concrete and jumped into the water, splashing water everywhere while getting a whistle blown at them by Stewart, the lifeguard that looked a little like Pauly Shore from MTV.

The guys being whistled was nothing out of the ordinary there because Tommy was at least warned several times a year about proper swimming pool behavior. I was surprised that he was even allowed back in after the beatdown he'd given out earlier in the summer. Maybe having Tommy around was good for business—maybe everyone felt safer knowing that Tommy was there because of his bully-beater reputation. I certainly did.

I sat there on the bench with my Braves hat on, watching all the kids play and laugh and enjoy the bright and sunny day. I was sitting alone with my thoughts and waiting for Mandy to walk by. I kept thinking I heard her behind me several times. When I would turn, pulling my heart out of my stomach, I discovered that it was not her. All those girls that sounded like Mandy were false alarms.

I had a new confidence about talking to her. At least I thought I did. I still couldn't believe that I rode to her house in the dark of night to tell her that I loved her. I wondered if she had heard me scream that as I rode off down the road. I hoped so.

———

Summer break was growing closer and closer to an end. The time for me to make my move had to be near. I had to pull off something daring, something like the night I went to her home. All I needed was for her to show up at the pool, and I could make my move. At least, that's what I planned. I was going all in. High school was closing in, little by little, and my window was shrinking. There were still several weeks before school started up again, but I couldn't waste any more time messing around. The summer, at least to me, had already rocketed by so quickly, I didn't see it flying by. I couldn't believe that it was already late July.

Before I could think of anything else, she walked past me completely out of nowhere with Courtney and Jennifer, gently tapping my shoulder as she walked by. I was utterly stricken by her, and my heart went upwards into my throat to the point I nearly choked. God, she was the most beautiful girl I had ever seen. I always thought that about her ever since I first laid eyes on her. Just her touch propelled all my senses into a complete frenzy. I couldn't believe it– she touched me and she was here at the pool. *My God,* I thought to myself, *what am I going to do?* I remember getting goosebumps on my arms.

I was stunned, taken completely out of my depth there by the pool. She had touched me. I sat there and watched her and her friends sit down alongside the fence. They took off their shirts and shorts, and suddenly, they were in their bathing suits. I didn't notice anyone else at that time. A bomb could have gone off there, and I wouldn't have known it. My eyes were locked on her and her alone. She looked at me looking at her. Our eyes locked from across the way. It was magical; that romantic stare was so magnetic between us.

My heart raced and was beating so hard that I could feel it banging against my chest and throughout my ears. I even recall trembling a bit. Across the way from me, in the light of day, was the girl that I had loved for so long and thought about for what seemed to be forever– forever, only if you measure in terms of time.

It had been about fifteen or twenty minutes since she and her friends had come into the pool. I tried to look around at other parts of the pool and other people as well, but my gaze always returned to her. I would catch Mandy looking at me from across the way. To be a kid in love is the craziest thing. First loves usually are; nothing ever quite like it on this earth, and nothing really matches it.

I wanted to go over there and start talking to her, confess my everlasting love for her; tell her that I have loved her for so long and the mere thought of us never being together would crush my heart and soul. That maddening confidence that I had earlier had gotten up and left, disappeared without a trace, and I was back to my old self again: nervous and scared.

A mutual friend of ours from school came over to sit with me dripping wet, Roger Bream. He started talking to me, catching up on what I had been doing over the summer. It was all small talk, and I was not really paying any attention at all. I kept my eyes looking over at Mandy. I heard Roger and laughed when he made funny observations about some of the kids there at the pool, but my mind was on Mandy.

I wanted to go over there and say something– I really did. Running into her at the pool was the whole reason I came there in the first place. It certainly was not for the water. Roger got up and wished me well in high school, and I told him that I'd see him later. I had decided while Roger talked on and on about nothing important at all that I was going to get up off the bench and go over there and talk to her. I was going to have to dig really deep within myself to do it, though. Some of that confidence was returning.

Finding my friends splashing about the pool laughing and whatnot, I got up from the bench and started toward the girls—not thinking about it, just doing it. I had to clear my mind because if I didn't, I would talk myself out of it. Talking myself out of stuff was the reason I would never talk to Mandy to begin with.

Actually, it was the reason for a lot of things. I never took chances really—was always afraid of things not working out like I'd want them to. So what would I do? I wouldn't dare take a chance. Looking back, there were so many opportunities that I never took because I talked myself out of doing anything. And it wasn't confined to the summer of 1991, but for a long time and even into my older years. Getting in my way was the worst thing I ever did. Sometimes you are your own worst enemy.

So, trance-like, I began walking toward her, not giving my brain a chance to stop me. I caught her eyes looking at me again. For that single moment in time, it was as if time itself ceased to exist, leaving only me and her left in the world. Our eyes met, and my heart began to melt like an ice cube in the sun. There she was, waiting on me. She smiled. That made me smile. For an instant, I thought things would be okay. For the first time, I thought that I was going to be okay and actually win one for a change and not get in my own way.

Before I could take another step towards my girl, I was broken out of my trance by a familiar voice. "Well...well...well." That gruff-sounding voice belonged to none other than Mark Pike, the kid who pushed me into the swimming pool earlier in the summer. I was not afraid of him, especially after I saw Tommy cash his lights out that day. I suppose it was watching him get the holy hell beaten out of him that stripped his intimidating stature from my eyes. I had not seen him since that day he pushed me into the water.

To me, he was just another prick bully who thought he could muscle his way through life without having to pay a toll. But I've learned we all have to pay a toll at some point. Sometimes it's a lot, and sometimes it's not. I was done paying a toll of fear to this guy.

"What's up?" I asked, hoping that he had turned over a new leaf as I turned around to face him.

"I got my ass whipped because of you a while back," Mark said, standing in front of me.

"Do you really want that again?" I asked, hoping that warning would be enough to scare him away. I snuck a quick glance over to the other side of the pool where Tommy was floating on his back. Of course, with all bullies, they are hard of hearing and stupid I've discovered over the years.

"I got backup this time," Mark pointed over to the right, and there was Tony. I had two of the biggest bullies in my town gunning for me. Tony was there for unfinished business from that day in Curt's yard when Todd whipped his ass. And Mark was just there to settle a score.

"You're dead," Mark told me as he grabbed me by my throat. Now, I was not a fighter, not by no means, but I'm going to tell you one thing: I was tired of the bullies. I was tired of being punked out all the time. For an instant, I wanted to be Tommy. For an instant, I wanted to beat Mark down as Tommy had earlier in the summer. But in the end, I wasn't

Tommy. I didn't have that intangible thing that set him apart from the guys that just took it.

Feeling all eyes on me there at the pool, especially Mandy's, I took my fingers and poked Mark's eyes. He shot back in pain and held his eyes with his hands doubled over. It was the only recourse that I had– the only thing that came to mind as my fight or flight sense kicked in. *One down*, I told myself. I jabbed him good, so good that I felt the watery parts of the eyes with the tips of my fingers. I thought for an instant that I had blinded the bastard. I hoped I had.

Before I could locate Tony and feel the rush of bringing a bully nearly to his knees, I felt a fist clock me across the face from the right. That meaty fist belonged to Tony. I fell to the wet concrete, dazed and seeing stars. God, it hurt so badly that I was hearing ringing in my ears. Then, I felt another hit to the face and then another. Tony hit me so hard that my face was numb. I felt him hitting me but didn't at the same time. The numbness helped. I only felt pressure when he would hit me. His fists came fast, and they came down hard against my jaw, head, and mouth. I was dazed, nearly completely out of it. Blood was beginning to pour from me.

Mark, with his eyes streaming with tears and squinting, leaned in and picked me up by my shirt and spit in my face and head-butted me on the nose– blood everywhere. I fell back down onto the concrete, and the two of them started stomping me there beside the fence with everyone watching, backing up and giving us space. I was a dead man, and all that I could manage to do was let them punish me.

Emerging from the water came my friends. Or so I was told. Mike was first out as he literally jumped on top of Tony, driving him down to the concrete face first. It was an even match between Mike and Tony because they were about the same size and girth. Plus, the advantage went to Mike because he was an avid wrestling fan. One time, out in my backyard, he put me in this leg lock that nearly broke both my ankles. He loved trying to use those wrestling moves that he saw on TV on us guys.

Tommy was next out of the water. He saw what was going on, and he slung his fist into Mark's ear, causing Mark to fall where I was lying. Tommy started stomping him like he did that day earlier in the summer.

It was complete bedlam there at the swimming pool. Stewart, the lifeguard who looked like Pauly Shore, crawled down off his perch and tried to intervene. No use, Tony and Mike pushed him back, sending him backpedaling into the water. There was no way the fight was going to be stopped. Everyone had stopped swimming and sunbathing and stood there watching it all unfold, cheering it on.

I rolled away from the ruckus and lay there face down on the concrete bleeding. I needed to get to my feet and fend for myself. I finally stood up on my two feet, with the help of the chain-linked fence that I was lying next to, and saw that Mark was getting an edge on Tommy.

I put my hand on Mark's shoulder from behind and spun him around and punched him as hard as I could. I think I knocked several of those black teeth out as Mark fell to his knees with blood pouring from his mouth. I lowered myself to face him, "This stops today, you got that!?" I managed to scream at him. I was tired of the bullies—tired of all the bullshit that came with them. I was washed over with rage out there at the pool. Adrenaline coursed throughout my body, keeping me up on my feet—otherwise, I would have fallen.

I don't know what exactly came over me. I just saw red. I then went over and grabbed Tony by his red hair and punched him several times as hard as I could in the back of the head. I fell down, Mike backed off. I got on top of Big Red, rolled him over, and put my hands around his throat. I squeezed as hard as I could until I saw his face turn blue. I wanted to choke the life out of that kid, and I was.

Seeing me spin out of control like I was, Pete and Curt rushed over there and tried to pry me off of Tony. It was no use, the two of them could not do it. Eventually, it took Tommy, Mike, Curt, and Pete to get me away. I had been pushed to the edge by those guys, and I was not going to take it anymore, especially not in front of Mandy.

As I was pulled away, kicking and screaming and cussing toward the exit, I saw Ricky and Todd come out of nowhere and start stomping on Mark and Tony. They were getting their licks in, too. Whatever was left of the two bullies, Ricky and Todd finished them off. *Good for them,* I thought later.

The police were called to the pool. Before we could get out of the gravel parking lot, a patrol car pulled up, and Officer Walker got out to see what was going on. He started with me first because I was bloodied and still trying to get back in there at them, with Tommy and Mike holding me back. I had taken most of the beating and by looks alone, it was me that Walker focused in on.

Officer Walker calmed me down and talked to me and the guys about what happened out front of the swimming pool next to his patrol car. I honestly thought I was going to jail, but Officer Walker knew all of us and knew that we weren't hell raisers, unlike Mark and Tony who were lying on the concrete being stomped by Ricky and Todd at that very moment.

Walker was cool about the whole thing and told us to go on our way and to stay away from the pool for a while. Now, if this sort of thing had happened in these days and times, let me tell you something, I wouldn't have been able to go home. I'd been in jail. Things weren't as serious back then as they appear to be now.

Officer Walker went inside and broke up the beatdown that Ricky and Todd were giving. Nothing ever legally came about the brawl at the pool.

That day was the last time I was ever at the swimming pool. We found out on the last day the swimming pool was open for the summer that we were banned. Usually, on the last day, two days before school reopened for the season, me and the guys would go there and hang out; you know, usual stuff. But we got checked at the door that day in August by Stewart: persona non grata.

"No way, dudes! Go on, get outta here. You guys are banned. No more." Stewart told us at the entrance to the pool.

"What the hell for?" Pete asked.

"Because every time you guys are here, something happens. You guys are bad for business."

That was the only consequence we had. I could live with that. I couldn't swim any damn way.

———

I never had any more trouble or problems with Mark later that summer, or what was left of it. Sure, I'd get stares from him from time to time when I got into high school. But nothing ever really came of it. By the time we hit sophomore year, Mark was a relic of the past. He had dropped out of school and out of mind. Good riddance. He and Tommy did, however, have some good fights. I never heard what became of him. I'd guess that he ended up like the white trash piece of shit he was as a kid. People like that hardly change for the better. They just grow up to be worse. Young pricks become old pricks.

Now, Tony, that was a different story altogether. He would for years always bark at me, looking as if he wanted to jump me. But he knew better. He knew that I had snapped that day at the swimming pool. The only thing that Tony could do was look at me and blow words past me. All that bully became after that day at the pool was a complete joke to me and others as well.

We still had immense tension between us, but nothing really ever came out of it. He, just as Mark Pike had done, dropped out of high school. I had heard he'd been in and out of jail most of the latter part of his teenage years and early twenties. Eventually, Tony was in a car accident where he was drunk behind the wheel. He flipped his car several times on an old country road in my hometown. He lived, but he lived as a paraplegic. I have no idea if he's even alive now. Don't really care. Serves him right.

Me and the guys converged back on Curt's front porch later to celebrate our victory. Curt's mom was cooking out and had invited all of us to eat. His dad was off to wherever. His mom didn't say much to us that day, I remember. She had already started drinking but not full-on as usual. She hadn't drunk enough to get lit up yet. I stayed my distance of course.

Curt had pulled me to the side of the house when we had all gotten there and told me that his dad and mom were fighting when he got home from the pool after we all had gone back to our houses to get a change of clothes. I asked what about.

"I don't exactly know," Curt said. "All I know is that I could hear them all the way out in the yard. I go into the house, and they are up in each other's faces, screaming. I couldn't really make it out or what it was about. But Dad said that he wanted a divorce."

I stood there and soaked in what Curt had told me. He looked worried and relieved at the same time. I think he just wanted some peace in this whole situation– whatever that entailed. Before I could say something else to my friend, Mike came over holding a Coke can and singing "Home Sweet Home" from Motley Crue. Me and Curt would discuss the matter later on.

We sat there on the front porch, which was huge and wrapped around the entire house, and ate freshly cooked hamburgers and hotdogs from the grill. We could not stop talking about the fight. Mike recounted his version, Tommy his version, and me, my version. Curt and Pete chimed in with theirs as well. The funny thing was that each of us had a different take on what happened. But no matter how differently the stories were told, no one could change the fact that we beat the bullies— slew the dragons, if you will. We felt like men sitting on that porch eating that day.

As we sat there, the pool closed for the day, and the swimmers and sunbathers all walked by Curt's house while we sat on the front porch. Those kids cheered and offered congratulations for us beating the bullies down and giving them a good show. We waved back to them like we were in a parade or something. For a little while, we were rock stars.

I was about to get up from the porch swing and go get another hot dog when I heard a voice so sweet, so heartbreaking that it could be none other than Mandy's. I turned around, and there she was: standing on the side of the street in front of Curt's house with her two friends.

"Come over here for a second," she directed, pointing at me.

Before I could allow the butterflies to take flight in my stomach, I stepped off the porch and walked across the grass toward her.

"Hey," I said, chewing what was left of my hot dog and nervously adjusting my Braves baseball cap. I couldn't chew like I wanted to because my jaw was hurting like hell. I thought for days that it was broken. But it turned out just bruised, much like my blackened eye.

"That was some show you put on back there," Mandy said.

"Thanks. I hate those guys," I said, not knowing exactly what to say.

"I'm glad you guys whipped them. They're jerks," Courtney said from behind Mandy.

"I was coming over there to talk to you when they started on me."

"I know. What was it you were going to ask?" Mandy quizzed, smiling.

"I forget. I got hit so hard that I don't remember," I said, rubbing my head laughing. The girls laughed too. That was a good sign. I did remember. But felt it better to be coy about it.

"I told the girls about you coming to the house the other night," Mandy said.

"That was so romantic," Jennifer said. "I wish Jeremy was like that."

"Yeah, I hope I didn't make your dad mad."

"You did, but that's okay. He'll totally get over it. Or he won't. It's whatever."

"I tried to call you the last few nights," I said, standing there as my friends sat on the porch eating and watching me.

"Yeah, I had to go stay with my aunt Julie because Dad had to go to South Carolina on some business thing. He didn't want me home alone, especially since that night you were at the house. He thought you might be crazy or something." We all laughed at that.

"Listen, are you doing anything tonight?" I asked, not knowing where my sudden boldness came from. Maybe it was the concussion talking for me. Mandy looked at her friends and then back at me.

"Nothing, why?" she replied with a smile.

"You think you might want to hang out with me later? Mike over there is going back home tomorrow, and we were going to all hang out with him over here at Curt's. I'd love it if you could come. Just to hang out, you know. Nothing major."

Mandy thought about it for a second, "Yeah, sounds cool. What time?"

"About eight-thirty. Before it gets dark," I replied.

"I'll tell my dad that I'm going over to Jennifer's, and I'll walk over here."

"I don't want you to have to walk," I said, feeling bad that I was not of age to drive yet.

"It's okay. I walk from the pool to home, anyway. It's not that far. What, like less than a mile? Yeah, I'll see you tonight then, okay? I'll meet you here," she said as she and her girls walked away.

I stood there on the side of the street and watched them walk away. Before Mandy got out of sight up the road, she turned and waved goodbye to me. I returned.

Standing there in a trance, still mystified by her speech, the guys started to make fun of me over on the porch.

"Oh Mandy," Tommy started. "I love you so much!" Everyone got a good laugh and squealed like girls as they mocked me. I was not offended though. My dream of having Mandy was almost a reality. I couldn't believe it, and neither could the guys. Maybe the summer was looking up.

CHAPTER 13

BIG CAT'S LAST NIGHT

1

IT WAS GETTING close to my date with Mandy. It was my first ever date and I wanted to impress her. I dressed in my cool clothes: shorts and a tropical buttoned-up shirt with my trusty Braves hat that was faded beyond comprehension. I wanted to make sure that I looked good for her. I stared into a newly bought mirror Dad had gotten for me which I hung in my room on the wall.

For over an hour, I tried on different shirts and shorts mixing the combinations, seeing what looked the best. I bet I spent nearly two hours prepping. Before I left my house, I checked my teeth, my breath, and most of all my deodorant and cologne. I thought I looked good and was hoping that Mandy would feel the same.

I was about to open the back door and walk out of my house when my mother came out of her bedroom in her robe. Her hair was all a mess. And it looked like she had been crying. I stopped and stared at her for a minute, wishing that she was better—wishing that she was the mom I remembered back when I was little. Hell, just earlier that morning when she had that moment of clarity. By the looks of her, she was on another mental break. It was only brief.

"What are you up to this evening?" she asked in a voice that I hadn't heard since Grandma Dixie's funeral. It was the voice of my sane mother. I was stunned by it.

"Just going over to Curt's to hang out with the guys," I replied, taking my hand off the door knob.

Mom went over to the kitchen table and sat down in a chair. "I can't believe my boy is going to be in high school soon," she said.

"Yeah," I replied standing there at the back door. "Yeah, I'm gearing up. Not much longer."

"I remember me and your dad walking you to your first day of kindergarten," Mom smiled, recalling that day in her head. "God, time goes by so fast. You remember when you were little you and I used to do those find-a-word puzzles, and we'd race to see who could complete theirs first. If you won, you got to stay up late."

I grinned and did remember that. God, it was a long time ago—before the mental problems became so demonstrative in our home.

"Yeah, I remember those nights. I remember you winning most of the time." We both laughed.

Man, it felt good doing it again. There for a moment in time—just like earlier that morning while I ate my Fruit Loops—it was like she was my mom again; like she had found her way out of the darkness of her mental illness or at the very least, was trying to. Maybe she was.

Mom got up from the chair and came over to me and did something that she hadn't done in years: she hugged me. I hugged her back and wanted to cry. I mean, the tears were at the ready. She pulled me away from her and looked at me smiling. It was a great moment between me and my mother.

That was until she said, "Now I want you to be careful out there tonight. They are watching us. They've been watching me for a long time, and now I think they're watching you, too." She leaned in and whispered in my left ear, "I think they're hiding in the attic, but I can't find them. I even checked the closets. But I believe your dad is hiding them here. I don't trust that man anymore. I think he's one of them."

That broke the magical moment between me and my mom. She

leaned back still looking at me, her arms on my shoulders now. I wanted to cry now because I knew that she would never come back from where she was. My mom was gone, lost to the darkness that had consumed her brain. There was help out there—I knew there was because there had been before—but she was so far down the road, that there was no turning back for her. Each day she slipped a little further down beyond that point of no return.

2

It was cloudy, kind of overcast, around eight that evening as I arrived at Curt's. The gang was all there ready to do our annual Vampire Watching/Sending Mike Back Home party from his backyard. Allow me to elaborate on this...

Curt had a really odd neighbor. I mean this guy stuck out like a sore thumb in the neighborhood of nicely mown lawns and well-manicured homes. In a neighborhood like we lived in if you were the least bit eccentric, people would notice and talk. And trust me, we had a lot of people that liked to talk. It wasn't just regulated to the old retired people in our neighborhood. It was the young ones, too.

The house that the suspected vampire dwelled in was a run-down two-story looking in need of dire repair. And the yard? Grass somehow didn't grow on that lot, front or back. It was just dirt. Dad told me years ago, long before I can remember, that the house and the lot it sat on were the nicest in the neighborhood. That was before the Colemans died, and the state took their place.

The house sat empty for years but the yard—when there was still grass—was taken care of by neighbors like my dad and others around the neighborhood. The house represented us as a neighborhood as a whole. Keeping the yard up was the right thing to do. Besides, if the house had gone to pot, property values in our hood would have gone down, Dad told me.

We first noticed the guy who moved into the house some years ago. I think we were in the fifth grade when he moved in. We knew something was strange when he arrived in town. The house that he bought was a benchmark for what homes in that neighborhood should look like. But when the alleged vamp bought the house, he let it go into a state of decay over the years. It didn't take long for the home to fall apart. That within itself was suspicious.

Everyone in the neighborhood wondered who the guy was, what he was about, and why he let such a wonderful, pleasant-looking house go to waste. However, no one that I knew of had ever talked to the man nor seen him about his place. He was a complete conundrum, a ghost.

One night, the guys and I were at Curt's playing night football. We had this Nerf neon orange football, and you were supposed to be able to see it in the dark. We could, but only a little bit. Most times we couldn't catch the damn thing, and if we did, it was luck. Mostly the football just hit us in the face and bounced to the ground.

Anyways, there we were out there playing in his enormous backyard when all of a sudden we heard this ear-piercing scream come from that spooky house that sat on the backside of Curt's property. We all stopped playing and looked at each other.

"Did you hear that?" I asked, looking at them and over at the house.

"Yeah, something came from that house," Pete said walking toward the house from the yard.

"What could that have been?" Curt asked the rest of us as we followed Pete cautiously.

"Sounded like a woman or something. Maybe a cat?" Tommy replied.

It did sound like a woman. I had watched enough horror movies to know when a woman screams that it isn't good. We walked over to a row of tall standing bushes that separated his house and Curt's. We all four crouched down and observed the place.

Nothing stirred for about ten minutes, and then the front door opened, and out came the dude who owned the house, carrying something over his shoulder. Now when I say this, understand that it was dark, and my vision was impaired by the bushes; but I, along with my friends, could have sworn that it was a body that he was carrying over his shoulder wrapped in plastic.

It looked like it, I'm telling you. As an adult, you tend to look back on things that you saw as a kid and think how stupid you were. But not this. Even as a full-grown man, I still think about that night in particular and cannot resolve what it was that we all had seen. If I had to swear on a Bible, it would say that it looked like a body that he was carrying.

Frightened to death and not believing what our eyes were showing us, the creepy guy opened his car's trunk, placed whatever it was he was carrying inside it, and slammed it shut. He then got into his car, backed out of the driveway, and headed off down the road.

That was just one instance with the guy. Of course, we all debated what it was that he was actually carrying, but there was no mistaking that he had something or someone in that trunk. Before that, a woman had screamed. Our young minds put two and two together and deduced that he must have killed that woman, put her in the trunk, and driven off someplace to dispose of her corpse. We had no proof of that. But there were things over the months that ensued that caused us to think that the guy was a vampire.

First, the man never came out during the day, never. The only time that you saw the creature of the night was, well, at night. Even then, you couldn't make out what he looked like as he got into his total black Toyota SUV and drove away, only to return before the sun came up the next morning. Seeing the man in the daylight? Forget about it. It never happened.

I never really got a good look at him, and I don't think anyone else in our neighborhood really did either. The vibe that I had gotten from our neighborhood was that he was a guy to stay away from. Suffice it to say, we never trick-or-treated him on Halloween. The neighborhood dads, mine included, had paid the guy a visit to get to know him since he was new to the neighborhood.

They would knock on the front door, and never once did the man ever open it. And this happened a lot. Eventually, they stopped trying and just kept an eye out. The consensus was that the house was a place to steer clear of. And everyone in the neighborhood did. One of the funny things was that no one had seen the man move into the house. No moving vans, no nothing. If he did move his stuff in, then he did it under the cover of night. Also, there was no electricity to the house. Never did a light come on there.

Secondly, there used to be a lot of dogs and cats in the neighborhood. After the guy moved in, we started noticing that the animals seemed to disappear, such as domesticated pets. It was like the animals vanished into thin air—even the dogs that were on tie-outs and in kennels had disappeared without a trace in our neighborhood. We noticed it, brought it up one night during a campout, and talked about it. The only resolution that we could draw was that the guy in the spooky house had taken them for some sort of ritual.

Thirdly, we watched one night while he moved something that looked like a casket into his basement! No lie, we all four witnessed it. With those three things, we tagged him as a vampire, a good ol' honest-to-God neighborhood vampire. And it was up to us to monitor him and take action, if necessary.

Of course, for some reason, we never were afraid of the guy. You would think that with all the stuff that we had seen over the years, we would be too scared to roam the streets and yards at night, especially late at night. We weren't and my only explanation for that is maybe, just maybe, we didn't believe he was a vampire like we held true. It could be that the things we might have seen were just our imaginations. The casket? Nah, that was real. We all saw it. But then again, we all witnessed the thing he was carrying over his shoulder that night too.

There was an off chance that we might've been wrong about the guy entirely. That thinking didn't stop us from having our annual "Watching the Vampire Night." If anything, it was always fun sitting there by that long line of thick bushes, watching a house, and waiting for something weird to happen—which sometimes it did. But sometimes it was quiet, too.

As an adult, I don't really honestly think he was a vampire. I don't believe in things like that. With that being said, I cannot put to rest the things that we had seen or had noticed. He may not have been a creature of the night, but he was something strange. Now, I think he might have been a serial killer. That's more plausible than a vampire, wouldn't you think?

As I grew up over the years I kept a check on the house. By the time me and my friends had moved away, so did the guy in the house some twelve years later, I was told. There was still no moving van or any signs that the man was gone. Honestly, he could've still been living there, and no one would really even know because no one saw him during the day. But the black Toyota SUV never returned. That was the key piece of evidence that he had left.

The last time that I was down that way, in the old neighborhood just to drive the streets I used to ride my bike on, the house was still there falling apart. Brown and green grass grew tall and sprawling here and there on the property. Windows had been busted out, maybe from kids or limbs from years of storms. It looked as if no one lived there and had not in decades. I still remember the house back in its glory days when my dad and the others from the neighborhood kept it up before the suspected vampire moved in.

3

The last couple of years on Mike's last night in town, nothing had occurred on our watch. I wasn't really anticipating anything happening that night because Mandy was coming over to see me. I couldn't care less if the guy was a vampire or a serial killer or whatever that night. I mean, this guy could have turned into a bat and flown over our heads, and I wouldn't have taken my eyes off Mandy. My thoughts were about her and her alone.

When I got to Curt's, Mandy was already there with the guys. They were all laughing and having a good time out in the yard as the sun was dipping into the east. Curt had a small campfire going in the same spot where we conducted our Dew Bashes, and Pete was roasting marshmallows over the fire. Tommy and Mandy were standing around the fire talking about trivial things in life like what was high school going to be like and such. Mike was off to the side and had his boom box out there that had one of my favorite bands in the world, R.E.M. playing my favorite song, "Losing My Religion".

That song had been played on the radio everywhere that summer, and I bought the cassette tape when the entire album came out. There was just something about that song that resonated with me back then, like there was an innocence about it. As I grew older, becoming a man, a husband, and a father, that song is still with me, and it takes me back to that summer of 1991 every time I listen to it. It's like portable magic.

I walked over to the fire, and Mandy saw me approaching, "You're going to tell me that I got here before you did, and you live a rock's throw from here?" Mandy joked.

"I had to make sure that I looked okay," I replied, looking into her eyes. She had the most beautiful eyes I had ever seen on a girl. I could get lost in them. If I did, that would be fine by me.

There we were, the two of us, standing by a campfire, speechless. The nervousness that I had over her for so long had long gone. No telling where those feelings went. But I was glad that they were vanquished. Finally.

"You look fine, don't worry," Mandy said.

"Listen, can I tell you something?" I asked, about to open my heart to her.

Just before I was about to start talking, Pete got the leg of his shorts on fire by the campfire, and he screamed out wildly, breaking everyone out of what they were doing. Pete ran around with his shorts on fire and me, Tommy, Curt, and Mike rushed over there and jumped on him, rolling him around the dewy grass. Yeah, we almost broke his ribs when we all dog-piled on him to extinguish the fire. The important thing was that the fire was put out, and his leg was saved. Years later, Pete couldn't grow hair on that side of his leg.

———

After that incident with the fire, we all repaired to the row of bushes and sat looking through the millions of small limbs, trying to see the creepy old house that the suspected vampire lived in. Mandy was new to all of it, and we filled her in on what had been happening since he moved in: our theories, and that we thought he may be a vampire. A long shot, but still plausible at the time.

I could tell that Mandy didn't know what to make of us out there. She would later admit to me that she thought we were all crazy, but she liked that kind of stuff. She said it was like being on an adventure. It kind of was now that I think back on it.

The night marched on, and all of us talked and laughed while we staked out the house from our plastic lawn chairs. Nothing to that point had happened at the home; didn't really expect it to but then hey, you never knew. Mike looked at me, mouthed something, and nodded his head to the side. He wanted to talk to me in private. He and I got up and walked away from the guys and Mandy.

"Why don't you and Mandy go ahead and leave, dude? Go somewhere instead of around a bunch of guys."

"What? No, this is your night, man. We ain't going to see you for like a year," I said.

"We'll see each other in a few weeks. Remember? We'll all be going to the same high school," Mike reminded me.

Of course, how could I have forgotten? I was so used to not seeing him for a full calendar year that my response was an automatic reaction to it.

"I don't want to leave, dude."

"Listen, you're okay. I'm cool with it. I understand this is your chance to talk to Mandy, finally. I want you to do this. Leave and go to the park or something. Just get her alone and tell her how you feel. Or you can sit here with a bunch of dudes. Your choice." Mike told me, smiling. "And if you sit here with us, I'm going to make fun of your ass forever."

I laughed to myself as I knew he'd never let me hear the end of it. "You sure? I don't want you to think I'm skipping out on you," I told him.

Mike knew that I would never put a girl over lifelong friends; that should've gone without saying. But I spoke it anyway.

"You're not. You got this awesome girl over there waiting on you. You can't talk about feelings with her with all of us around. You know we'll start making fun of you when you do." And he was right, they would. I stood there and looked at the Big Cat there in the darkness. Then, just as we did every time just before he got into his dad's car and left for the summer, we hugged like brothers.

"See you at school," I said to him as I gave him one good last look.

He smiled back at me and winked. "Yeah."

4

Me and Mandy left the backyard and walked down the road to the park in the darkness. We crawled under the fence that me and the guys crawled under all the time, and we walked hand-in-hand across the swarthy, lonely park, and over to the baseball field. Holding her hand was nerve-racking, to say the least. But I did it like I had been doing with her forever. Halfway to where we were going it felt normal, felt right. Most of all, it felt as if it belonged there—my hand holding hers.

Off to the right, sat an old bench facing the baseball field on the first base side. I used to sit there many times by myself to ponder everything and anything that my mind issued out. I had seen Mandy sit there earlier in the summer and thought about how significant it was to see the girl of my dreams sitting on the same bench where I wondered about the world.

There we were, the two of us, about to talk deeply for the very first time. You couldn't ask for a better scene for the two of us. The clouds from the overcast sky had cleared and the moon and stars began to show themselves off in brilliant, sparkling white light that twinkled off miles away from where we were. It was the perfect summer night. I don't think I had one like that afterward. In fact, I know that I didn't.

We both sat there, holding hands. I never in my wildest dreams thought I would end up there with Mandy, never in a million years. I always hoped and prayed for that to happen, but I never thought it would. I always thought I would be disappointed and never be with the girl I thought was my soul mate.

"It's pretty out here tonight," Mandy said, looking around up at the stars that shimmered like diamonds.

"Yeah, I come here just to be alone sometimes. Clear my head. It's always quiet. Good place to think, you know?" I was trying to figure out what else to say to her, to keep the conversation going when she spoke.

"I thought that you coming to the house the other night was so cool. Nobody has ever done that before. I mean, I've read about stuff like in books and watched it in movies, but never had it happen to me," Mandy said, tightening her grip on my hand.

"I had to. Look… Mandy," I turned to face her. I was going to tell her everything that I had been feeling since the first time I saw her. I had so much that I wanted to tell her. Where was I even to begin?

"Since the first time you showed up at school, I liked you…a lot. I don't know what you call it, fate, maybe? But I knew as soon as I saw you that I liked you. I know that might sound crazy, maybe even stalker-like, but I've wanted to tell you for so long how I feel. I can't believe that we're here right now. There's so many things that I want to tell you, that I don't know where to begin."

"You've liked me all this time and never said anything?" Mandy asked as if she was hurt.

"Yeah. I could never get the nerve up to talk to you. I mean, I talked about you so much to the guys that they got tired of hearing me because they knew I wouldn't ever do anything about it. But the other night, I felt like I needed you to know. I guess what I'm trying to say is that I like you with everything I got. And I know that we really don't know each other at all. And I know that all of this might sound crazy, but that is the truth."

Mandy sat there, looking as if she was going to cry. She had never heard anyone talk to her like that before, she told me. "You had my heart the day you sat down at your desk in Mrs. Vogol's class," I finally admitted.

Those words just came rolling out of my mouth before my mind had a chance to stop them. But they were honest, those words—as honest as a kid can be at my age, confessing his innermost thoughts to the girl of his dreams.

God, it was so good to finally get that off my chest. That in and of itself was a win for me. Hell, the whole night up to that point was a win for me. I had been carrying all of that on me for so long, it was like a weight had been lifted off of me. Mandy sat there, clutching my hand tightly. She began to cry a bit looking off into the distance, keeping her face turned away from mine. She did not want me to see her weep.

We sat for a few moments looking around in the darkness, and then she spoke, pulling her hand away from mine and wiping her tears away, "I'm leaving tomorrow."

My heart sank into the pit of my stomach. I thought that I was going to throw up. Had I heard her right?

"Leave? What do you mean?" I asked, afraid of what leaving entailed. My heart fell into my stomach like I was going downhill on a rollercoaster.

"My dad is taking this new job in South Carolina. He called me earlier before I came to Curt's. I guess his trip went good. We're supposed to drive down there and try to find a place to live. He wants us out of here by the end of the week. That's why he was in South Carolina. I had no idea he was thinking about taking a job down there. But I guess we're going to be living down there now. Not that I want to."

Now I wanted to cry. The girl of my dreams, the girl that I lost sleep over, the girl that I finally got the nerve up to talk to was going to live miles and miles away from me. It wasn't fair. Life wasn't fair. The whole summer had been a case study of unfairness from Mom going off the rails, to nearly getting kidnapped, to Grandma Dixie's death, and now this.

"You can't leave," I muttered, not to her but to myself. But she heard it, no way she didn't.

"I know. It's not fair," Mandy said, wiping the tears from her eyes. "I don't want to go. I don't want to leave my friends. And now you."

My whole world was crumbling down. A while ago, I was on top of the world. But at that moment, sitting there under the stars, I was in hell. Everything that I thought was going to happen between us was in dire straits. It hurt, it sucked, and it wasn't right. How could this happen? To get so close but be so far away.

"This sucks," I said after some more considerable silence. That was all I could say at the time. What else was there to say really? The pain was too much.

"I think you're awesome, though. And I could see myself being with you for the rest of my life," Mandy said.

You say things like that when you are thirteen years old, meaning every word. I think we all have made bold proclamations at some point during that age. Being out there in the darkness, just the two of us, she meant that statement. I felt it deep inside.

When you're young, words are the most powerful weapons you have. They build and destroy, conquer and surrender, and hate and love. When you're young, words possess a certain mystical power. And when they're spoken by kids who are in love, the magic of those measured words is a force of the incalculable, oftentimes unbeknownst to those who wield them.

Moments passed—silent moments—before I spoke to her. "I have dreamed about you so many times that I lost count. I don't know how I can go on without you now that I know how you feel," I said, feeling my mind being scattered about.

I was feeling at that point the worst I had ever felt in my life. I had everything in the palm of my hand and it was slipping away. I just kept thinking that it wasn't fair, not at all.

"I'm sorry. This isn't how I wanted things to be. I kind of knew that you liked me last year, I just wished you would have said something back then. I really liked you, too," Mandy said, still crying softly. That's what I get for waiting, I guess. I missed out on being with her.

Mandy's crying was a mixture of everything, not just me. She was crying because she didn't want to move away. This town was supposed to be her forever home. They had moved here after her mother died, and she and her dad needed a fresh start. It was hard for her to live in the same house where they all lived as a happy nuclear family. They had managed it for about a year– she told me later on a few weeks down the road– but the absence of Shannon, her mom, was too great.

I had laid it on the line to her, opened my heart, and exposed my feelings toward her, and all I got in return was that she felt the same way and that she was moving away—didn't seem right, not right at all. It seemed sitting there under the stars that night, the universe was laughing at me as if it had just played the cruelest joke. I felt numb.

I needed to try to stop the emotional bleeding somehow. There had to be something that we could do. I refused to believe that after all of this, it was going to be just over. I couldn't wrap my head around that notion.

"What do we do about this?" I asked, hoping to salvage what we seemed to have. It was a thin question, but it needed to be asked.

There was a long pause between us.

Finally, she said, "We can make it work somehow. We can promise to call each other every day and write, and we can visit each other during school breaks if our parents will let us. I think that I can talk my dad into that at least. Maybe," Mandy suggested.

Could that work? Keep in mind, this was before cell phones, texting, the internet, email, and all of that. It could have worked...maybe...but with us being only thirteen, could we make that kind of commitment? That kind of long-distance devotion to the other? No. I can safely answer that one as difficult as it was sitting there beside her, desperately wanting her forever. I knew better to make nighttime promises that would melt in the sunlight.

"That's not going to work," I said lowly and defeated after some thought.

"Yes, it can. We can make it work. If we love each other strong enough we can make it work." she said, turning to look at me with those sad green eyes.

I wanted to say that was a good idea, but I knew better. It would never work—long-distance stuff never worked. I think we both knew that, but Mandy wanted to hold on to that magic that we had between the two of us. And I wanted to hang onto it just as much if not more than she did. I never wanted to let her go now that I had her. But what could I do? I was just a kid at the end of the day who really wasn't in charge of my life whatsoever.

Her dad was leaving to take a new job, and Mandy had to go with him. We were just thirteen-year-old kids in love. No matter how much love there is, when you're young, you're at the mercy of the adults who still control your life. It's not fair, but that's how things are and will forever be.

We sat there quietly beside each other, looking about the darkness, watching shadows race across and dance throughout the landscape. There were so many things that ran throughout our minds that when I was going to say something, the thought would elude me only to be replaced with something else. I couldn't manage to hang on to anything, not one thought in particular. All there was was pain. *It wasn't fair*, I kept thinking.

Mandy was the same way, I'm sure. Fate had dealt us a horrible hand, and there was nothing we could do about it. We were just stupid kids in love. And what did that get you? Nothing but a broken heart.

I was going to say something to her, but before I did, she leaned in and kissed me. It was my first kiss and hers as well. I still remember it fondly, and it was the kiss that I measured all others against after Mandy. We kissed passionately, not like teenagers, but like two kindred souls knowing that our time was drawing to a close.

It was such a wonderful feeling; nothing that I thought it would be. I didn't really know if I was even doing it right, and she didn't either, she confessed later. But it didn't matter. We were doing it out of passion and love. It was the best kiss I ever had in my life. The first cut is always the deepest.

I got lost with her there in the darkness on that bench. I had never felt that way before and knew that if I ever lost her, my life would fall apart. I know I was only thirteen years old and had a lot to learn about the world in front of me, but nothing at that moment in time could tell me any different. I loved her, no matter how young I was. Love is love.

As we kissed under the stars that night, I could feel her love, and I never wanted to let her go. I had gone through so much emotionally just to get her, and now she was telling me that she was having to go away.

I couldn't stop kissing her. I didn't want it to end. I wished that we could stay like that forever, but I knew there had to be an end sometime. It was the most heartbreaking moment of my life at the time, but at the same time, the most exhilarating. I wouldn't have traded that kiss for anything in the whole world that night under the stars.

5

Later that night, I walked her to Jennifer's after we left the park. We held hands the entire way. We talked about how cool it would have been if we had the whole summer to spend with each other. It would have been great, we both decided. I missed a huge opportunity with her, and I knew that and took full responsibility for it. God, the things we could've done. It would have been sublime.

We paced ourselves slowly on the way back to Jennifer's house, getting to know each other a little better under the streetlights we walked under on the sidewalks. With every step that we took, the realization set in that eventually we were going to make it to her friend's house. And from there, I was going to have to let her go for good.

It was going to be hard, and I didn't know if I could do it to tell you the truth—didn't want to let her go. I mean, how in the hell do you let go of something just when you got it? I can tell you that I had the biggest lump in my throat on that long walk to and from her friend's house that night.

I wanted to walk that walk for eternity, holding her soft hand the whole way there. How fair was it to finally get something only to have it taken from you within twenty-four hours? It wasn't. But I blame myself. Perhaps the fates, too.

I was mad as hell and heartbroken all at the same time. Things were changing, no matter how Tommy spun it. Things were going to change, and there wasn't anything I could do about it. Me losing Mandy as quickly as I got her was evidence of that. Why couldn't I have spoken up sooner to her? Why didn't I just go up to her when I first met her, take her by the hand, and show her how I felt? Then I realized that only happens in the movies. But what I did at her house the other night was in the movies, too, but I managed to do that, right?

Of course, I know that wouldn't have changed anything. Her dad would still get that new job in South Carolina, no matter what I did in the past. It was as if the future was already written, and I wasn't able to do anything about it but stand there and watch as my life fell apart. Actors in a play called "Life" are what we are: acting the parts, saying the lines, and not knowing what the next page of the script is, but we are characters in this play, make no mistake.

———

Finally, we made it to Jennifer's home. We both stood out there on the sidewalk and held hands looking at each other. Neither one of us wanted to let go. But one of us had to make the first move. As it pained me, I slowly took my hands from hers and put them in my back pockets.

I can't really describe what happened there between us that night on the sidewalk. There were no words uttered; didn't need to be, I guess. She knew how I felt, and I knew how she felt. Words would just get in the way at that moment. We stood facing each other, close, and gazed into each other's eyes that summer night.

I leaned in and kissed her on her soft lips. Afterward, we hugged.

"I'll try to see you tomorrow, okay?" she whispered in my ear, hugging me tightly.

I just nodded. I was about to cry. Those butterflies that had vanished were back in earnest, swarming around in my stomach and making me feel like I was going to throw up.

"Good night," I told her as I gently pulled away from her. "Before I go," I reached up and took my Braves hat off my head and gave it to her. "I want you to have this. You might want to wash it though. A little sweaty." We both smiled through the tears.

Mandy, with tears in her eyes, smiled. She took the hat and held it in her small hands. I gave her one good last look as I turned and started back down the walkway.

"I love you!" Mandy shouted in the night.

I turned, still walking backward facing her with my hands plunged into my pockets, "Love you, too!" I smiled, but it only hid the pain.

———

I must have walked the streets of my small town for hours, trying to make sense of everything that had happened. I couldn't make sense of it.

God, it made no sense to me. I just remember walking around everywhere in town. Not thinking of one thing in particular but everything at the same time.

I wanted to scream out loudly for the whole world to hear. But what would that accomplish? I was still going to feel that immense pain in my heart. I thought earlier that night that things would be okay, that maybe Tommy was right that things wouldn't change. But he was wrong. Things had already changed: I had changed. Everything was changing around me, damn it. I wanted to run away; just run in one direction and never look back. Run away from the pain of Mandy; run away from the pain of seeing my mother; run away from high school; run away from Dad never being home; run away from Grandma Dixie's memory and the pain it still held; run away from it all.

I wanted to run away and disappear to never be heard from again. I wanted things right. I wanted my mom to be normal again, not the emotional rollercoaster she had become.

I wanted my dad to snap out of his funk due to Grandma Dixie's death, talk to me again, and show up at home to deal with Mom.

I wanted to never have to go to high school and worry about if me and my friends were still going to be friends at the end of it.

I wanted my grandma back from the dead.

I wanted that guy who chased me earlier in the summer to die because I probably wasn't the first kid he tried to snatch.

I wanted Mandy because I didn't think our story should be ending right as it got started.

I remember standing under a streetlight crying and wishing that I was dead; then wishing that things would be normal for me and that I would get a win. Just a win was all I needed. Just a win. Just one.

———

I had finally made it to Curt's house, and I knew that he and the rest of the guys would want the scoop on what happened with Mandy. I really thought about going back to my house and crashing into the confines of my own bedroom. But I could use those crazy guys to put my back up against. That was the one constant thing about our gang...we could always rely on each other.

I needed something, anything to take the edge off. I opened the front door to Curt's house, which was always unlocked, and went inside. His mother was gone to parts unknown, and his dad hadn't come back yet. It was dimly lit inside, and I knew the house so well that I felt my way around the living room and up the stairs. Before I opened Curt's bedroom door, I closed my eyes and tried to gather myself. The last thing that I wanted to do was break down there in front of my friends. I opened the door and saw them sitting like they always did: usual positions.

"Well?" Curt asked. I just shook my head and lay down on his bed next to Tommy.

"That good, huh?" Tommy asked, seeing that things had gone sideways.

"She's moving with her dad to South Carolina. She'll be gone by the end of the week," I said looking up at the ceiling and feeling my eyes well up with tears.

"Moving? No way, man," Curt said, not believing what I just said.

I rose on the bed and looked at my brood, "Yeah. I told her how I felt, we kissed, I walked her to Jennier's, and that's it," I summarized.

"I can't believe it. How does she feel about you?" Pete asked, pausing his *Mike Tyson's Punch-Out* game.

"The same way I feel about her. She said that she liked me for a while. God, this ain't fair," I said crying for the loss that devastated me.

I broke down there in front of them, something that I told myself I wouldn't do. I couldn't help it. The thought of her never being around me was like a stake being driven through my heart. The guys just sat there and looked down at the floor. They didn't know what to say, and I did not expect them to. They just let me be.

I guess everything that I was feeling over the last several weeks had finally come to a head. The only thing I knew to do was just cry. What words could they offer me to make me feel better? There weren't any. I was alone even though I had the support of my friends.

Everything that night hurt—hurt badly—and the only thing that I could think about was what I was going to do now that the girl that I loved was leaving. That seemed to be the cherry on top of the summer. Things felt weird; seemed like everything was a dream that had been going on that summer. And if it was a dream I couldn't wait to wake up. Mandy was gone out of my life forever, and I had the task of putting my life back together at the young age of thirteen.

CHAPTER 14
THE DAY AFTER

1

I COULDN'T SLEEP that night after learning that Mandy was leaving. We both knew how the other felt. I had waited for years to hear her say it and years to tell her what was in my soul. All that waiting, all that build-up, all those sleepless nights, those future plans, everything was shot to hell. Life has a funny way of sucking sometimes. Nothing you can do about it but work with what you got.

How could her dad be leaving, I asked myself still in disbelief hours after I left Mandy standing in front of Jennifer's house. If there was ever a crossroads in my life up to that point, it was right there. At thirteen, it was the biggest crossroads of my young life. I didn't know what else to do. There was nothing that I could do, really, but just take it. Sit back and just take it.

2

That next day, I was tired; had not slept at all. I stayed up all night, questioning everything under the sun. The summer had turned into a period of my life that I was ready to forget, lock away in a trunk to never see again. The beginning of summer had promise and had something pure about it when it first started, even if there were ominous things off on the horizon. But events happened during the summer that caused that promise to turn into nothing but dust in the wind.

I was disappointed in what happened. I could've just as easily laid in bed for the rest of summer and woke up to go to my first day of high school. I had no desire to face the world as a kid of thirteen. I was as empty as a kid could be at that point in time. Never did I feel more lost than I did the night after leaving Mandy in front of Jennifer's house.

3

I did my normal home routine at home that next day: ate cereal, watched some cartoons, got out of my pajamas, and walked out of the house. I wasn't hassled by my Mom and her mental illness. My life was falling apart, and nobody in that house seemed to care. Why would they? They both had their problems to deal with, and their child who suffered a massive broken heart wasn't something that they wanted to deal with, or in Mom's case, could deal with. I walked outside into the sunshine and took a long look around the neighborhood. Things looked and felt the same as they always did. Me? I didn't feel the same. I didn't know if I ever would.

I stood out there on my back porch and watched as a group of kids walked by the house on the street going to the pool for the day—a lot of foot traffic on our street due to that pool on those summer days. Deciding that I needed some interaction of some kind, I got on my bike and went over to Curt's house where all the guys sat on the front porch laughing and talking.

They saw me pull up into the yard from the street and they shut up quickly. No doubt they were discussing my problem. "

"What's up?" I asked as I put my bike down in the yard and leaped upon the porch to sit beside Pete.

"How you doing?" Pete asked for everyone.

I looked around at the street in front of us and then off in the distance down the road, "Fine, I guess."

"We're sorry that things didn't turn out right, dude," Curt said. "But at least you knew how she felt, and you told her how you felt. I couldn't have done something like that."

The guys all agreed. They were just making me feel better about finally getting the courage up to tell her how I felt. I appreciated that gesture, really.

"Doesn't matter though. She's leaving," I said, still staring off into space as cars passed on the street early that afternoon.

There was that moment of awkward silence between us there on the porch. I wasn't much for talking, but I did come there for some support. It wasn't fair for me to drag them down into my own despair.

"You guys want to go play baseball?" I suggested, shattering the silence.

4

We went to the baseball field and played our usual game of sandlot rules baseball. I was pitching to Pete, Tommy was in the outfield, and Curt was in the infield, in case grounders hit around the vicinity of second and first. If the past held true, the kids that finished swimming would leave the pool and walk over to where we were to play with us. And only then would we have enough to play a real game. But until then, we made do with what we had and still had fun.

The later the afternoon progressed, the more kids joined our game and the hotter it got. It was not very long before we had enough to divide into two teams and play baseball. I had been pitching the entire day, and I will be honest with you: Mandy didn't weigh on my mind as much as I thought she would.

The game took my mind off her. But Mandy's memory was still there, leaving her fingerprints all over my mind. Having to be busy doing something made it much easier for me to cope, at least for that time out there on the baseball field. I was getting ready to take the mound against the team we made from all the kids from the swimming pool and was ready to have the best game of my life. I was going to dedicate it to Mandy—dedicate it to the summer that was going to be lost forever.

I toed the worn-out pitching rubber on the mound and looked at the batter. I reached up to tug at the bill of my Braves hat and realized that I didn't have it anymore. It was with Mandy. I took a deep breath at that realization and ran my fingers through my sweaty hair. I stepped back with my right leg and was about to kick and fire when all of a sudden, Pete yelled loudly at me from shortstop breaking my focus. I turned around to see what was going on.

He pointed down the first base side of the field and when I turned to see what it was, I saw what stopped the game from getting underway: Mandy was standing at the fence watching, wearing my Braves hat. I looked at Pete who motioned for me to go over there. I was hesitant. I didn't really want to talk to her anymore. It would hurt too much.

It was going to hurt talking to her one last time. I thought last night was a clean break, but her coming back to say whatever she had to say was going to drive me even darker. I didn't want to talk to her, but how could I not?

I stepped off the mound, much to the cussing and booing of the opposing team and even some on my team. They had no idea what I was doing. *I* didn't even know what I was doing, to tell you the truth. But when I saw her, I couldn't resist. Even if she was walking away from me forever, I had to go over there and hear her voice one last time —smell her honeysuckle hair, and look into those deep, entrancing eyes.

I walked over there to her, and she was all smiles. *How could she be smiling at a time like this*, I questioned myself as I stood before her with the fence separating us.

"Do you still feel the same way you did last night?" she asked, seeming like she was holding something back from me.

I stood there in front of her dumbfounded by her question. "Of course, why wouldn't I?" I responded to the stupid question. I had felt that way for years, not just last night.

"My dad decided after a long talk between us that the job wasn't worth taking me away from my friends and school. He said he was too old to start over after he had given it more thought, and it wasn't fair for me to have to leave a place that I loved." Mandy said with a huge smile.

My heart sank deeply into the pit of my stomach. Had things

changed that quickly? "You're staying?" I asked cautiously, wanting to hear the word yes.

She nodded, smiled, and then threw her arms around me across the waist-high fence, "Yes, I'm staying!" she screamed loudly. I threw my baseball glove off my left hand and flung my arms around her. I hugged her tightly, and then we kissed. The guys out on the baseball field were giving us catcalls and mocking us and even some were cussing for holding up the game. They didn't understand.

Forgetting all about the game, I leaped across the three-foot high fence and got beside her. We walked hand-in-hand away from the ball field and went down to the lower part of the park, to the center where park benches sat underneath the tall pine trees casting out ample shade from the summer sun.

"Where the hell is he going?" a kid who was ready to bat against me asked, watching the two of us leave.

"He's going with his girlfriend." I heard Curt say. I turned to look at him, and he had a huge grin on his face. I smiled back.

CHAPTER 15
THE BEGINNING/THE MIDDLE/THE END

1

I HAD GOTTEN the girl of my dreams during that summer. Never in a million years did I think that it would ever happen. I dreamed about it, talked about it, and thought about it so much that it literally consumed me in every respect of the word. But there I was, with Mandy Fields. The guys were happy as hell for me too. I had proven them all wrong, but to hear them tell it, they each knew I'd eventually get her. Yeah, right.

Mandy and I spent the rest of the summer of 1991 together, hanging out with each other. We hung around the guys, too, and had a ball, but she and I also had our private times. Eventually, I met her dad in the fall of 1991, who I clicked with instantly because he and I had an affinity for baseball. We even went to a few Braves games later the next summer.

Mandy and I would go on to lose our virginity to each other that following summer in '92 at the end of our freshman year of high school in her bedroom while her dad was away on business. God, I was so nervous. So was she. But it was fine after we got going. I never forgot how she felt in my arms that night. It was like our first kiss out at the park; I never forgot that either.

I told Mandy about my parents when she asked about them later that summer just before high school. I told her the real and the raw and that I would never ask her to my house. It just wasn't a good place to be. So we never went. My mom and dad never met her which was sad because Mandy was great. All Dad knew was that I had a girlfriend, and that was about the extent of it. I kept my life private from him. Mom? She was too out of it to understand. I wished that I could have shared my happiness with them, but I knew that I could never. Both were in their own worlds, bedeviled.

Going out of the summer of 1991 and into the rank and file of high school, things were glaringly different, just as I thought and feared they would be, for not only me and the guys, but for Mandy and me.

2

Our romance had lasted and blossomed for three years, almost well past our junior year of high school. We just ran out of gas you could say, and neither one of us wanted to refuel and go more miles. Things had happened between us; things were said and done that couldn't be repaired. Those kinds of things happen when you're young and growing in the spring of your life.

The bridges that we had crossed together for nearly four years were burned, never to be walked over ever again. It was sad when it was over, but everything has to end, no matter how good or bad. I guess if things didn't end badly, they wouldn't end at all. Very rarely do things end well.

High school had eventually divided the two of us. I thought that we would make it out alive with our relationship still intact—maybe even stronger—than before we went in. But that was completely hopeful thinking on my part. There were so many changes that occurred in those nearly four years. What it came down to was that we outgrew each other. How do you like that? I outgrew the girl of my dreams. However, she had outgrown me too.

We were thirteen-year-old starry-eyed kids in love in 1991, and when 1994 came, that love that I always thought would burn as brightly as the sun was retreating, waning into the recesses of darkness and cold. I learned that there was nothing quite like young love. I also discovered there's nothing like a young breakup either.

I loved her, but not like I had back when I first saw her in those years in school. Mandy would later confess to me that she, too, had lost that spark she had for me back in '91. Do I blame her? Absolutely not. We were kids treading on things that even adults in their midlife can't grasp and fully understand. Who really understands love? If adults can't, what chance do kids have? Zero. Nobody told me that love only gets more complicated as you grow.

Our relationship crashing and burning was a causality of high school, just as I feared long ago. If anything, I lay the blame on life. People change; there is no getting around that, especially when you're young and still have years to grow, years to change, and years to form different opinions that contradict the ones that you used to have. During the years that Mandy and I were together, we grew, but unfortunately, we grew apart.

Had I known back in '91 how things would have ended up, I would have spared myself the heartache and total depression and just loved her from a safe distance as I had. But who knew the future? I had gotten way too close to the sun, and my wax wings had melted, sending me into a complete freefall. Grief is eventually the price that you pay for love.

I cannot go to a certain point in our relationship where things spun out of control and decayed. It happened over time, and I guess I ignored the writing on the wall. She did as well, I guess. Things like getting part-time jobs, playing sports, friend influences, family obligations, school, and the greatest backbreaker of all, the opposite sex, were all stressors that proved too much for us to handle. High school is hell, don't let anyone tell you any different. It emotionally robs you while you're watching it happen.

We were still kids trying to figure out life and everything there was to know about it. So much got in our way, and the more that we were apart, the more that we ventured off by ourselves. It had gotten to where she and I were hardly ever together and when we were, things seemed forced, like we were different people. It wasn't organic like before. Things were wilting between us in those high school years. It's hard to explain love when you're sixteen and seventeen years old, and it gets only more complicated as you get older. Don't let them lie to you about that.

Like a guest that had stayed too long, it was finally time to leave. I remember sitting in my car with her the night that things had finally gone down. It was Spring Break that junior year for us at high school, and the two of us had barely seen each other that entire week due to work and other obligations. We had barely talked on the phone. Things couldn't keep going the way they had been, and I knew it. She did, too. We both were waiting for the other to say it, to say things were finished. Neither she nor I could bring ourselves to do it over the last several months. We both limped across the finish line.

I recall the night in question when the end came. I remember that it was drizzling outside, and the windows in my car were fogged up pretty good there in her dad's driveway. We had been to a movie that night and things seemed to go well. But it also seemed fake, like she was withholding something from me. Maybe I was, too. Matter of fact, I was, if I'm being honest.

I cannot fault her for that because I was the same way. A normal teenage couple would have split when things began to get weird, but not us. We had a history, and that had given us a false sense of security. We had become complacent, ignoring the signs that our relationship had run its course.

We sat in my car for a while, awkwardly talking about things going on at work and such. I remember OMD's, "So In Love" was playing lowly on the radio. But it was only background noise, seeming to set the tone for what we both knew was about to be said. The end was coming, or maybe it had already been there, like a cancer growing in the dark. Either way, we both knew the jig was up.

It was all stall tactics, sitting in my car and small-talking our way through the impending doom of our relationship. I was hoping that the night would just end as they all had: with a kiss goodbye, a "see you later," and a "love you." I guess I was hoping that I could, or she would put our last goodbye until the next time we met—just stall it until we couldn't anymore.

We were past that, way past that. We hit that bump of silence once again in my car, like we had many times in recent times. There was nothing to say anymore, and the things that we had in common back then when our relationship was new and vibrant had gone into an entirely new direction. We were different people.

"Mandy," I asked, never forgetting what I said to her in my car on that rainy night. "This ain't working anymore, is it?" I asked her, already knowing the answer.

I wanted to hear her say it. Mandy sat there and tried to look through the foggy windows hoping that I wouldn't see the tears flow from her eyes. But I saw them. I had them too.

"No," she said as her voice cracked.

I never forgot that sound of her voice cracking. There was pain in that crack. It hurt her to reply. It hurt me to hear it. In that car, I felt as if someone had stabbed me with a pitchfork in the gut. I was hurting badly. It was coming to an end, and even though we both knew it, it still hurt like hell. No matter how much love you have for someone when the end comes, it hurts and hurts badly.

The two of us sat there for almost an hour just thinking to ourselves, not uttering one single word. What was there left to say? Mandy and I both knew that it was over, down for the count, and nothing was going to change that.

Like I said earlier, too many things had happened, and too much was said over the scope of our relationship for there to be any hope for a future. We had things like jealousies that ran all over the two of us. She thought I liked this girl Amber in my Chemistry lab, and I thought she was in love with this baseball player named Max. Maybe there was some truth to both accounts. But we never did anything out of the way to hurt the other. We stayed together through all of that and most of all, faithful.

The girl of my dreams for as long as I could recall was slipping away into the night. I hated seeing it happen, but it was for the best.

"I still love you," Mandy said to me with her eyes bloodshot and stinging.

"I know," I replied, feeling that she still loved me, but was not in love with me any longer. "I still love you. I can't change that."

"It's not like it used to be, is it?" Mandy asked, knowing the answer because she felt the same as me.

"No. I wish that we never grew up. I wish that we could've stayed like we were back in '91," I told her.

That was the truth of the matter. Back then, she was my everything, my every thought, my entire world but as we had gotten older, and high school came into the picture, things were not the same. The innocence that we had back then had been stolen and replaced with something else that neither of us could define. All we knew for sure was that something was off. What it was exactly we didn't know– couldn't find the origins.

We kissed one last time and said our goodbyes to each other promising that we would remain friends. But that never happens, does it? Mandy and I parted ways on that rainy night. I thought about her for months and dropped fifteen pounds because I had no interest in eating anymore.

After we broke up, depression had set in, and I wondered why. I had disconnected myself from her in the relationship long ago, but for some reason it finally being over had done something to me. Eventually, I was able to shake it and get back to where I was mentally. I was never truly the same after Mandy and her memory remained with me well into adulthood. She made such an imprint upon me that I never forgot her and our times together, both good and bad.

We'd see each other in the hallways at school after the breakup and smile and wave. It hurt me as it did her. I didn't see her during the summer break before that August that started our senior year of high school. By then, her absence was somewhat easier to manage. It wasn't that I had forgotten her, but rather got used to the fact she wasn't in my life. As I'm certain she did. She and I had moved on like kids our age often do—with a brisk step toward the future and whatever it held. She had a new boyfriend and me with a new girlfriend the next time we saw each other at that first football home game. It was okay. She was doing good, and so was I. We never hated each other, nor did we speak badly of the other. Things were all good between us. That's the best you can hope for.

Some people come into your life, and you can forget and move on. Then some come in, and for whatever reason, their memory stays long after they have left. It's those people that are the most important. Hold them in your memory and heart for as long as you can because it's those memories that will keep you warm on your coldest nights.

I heard that she had done well for herself later on after high school. Mandy had gotten married, had two children, and after graduating from Duke University, became a doctor, practicing nearby where I live now in Claxton. Good for her. I always knew that she would do well for herself. The last time I ever saw Mandy Fields was walking across the graduation stage to accept her diploma. She was beautiful in her cap and gown. But I don't remember her like that. I remember Mandy as my first kiss under the stars that night at the baseball field. I remember how much in love I was with her and how I'd never let her go no matter what. I remember all the good times we shared growing up in those first three years of high school. I will always miss Mandy Fields. But she lives on in my heart and in my heart it's still the summer of 1991, and I'm still nervous trying to talk to her.

3

High school and the progression of time not only crushed my relationship with Mandy but with my friends as well. I lost them, too, in the wreckage of growing up. I knew back in '91 that things would change. God, I felt it deep in my bones, but I held out for hope that maybe I was being too paranoid. Not the case. Sometimes the things you fear the most have a way of coming true. It's not paranoia if it happens, is it?

The five of us, including Big Cat, entered high school not knowing what was waiting for us beyond those heavy, steel doors that led into the four-year institution. Even if we would've known, we still had to go there, no way out. I can tell you that we left much differently than we went in. A lot can change in four years. And it did.

Things didn't sting at first because we still had to rely on each other to navigate through high school socially. We needed each other for that reason. Call it fate, call it Karma, call it whatever you want, but the five of us never had one, single class together in the four years that we attended that school. It seemed that the school Gods had split us up for a reason making us befriend those we barely knew. We didn't have a choice but to make friends. It was the only way we each could survive.

We all made friends with other kids that we had stuff in common with as a means to an end; nothing personal. It was making those other friends that caused us to slowly peel away from the group that we had. We found it interesting that there were others out there who had the same interests we had. And then the girlfriends came into the picture. Jobs would later come.

I had friends that Pete, Mike, Tommy, and Curt didn't like, and they had friends that I didn't favor. That was a problem for us because each of us would bring our new friends to things like Dew Bashes, campouts, and other such traditions that only we did as a group. When others began to join in, that was when lines were drawn, and we went our own ways. It was sad seeing the decay of our friendships, but it was happening live and in stereo. Late in our junior year of high school, we all had pretty much formally disbanded. I guess looking back, there wasn't much to disband. Tommy was already gone during the summer of 1994.

There wasn't a scene like Mandy and I had in my car in her dad's driveway that rainy night when things were over. The guys and I just ceased hanging around each other little by little, and before you knew it, nothing at all. I can't say precisely when the end officially came, but it did.

Going in opposite directions as we did hadn't taken long. By the end of our freshman year, we all were doing things separately with other friends that we had made in high school. And even though the guys lived right there in the same neighborhood, we barely got together anymore. We would hang out on occasion but it was only that: occasionally. Around our junior year, we weren't even doing that.

As with Mandy, things had gotten unattended and eventually, our friendship which we thought was solid as a rock, withered away leaving us to be only faces in the school halls and faces down the street. It didn't take too long for the guilt of not being best friends to wane. Emotions as a kid tend to run quickly. I blame it on hormones personally. You lose and then you move on. Moving on is much easier when you're a kid. As an adult? Not so much.

I had been with those guys for so long that the hurt of not having them in my life as much literally shook the very foundation that I had built my mental state upon. The five of us might not have had a future anymore, but we would always have the past and no one, not even Father Time, could steal that away. I still love them. I still think about them and smile at the times we all had with each other. Nothing can steal that away from me. Nothing.

I hated high school for what it did to me and my friends. I blamed the school for separating us from each other. But in retrospect, I guess we all made choices that broke the friendship.

We could have gotten together after school instead of hanging out with new friends that we befriended in high school. We made that decision, not the school. Just as I thought that it was our destiny to meet, it was our destiny to disband. And even though I blamed the high school for tearing us apart, I guess the blame lay solely on our shoulders. Where else should it lie? I think we all left each other separately over time. But there were no hard feelings at all. It hurt, don't get me wrong, but I loved them too much to be mad at them. I love those guys even though I haven't seen them in decades. They were the best friends that I ever had.

———

Mike went on to the University of Tennessee after high school and got a degree. I think it was in communications or something. I don't really know. He had lost touch with me and the guys during high school. It sucked. All I know was that he graduated college, got into school debt, and wasn't doing what he had gone to college to do. The last I heard was that he was working in a factory making good money. I heard from a friend of a friend that he had gotten divorced some time ago after a twelve-year marriage that ended badly.

It was bad for him at first, but he had met a really awesome woman, and they hit it off. With Mike having two kids and she having two kids, they merged the two families, and Mike got remarried. Things as far as I know, or at least the last I had heard, were going really well for them. I'm glad. Mike was always a great guy. The summers that he would come and visit were always a treat. I have missed him greatly over the years. Never has been a Big Cat again in my life.

————

Tommy left Claxton during the summer of 1994. His parents had gotten killed in a car accident. He went to live with his aunt in Nashville. I had not heard from him since. I would ask Pete from time to time during our high school years—those times when we would see each other out in town or briefly in school—if he had heard from Tommy. Pete would always say, "Not in a while." Where Tommy is now I haven't a clue. I tried looking him up on Facebook one day when I was thinking about him saving my life that day at the swimming pool. He wasn't there, or at least I couldn't find him. There were others with his name, but it wasn't my friend. I wondered if the picture profiles that I was looking at were him. If he and I passed nowadays in a store, I would not know him. And that's a sad thought given our history. Wherever he is, I hope he's doing well.

————

Pete, during high school, didn't tell his dad that he wanted to stop playing football. He kept on doing something that he didn't like but pretended for everyone that he did. In high school, he was the star running back. Of course he was. He was really good. But with all that acclaim that he had gotten from coaches and teachers and students, he became insufferable. I hated being around him. He got cocky and started to be a prick to me. I stopped talking to him after he thought he was better than me. That was not the Pete Hembree I knew. That was what high school and a letterman jacket had turned him into. Eventually, Pete got hurt playing in a game during week 6. A torn ACL put him down and out his senior year. He never played football again. That was his out, I think. He went around blaming his injury on why he didn't play college, but I knew secretly from a conversation that we had up on the water tower back in the summer of 1991 that his heart wasn't in it. His torn ACL was his way of being done...finally.

Pete graduated high school and leaped right into the workforce thereafter. He's doing pretty good for himself. He's got a wonderful family, a good job, and coaches little league football with his dad, I hear.

4

Matt was snapped back from the past by an alert on his phone. He looked down and saw that it was just an email chime, letting him know that his Chase credit card was offering a special rate for qualified cardholders. He blinked his eyes and noticed that tears were welling up in them. He raised his hand and quickly wiped them. He looked around his backyard and felt something...it was sadness.

He missed those days, those friends. He missed the days of being a kid, holding hands with Mandy. He longed—if only for a moment in time—for the summer of 1991; to be back there, once again to smell the grass, to feel the sun on his young skin, to laugh until he cried with something stupid Curt, Pete, Tommy, or Mike said. As crazy as it sounded in his head, he wanted to see his mom and dad again, just to see them one last time in that land of long ago. Matt, sitting on his patio in a chair, began to tear up again as he thought back on all the campouts he and his friends did, all the video games they played, the endless miles they put on their bikes...the everything that was lost forever. Yes, the tears came.

Then Mandy came into his thoughts. He remembered her, those times they shared in a flurry; fast images popping in his field of vision. He remembered the times they sat on her front porch swing in the fall and held hands and talked about the future where they were married, living in a nice house with a white picket fence with two kids and a cat. He smiled as though he could still smell the scent in her hair, honeysuckle.

"Matt?! Are you okay?!" Mia yelled, standing out on the back porch, worried about her husband who had been out there for nearly three hours.

Matt batted his eyes, taking himself out of the past to look across the backyard and over to his house where Mia was standing on the back porch, hands in her back pockets.

"What?!"

"Are you okay?!" Mia again yelled.

He got up from his chair, stretching his tired back out, and walked slowly across the backyard toward his wife. He reached up and wiped his eyes, just in case there were any tears left in them, and walked up the steps, over to his wife. He reached out and gave her the biggest hug he had ever given her. After a couple of minutes, he pulled back and looked into her eyes,

"I'm okay. I've just been thinking about stuff."

"About?" Mia asked.

Matt gave a half-hearted smile and said, "How much time you got?"

Mia looked at him curiously as the two of them turned and walked inside the house.

AUTHOR'S NOTES

This book was perhaps the most difficult for me to write. Not that I couldn't figure it out, but because I wanted to get this right. This novel is the one that means the most to me, not only as a writer but as a person. Most writers—myself included—write confessional fiction. What that means is that we as writers put some of *us* into the characters and the situations in our stories. I'm no different, especially here.

When I say that I "wanted to get this right," I don't mean that I mailed in the other books that I have written. This book was about a time that no longer exists but in the rooms of my mind. Sometimes I like to go into those rooms and walk around, feel the memories as they wrap themselves around me like a warm blanket. This book is about memories of a time long ago that will never be again in my life. Sometimes I wish that I could visit those old times; see myself as a kid doing kid things on any random day. Don't we all?

It was important for me to get the feel of this book—that utter authenticity—of how things were back in those summers growing up. I didn't take just *one* summer in my life, but several, and condensed it down for the sake of the narrative.

One of the themes of this novel is change. Change is something that everyone can relate to because we've all undergone many changes in our lives—most of the time by circumstance itself that sparked those changes—welcomed or not. Let's face it, when you're a kid things are changing all the time. Life is nothing but constant change. Sometimes for the better, sometimes for the worse.

Another important theme in this novel is time—memories of those I love and how quickly I grew up and lost that innocent wonder. This book is about having memories that I can look back on and smile with a sense of youthful wonderment. Who hasn't ever gone back to the good places in our minds and revisited old familiar scenes and smiled—to feel all warm and gooey inside? That's what this book is for me; my warm and gooey place to smile—to shake hands with the ghosts that haunt the mansion that is my mind; to remember things as they were; to feel it all over again. I know that I can't ever go back in time to see it all and see things through adolescent lenses, but *memories* of that time—days gone by—are what take me back any time I want.

This is my love letter to those times past; a love note to the friends that I had and the memories that have not yet faded from my memory. One day all these memories will fade, and I won't be able to recall them nor their accuracy. What's scary is that many of the memories have already faded away, dissolved into that world where there is nothing but a barren wasteland of "Gee, wasn't there something here before?"

This novel is my farewell wave to all those summers spent chasing fireflies; walking barefooted in the cool grass at night; to all the times spent trading baseball cards; the bicycle rides around town that never seemed to end; the campouts in my best friend's backyard on a Friday night; the hundreds of games of H-O-R-S-E; the friendships that were and the ones that didn't last; to spending all my money buying comic books; to staying up all night just because it was summer and there was no school the next day; the crushes I had on that certain somebody in school; the music that I listened to that inadvertently became the sound-track to my life; to what was…and what will never be again.

As always, thank you for taking yet another journey with me…

See you in time!
December 2, 2023

ALSO BY MATTHEW MCCONKEY

Home Again

Scarecrows and Shadows

Maple Lane

Everything Fades in Time